Disney

FROZEN

ALSO AVAILABLE FROM JOE BOOKS INC

Disney Frozen Cinestory Comic

Disney Cinderella Cinestory Comic

Disney 101 Dalmatians Cinestory Comic

Disney Big Hero 6 Cinestory Comic

Disney•Pixar Inside Out Cinestory Comic

Disney Princess Comics Treasury

Disney•Pixar Comics Treasury

Disney Darkwing Duck: The Definitively Dangerous Edition

Disney Phineas and Ferb Colossal Comics Collection

Disney Frozen: The Story of the Movie in Comics

Disney•Pixar Inside Out: The Story of the Movie in Comics

Disney

FROZEN

FUNBOOK

 JOE BOOKS INC

JOE BOOKS INC
HarperCollinsPublishers
Published in the United States by Joe Books
Publisher: Adam Fortier
President: Steve Osgoode
COO: Jody Colero
CEO: Jay Firestone
567 Queen St W, Toronto, ON M5V 2B6
www.joebooks.com

HarperCollins Books may be purchased for educational, business, or sales promotional use through our Special Markets Department.
HarperCollins Publishers Ltd
2 Bloor Street East, 20th Floor
Toronto, Ontario, Canada
M4W 1A8
www.harpercollins.ca
Library and Archives Canada Cataloguing in Publication information is available upon request.
ISBN 978-1-926516-90-5
(Joe Books edition, US)
First Joe Books and HarperCollins Publishers Ltd Edition: June 2015

1 3 5 7 9 10 8 6 4 2

Printed in USA through Avenue4 Communications at Cenveo/Richmond, Virginia
For information regarding the CPSIA on this printed material, call: (203) 595-3636 and provide reference # RICH - 623964

DISNEY PUBLISHING WORLDWIDE GLOBAL MAGAZINES, COMICS AND PARTWORKS
Bianca Coletti (Editorial Director) • Editorial Team: Guido Frazzini (Director, Comics), Stefano Ambrosio (Executive Editor, New IP), Carlotta Quattrocolo (Executive Editor, Franchise), Camilla Vedove (Senior Manager, Editorial Development), Behnoosh Khalili (Senior Editor), Julie Dorris (Senior Editor), Christopher Meyer, Kristen Ginter, Virpi Korhonen

FOR JOE BOOKS
DESIGNER Ester Salguero and Ernesto Lovera • COVER DESIGNER: Heidi Roux • EDITOR Rob Tokar • SENIOR EDITOR Carolynn Prior • SENIOR EDITOR Robert Simpson • EXECUTIVE EDITOR Amy Weingartner • PRODUCTION COORDINATOR Stephanie Alouche
SPECIAL THANKS TO DISNEY PUBLISHING:
Curt Baker • Manny Mederos • Beatrice Osman • Christopher Triose
Dedication
For Abby and Meaghan Alouche -

CONTENTS

WELCOME TO ARENDELLE — 12

FROZEN: THE STORY OF THE MOVIE IN COMICS! — 16

COMIC: HOW TO SCARE A TROLL — 67

COMIC: WINTER SURPRISE — 71

COMIC: WHERE'S MY HEAD? — 72

COMIC: SNOW RECORD — 76

COMIC: ROYAL SKATING DAY — 77

COMIC: THE SNOW TROLL — 83

COMIC: OPEN YOUR EYES 84

 COMIC: ICE SURPRISE 86

 COMIC: THE KING OF HUGS 87

 COMIC: A NEW HAIRSTYLE 93

 COMIC: MORNING LESSON 94

 COMIC: CAMPING NIGHT 96

 COMIC: SWEET TRICK 97

 COMIC: SWIM DREAM 98

 ACTIVITY: OLAF'S ACTIVITY CORNER 101

ACTIVITY: FJORD-HOPPING WITH SVEN 102

 ACTIVITY: REACH ELSA 104

 ACTIVITY: SISTERS: THEY HAVE DIFFERENCES 106

 ACTIVITY: WELCOME TO ARENDELLE 108

 ACTIVITY: SNOWFLAKES PATH 110

 ACTIVITY: HIDE AND SEEK 111

 ACTIVITY: OLAF'S DREAMS 112

 ACTIVITY: LOST IN THE SNOW 113

 ACTIVITY: ICY REFLECTIONS 114

ACTIVITY: MARSHMALLOW'S CHASE 115

 ACTIVITY: ICE HARVESTERS 116

 ACTIVITY: ELSA'S AMAZING POWER 118

 ACTIVITY: LET'S BUILD A SNOWMAN! 120

 ACTIVITY: ELSA FLEES... ANNA PURSUES 122

 ACTIVITY: TRUE FRIENDS 124

ACTIVITY: THE ICE PALACE 126

 ACTIVITY: SISTERS' MATCH 128

 ACTIVITY: PARTY PREPS 130

ACTIVITY: NOBLE PORTRAITS 132

 ACTIVITY: TO A SECRET PLACE 133

 CINESTORY SCENE #1 "KRISTOFF'S BOYHOOD DREAM" 135

 CINESTORY SCENE #2 "ANNA AND ELSA AT PLAY" 149

 CINESTORY SCENE #3 "THE CORONATION" 160

 CINESTORY SCENE #4 "ELSA FINDS HERSELF" 199

FROZEN FEVER 208

 ACTIVITY SOLUTIONS 240

CREDITS

FROZEN: THE STORY OF THE MOVIE IN COMICS!
Adaptation: Alessandro Ferrari • Pencils/Inks: Massimiliano Narciso • Color: Kawaii Creative Studio

HOW TO SCARE A TROLL
Writer: Alessandro Ferrari • Artist: Iboix Estudi • Colorist: Charles Pickens • Letterer: Patrick Brosseau

WINTER SURPRISE
Writer: Alessandro Ferrari • Artist: Iboix Estudi • Colorist: Charles Pickens • Letterer: Patrick Brosseau

WHERE'S MY HEAD?
Writer: Alessandro Ferrari • Artist: Iboix Estudi • Colorist: Charles Pickens • Letterer: Patrick Brosseau

SNOW RECORD
Writer: Alessandro Ferrari • Artist: Iboix Estudi • Colorist: Charles Pickens • Letterer: Patrick Brosseau

ROYAL SKATING DAY
Writer: Alessandro Ferrari • Layout: Elisabetta Melaranci • Cleanup: Arianna Rea, Federica Salfo • Ink: Michela Frare, Cristina Stella • Color: Dario Calabria

THE SNOW TROLL
Writer: Alessandro Ferrari • Layout: Elisabetta Melaranci • Cleanup: Federica Salfo • Ink: Michela Frare • Color: Dario Calabria

OPEN YOUR EYES
Writer: Alessandro Ferrari • Layout: Arianna Rea • Cleanup: Federica Salfo • Ink: Michela Frare, Cristina Stella • Color: Dario Calabria

ICE SURPRISE
Writer: Alessandro Ferrari • Layout: Elisabetta Melaranci • Cleanup: Rosa la Barbera • Color: Greta Grippa

THE KING OF HUGS
Writer: Alessandro Ferrari • Layout: Elisabetta Melaranci • Cleanup: Arianna Rea, Federica Salfo • Ink: Michela Frare, Cristina Stella • Color: Dario Calabria

A NEW HAIRSTYLE
Writer: Alessandro Ferrari • Layout: Elisabetta Melaranci • Cleanup: Arianna Rea, Federica Salfo • Ink: Michela Frare, Cristina Stella • Color: Dario Calabria

MORNING LESSON
Writer: Alessandro Ferrari • Layout: Elisabetta Melaranci • Cleanup: Arianna Rea, Federica Salfo • Ink: Michela Frare, Cristina Stella • Color: Dario Calabria

CAMPING NIGHT
Writer: Alessandro Ferrari Layout: Arianna Rea Cleanup: Rosa la Barbera Color: Greta Grippa

SWEET TRICK
Writer: Alessandro Ferrari • Layout: Elisabetta Melaranci • Cleanup: Arianna Rea, Federica Salfo • Ink: Michela Frare, Cristina Stella • Color: Dario Calabria

FROZEN CINESTORY
Adapted by: Robert Simpson, Erik Burnham and Josh Elder • Lettering and Layout: Salvador Navarro, Eduardo Alpuente and Alberto Garrido

FROZEN FEVER CINESTORY
Adapted by: Paul Kupperberg • Lettering and Layout: Eduardo Alpuente, Alberto Garrido, Puste and Ester Salguero

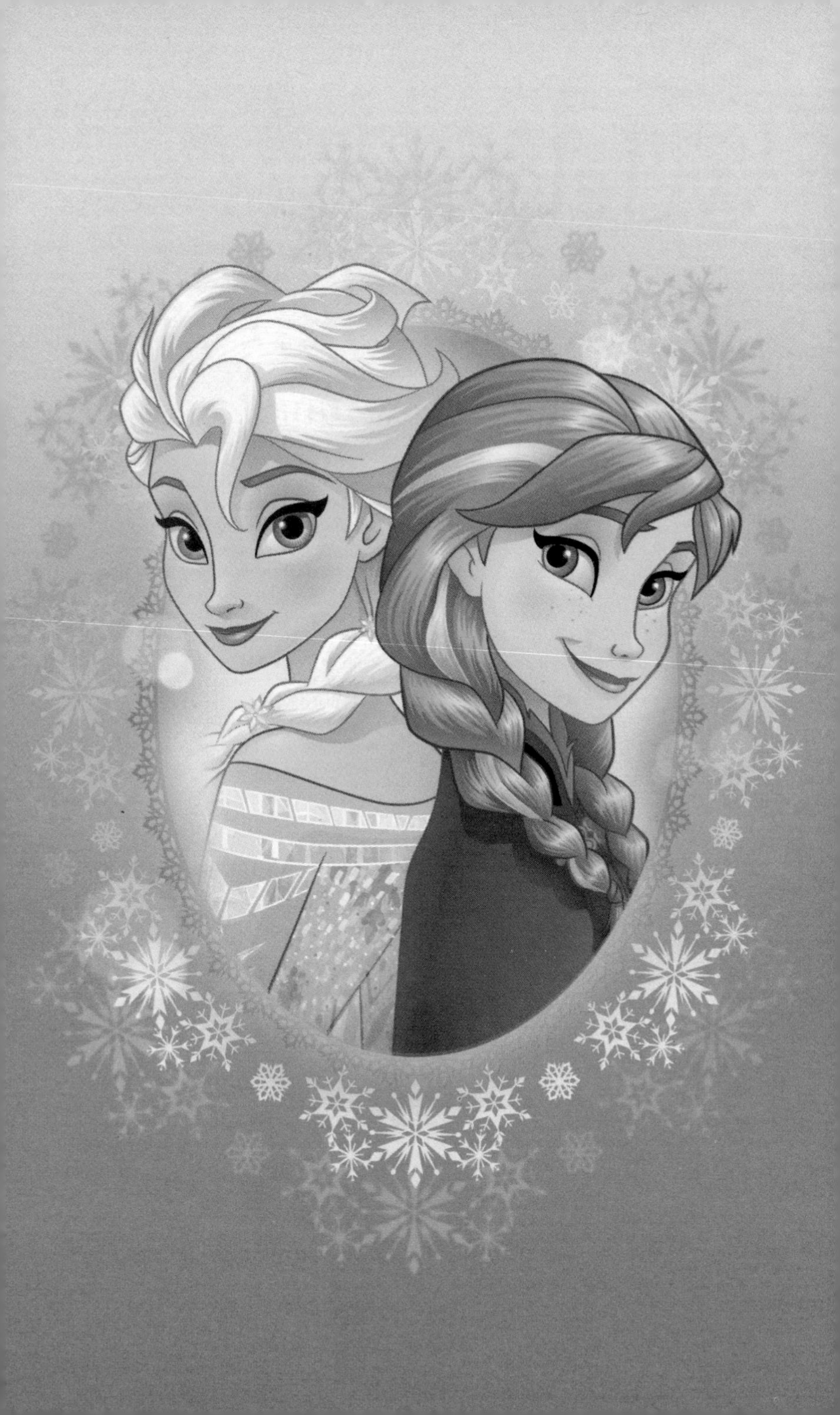

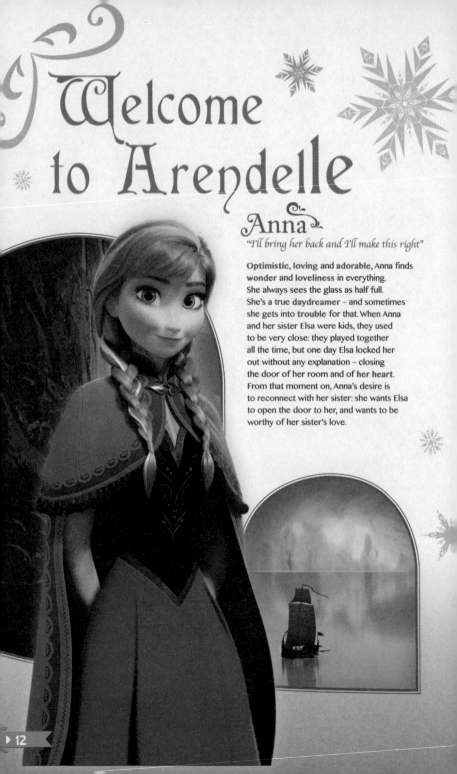

Welcome to Arendelle

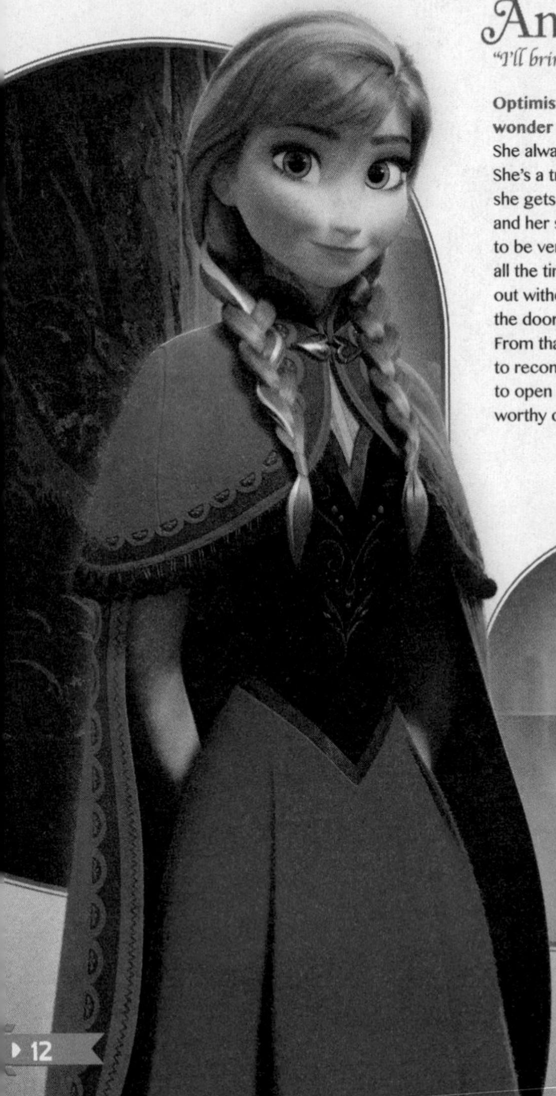

Anna

"I'll bring her back and I'll make this right"

Optimistic, loving and **adorable**, Anna finds **wonder** and **loveliness** in everything. She always sees the glass as half full. She's a true **daydreamer** – and sometimes she gets into **trouble** for that. When Anna and her sister Elsa were kids, they used to be very close: they played together all the time, but one day Elsa locked her out without any explanation – closing the door of her room and of **her heart**. From that moment on, Anna's desire is to reconnect with her sister: she wants Elsa to open the door to her, and wants to be worthy of her sister's love.

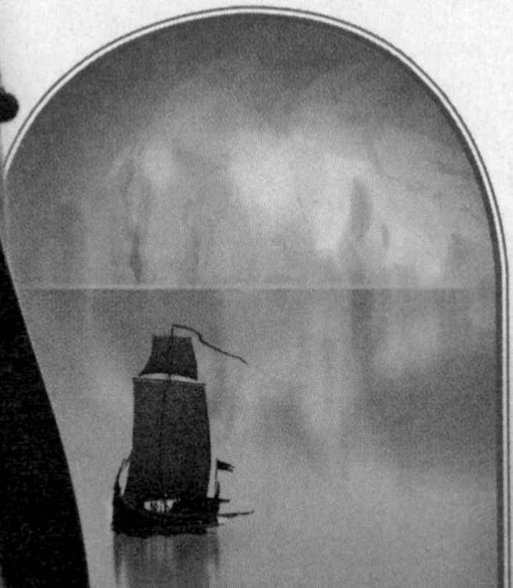

Elsa

"I never knew what I was capable of"

Elsa is the heir to the throne of Arendelle. She's a **natural leader**, she's **controlled**, **regal** and **graceful**: everybody in the kingdom loves her. But she has a **dark secret**, a secret she hides even from her sister Anna. Elsa has the **power** to **create ice** and **snow** with her hands, but she's not able to control it at all times. She needs to wear **gloves** most of the time, otherwise she'd **freeze anything she touches**. That's why she shut Anna out – to protect Anna from her powers. She'll soon learn, though, how important it is to open your heart and let the ones that love you in.

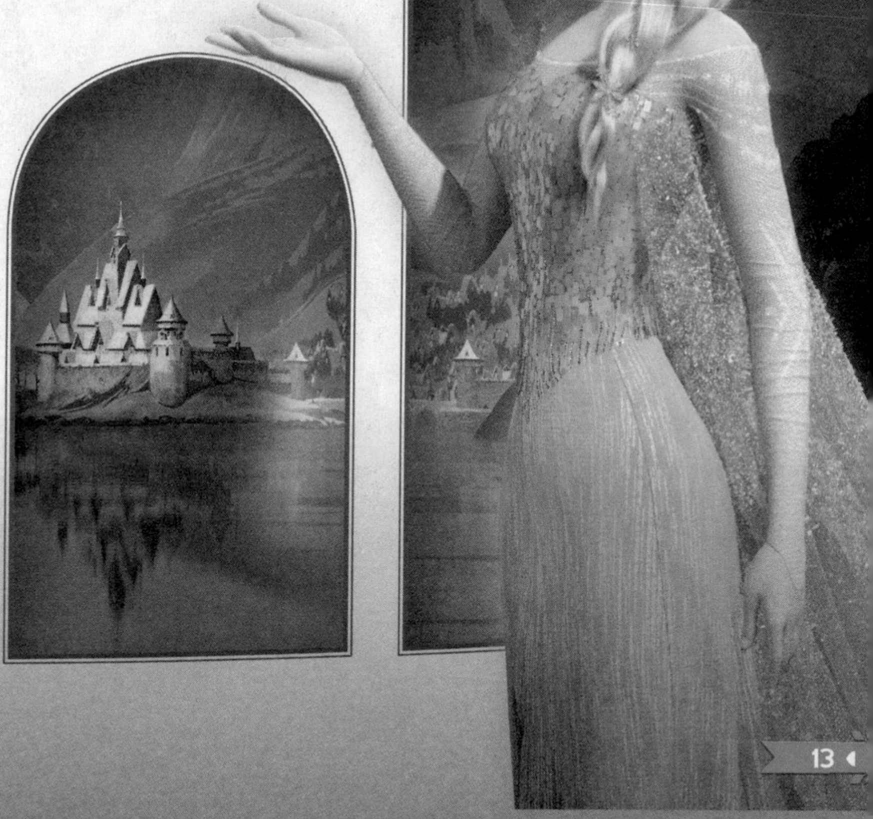

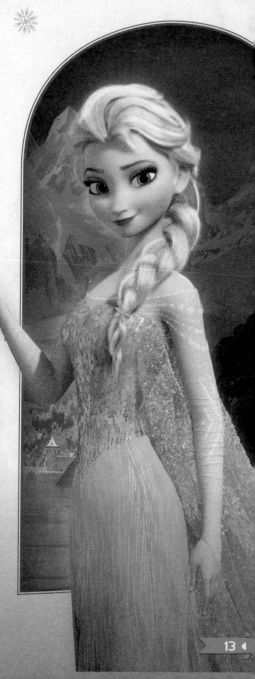

Kristoff

"Doesn't sound like true love."

Together with his reindeer – and **best friend** –
Sven, Kristoff gets blocks of ice from the
North Mountain and takes them to Arendelle
on his sledge to sell. He spends a lot of time
outside and he enjoys his work. Kristoff deeply
believes that sooner or later **people always
end up hurting you**, so he avoids getting
close to anyone – even to the love of his life.
Anna asks his help to meet up with her sister
Elsa. Two people in the whole kingdom
could not be more different...

Sven

Sven and Kristoff have been **inseparable
life companions** since they were little.
This friendly reindeer is crazy for
carrots, and would do anything for his
human friend. Although he cannot
speak, Kristoff speaks for the two
of them, often putting words from his
own conscience into the animal's mouth.

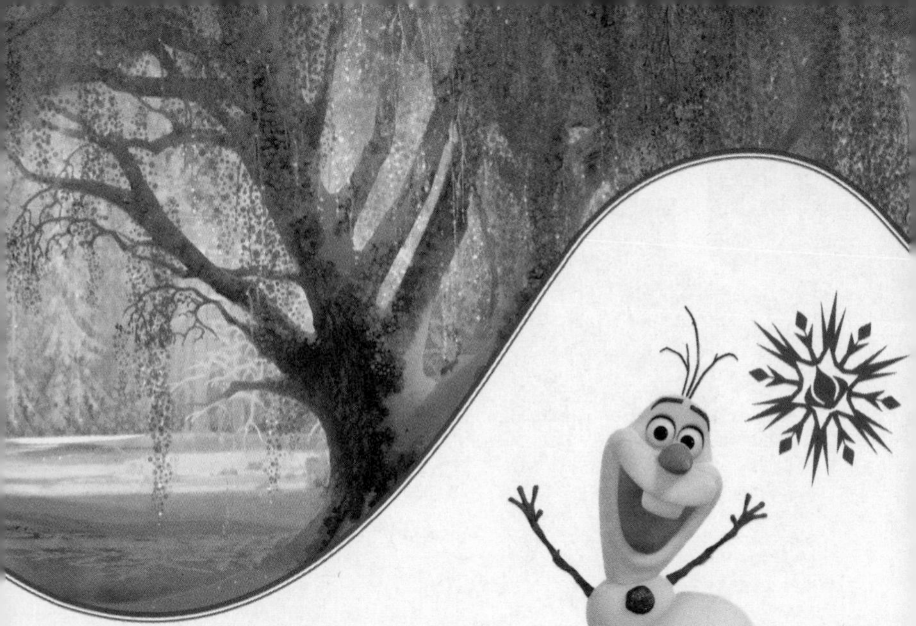

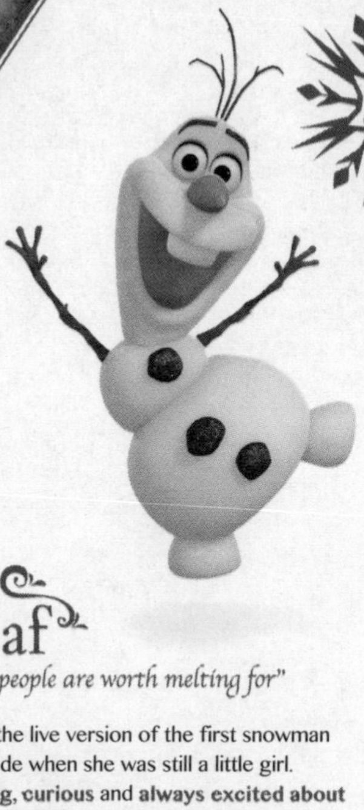

Olaf

"Some people are worth melting for"

Olaf is the live version of the first snowman Elsa made when she was still a little girl. **Trusting, curious** and **always excited about the world**, Olaf has a **big heart** and is always ready to help others no matter what. Due to his **magical nature**, Olaf can divide his body into pieces – each of them moving independently – and easily put himself back together. **His greatest dream is to see summer**: he has no idea that heat could melt him!

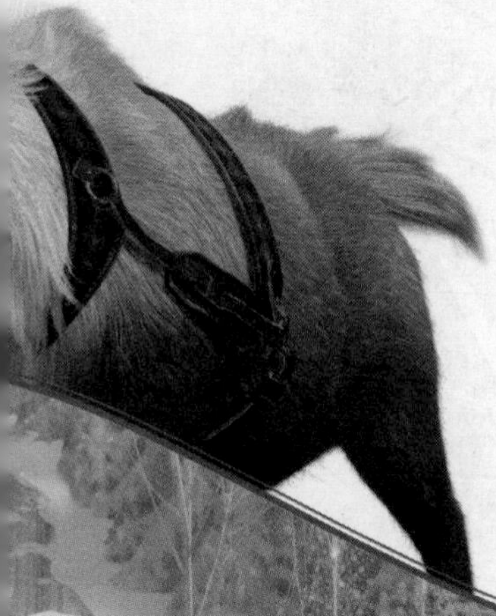

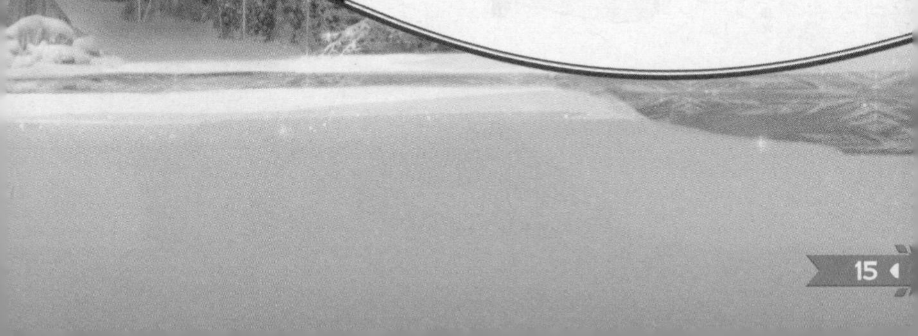

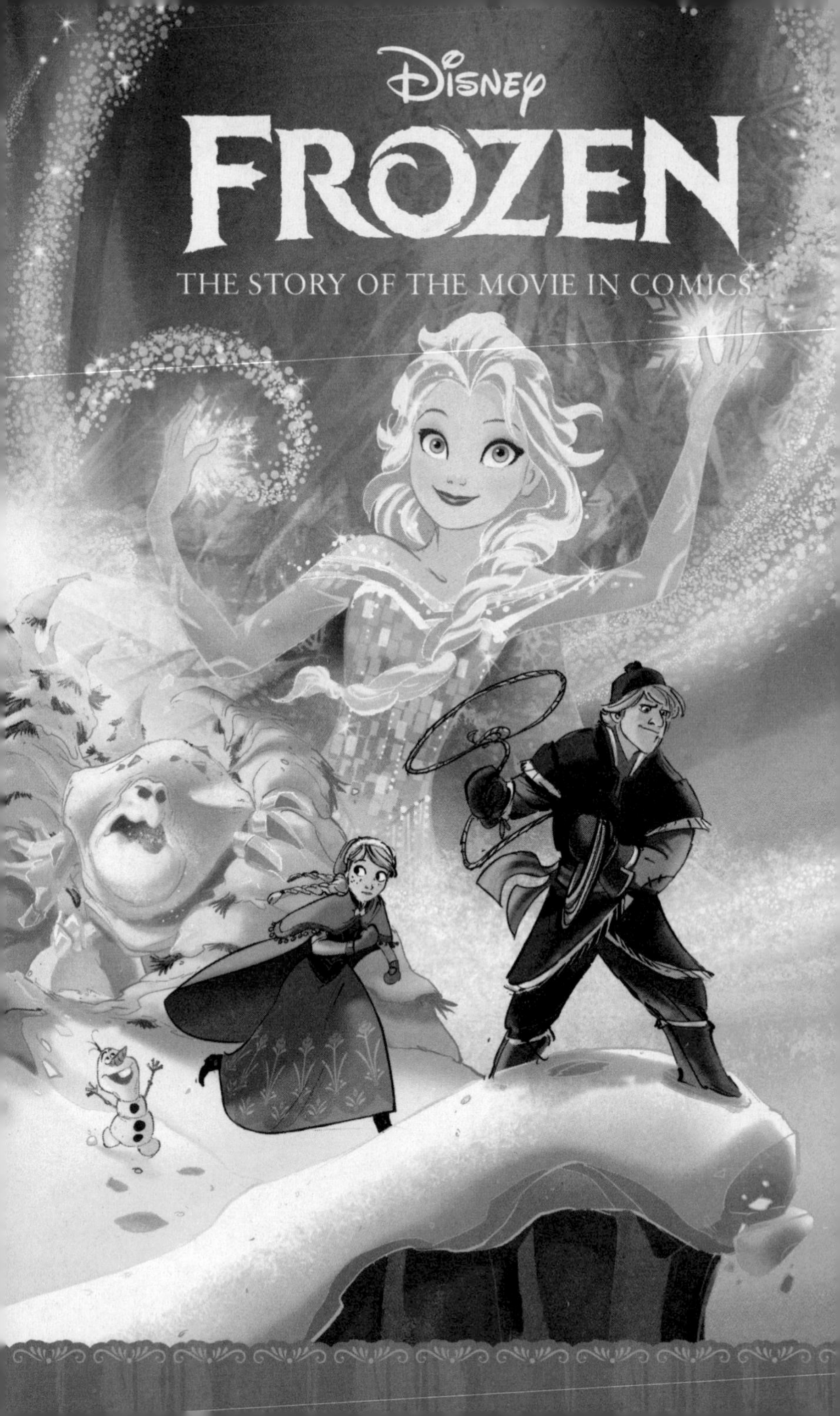
Disney
FROZEN
THE STORY OF THE MOVIE IN COMICS

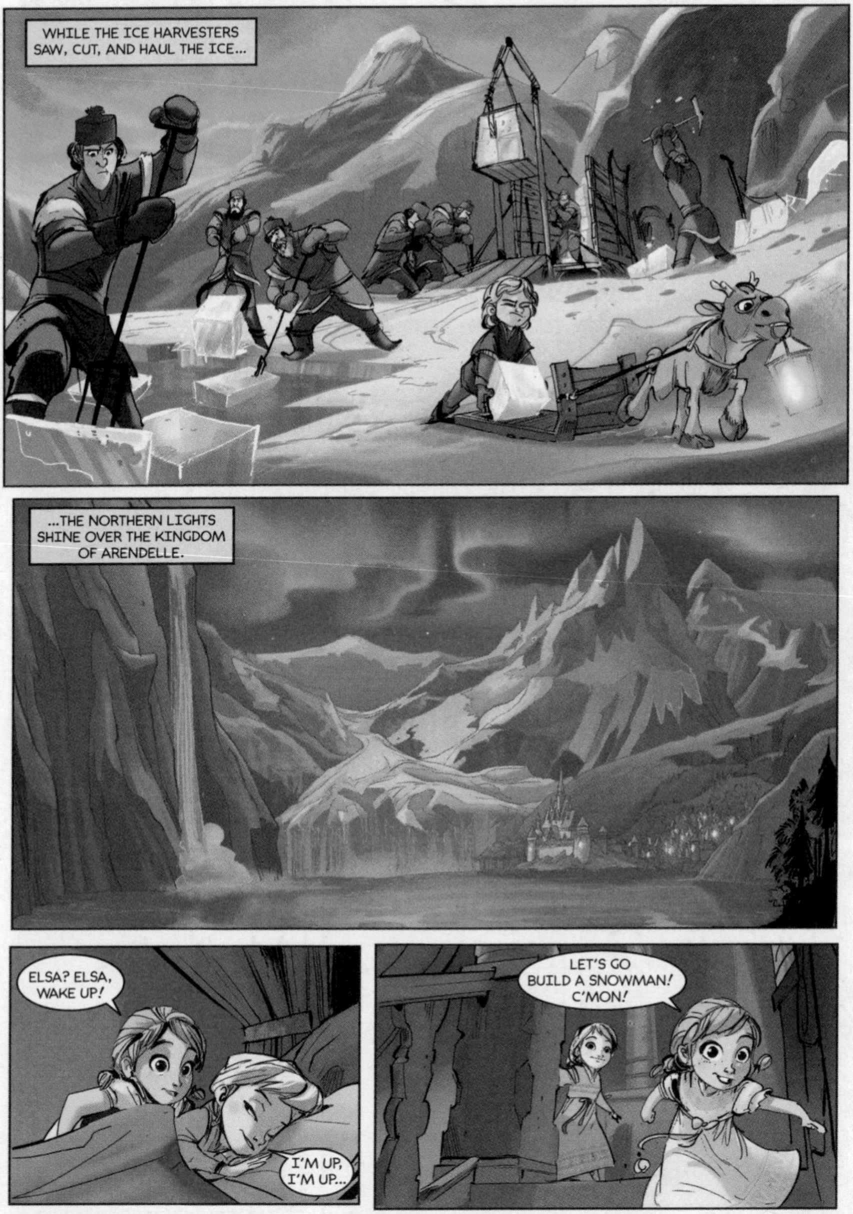
WHILE THE ICE HARVESTERS SAW, CUT, AND HAUL THE ICE...
...THE NORTHERN LIGHTS SHINE OVER THE KINGDOM OF ARENDELLE.
ELSA? ELSA, WAKE UP!
I'M UP, I'M UP...
LET'S GO BUILD A SNOWMAN! C'MON!

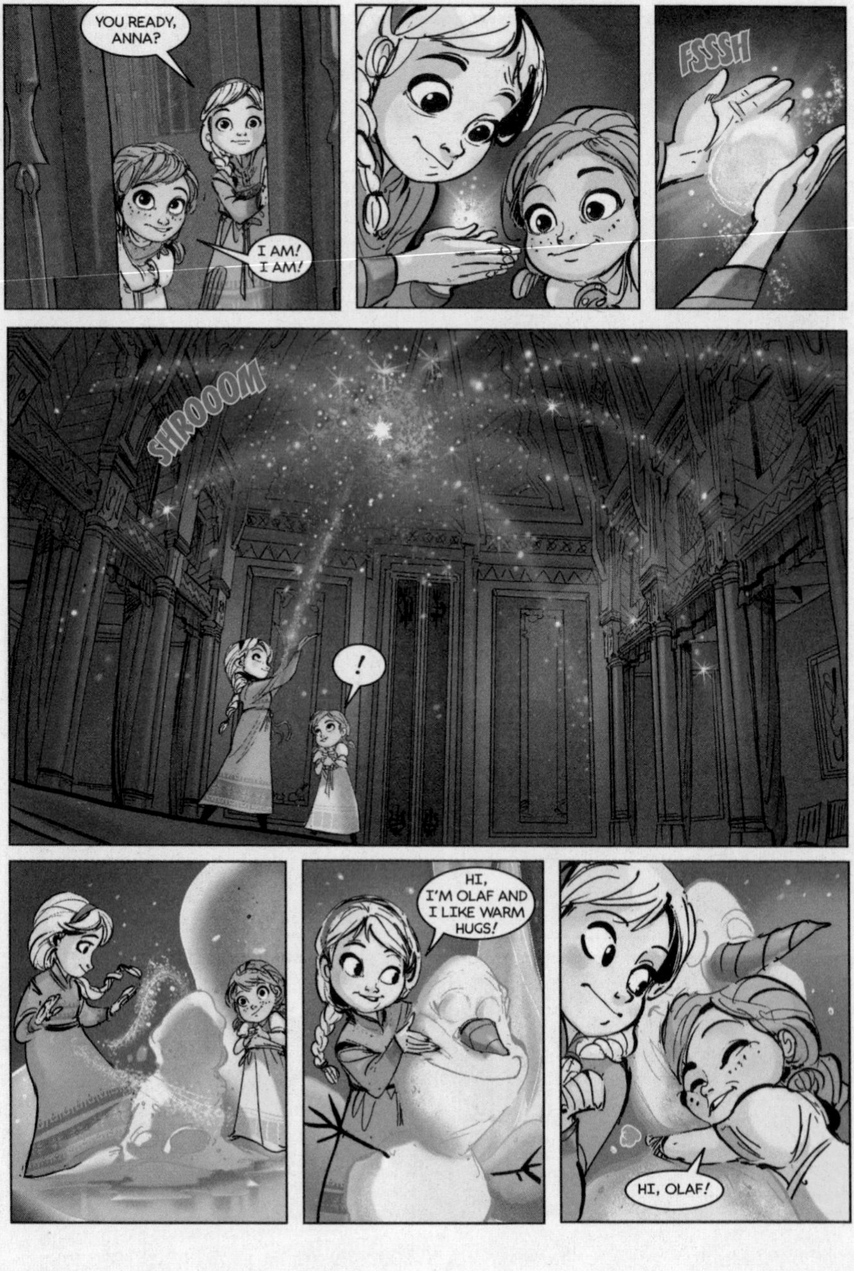
YOU READY, ANNA?
I AM! I AM!
FSSSH
SHROOOM
!
HI, I'M OLAF AND I LIKE WARM HUGS!
HI, OLAF!

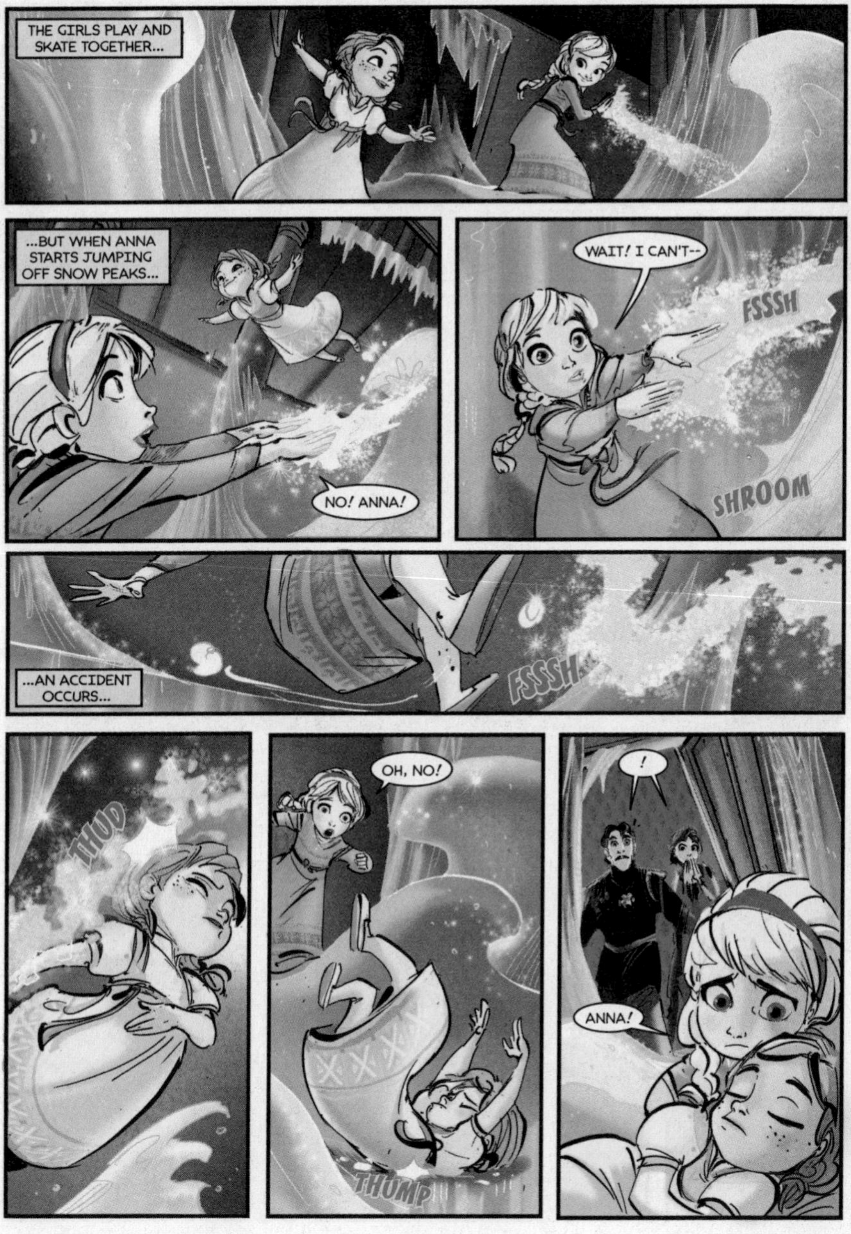

THE GIRLS PLAY AND SKATE TOGETHER...
...BUT WHEN ANNA STARTS JUMPING OFF SNOW PEAKS...
NO! ANNA!
WAIT! I CAN'T--
FSSSH
SHROOM
...AN ACCIDENT OCCURS...
FSSSH
THUD
OH, NO!
THUMP
!
ANNA!

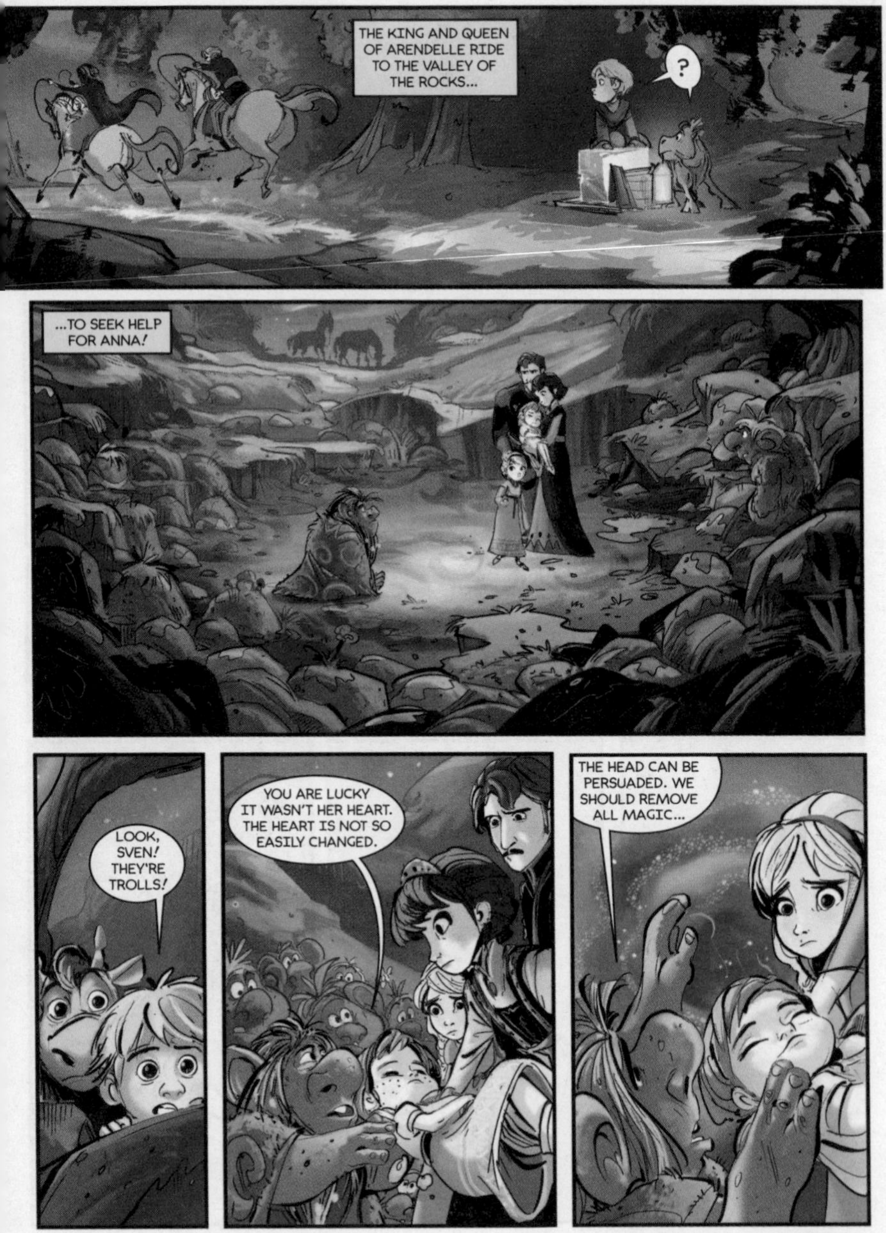
THE KING AND QUEEN OF ARENDELLE RIDE TO THE VALLEY OF THE ROCKS...
?
...TO SEEK HELP FOR ANNA!
LOOK, SVEN! THEY'RE TROLLS!
YOU ARE LUCKY IT WASN'T HER HEART. THE HEART IS NOT SO EASILY CHANGED.
THE HEAD CAN BE PERSUADED. WE SHOULD REMOVE ALL MAGIC...

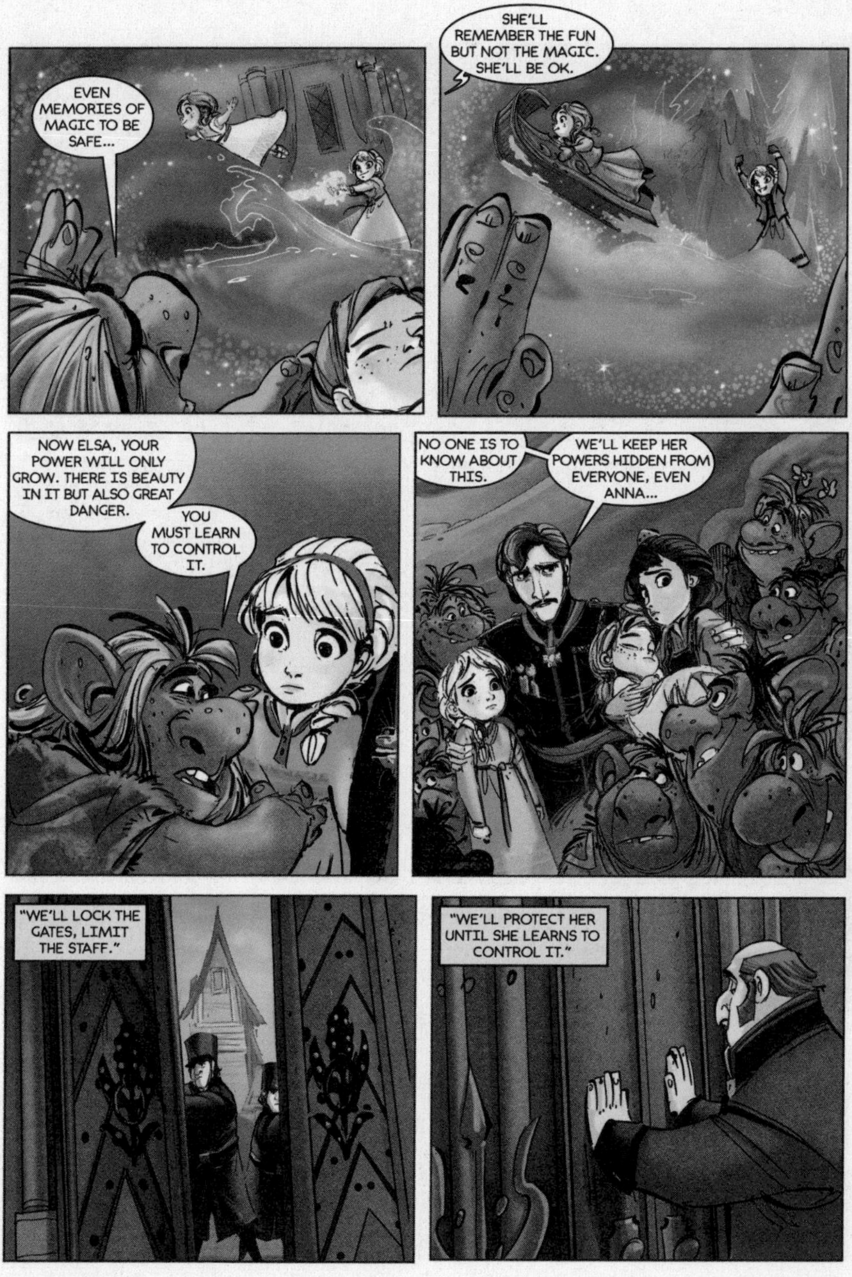
EVEN MEMORIES OF MAGIC TO BE SAFE...
SHE'LL REMEMBER THE FUN BUT NOT THE MAGIC. SHE'LL BE OK.
NOW ELSA, YOUR POWER WILL ONLY GROW. THERE IS BEAUTY IN IT BUT ALSO GREAT DANGER.
YOU MUST LEARN TO CONTROL IT.
NO ONE IS TO KNOW ABOUT THIS.
WE'LL KEEP HER POWERS HIDDEN FROM EVERYONE, EVEN ANNA...
"WE'LL LOCK THE GATES, LIMIT THE STAFF."
"WE'LL PROTECT HER UNTIL SHE LEARNS TO CONTROL IT."

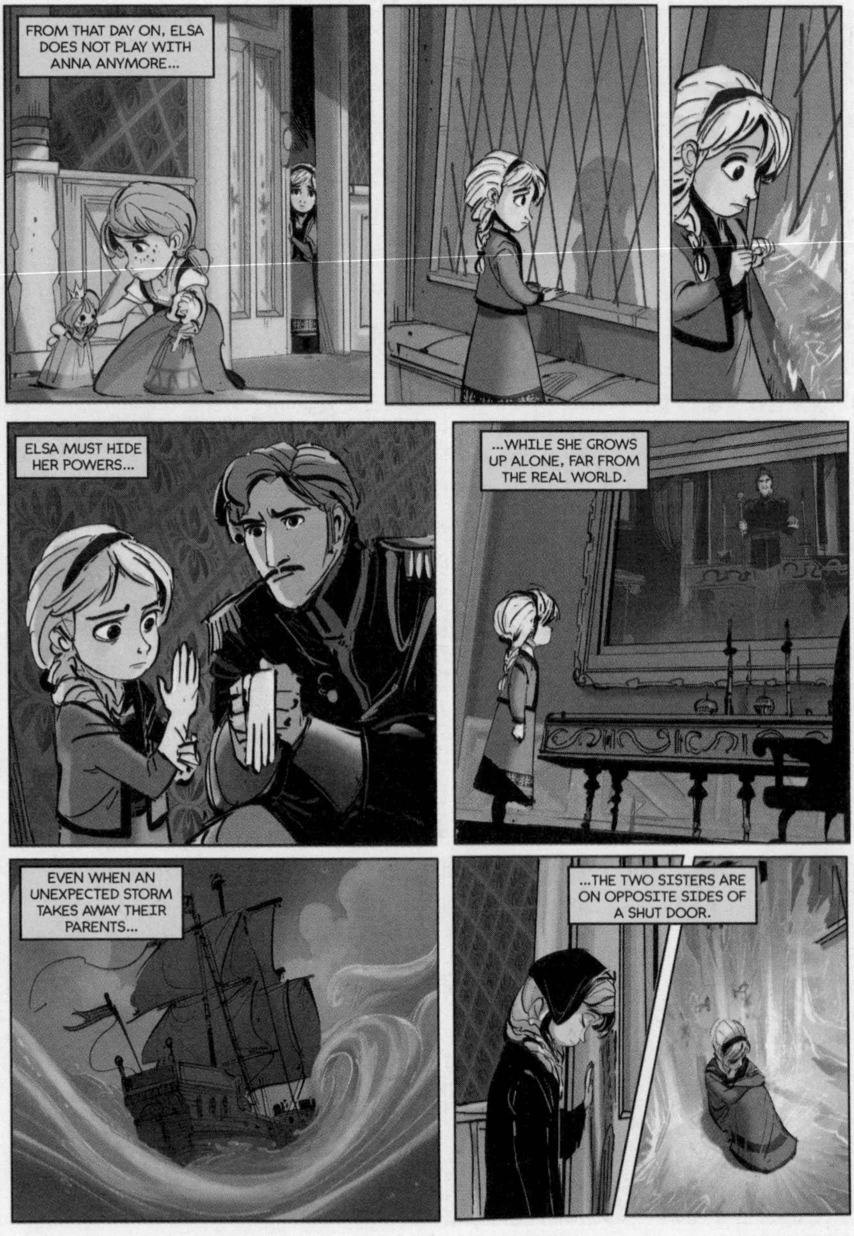
FROM THAT DAY ON, ELSA DOES NOT PLAY WITH ANNA ANYMORE...
ELSA MUST HIDE HER POWERS...
...WHILE SHE GROWS UP ALONE, FAR FROM THE REAL WORLD.
EVEN WHEN AN UNEXPECTED STORM TAKES AWAY THEIR PARENTS...
...THE TWO SISTERS ARE ON OPPOSITE SIDES OF A SHUT DOOR.

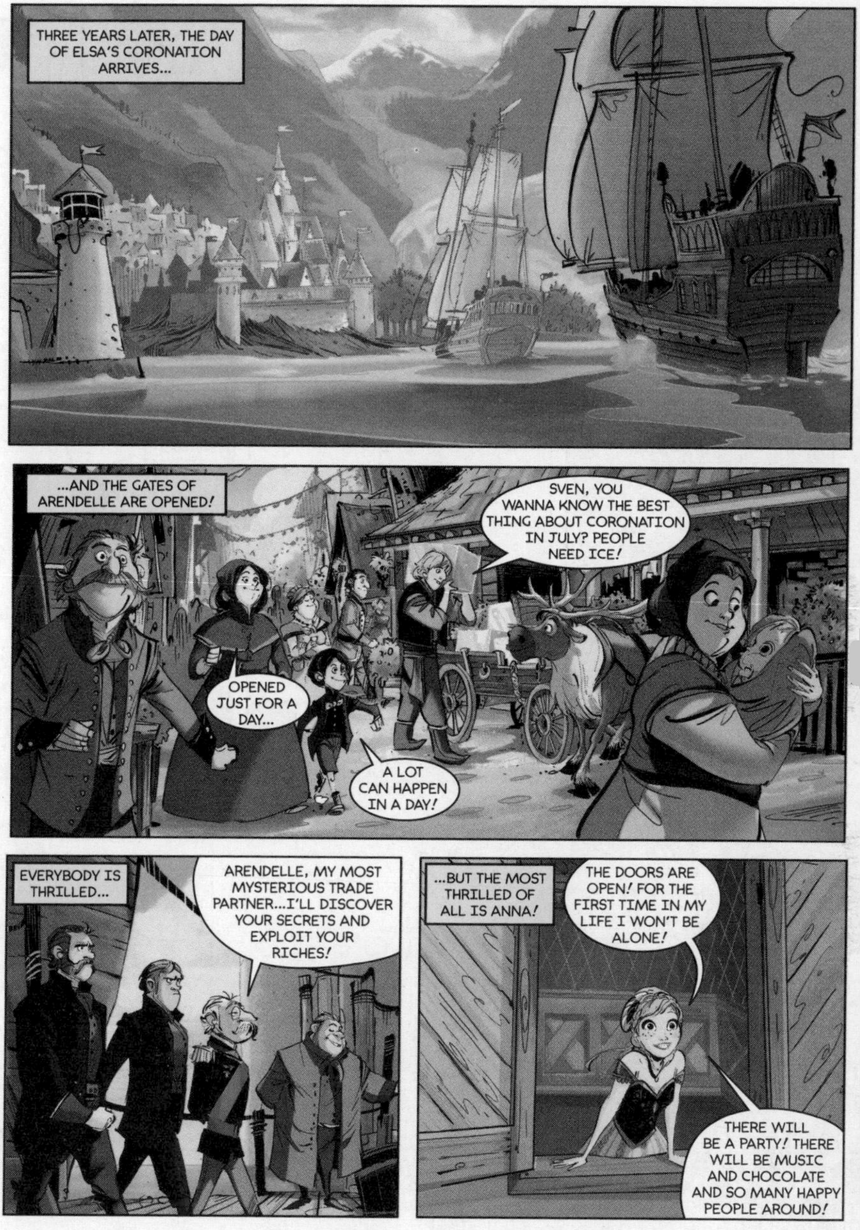

THREE YEARS LATER, THE DAY OF ELSA'S CORONATION ARRIVES...
...AND THE GATES OF ARENDELLE ARE OPENED!
SVEN, YOU WANNA KNOW THE BEST THING ABOUT CORONATION IN JULY? PEOPLE NEED ICE!
OPENED JUST FOR A DAY...
A LOT CAN HAPPEN IN A DAY!
EVERYBODY IS THRILLED...
ARENDELLE, MY MOST MYSTERIOUS TRADE PARTNER...I'LL DISCOVER YOUR SECRETS AND EXPLOIT YOUR RICHES!
...BUT THE MOST THRILLED OF ALL IS ANNA!
THE DOORS ARE OPEN! FOR THE FIRST TIME IN MY LIFE I WON'T BE ALONE!
THERE WILL BE A PARTY! THERE WILL BE MUSIC AND CHOCOLATE AND SO MANY HAPPY PEOPLE AROUND!

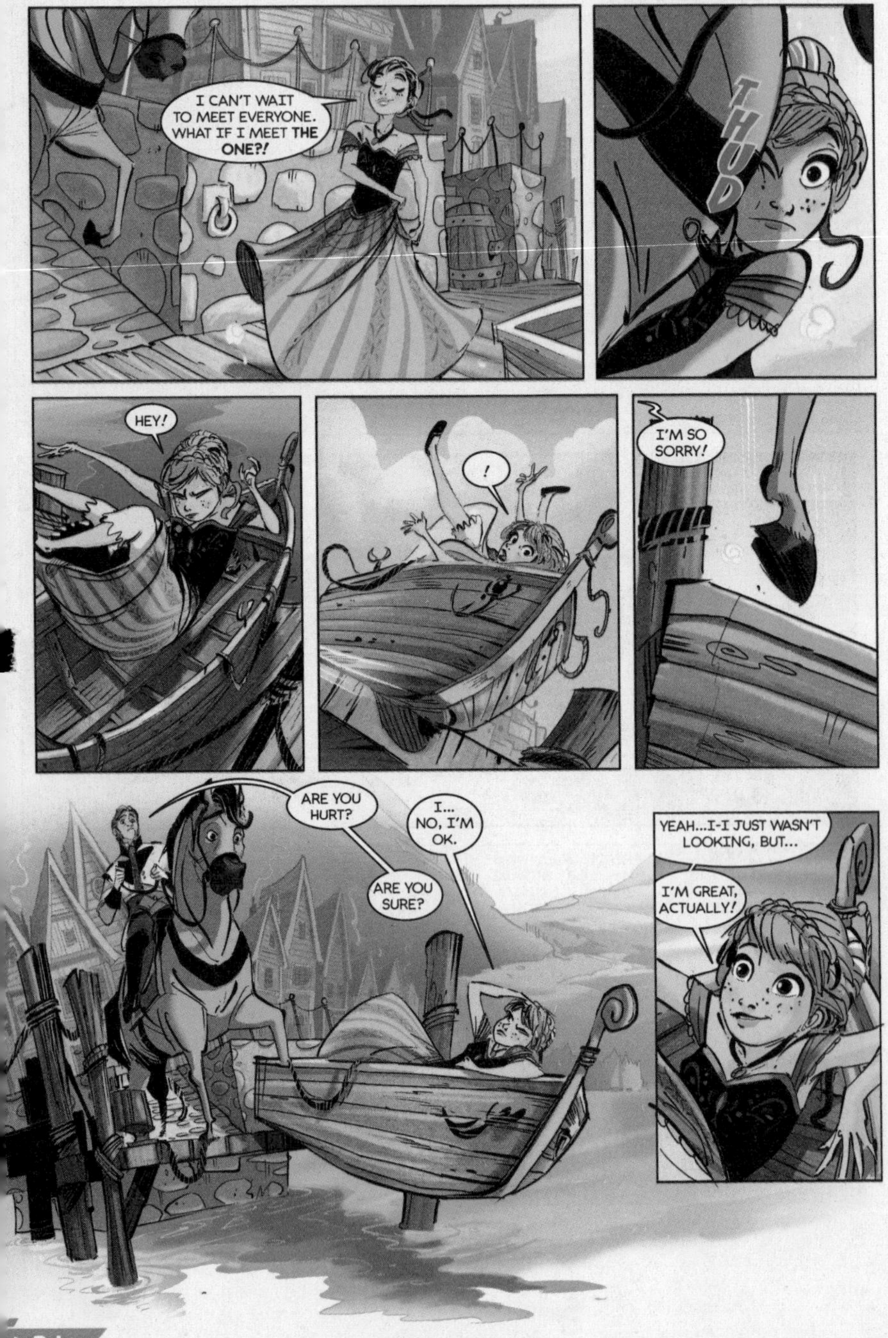
I CAN'T WAIT TO MEET EVERYONE. WHAT IF I MEET THE ONE?!
THUD
HEY!
!
I'M SO SORRY!
ARE YOU HURT?
ARE YOU SURE?
I... NO, I'M OK.
YEAH...I-I JUST WASN'T LOOKING, BUT...
I'M GREAT, ACTUALLY!

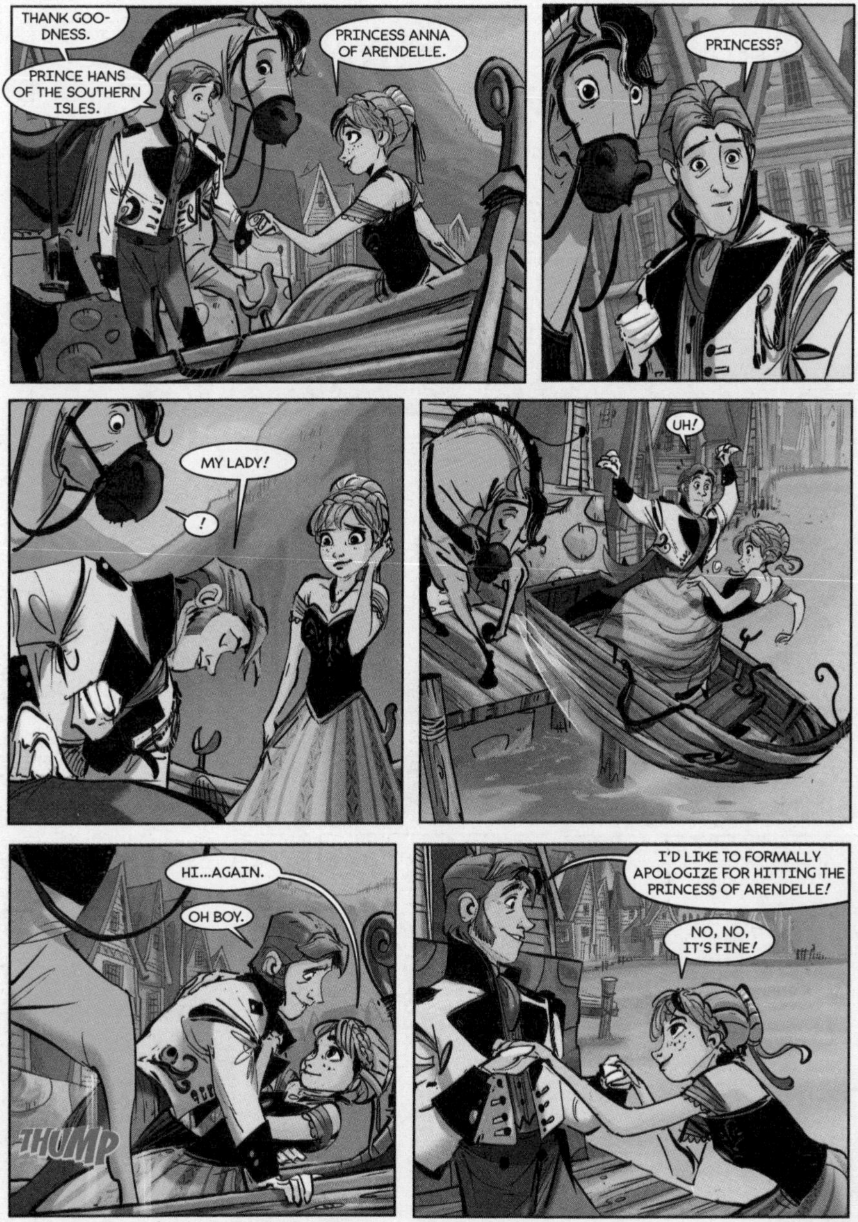
THANK GOO-DNESS.
PRINCE HANS OF THE SOUTHERN ISLES.
PRINCESS ANNA OF ARENDELLE.
PRINCESS?
MY LADY!
!
UH!
HI...AGAIN.
OH BOY.
THUMP
I'D LIKE TO FORMALLY APOLOGIZE FOR HITTING THE PRINCESS OF ARENDELLE!
NO, NO, IT'S FINE!

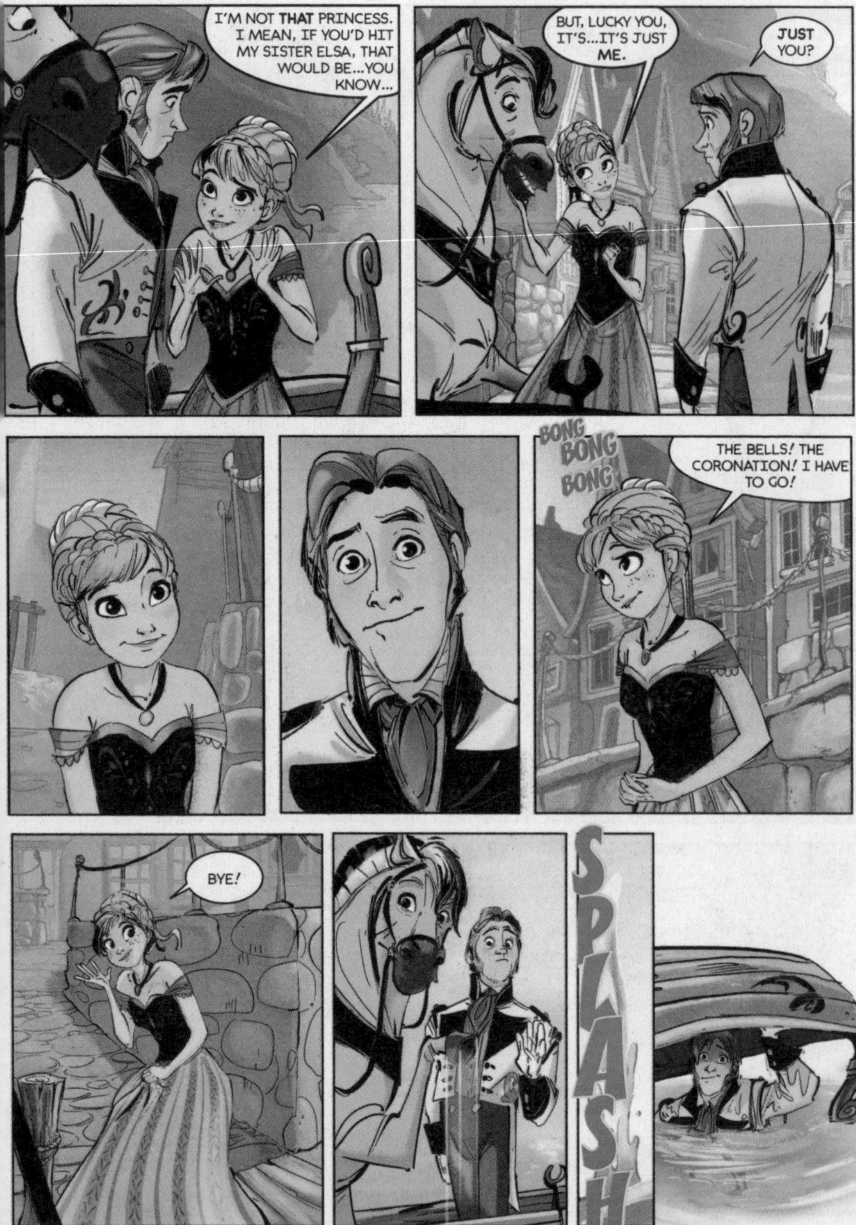
I'M NOT THAT PRINCESS. I MEAN, IF YOU'D HIT MY SISTER ELSA, THAT WOULD BE...YOU KNOW...
BUT, LUCKY YOU, IT'S...IT'S JUST ME.
JUST YOU?
BONG BONG BONG
THE BELLS! THE CORONATION! I HAVE TO GO!
BYE!
SPLASH

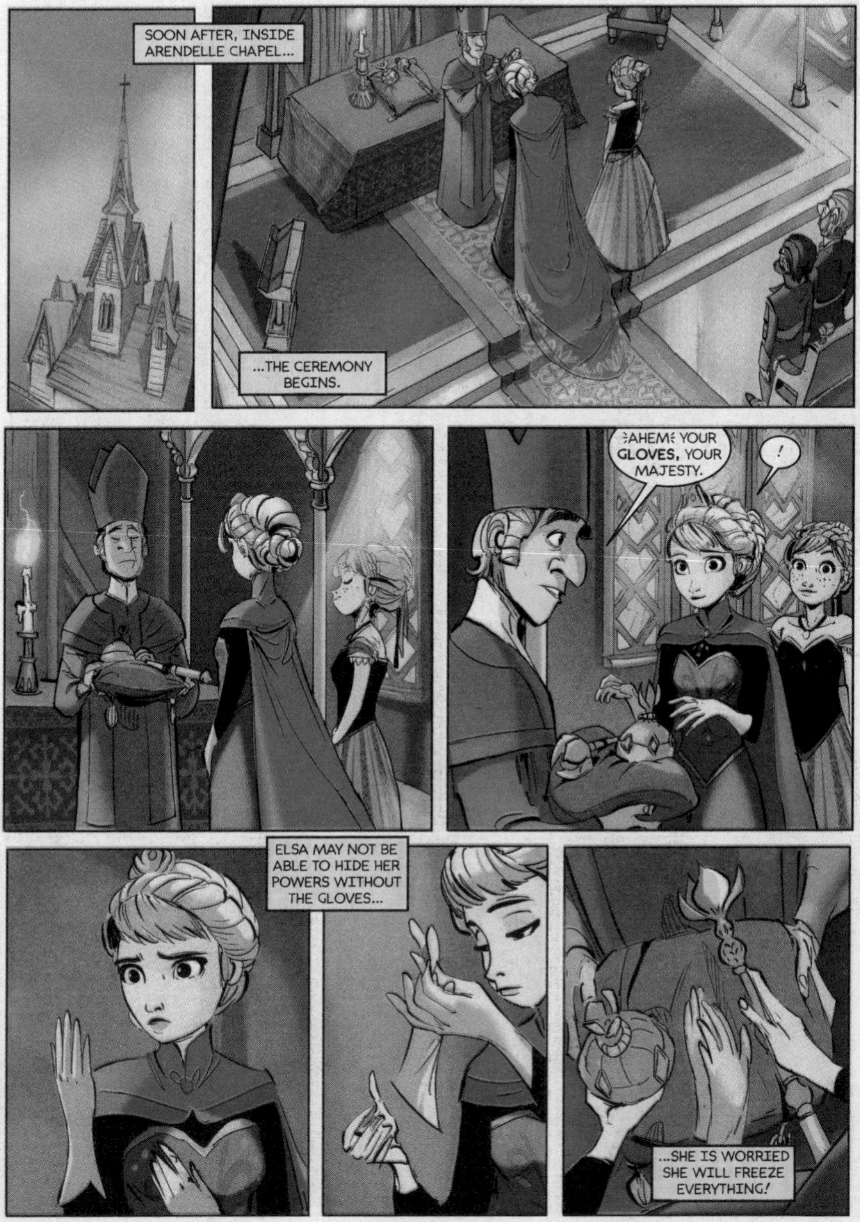
SOON AFTER, INSIDE ARENDELLE CHAPEL...
...THE CEREMONY BEGINS.
AHEM YOUR GLOVES, YOUR MAJESTY.
!
ELSA MAY NOT BE ABLE TO HIDE HER POWERS WITHOUT THE GLOVES...
...SHE IS WORRIED SHE WILL FREEZE EVERYTHING!

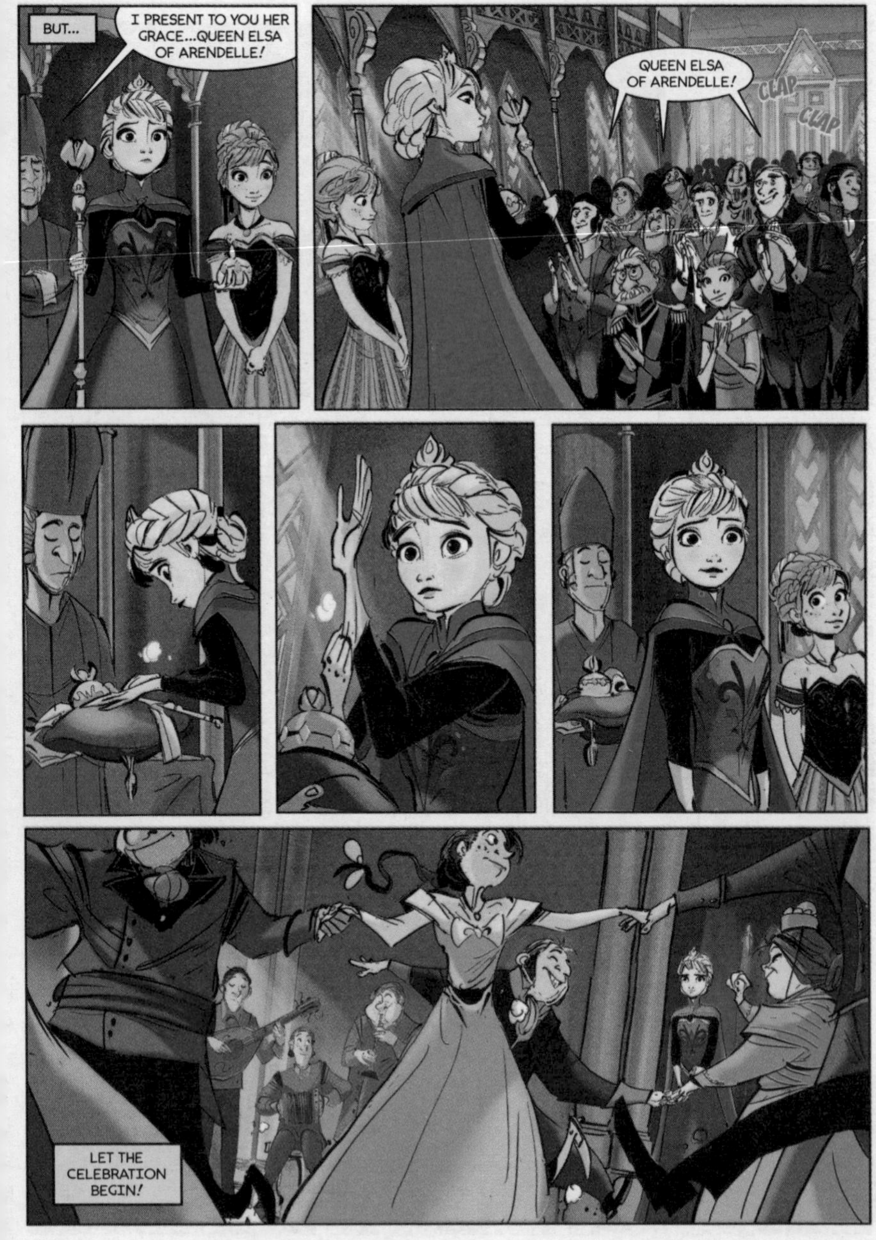
BUT...
I PRESENT TO YOU HER GRACE...QUEEN ELSA OF ARENDELLE!
QUEEN ELSA OF ARENDELLE!
CLAP
CLAP
LET THE CELEBRATION BEGIN!

HI.

UH? H-HI.

WHAT IS THIS AMAZING SMELL?

?

SNIFF SNIFF

CHOCOLATE!

I WISH IT COULD BE LIKE THIS ALL THE TIME!

ME, TOO. BUT IT CAN'T.

WHY NOT?

IT JUST CAN'T.

BOOF!

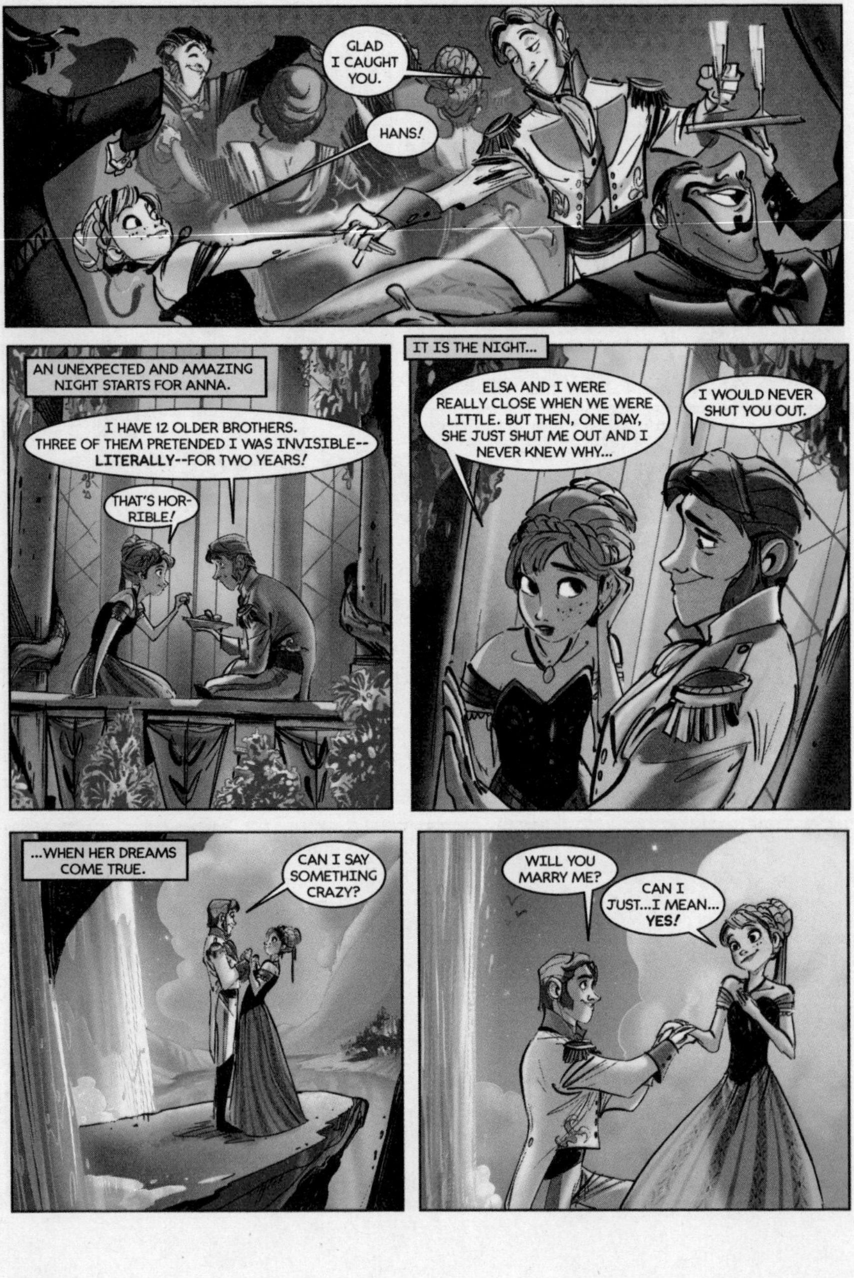
GLAD I CAUGHT YOU.
HANS!
AN UNEXPECTED AND AMAZING NIGHT STARTS FOR ANNA.
I HAVE 12 OLDER BROTHERS. THREE OF THEM PRETENDED I WAS INVISIBLE-- **LITERALLY**--FOR TWO YEARS!
THAT'S HOR-RIBLE!
IT IS THE NIGHT...
ELSA AND I WERE REALLY CLOSE WHEN WE WERE LITTLE. BUT THEN, ONE DAY, SHE JUST SHUT ME OUT AND I NEVER KNEW WHY...
I WOULD NEVER SHUT YOU OUT.
...WHEN HER DREAMS COME TRUE.
CAN I SAY SOMETHING CRAZY?
WILL YOU MARRY ME?
CAN I JUST...I MEAN... **YES!**

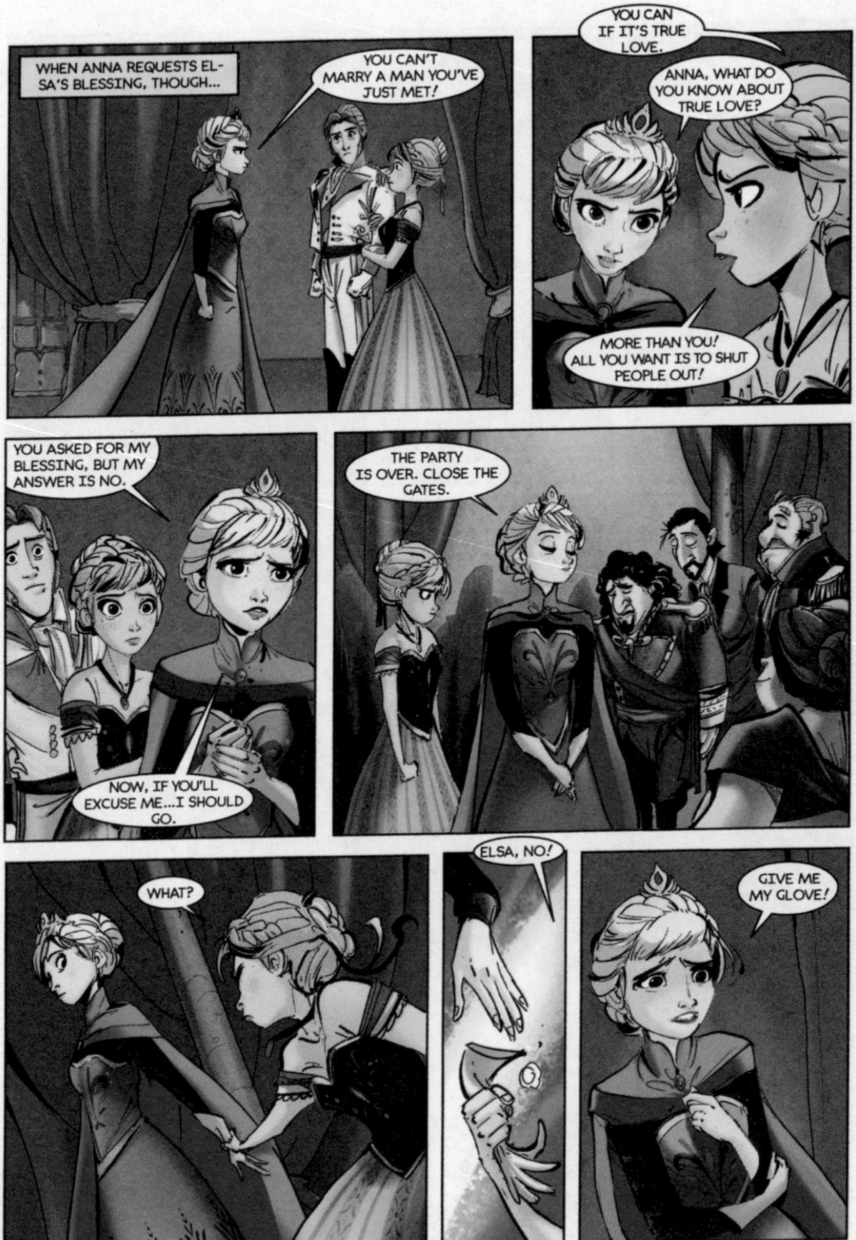
WHEN ANNA REQUESTS ELSA'S BLESSING, THOUGH...
YOU CAN'T MARRY A MAN YOU'VE JUST MET!
YOU CAN IF IT'S TRUE LOVE.
ANNA, WHAT DO YOU KNOW ABOUT TRUE LOVE?
MORE THAN YOU! ALL YOU WANT IS TO SHUT PEOPLE OUT!
YOU ASKED FOR MY BLESSING, BUT MY ANSWER IS NO.
NOW, IF YOU'LL EXCUSE ME...I SHOULD GO.
THE PARTY IS OVER. CLOSE THE GATES.
WHAT?
ELSA, NO!
GIVE ME MY GLOVE!

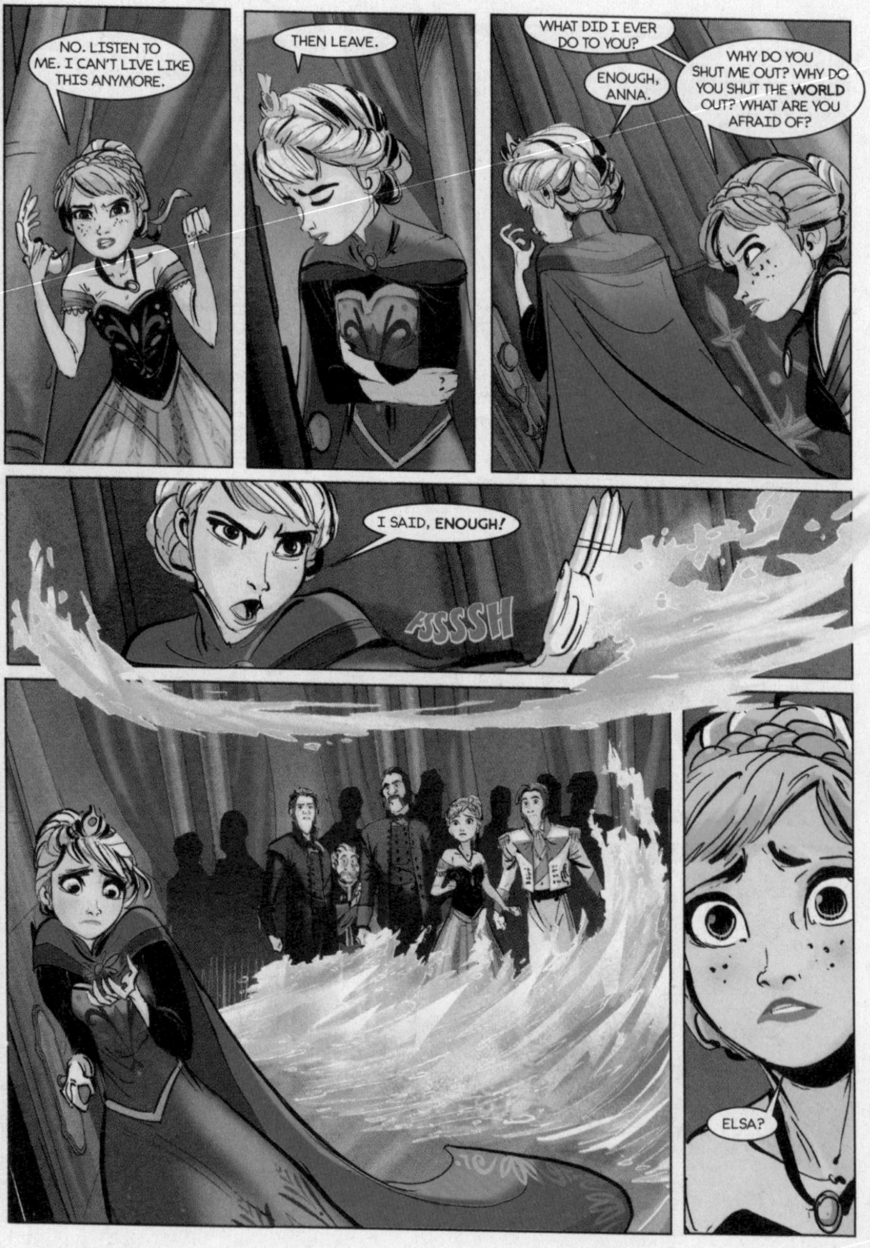
NO. LISTEN TO ME. I CAN'T LIVE LIKE THIS ANYMORE.
THEN LEAVE.
WHAT DID I EVER DO TO YOU?
ENOUGH, ANNA.
WHY DO YOU SHUT ME OUT? WHY DO YOU SHUT THE **WORLD** OUT? WHAT ARE YOU AFRAID OF?
I SAID, **ENOUGH!**
FSSSSH
ELSA?

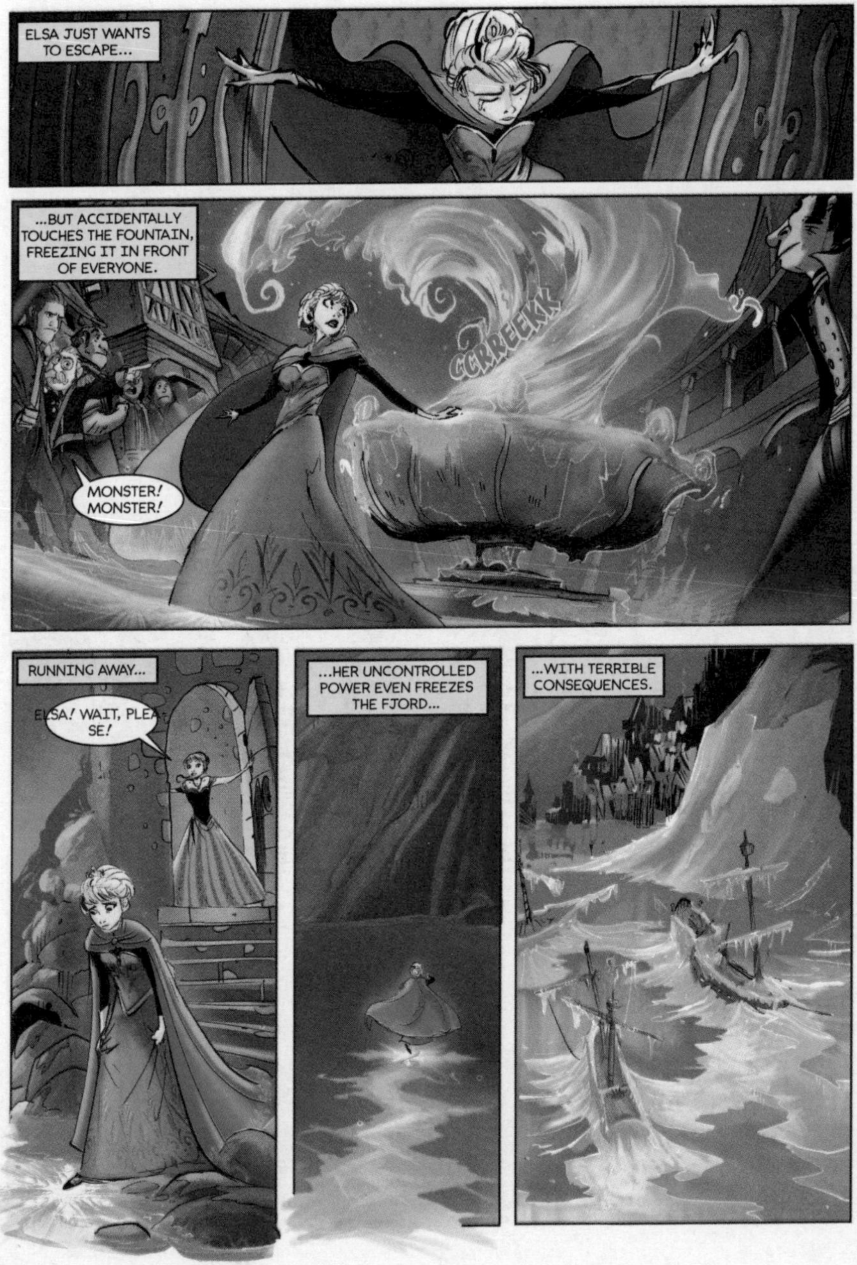
ELSA JUST WANTS TO ESCAPE...
...BUT ACCIDENTALLY TOUCHES THE FOUNTAIN, FREEZING IT IN FRONT OF EVERYONE.
CCRREEKK
MONSTER! MONSTER!
RUNNING AWAY...
ELSA! WAIT, PLEASE!
...HER UNCONTROLLED POWER EVEN FREEZES THE FJORD...
...WITH TERRIBLE CONSEQUENCES.

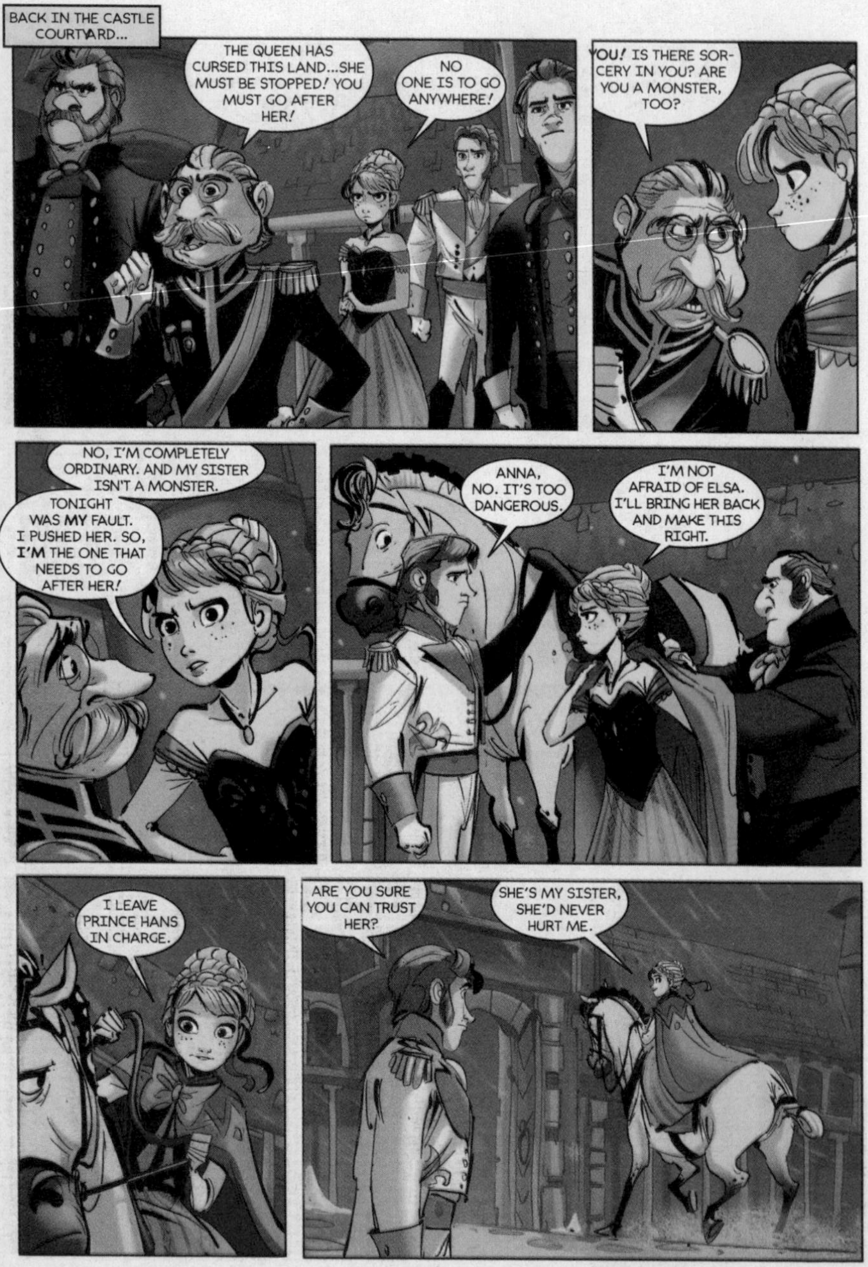
BACK IN THE CASTLE COURTYARD...
THE QUEEN HAS CURSED THIS LAND...SHE MUST BE STOPPED! YOU MUST GO AFTER HER!
NO ONE IS TO GO ANYWHERE!
YOU! IS THERE SORCERY IN YOU? ARE YOU A MONSTER, TOO?
NO, I'M COMPLETELY ORDINARY. AND MY SISTER ISN'T A MONSTER.
TONIGHT WAS MY FAULT. I PUSHED HER. SO, I'M THE ONE THAT NEEDS TO GO AFTER HER!
ANNA, NO. IT'S TOO DANGEROUS.
I'M NOT AFRAID OF ELSA. I'LL BRING HER BACK AND MAKE THIS RIGHT.
I LEAVE PRINCE HANS IN CHARGE.
ARE YOU SURE YOU CAN TRUST HER?
SHE'S MY SISTER, SHE'D NEVER HURT ME.

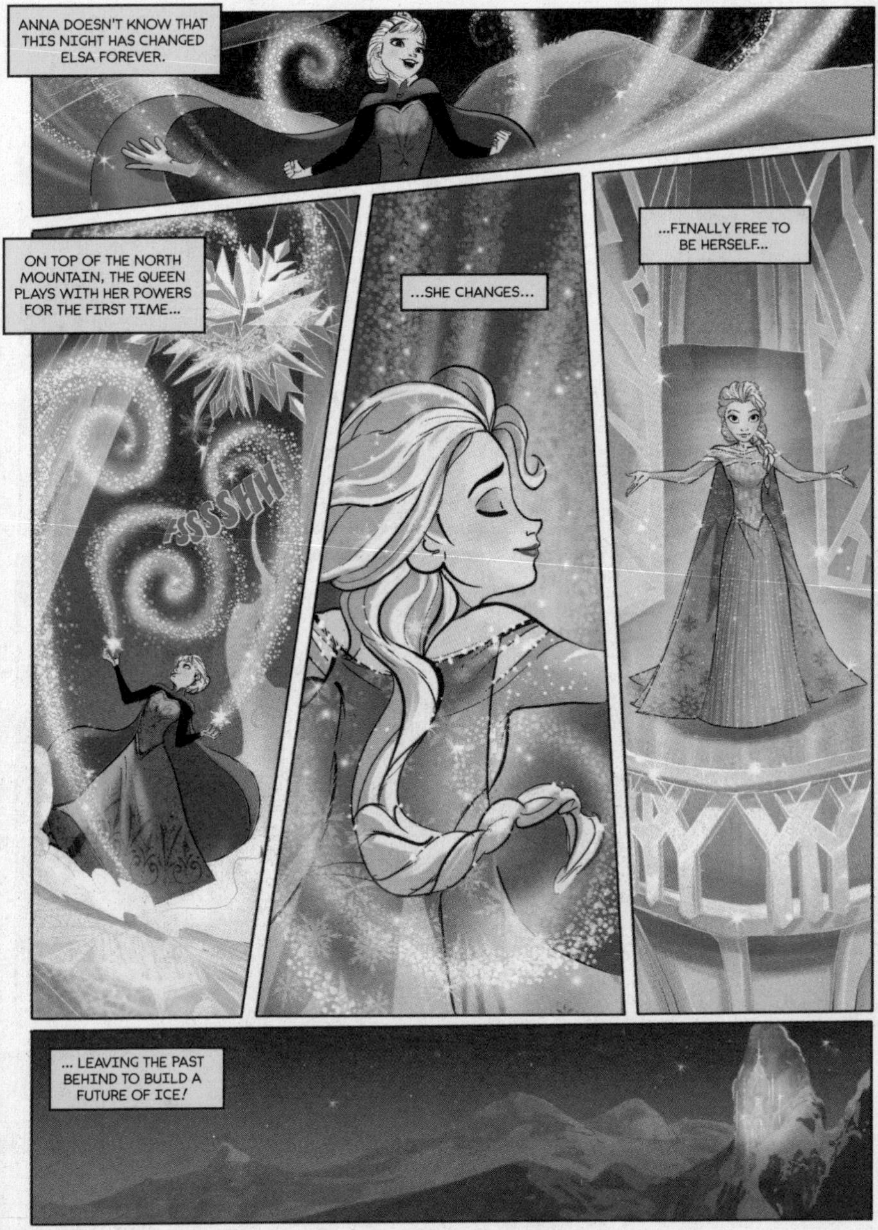
ANNA DOESN'T KNOW THAT THIS NIGHT HAS CHANGED ELSA FOREVER.
ON TOP OF THE NORTH MOUNTAIN, THE QUEEN PLAYS WITH HER POWERS FOR THE FIRST TIME...
FSSSSHH
...SHE CHANGES...
...FINALLY FREE TO BE HERSELF...
... LEAVING THE PAST BEHIND TO BUILD A FUTURE OF ICE!

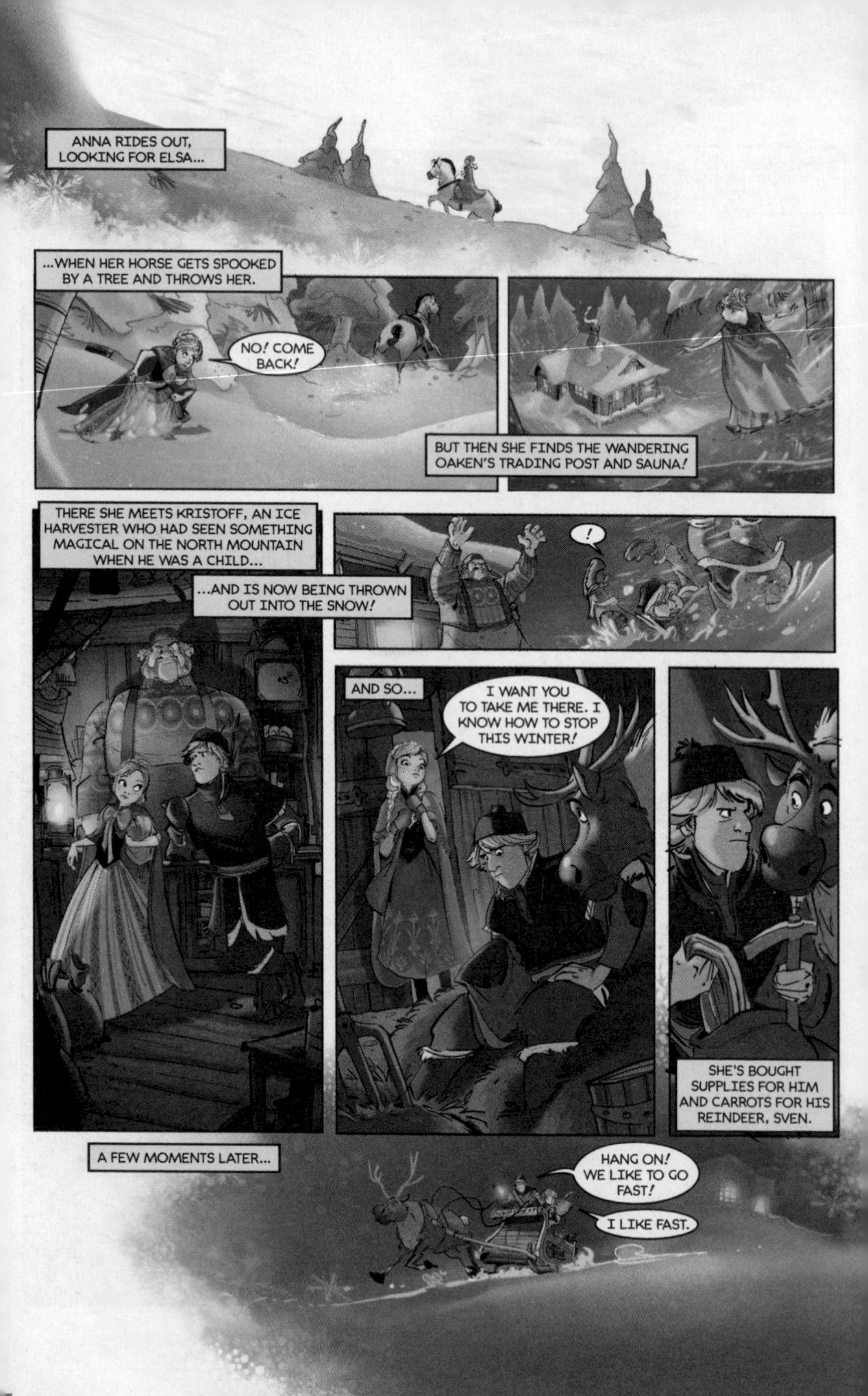
ANNA RIDES OUT, LOOKING FOR ELSA...
...WHEN HER HORSE GETS SPOOKED BY A TREE AND THROWS HER.
NO! COME BACK!
BUT THEN SHE FINDS THE WANDERING OAKEN'S TRADING POST AND SAUNA!
THERE SHE MEETS KRISTOFF, AN ICE HARVESTER WHO HAD SEEN SOMETHING MAGICAL ON THE NORTH MOUNTAIN WHEN HE WAS A CHILD...
...AND IS NOW BEING THROWN OUT INTO THE SNOW!
!
AND SO...
I WANT YOU TO TAKE ME THERE. I KNOW HOW TO STOP THIS WINTER!
SHE'S BOUGHT SUPPLIES FOR HIM AND CARROTS FOR HIS REINDEER, SVEN.
A FEW MOMENTS LATER...
HANG ON! WE LIKE TO GO FAST!
I LIKE FAST.

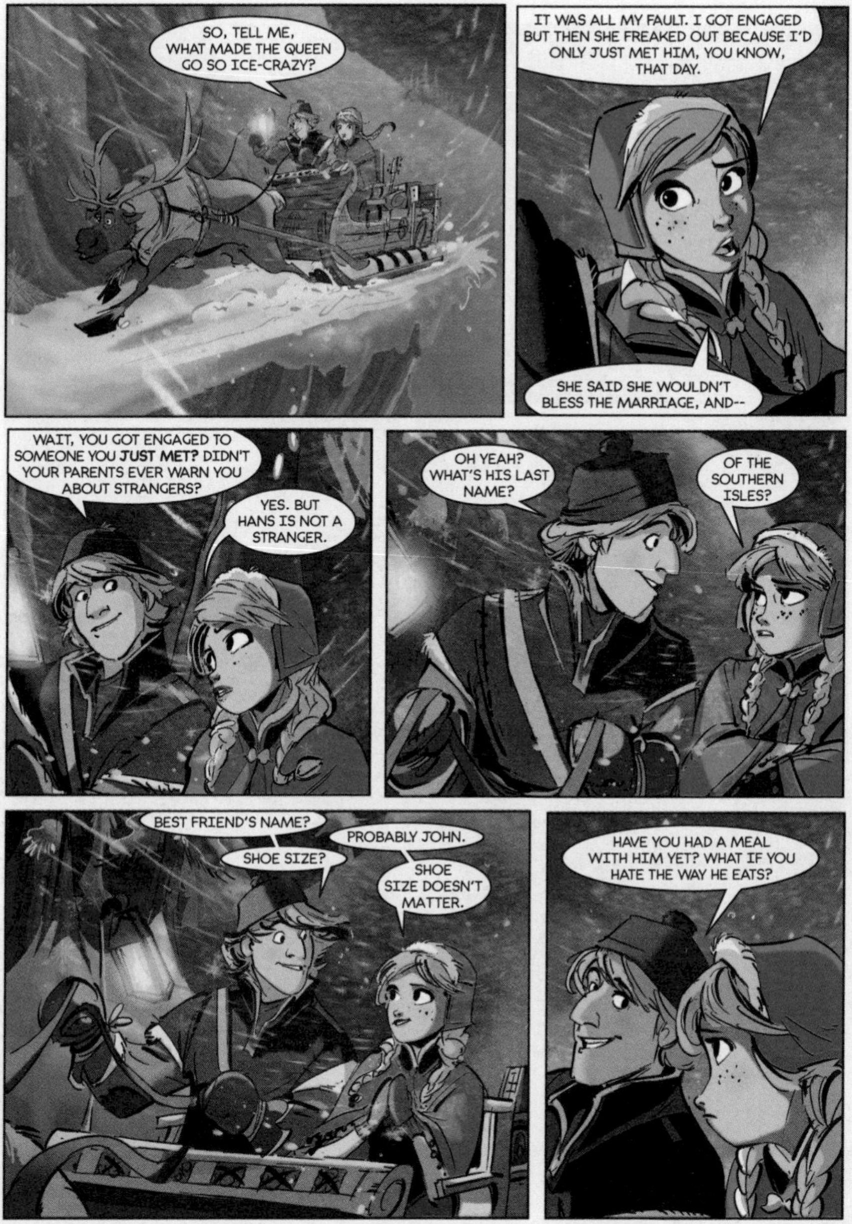
SO, TELL ME, WHAT MADE THE QUEEN GO SO ICE-CRAZY?
IT WAS ALL MY FAULT. I GOT ENGAGED BUT THEN SHE FREAKED OUT BECAUSE I'D ONLY JUST MET HIM, YOU KNOW, THAT DAY.
SHE SAID SHE WOULDN'T BLESS THE MARRIAGE, AND--
WAIT, YOU GOT ENGAGED TO SOMEONE YOU **JUST MET?** DIDN'T YOUR PARENTS EVER WARN YOU ABOUT STRANGERS?
YES. BUT HANS IS NOT A STRANGER.
OH YEAH? WHAT'S HIS LAST NAME?
OF THE SOUTHERN ISLES?
BEST FRIEND'S NAME?
PROBABLY JOHN.
SHOE SIZE?
SHOE SIZE DOESN'T MATTER.
HAVE YOU HAD A MEAL WITH HIM YET? WHAT IF YOU HATE THE WAY HE EATS?

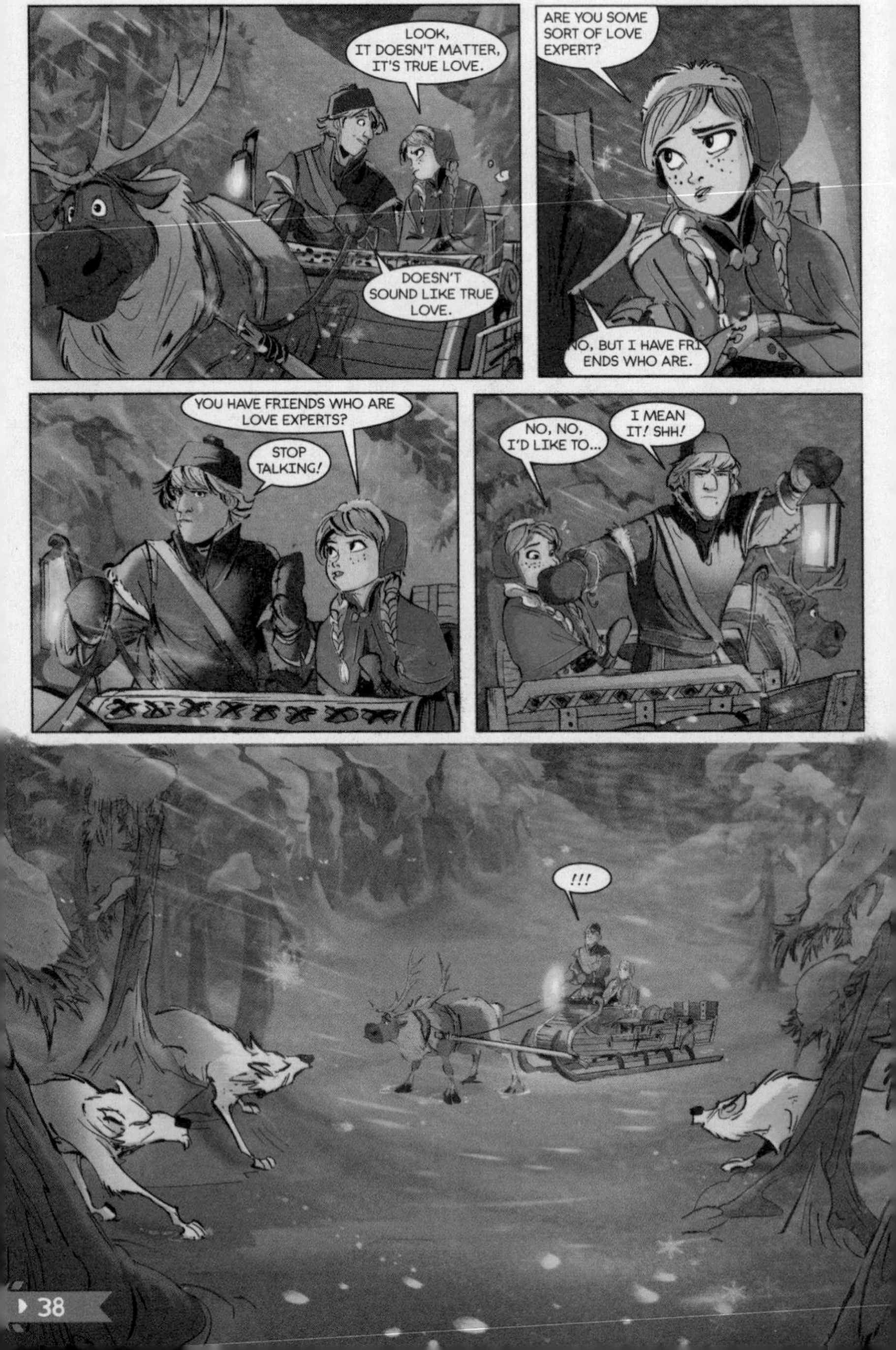

LOOK, IT DOESN'T MATTER, IT'S TRUE LOVE.
DOESN'T SOUND LIKE TRUE LOVE.
ARE YOU SOME SORT OF LOVE EXPERT?
NO, BUT I HAVE FRIENDS WHO ARE.
YOU HAVE FRIENDS WHO ARE LOVE EXPERTS?
STOP TALKING!
NO, NO, I'D LIKE TO...
I MEAN IT! SHH!
!!!

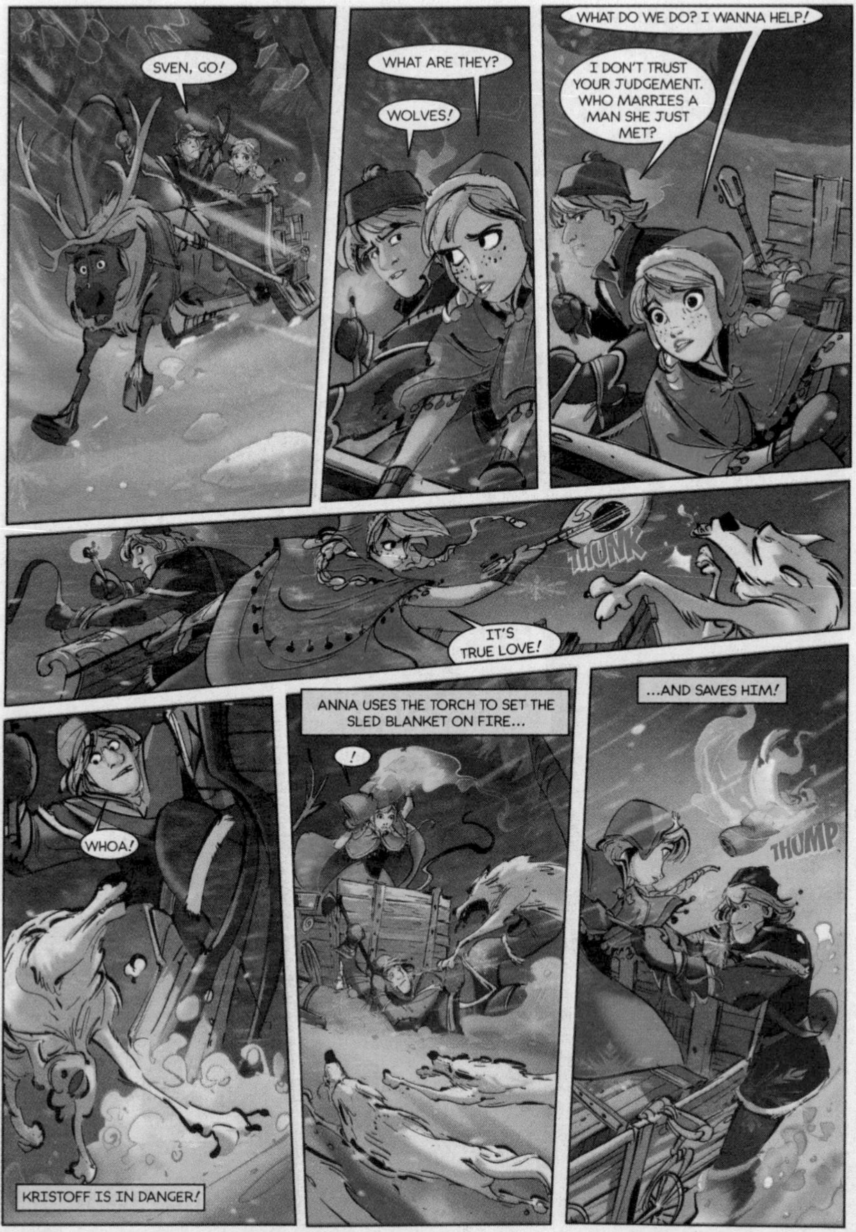
SVEN, GO!
WHAT ARE THEY?
WOLVES!
WHAT DO WE DO? I WANNA HELP!
I DON'T TRUST YOUR JUDGEMENT. WHO MARRIES A MAN SHE JUST MET?
THUNK
IT'S TRUE LOVE!
WHOA!
KRISTOFF IS IN DANGER!
ANNA USES THE TORCH TO SET THE SLED BLANKET ON FIRE...
!
...AND SAVES HIM!
THUMP

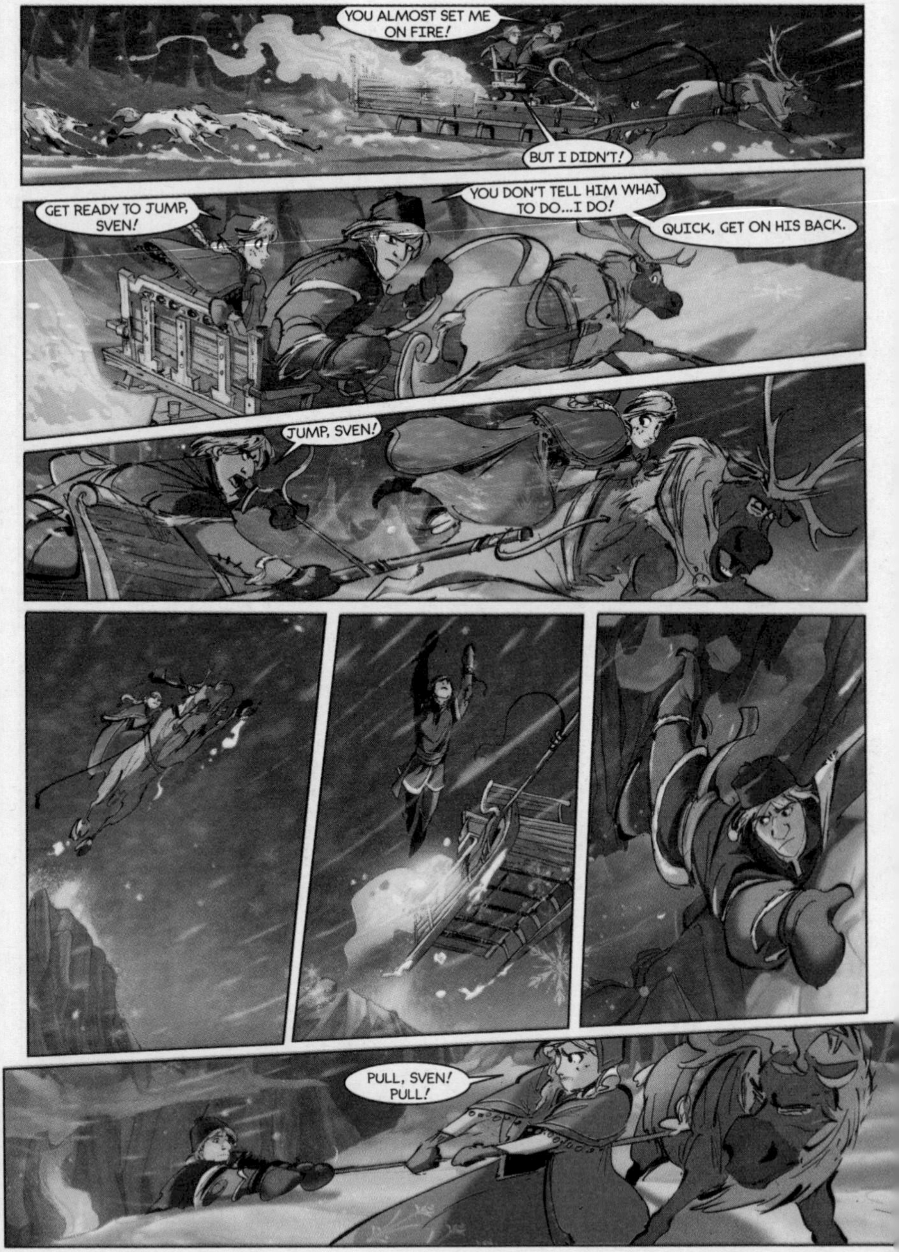
YOU ALMOST SET ME ON FIRE!
BUT I DIDN'T!
GET READY TO JUMP, SVEN!
YOU DON'T TELL HIM WHAT TO DO...I DO!
QUICK, GET ON HIS BACK.
JUMP, SVEN!
PULL, SVEN! PULL!

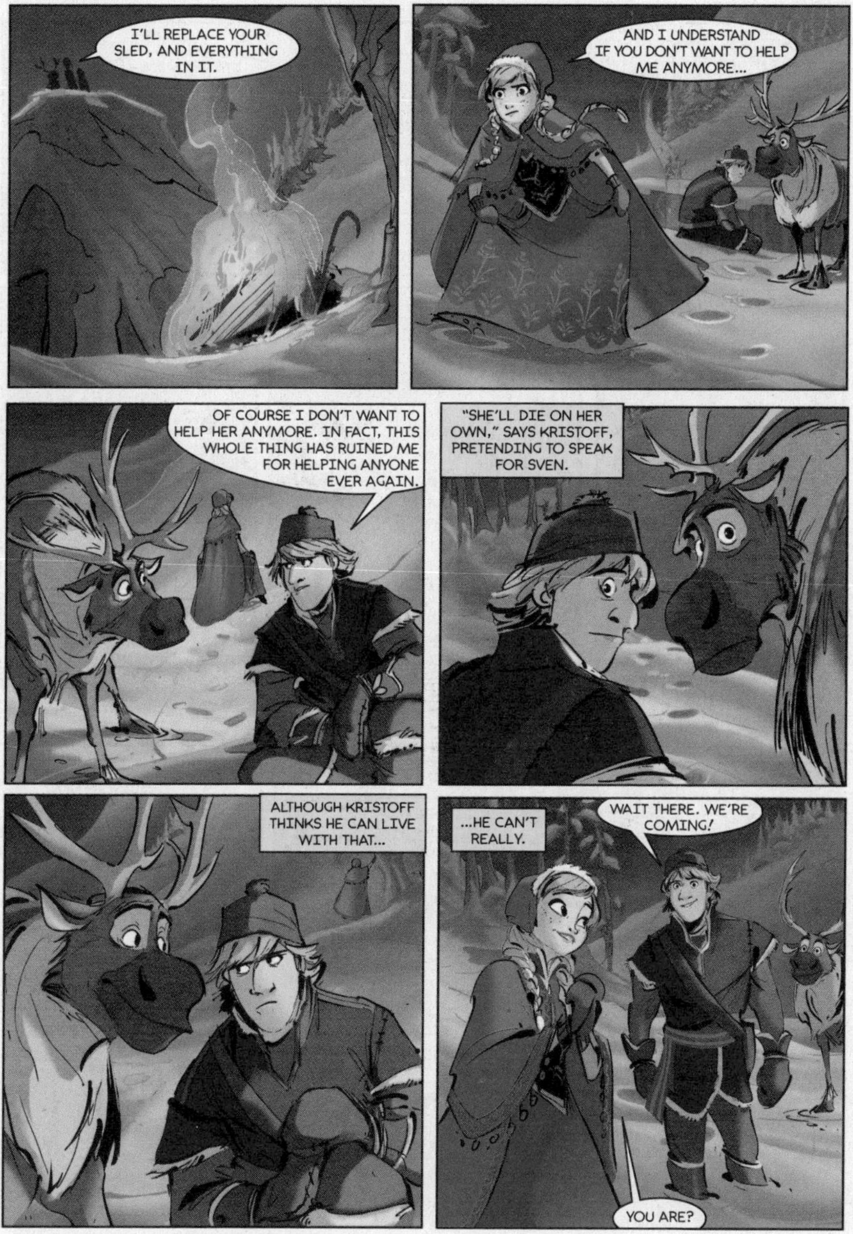
I'LL REPLACE YOUR SLED, AND EVERYTHING IN IT.
AND I UNDERSTAND IF YOU DON'T WANT TO HELP ME ANYMORE...
OF COURSE I DON'T WANT TO HELP HER ANYMORE. IN FACT, THIS WHOLE THING HAS RUINED ME FOR HELPING ANYONE EVER AGAIN.
"SHE'LL DIE ON HER OWN," SAYS KRISTOFF, PRETENDING TO SPEAK FOR SVEN.
ALTHOUGH KRISTOFF THINKS HE CAN LIVE WITH THAT...
...HE CAN'T REALLY.
WAIT THERE. WE'RE COMING!
YOU ARE?

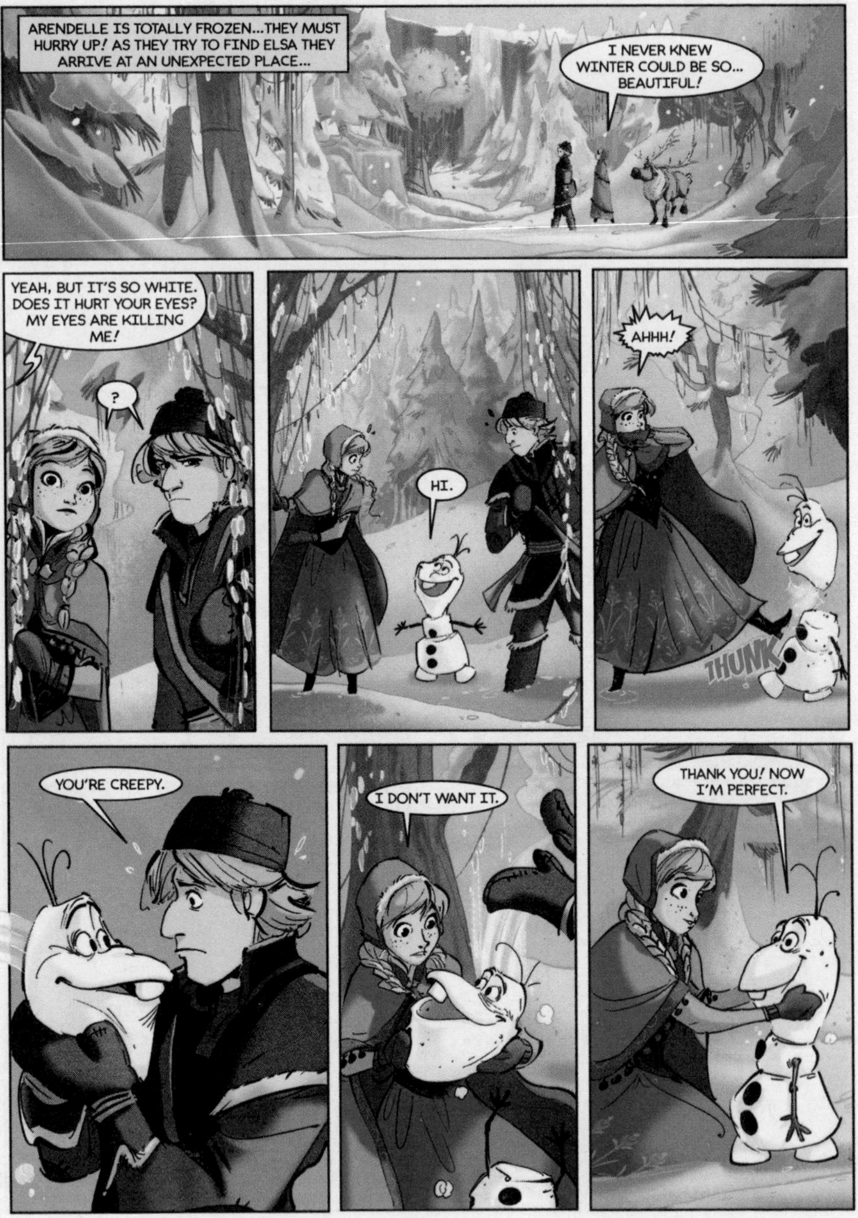
ARENDELLE IS TOTALLY FROZEN...THEY MUST HURRY UP! AS THEY TRY TO FIND ELSA THEY ARRIVE AT AN UNEXPECTED PLACE...
I NEVER KNEW WINTER COULD BE SO... BEAUTIFUL!
YEAH, BUT IT'S SO WHITE. DOES IT HURT YOUR EYES? MY EYES ARE KILLING ME!
?
HI.
AHHH!
THUNK
YOU'RE CREEPY.
I DON'T WANT IT.
THANK YOU! NOW I'M PERFECT.

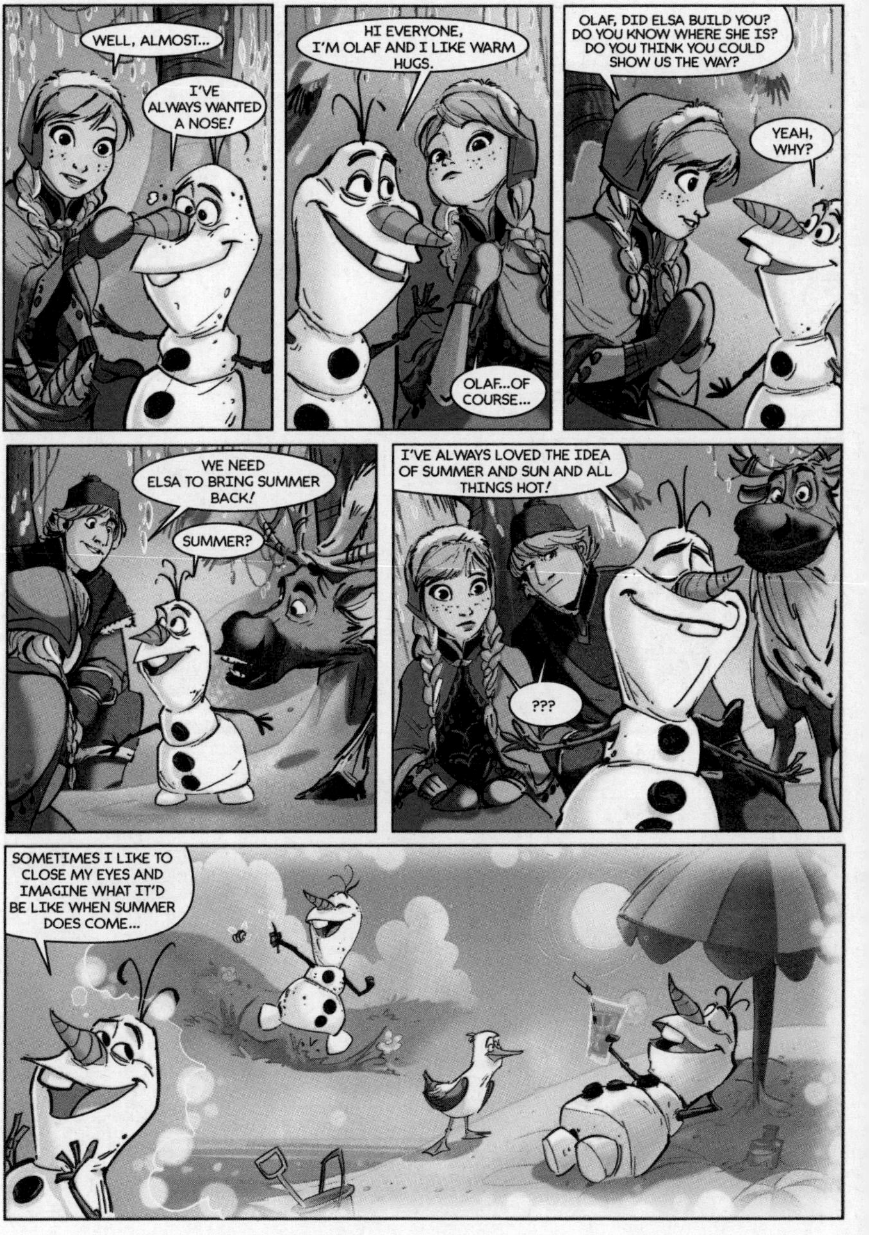
WELL, ALMOST...
I'VE ALWAYS WANTED A NOSE!
HI EVERYONE, I'M OLAF AND I LIKE WARM HUGS.
OLAF...OF COURSE...
OLAF, DID ELSA BUILD YOU? DO YOU KNOW WHERE SHE IS? DO YOU THINK YOU COULD SHOW US THE WAY?
YEAH, WHY?
WE NEED ELSA TO BRING SUMMER BACK!
SUMMER?
I'VE ALWAYS LOVED THE IDEA OF SUMMER AND SUN AND ALL THINGS HOT!
???
SOMETIMES I LIKE TO CLOSE MY EYES AND IMAGINE WHAT IT'D BE LIKE WHEN SUMMER DOES COME...

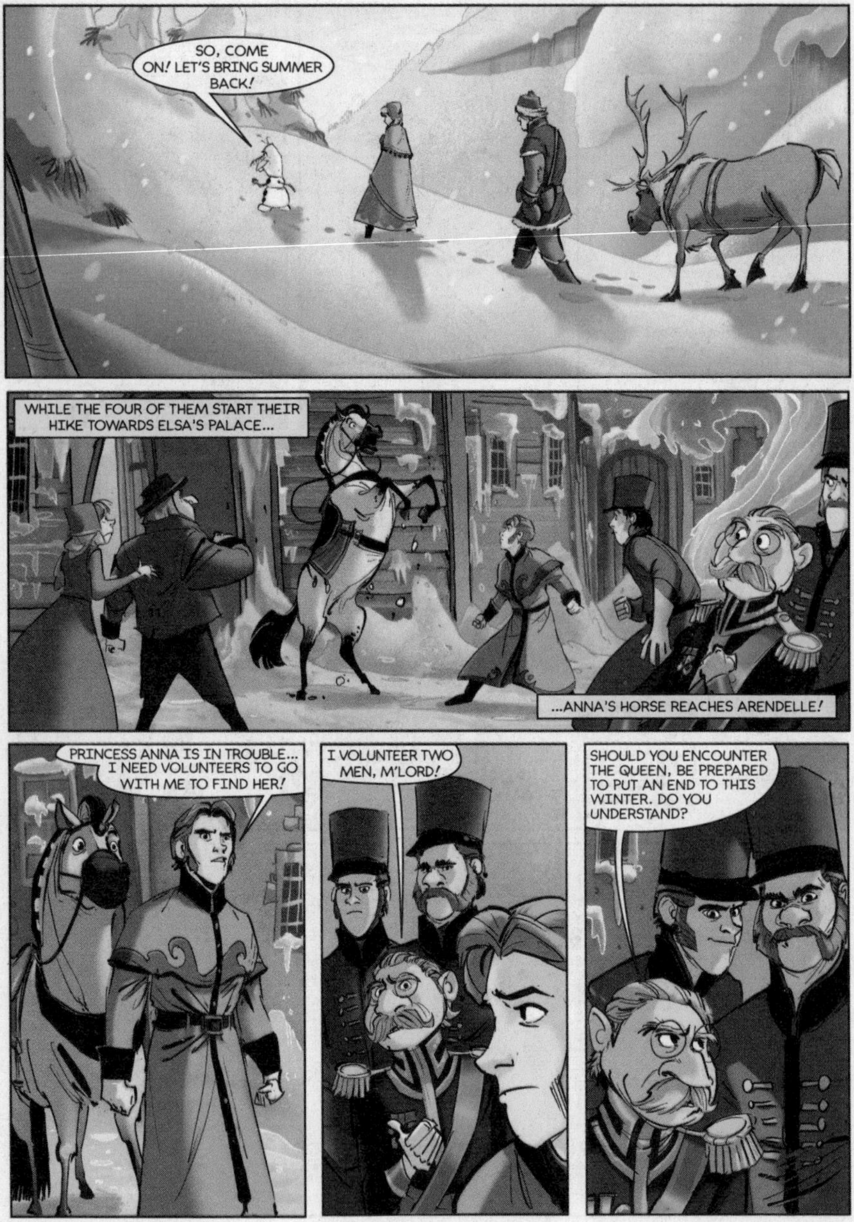
SO, COME ON! LET'S BRING SUMMER BACK!
WHILE THE FOUR OF THEM START THEIR HIKE TOWARDS ELSA'S PALACE...
...ANNA'S HORSE REACHES ARENDELLE!
PRINCESS ANNA IS IN TROUBLE... I NEED VOLUNTEERS TO GO WITH ME TO FIND HER!
I VOLUNTEER TWO MEN, M'LORD!
SHOULD YOU ENCOUNTER THE QUEEN, BE PREPARED TO PUT AN END TO THIS WINTER. DO YOU UNDERSTAND?

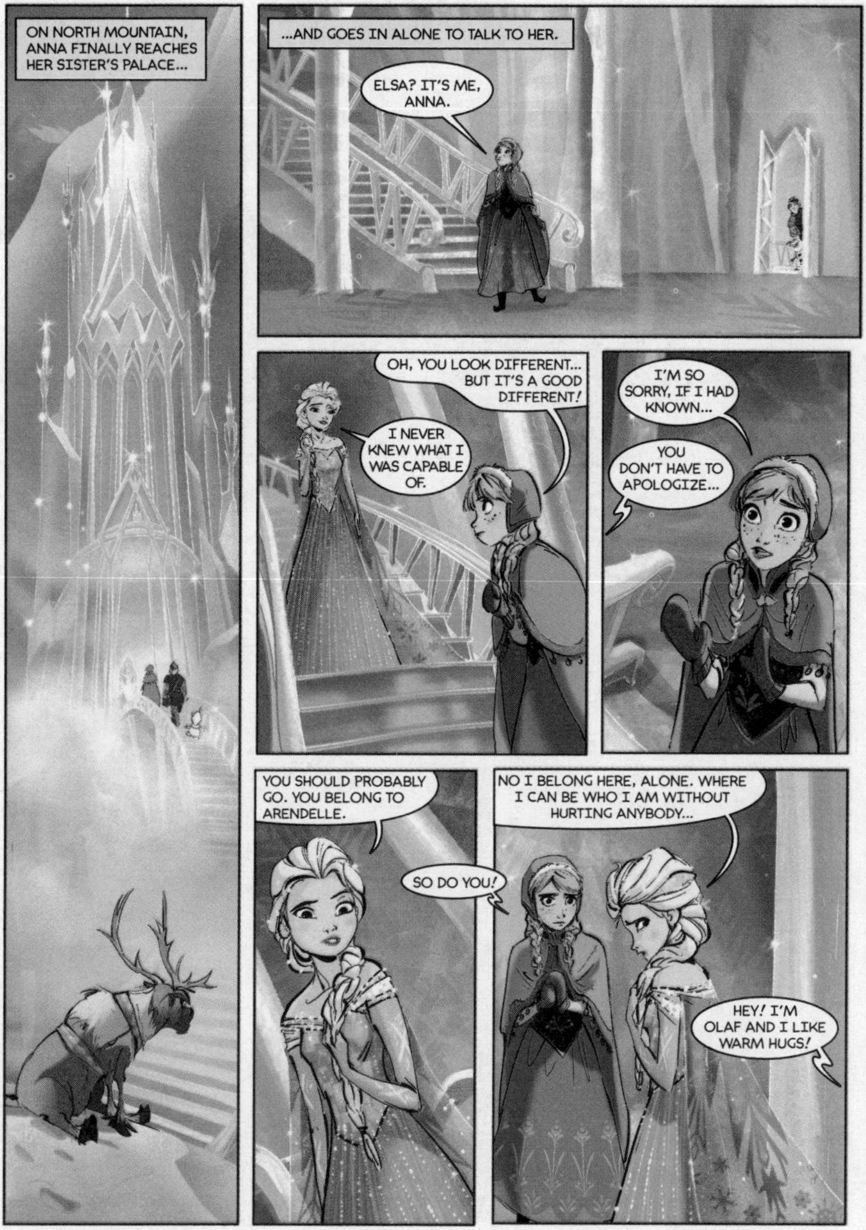
ON NORTH MOUNTAIN, ANNA FINALLY REACHES HER SISTER'S PALACE...
...AND GOES IN ALONE TO TALK TO HER.
ELSA? IT'S ME, ANNA.
OH, YOU LOOK DIFFERENT... BUT IT'S A GOOD DIFFERENT!
I NEVER KNEW WHAT I WAS CAPABLE OF.
I'M SO SORRY, IF I HAD KNOWN...
YOU DON'T HAVE TO APOLOGIZE...
YOU SHOULD PROBABLY GO. YOU BELONG TO ARENDELLE.
SO DO YOU!
NO I BELONG HERE, ALONE. WHERE I CAN BE WHO I AM WITHOUT HURTING ANYBODY...
HEY! I'M OLAF AND I LIKE WARM HUGS!

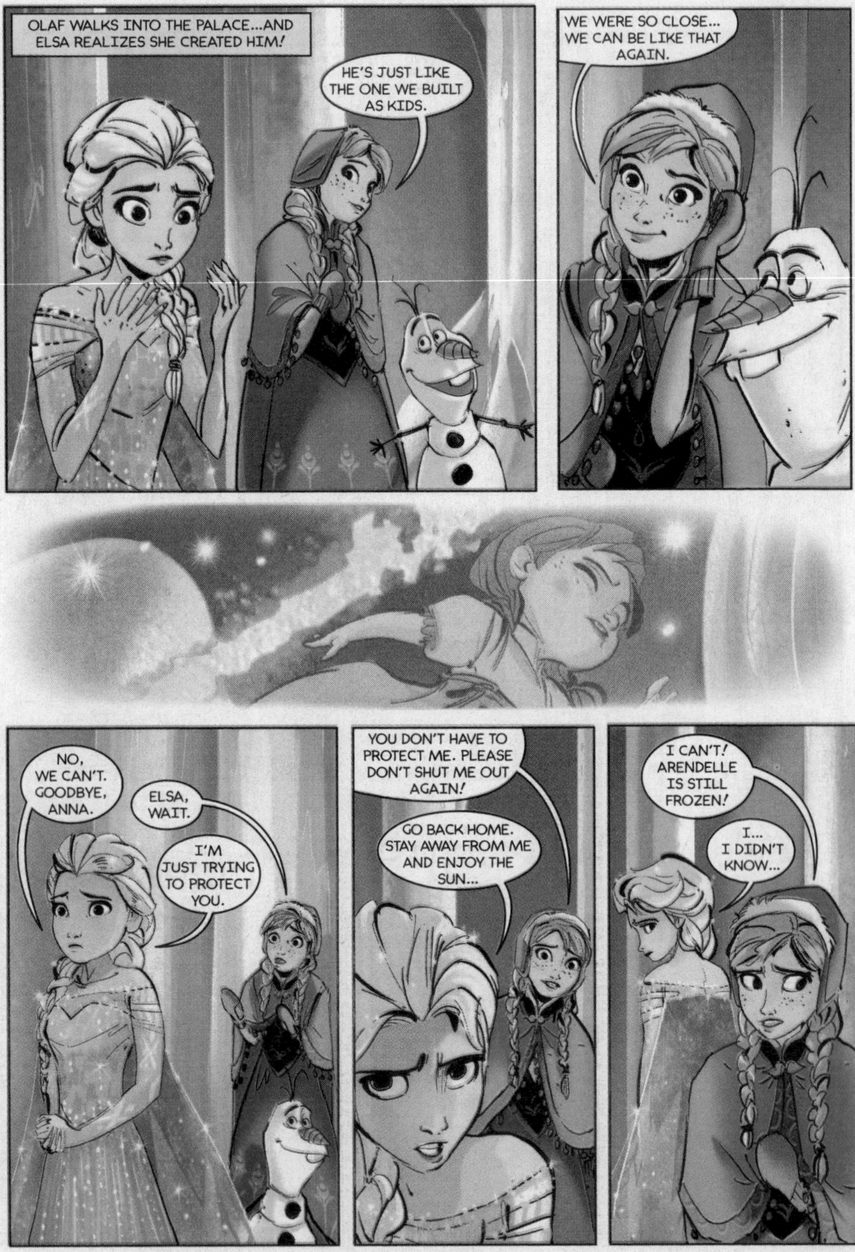
OLAF WALKS INTO THE PALACE...AND ELSA REALIZES SHE CREATED HIM!
HE'S JUST LIKE THE ONE WE BUILT AS KIDS.
WE WERE SO CLOSE... WE CAN BE LIKE THAT AGAIN.
NO, WE CAN'T. GOODBYE, ANNA.
ELSA, WAIT.
I'M JUST TRYING TO PROTECT YOU.
YOU DON'T HAVE TO PROTECT ME. PLEASE DON'T SHUT ME OUT AGAIN!
GO BACK HOME. STAY AWAY FROM ME AND ENJOY THE SUN...
I CAN'T! ARENDELLE IS STILL FROZEN!
I... I DIDN'T KNOW...

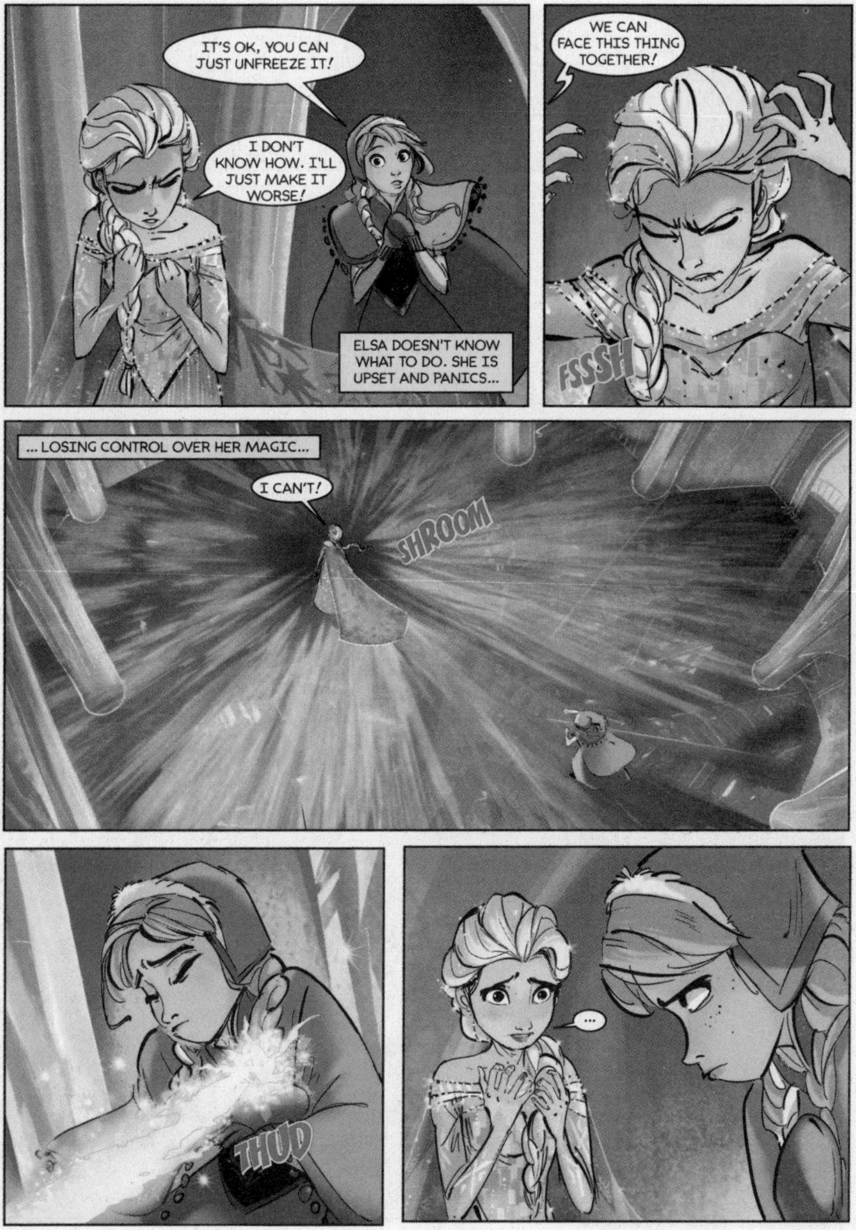
IT'S OK, YOU CAN JUST UNFREEZE IT!
I DON'T KNOW HOW. I'LL JUST MAKE IT WORSE!
ELSA DOESN'T KNOW WHAT TO DO. SHE IS UPSET AND PANICS...
WE CAN FACE THIS THING TOGETHER!
FSSSH
... LOSING CONTROL OVER HER MAGIC...
I CAN'T!
SHROOM
THUD
...

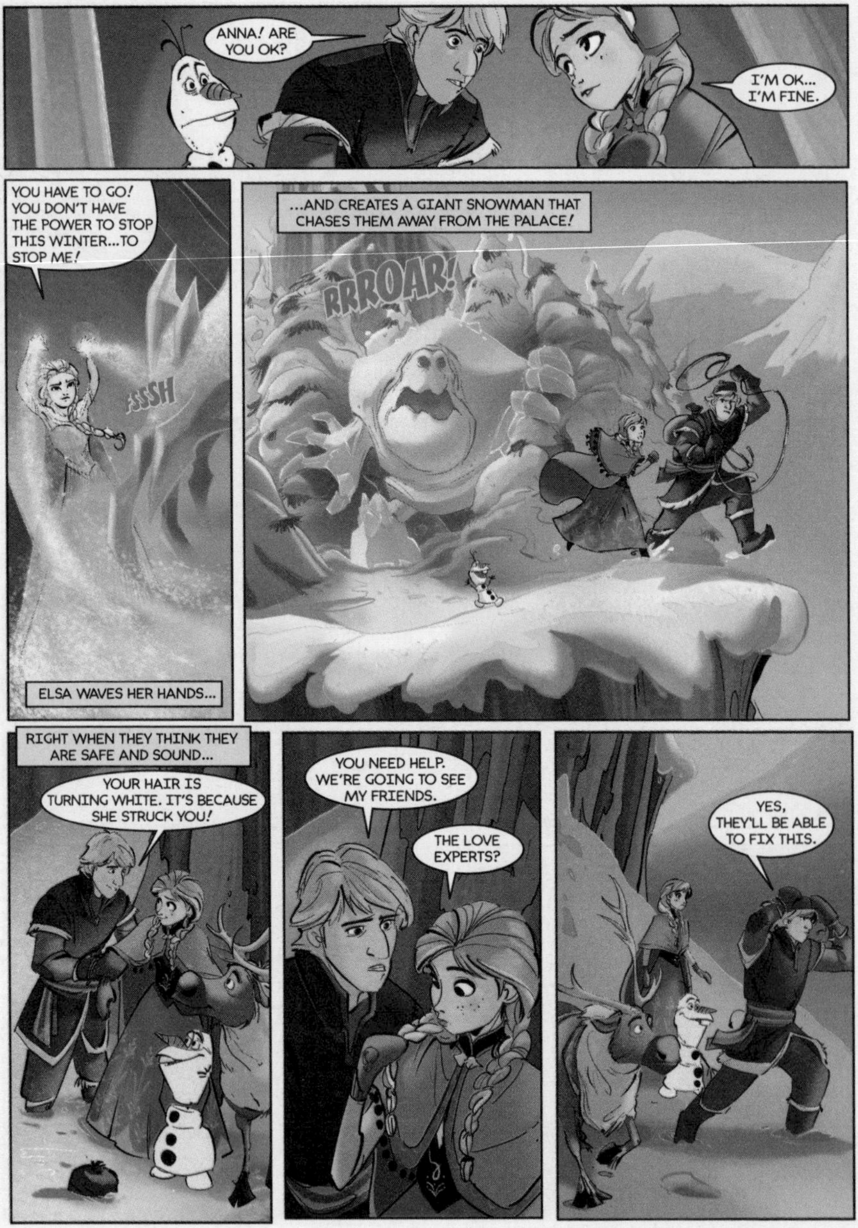
ANNA! ARE YOU OK?
I'M OK... I'M FINE.
YOU HAVE TO GO! YOU DON'T HAVE THE POWER TO STOP THIS WINTER...TO STOP ME!
FSSSH
ELSA WAVES HER HANDS...
...AND CREATES A GIANT SNOWMAN THAT CHASES THEM AWAY FROM THE PALACE!
RRROAR!
RIGHT WHEN THEY THINK THEY ARE SAFE AND SOUND...
YOUR HAIR IS TURNING WHITE. IT'S BECAUSE SHE STRUCK YOU!
YOU NEED HELP. WE'RE GOING TO SEE MY FRIENDS.
THE LOVE EXPERTS?
YES, THEY'LL BE ABLE TO FIX THIS.

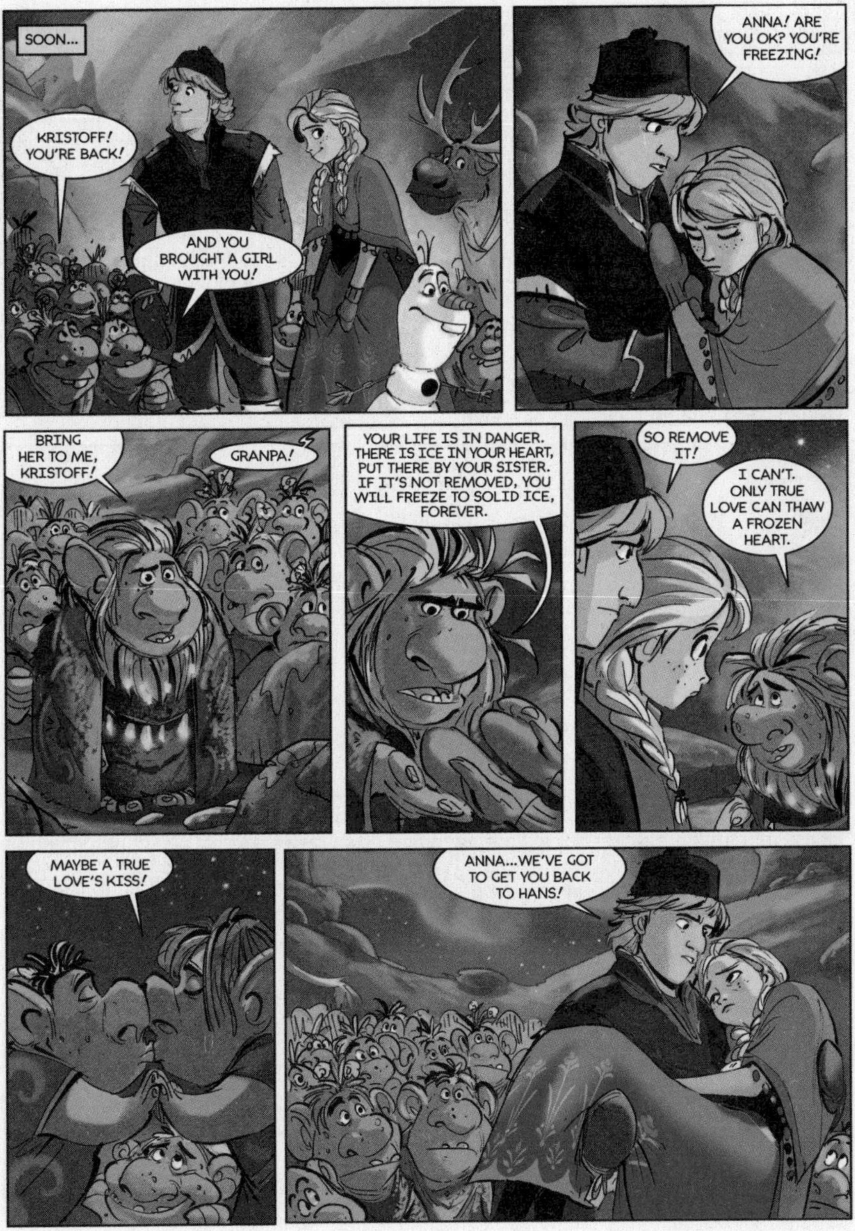
SOON...
KRISTOFF! YOU'RE BACK!
AND YOU BROUGHT A GIRL WITH YOU!
ANNA! ARE YOU OK? YOU'RE FREEZING!
BRING HER TO ME, KRISTOFF!
GRANPA!
YOUR LIFE IS IN DANGER. THERE IS ICE IN YOUR HEART, PUT THERE BY YOUR SISTER. IF IT'S NOT REMOVED, YOU WILL FREEZE TO SOLID ICE, FOREVER.
SO REMOVE IT!
I CAN'T. ONLY TRUE LOVE CAN THAW A FROZEN HEART.
MAYBE A TRUE LOVE'S KISS!
ANNA...WE'VE GOT TO GET YOU BACK TO HANS!

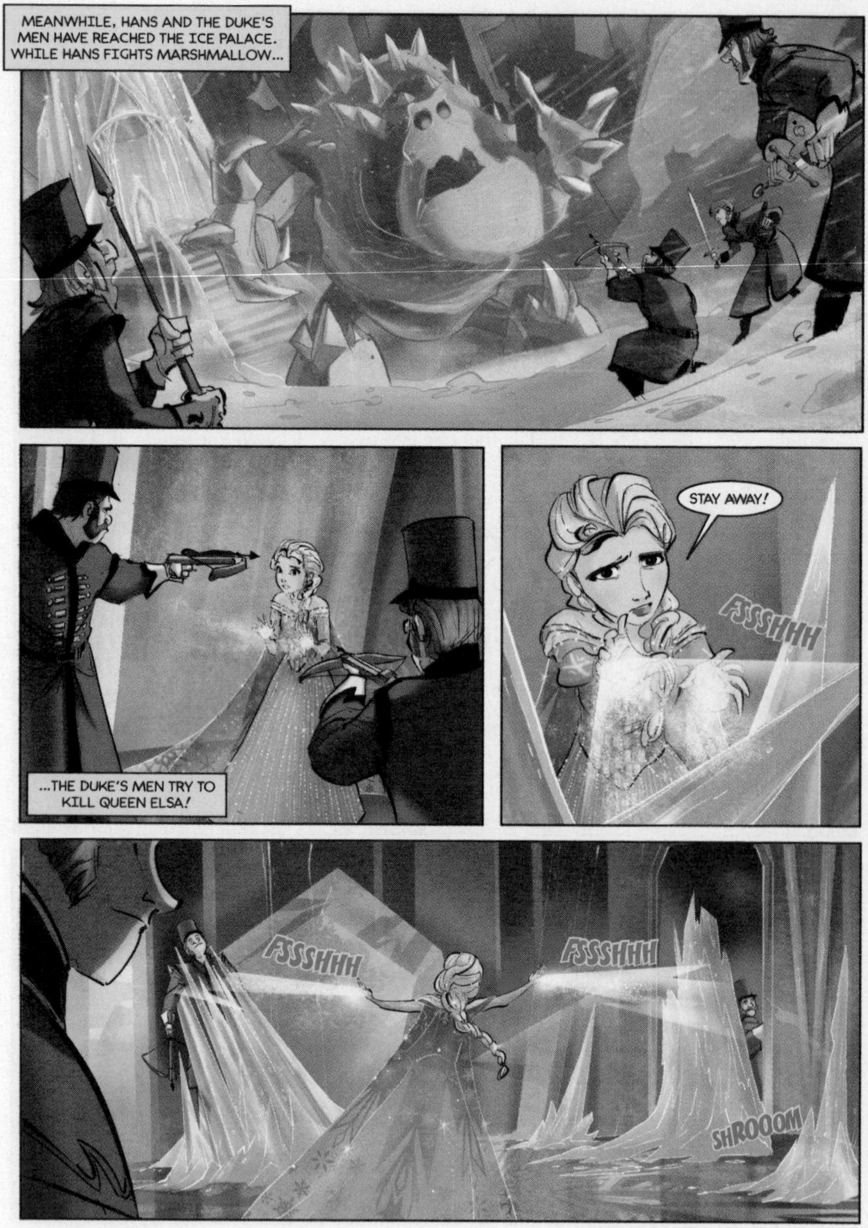
MEANWHILE, HANS AND THE DUKE'S MEN HAVE REACHED THE ICE PALACE. WHILE HANS FIGHTS MARSHMALLOW...
...THE DUKE'S MEN TRY TO KILL QUEEN ELSA!
STAY AWAY!
FSSSHHH
FSSSHHH
FSSSHHH
SHROOOM

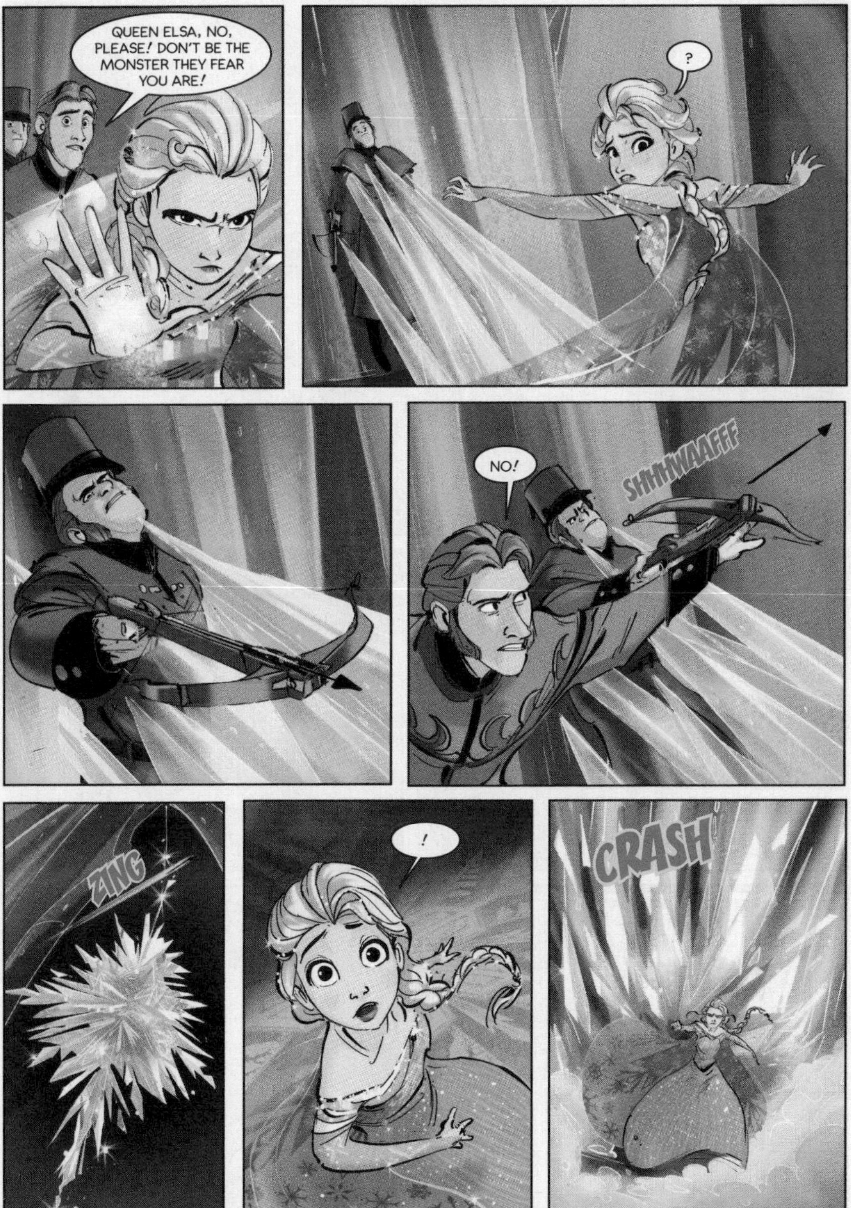
QUEEN ELSA, NO, PLEASE! DON'T BE THE MONSTER THEY FEAR YOU ARE!
?
NO!
SHHHWAAFFF
ZING
!
CRASH

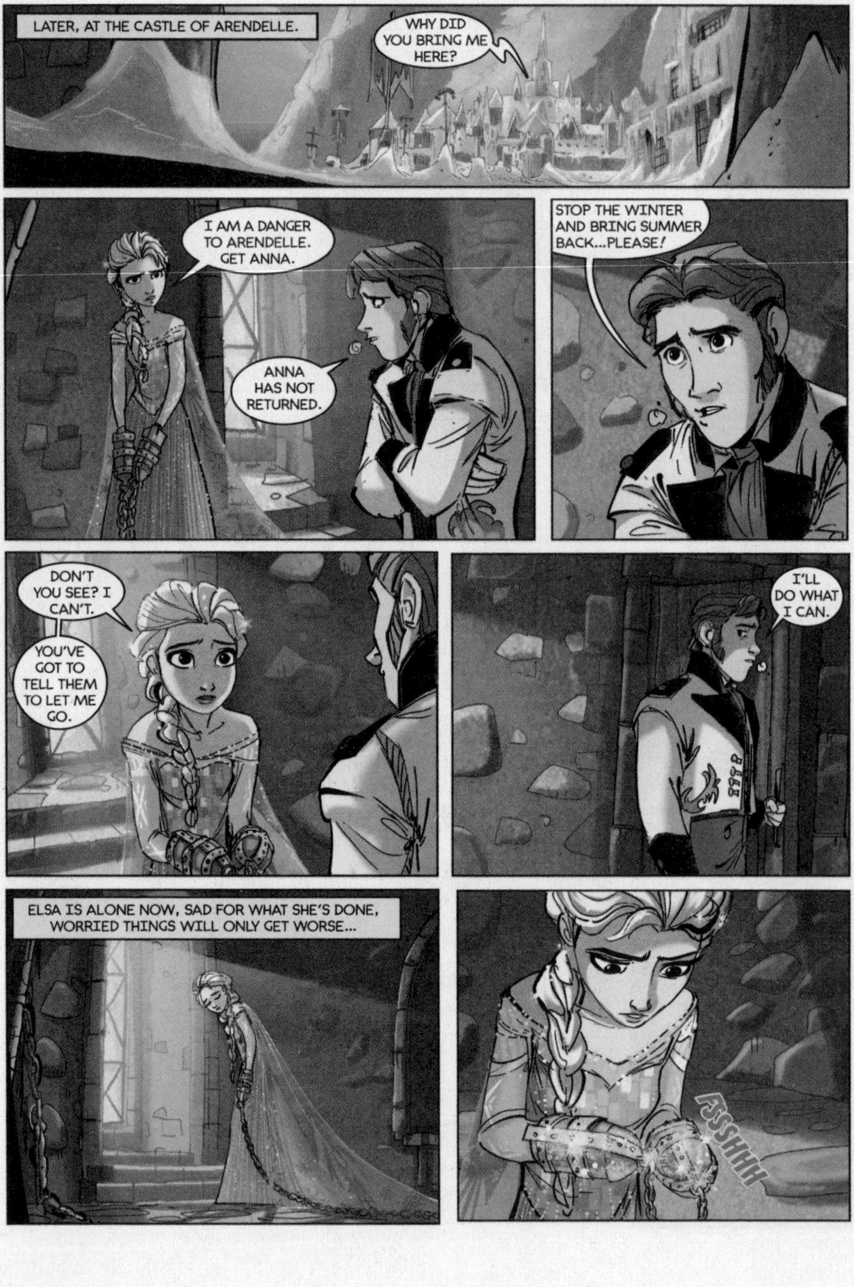
LATER, AT THE CASTLE OF ARENDELLE.
WHY DID YOU BRING ME HERE?
I AM A DANGER TO ARENDELLE. GET ANNA.
ANNA HAS NOT RETURNED.
STOP THE WINTER AND BRING SUMMER BACK...PLEASE!
DON'T YOU SEE? I CAN'T.
YOU'VE GOT TO TELL THEM TO LET ME GO.
I'LL DO WHAT I CAN.
ELSA IS ALONE NOW, SAD FOR WHAT SHE'S DONE, WORRIED THINGS WILL ONLY GET WORSE...
FSSSHHHH

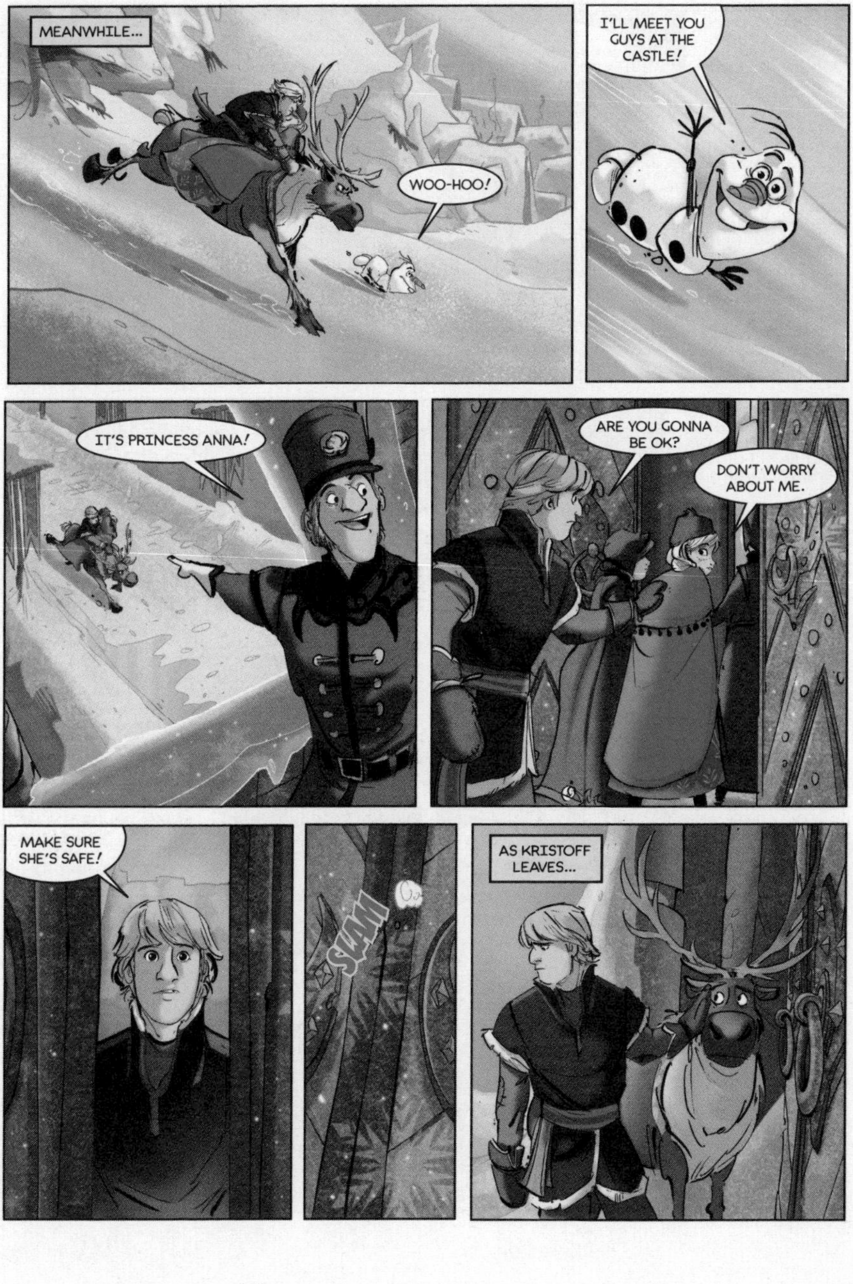
MEANWHILE...
WOO-HOO!
I'LL MEET YOU GUYS AT THE CASTLE!
IT'S PRINCESS ANNA!
ARE YOU GONNA BE OK?
DON'T WORRY ABOUT ME.
MAKE SURE SHE'S SAFE!
SLAM
AS KRISTOFF LEAVES...

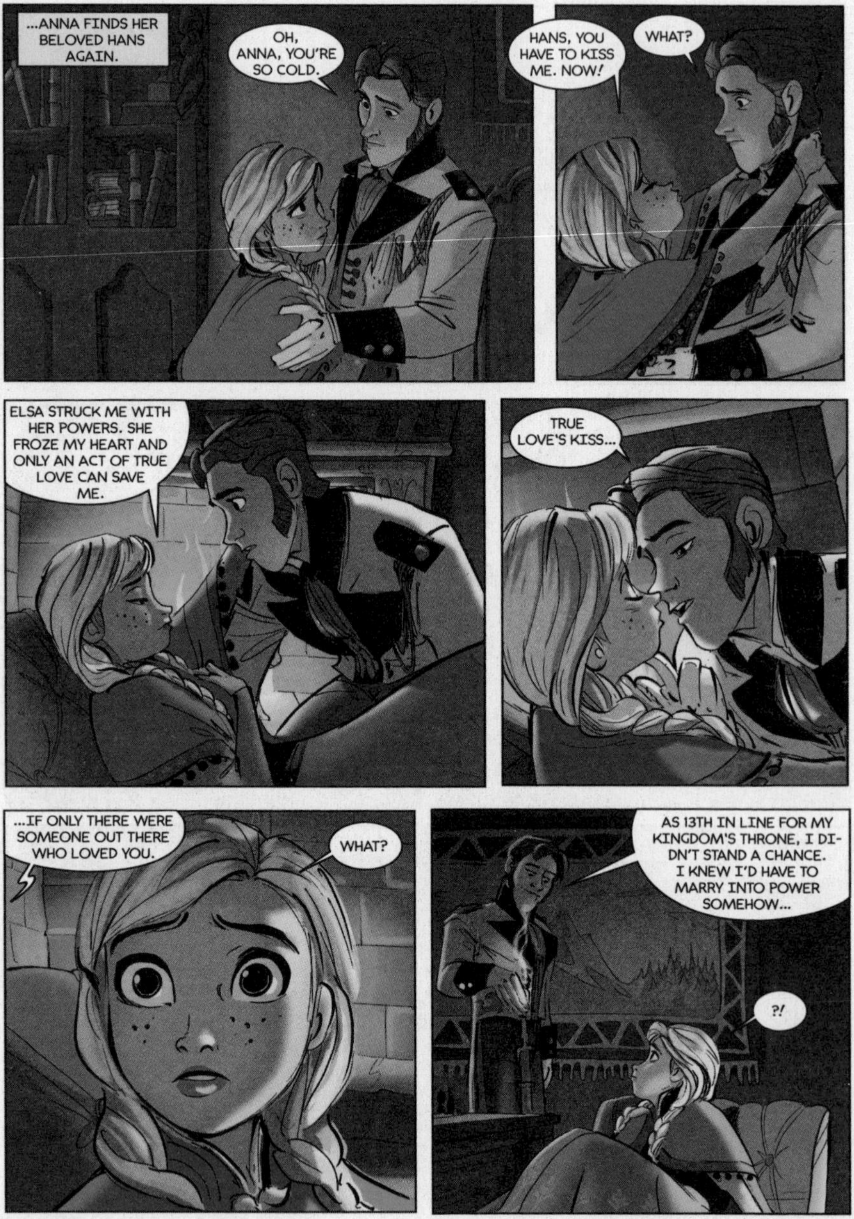

...ANNA FINDS HER BELOVED HANS AGAIN.
OH, ANNA, YOU'RE SO COLD.
HANS, YOU HAVE TO KISS ME. NOW!
WHAT?
ELSA STRUCK ME WITH HER POWERS. SHE FROZE MY HEART AND ONLY AN ACT OF TRUE LOVE CAN SAVE ME.
TRUE LOVE'S KISS...
...IF ONLY THERE WERE SOMEONE OUT THERE WHO LOVED YOU.
WHAT?
AS 13TH IN LINE FOR MY KINGDOM'S THRONE, I DIDN'T STAND A CHANCE. I KNEW I'D HAVE TO MARRY INTO POWER SOMEHOW...
?!

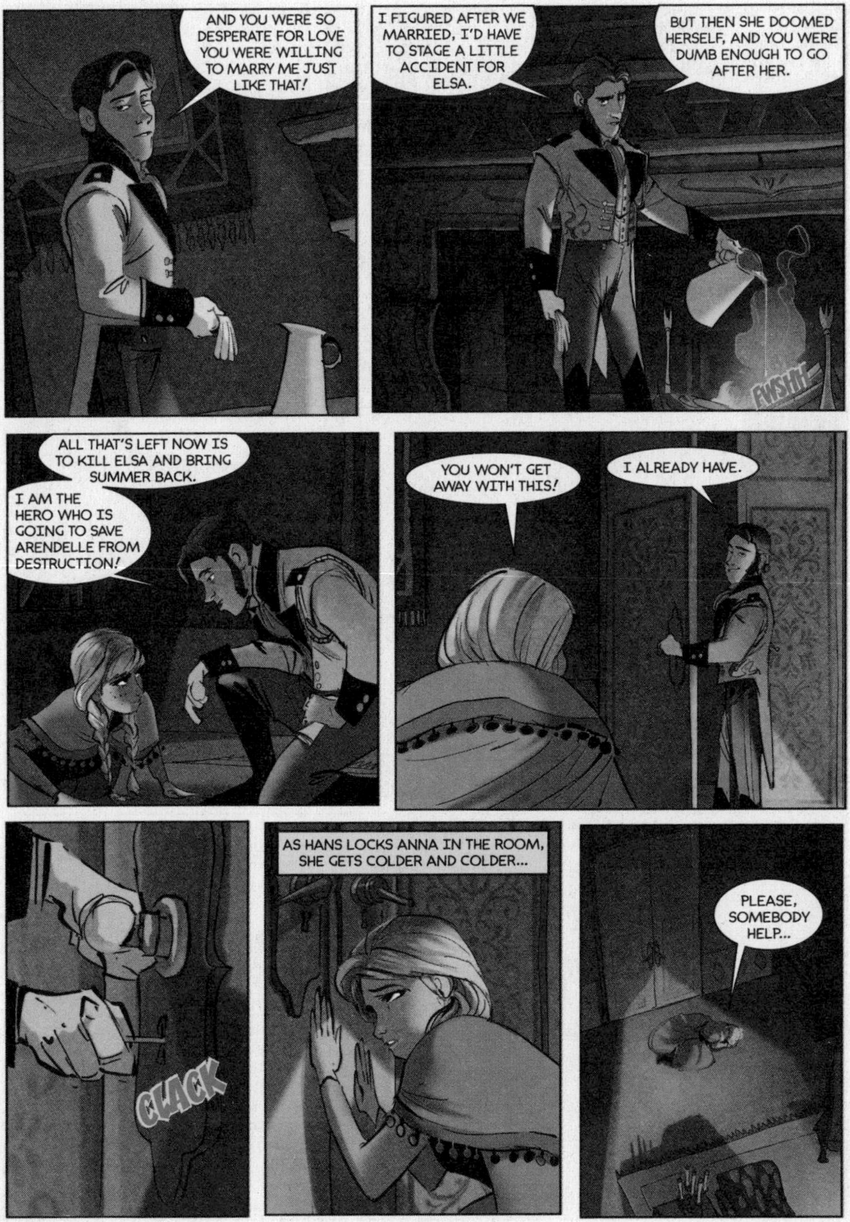
AND YOU WERE SO DESPERATE FOR LOVE YOU WERE WILLING TO MARRY ME JUST LIKE THAT!
I FIGURED AFTER WE MARRIED, I'D HAVE TO STAGE A LITTLE ACCIDENT FOR ELSA.
BUT THEN SHE DOOMED HERSELF, AND YOU WERE DUMB ENOUGH TO GO AFTER HER.
FVSHH
ALL THAT'S LEFT NOW IS TO KILL ELSA AND BRING SUMMER BACK.
I AM THE HERO WHO IS GOING TO SAVE ARENDELLE FROM DESTRUCTION!
YOU WON'T GET AWAY WITH THIS!
I ALREADY HAVE.
CLACK
AS HANS LOCKS ANNA IN THE ROOM, SHE GETS COLDER AND COLDER...
PLEASE, SOMEBODY HELP...

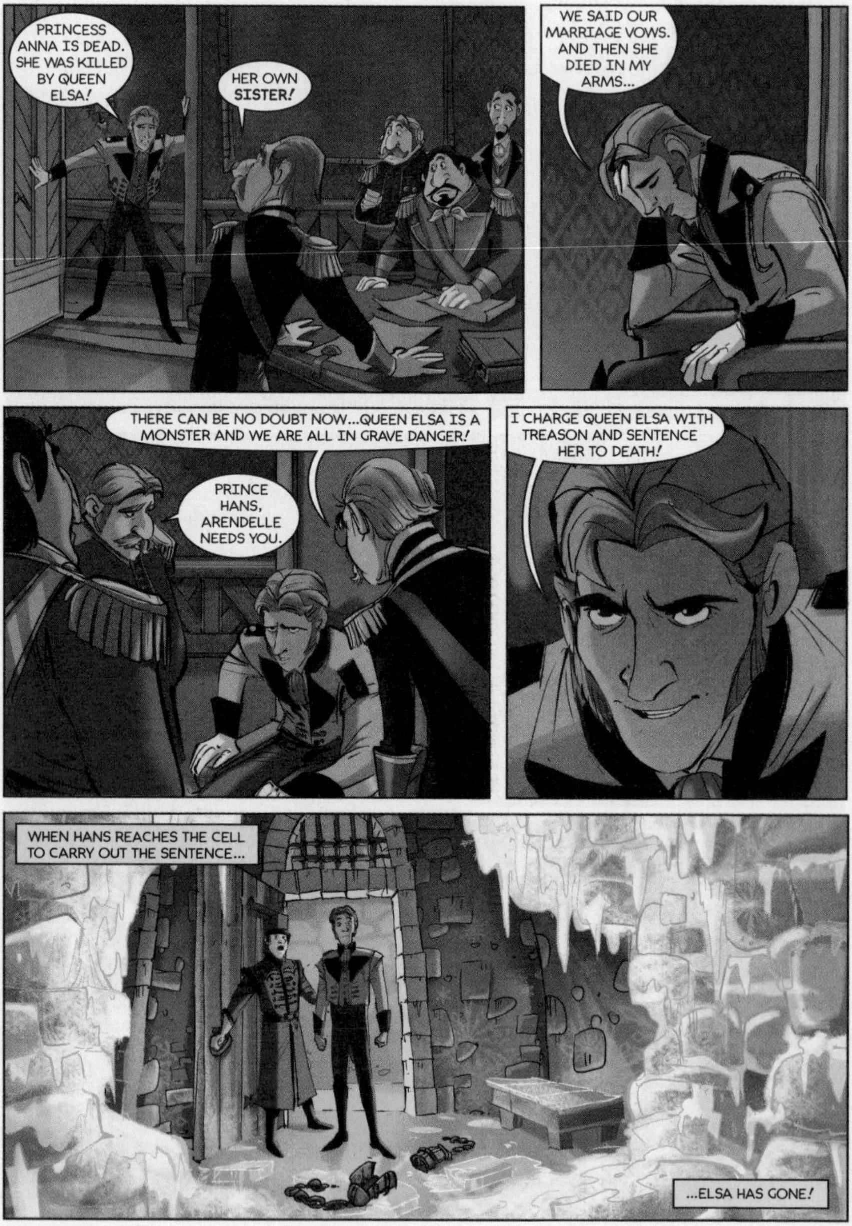
PRINCESS ANNA IS DEAD. SHE WAS KILLED BY QUEEN ELSA!
HER OWN **SISTER!**
WE SAID OUR MARRIAGE VOWS. AND THEN SHE DIED IN MY ARMS...
THERE CAN BE NO DOUBT NOW...QUEEN ELSA IS A MONSTER AND WE ARE ALL IN GRAVE DANGER!
PRINCE HANS, ARENDELLE NEEDS YOU.
I CHARGE QUEEN ELSA WITH TREASON AND SENTENCE HER TO DEATH!
WHEN HANS REACHES THE CELL TO CARRY OUT THE SENTENCE...
...ELSA HAS GONE!

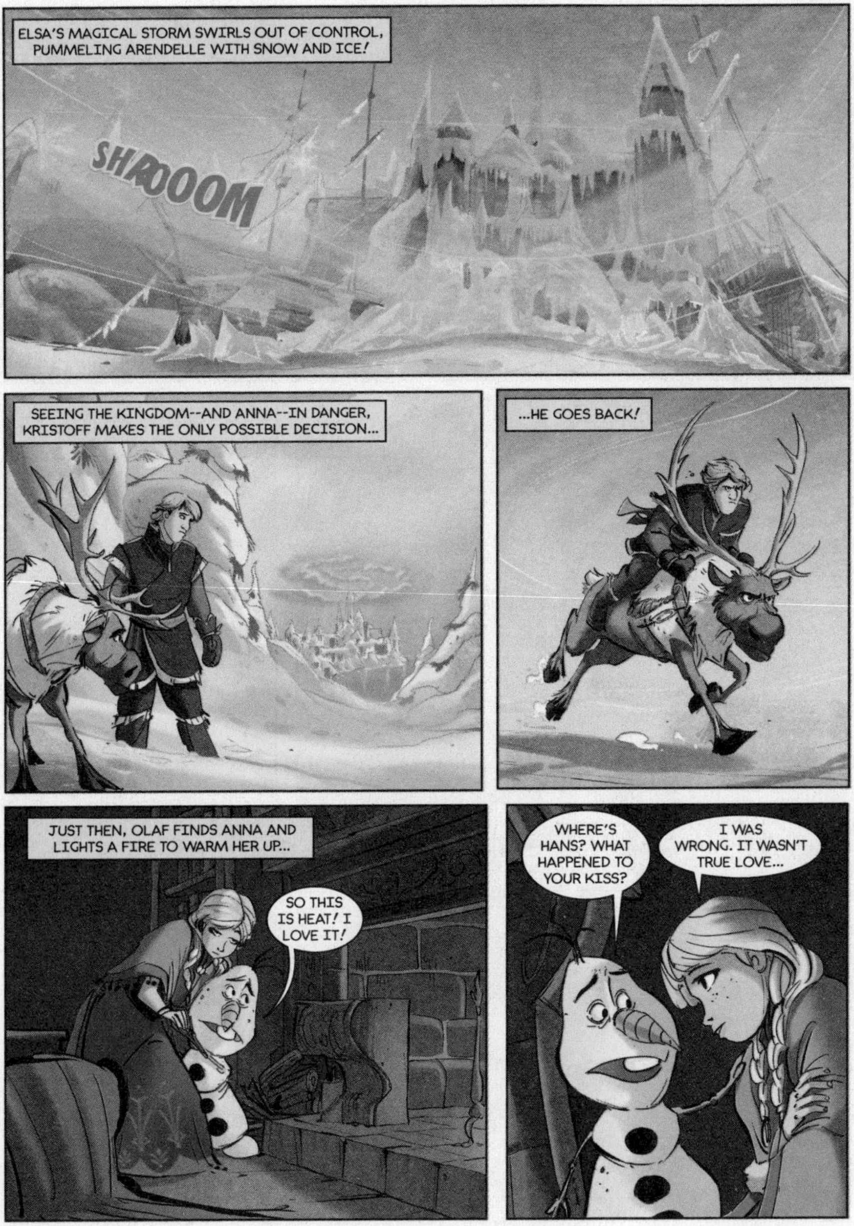
ELSA'S MAGICAL STORM SWIRLS OUT OF CONTROL, PUMMELING ARENDELLE WITH SNOW AND ICE!
SHROOOM
SEEING THE KINGDOM--AND ANNA--IN DANGER, KRISTOFF MAKES THE ONLY POSSIBLE DECISION...
...HE GOES BACK!
JUST THEN, OLAF FINDS ANNA AND LIGHTS A FIRE TO WARM HER UP...
SO THIS IS HEAT! I LOVE IT!
WHERE'S HANS? WHAT HAPPENED TO YOUR KISS?
I WAS WRONG. IT WASN'T TRUE LOVE...

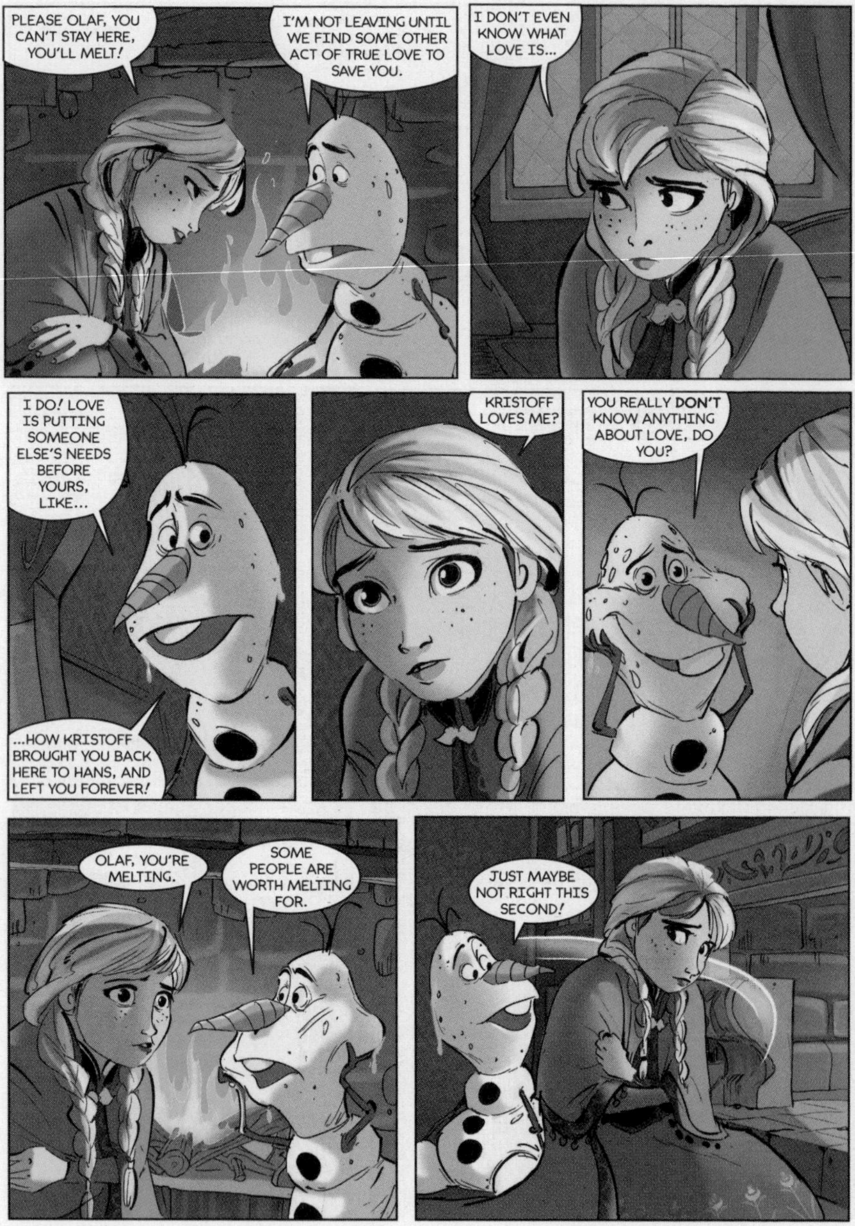
PLEASE OLAF, YOU CAN'T STAY HERE, YOU'LL MELT!
I'M NOT LEAVING UNTIL WE FIND SOME OTHER ACT OF TRUE LOVE TO SAVE YOU.
I DON'T EVEN KNOW WHAT LOVE IS...
I DO! LOVE IS PUTTING SOMEONE ELSE'S NEEDS BEFORE YOURS, LIKE...
...HOW KRISTOFF BROUGHT YOU BACK HERE TO HANS, AND LEFT YOU FOREVER!
KRISTOFF LOVES ME?
YOU REALLY **DON'T** KNOW ANYTHING ABOUT LOVE, DO YOU?
OLAF, YOU'RE MELTING.
SOME PEOPLE ARE WORTH MELTING FOR.
JUST MAYBE NOT RIGHT THIS SECOND!

SUDDENLY, A WINDOW BLOWS OPEN! WHEN OLAF RUNS TO CLOSE IT...

?

SWOOSH

BAM

CRACK

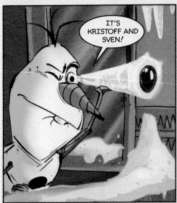

IT'S KRISTOFF AND SVEN!

THEY'RE COMING BACK!

MAYBE I WAS WRONG. I GUESS KRISTOFF DOESN'T LOVE YOU ENOUGH TO LEAVE YOU BEHIND!

HELP ME UP, OLAF. PLEASE. I NEED TO GET TO KRISTOFF.

WHY?

OH, I KNOW WHY. THERE'S YOUR TRUE LOVE...

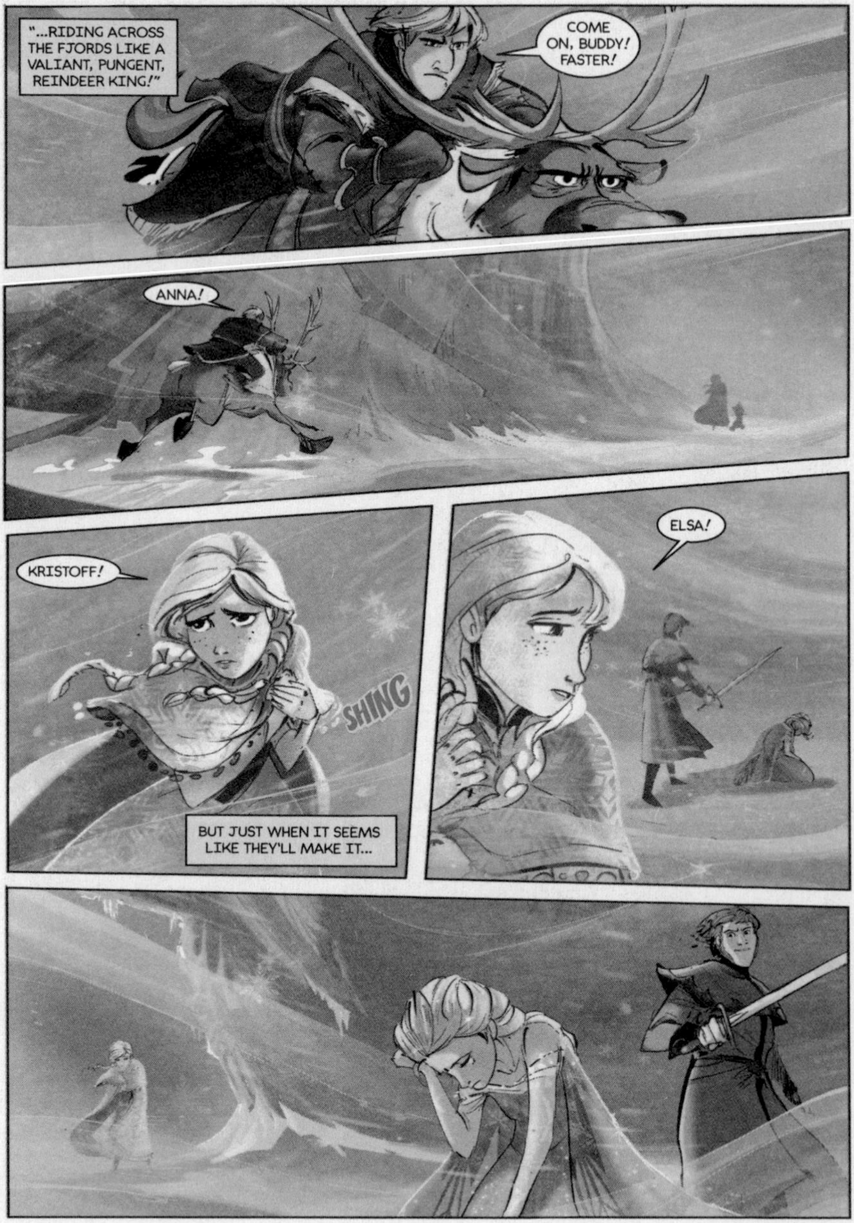

"...RIDING ACROSS THE FJORDS LIKE A VALIANT, PUNGENT, REINDEER KING!"
COME ON, BUDDY! FASTER!
ANNA!
KRISTOFF!
SHING
BUT JUST WHEN IT SEEMS LIKE THEY'LL MAKE IT...
ELSA!

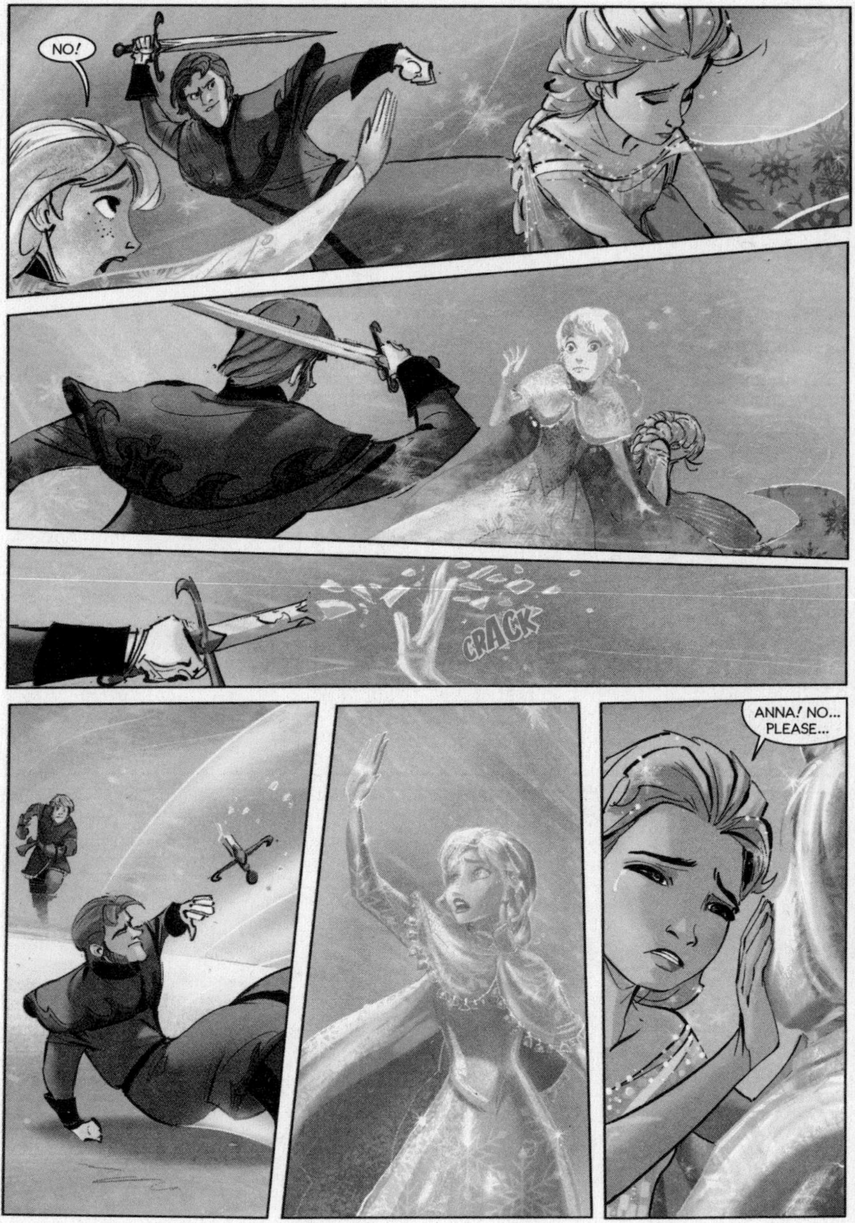
NO!
CRACK
ANNA! NO...
PLEASE...

IN THE SILENCE OF THE FJORD, EVERYONE LOOKS AT ANNA, FROZEN SOLID...

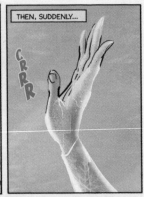

THEN, SUDDENLY...

CRRR

...THE ICE MELTS...

CRRR

...AND ANNA COMES BACK TO LIFE!

YOU SACRIFICED YOURSELF FOR ME?

I LOVE YOU...

AN ACT OF TRUE LOVE WILL THAW A FROZEN HEART!

LOVE WILL THAW... LOVE, OF COURSE!

FWIIIS

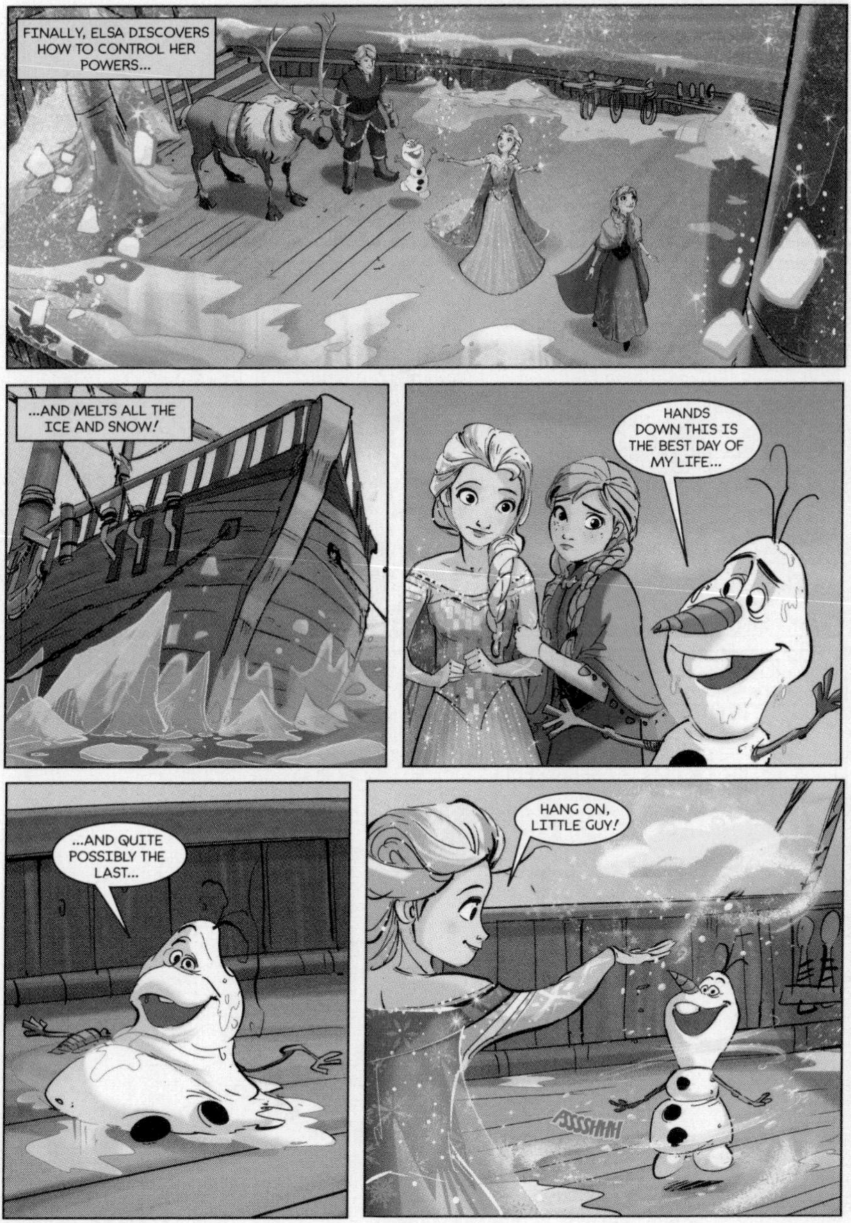
FINALLY, ELSA DISCOVERS HOW TO CONTROL HER POWERS...
...AND MELTS ALL THE ICE AND SNOW!
HANDS DOWN THIS IS THE BEST DAY OF MY LIFE...
...AND QUITE POSSIBLY THE LAST...
HANG ON, LITTLE GUY!

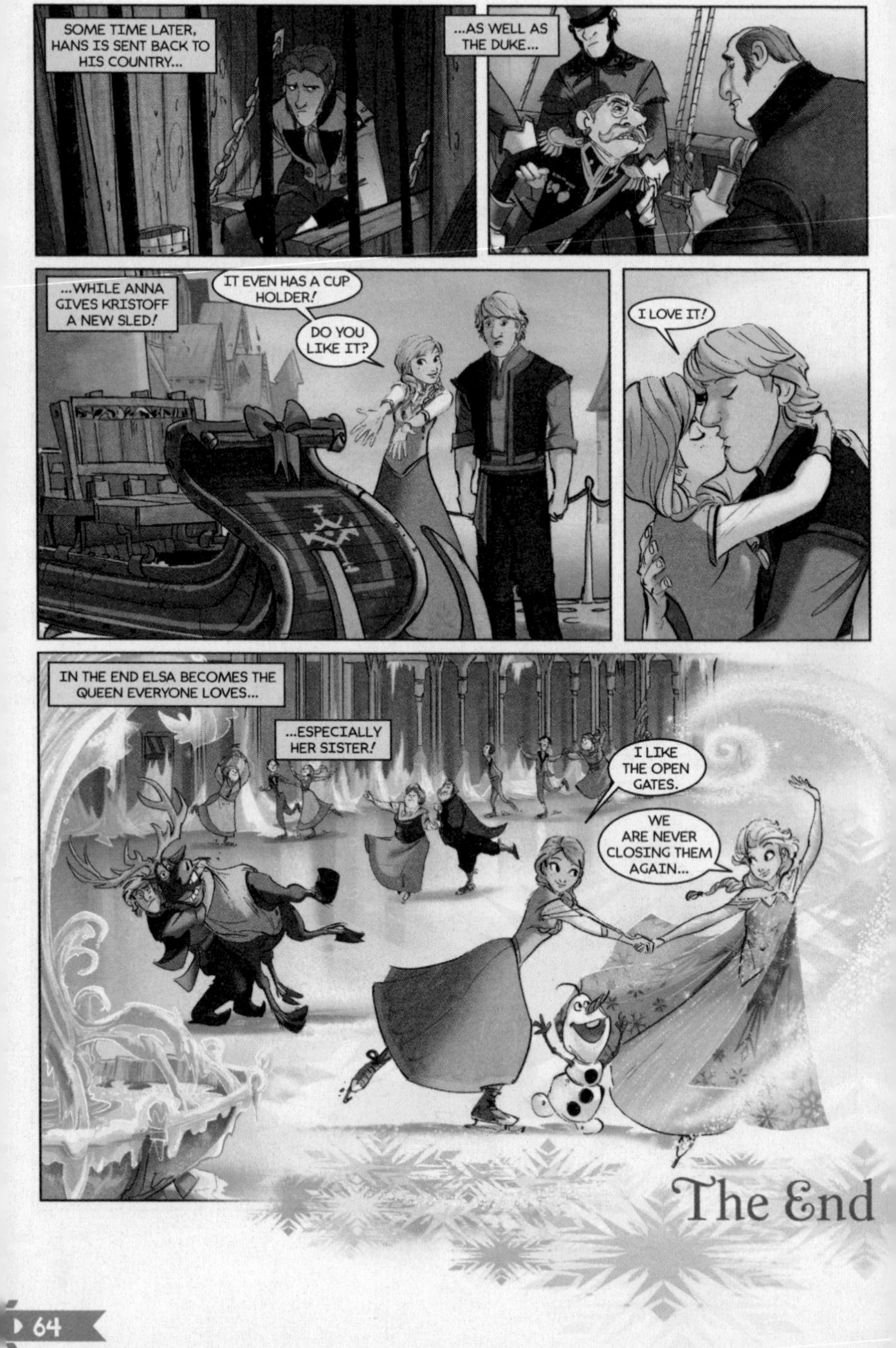
SOME TIME LATER, HANS IS SENT BACK TO HIS COUNTRY...
...AS WELL AS THE DUKE...
...WHILE ANNA GIVES KRISTOFF A NEW SLED!
IT EVEN HAS A CUP HOLDER!
DO YOU LIKE IT?
I LOVE IT!
IN THE END ELSA BECOMES THE QUEEN EVERYONE LOVES...
...ESPECIALLY HER SISTER!
I LIKE THE OPEN GATES.
WE ARE NEVER CLOSING THEM AGAIN...

The End

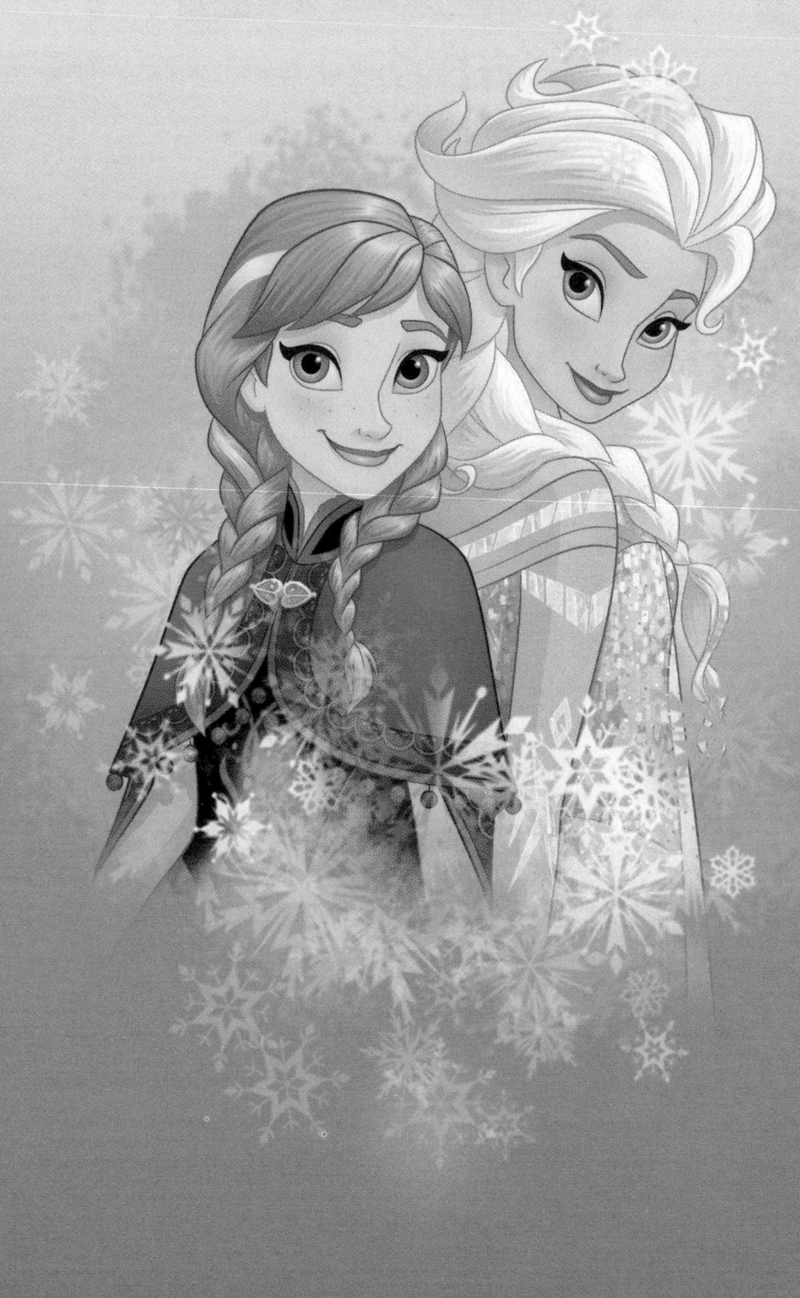

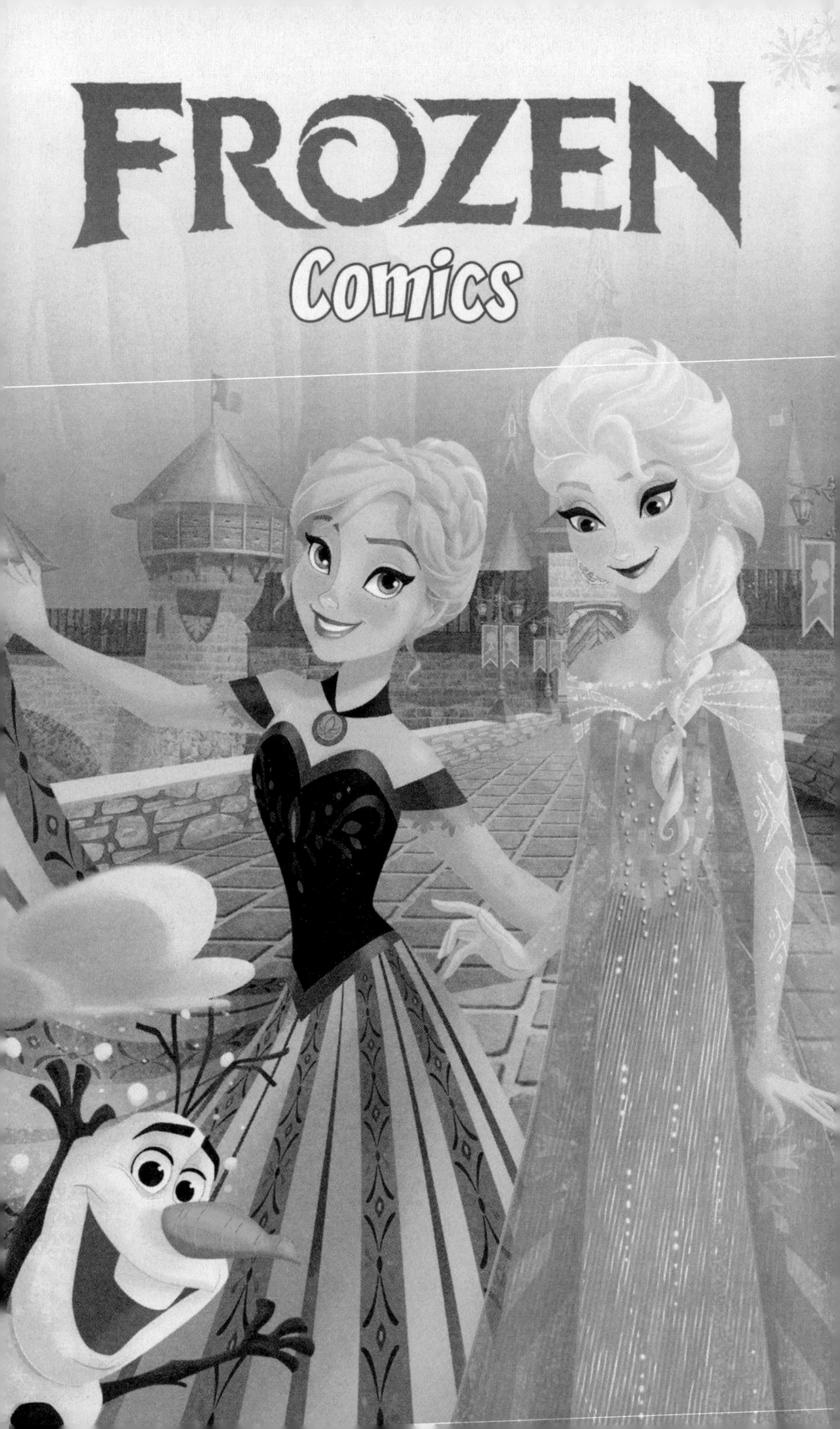
FROZEN
Comics

HOW TO SCARE A TROLL

Writer: Alessandro Ferrari
Artist: Iboix Estudi
Colorist: Charles Pickens
Letterer: Patrick Brosseau

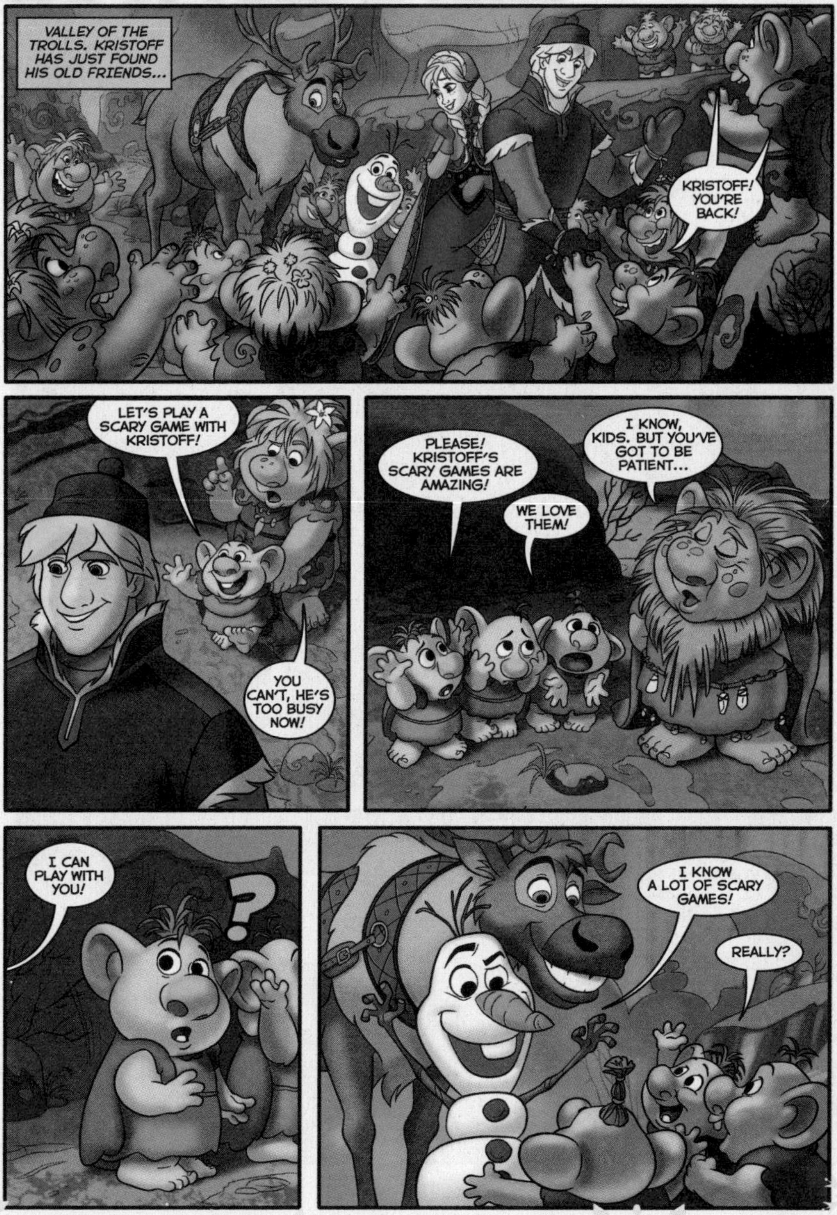
VALLEY OF THE TROLLS. KRISTOFF HAS JUST FOUND HIS OLD FRIENDS...
KRISTOFF! YOU'RE BACK!
LET'S PLAY A SCARY GAME WITH KRISTOFF!
YOU CAN'T, HE'S TOO BUSY NOW!
PLEASE! KRISTOFF'S SCARY GAMES ARE AMAZING!
WE LOVE THEM!
I KNOW, KIDS. BUT YOU'VE GOT TO BE PATIENT...
I CAN PLAY WITH YOU!
?
I KNOW A LOT OF SCARY GAMES!
REALLY?

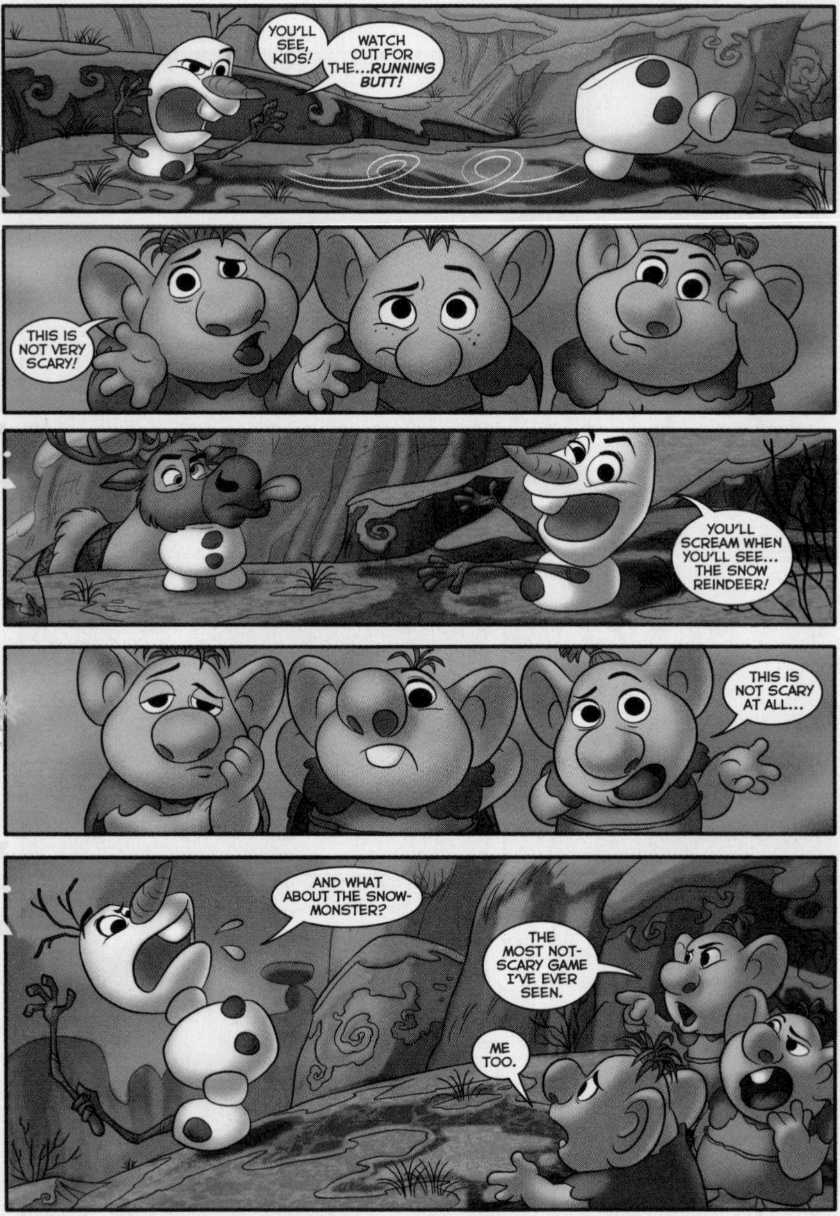
YOU'LL SEE, KIDS!
WATCH OUT FOR THE...RUNNING BUTT!
THIS IS NOT VERY SCARY!
YOU'LL SCREAM WHEN YOU'LL SEE... THE SNOW REINDEER!
THIS IS NOT SCARY AT ALL...
AND WHAT ABOUT THE SNOW-MONSTER?
THE MOST NOT-SCARY GAME I'VE EVER SEEN.
ME TOO.

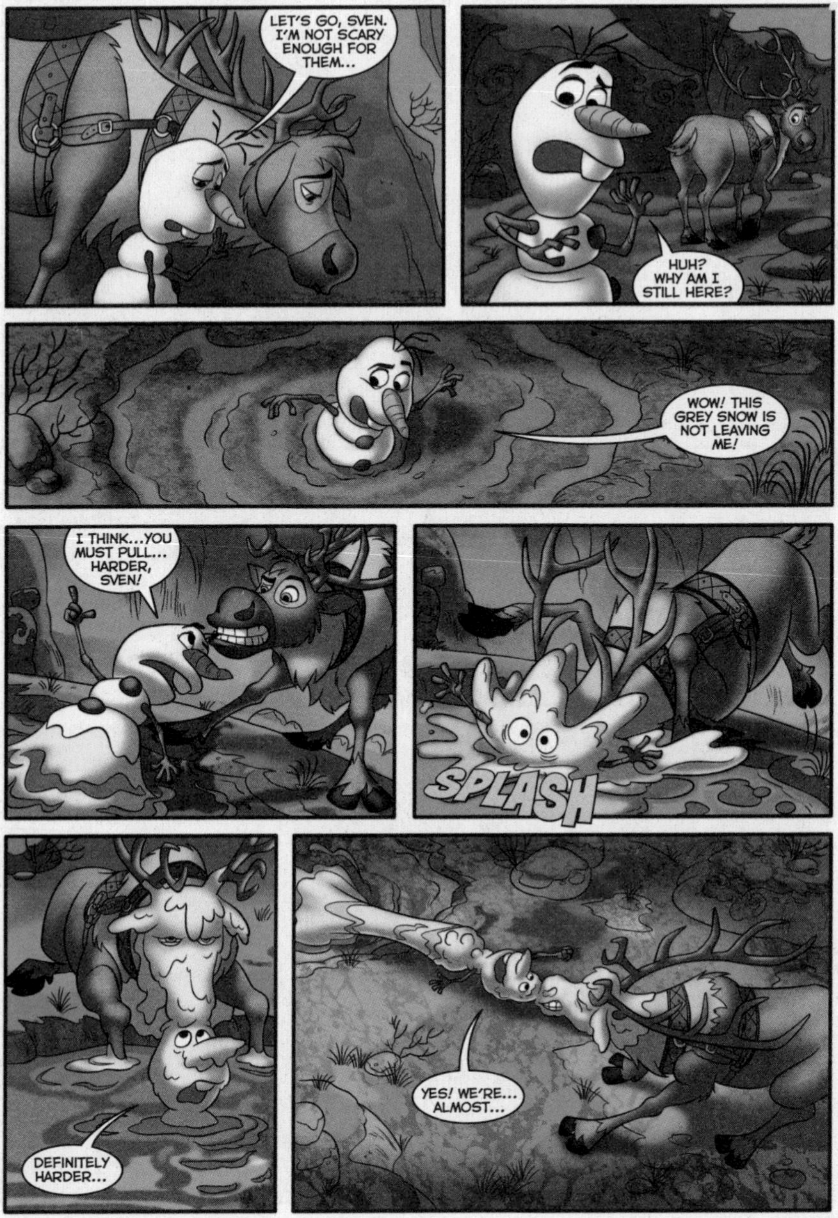
LET'S GO, SVEN. I'M NOT SCARY ENOUGH FOR THEM...
HUH? WHY AM I STILL HERE?
WOW! THIS GREY SNOW IS NOT LEAVING ME!
I THINK...YOU MUST PULL... HARDER, SVEN!
SPLASH
DEFINITELY HARDER...
YES! WE'RE... ALMOST...

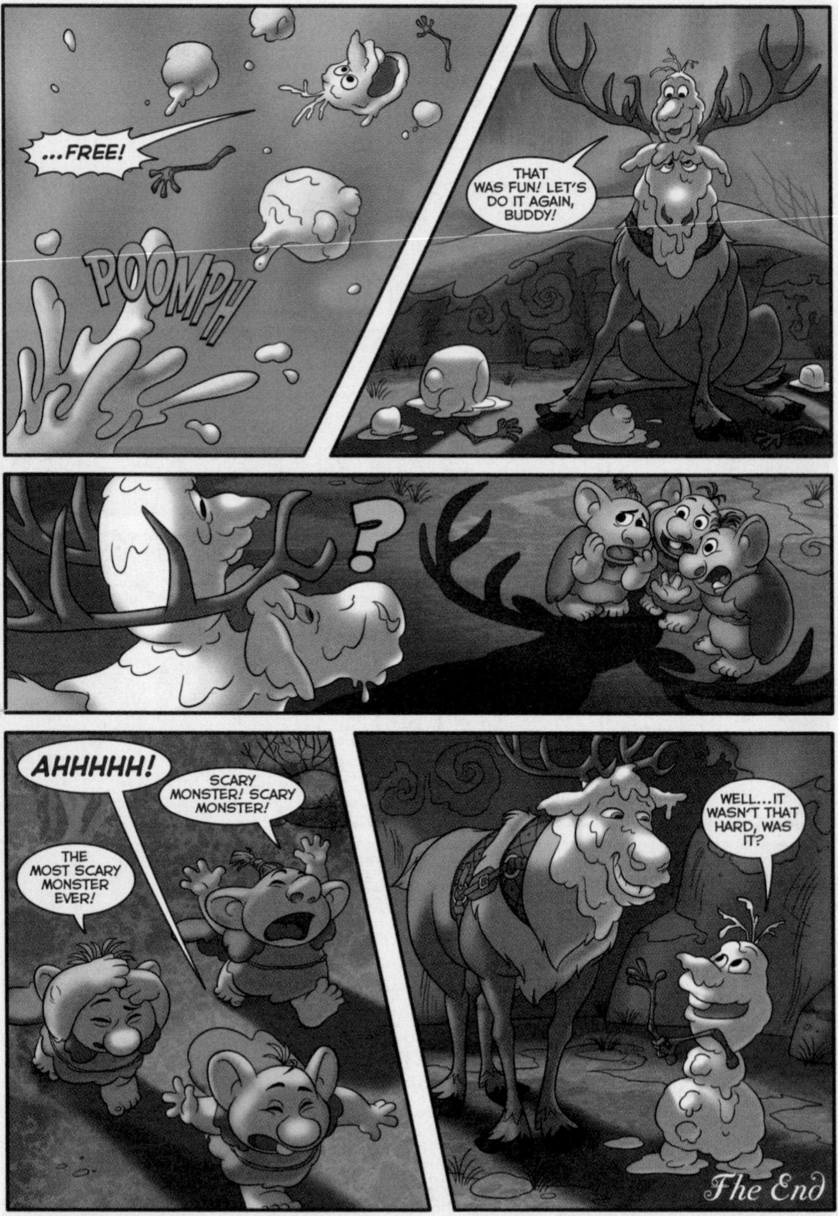
...FREE!
POOMPH
THAT WAS FUN! LET'S DO IT AGAIN, BUDDY!
?
AHHHHH!
SCARY MONSTER! SCARY MONSTER!
THE MOST SCARY MONSTER EVER!
WELL...IT WASN'T THAT HARD, WAS IT?
The End

WINTER SURPRISE

WRITER: ALESSANDRO FERRARI
ARTIST: IBOIX ESTUDI
COLORIST: CHARLES PICKENS
LETTERER: PATRICK BROSSEAU

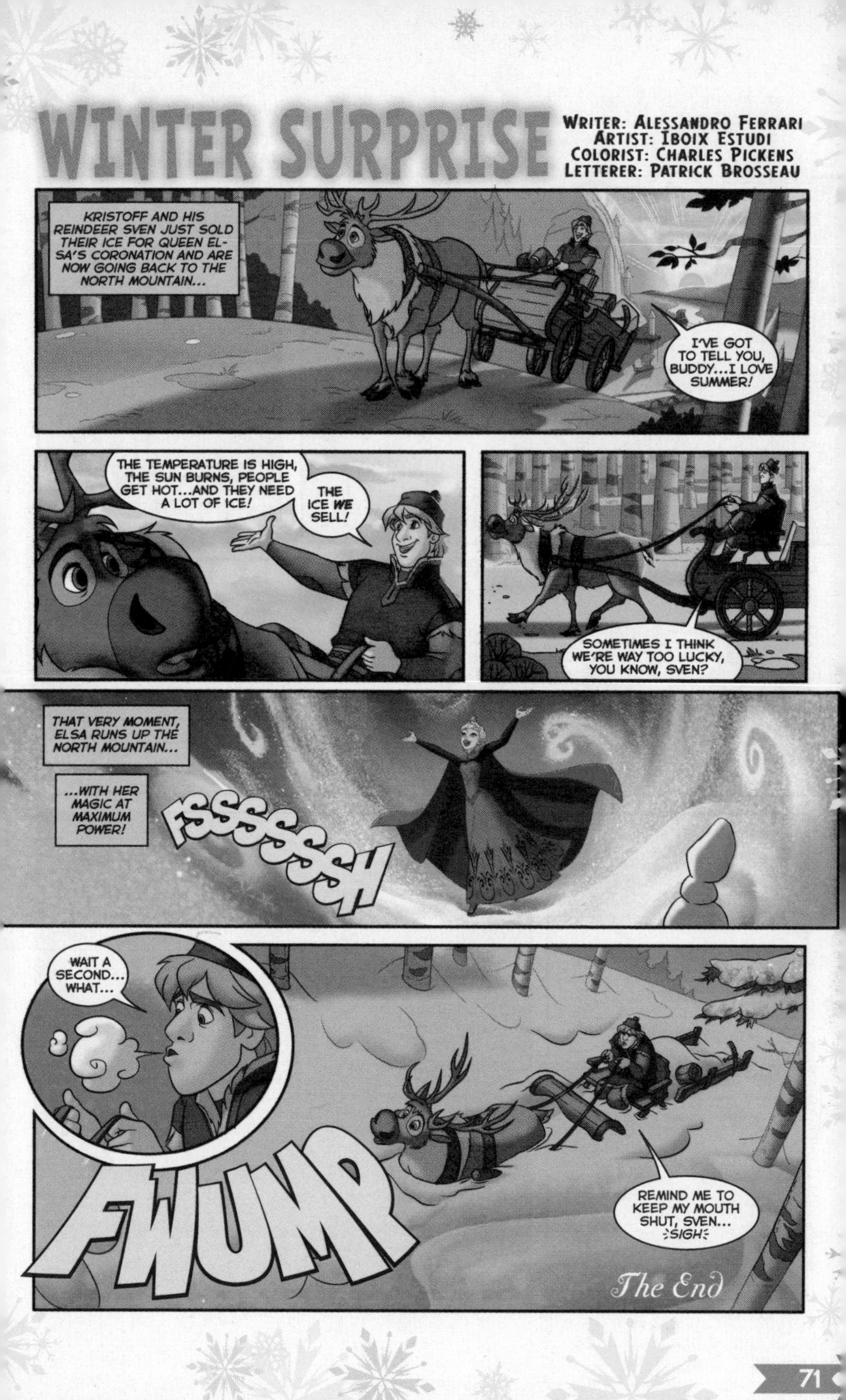

KRISTOFF AND HIS REINDEER SVEN JUST SOLD THEIR ICE FOR QUEEN ELSA'S CORONATION AND ARE NOW GOING BACK TO THE NORTH MOUNTAIN...
I'VE GOT TO TELL YOU, BUDDY...I LOVE SUMMER!
THE TEMPERATURE IS HIGH, THE SUN BURNS, PEOPLE GET HOT...AND THEY NEED A LOT OF ICE!
THE ICE WE SELL!
SOMETIMES I THINK WE'RE WAY TOO LUCKY, YOU KNOW, SVEN?
THAT VERY MOMENT, ELSA RUNS UP THE NORTH MOUNTAIN...
...WITH HER MAGIC AT MAXIMUM POWER!
FSSSSSSH
WAIT A SECOND... WHAT...
FWUMP
REMIND ME TO KEEP MY MOUTH SHUT, SVEN... SIGH
The End

WHERE'S MY HEAD?

WRITER: ALESSANDRO FERRARI
ARTIST: IBOIX ESTUDI
COLORIST: CHARLES PICKENS
LETTERER: PATRICK BROSSEAU

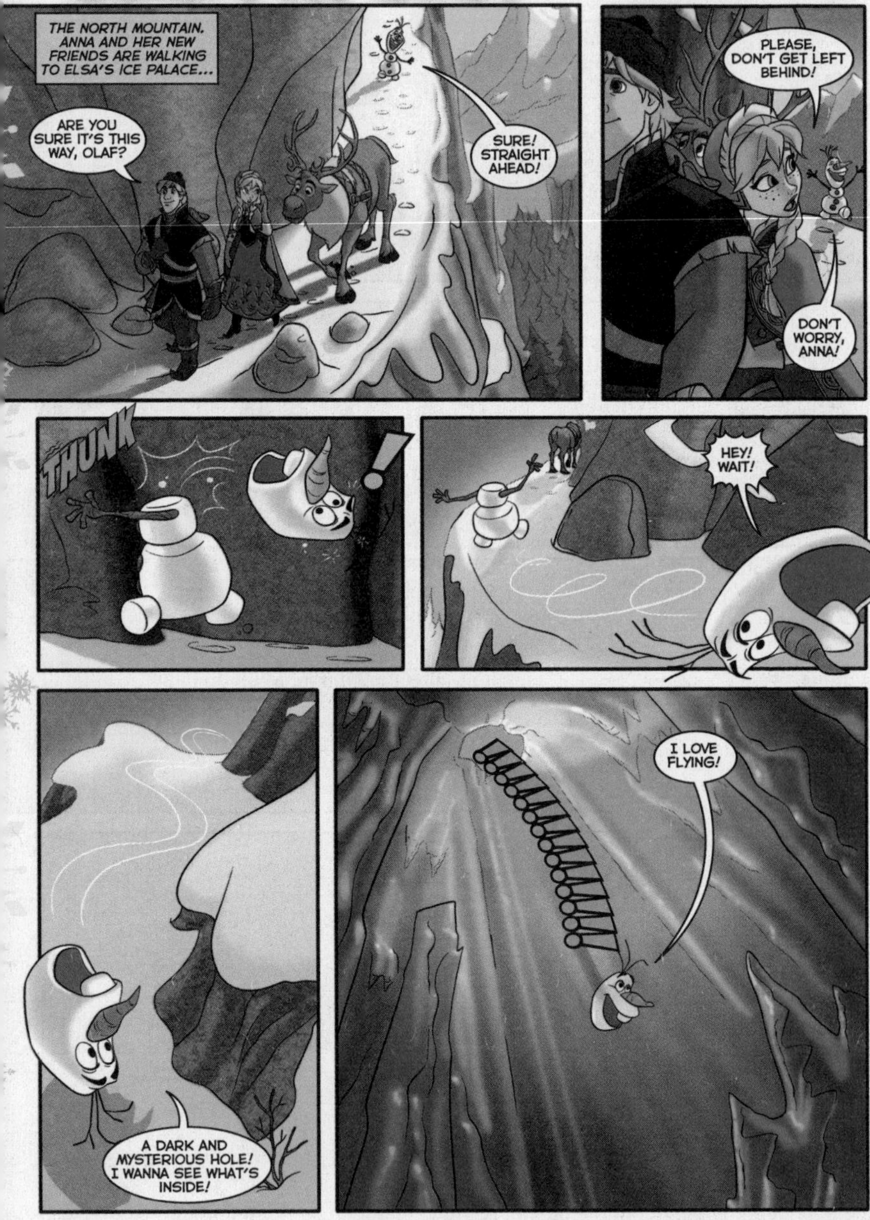

THE NORTH MOUNTAIN. ANNA AND HER NEW FRIENDS ARE WALKING TO ELSA'S ICE PALACE...
ARE YOU SURE IT'S THIS WAY, OLAF?
SURE! STRAIGHT AHEAD!
PLEASE, DON'T GET LEFT BEHIND!
DON'T WORRY, ANNA!
THUNK
!
HEY! WAIT!
A DARK AND MYSTERIOUS HOLE! I WANNA SEE WHAT'S INSIDE!
I LOVE FLYING!

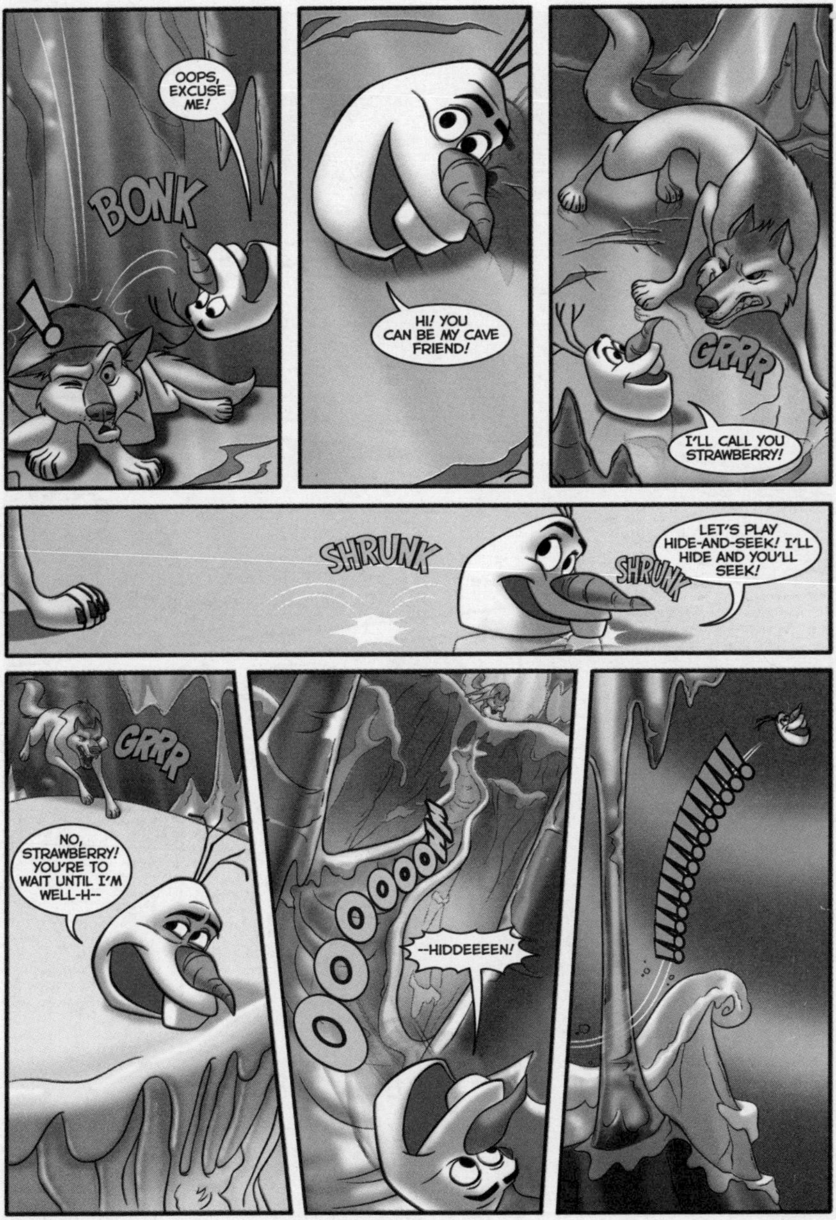
OOPS, EXCUSE ME!
BONK
!
HI! YOU CAN BE MY CAVE FRIEND!
GRRR
I'LL CALL YOU STRAWBERRY!
SHRUNK
SHRUNK
LET'S PLAY HIDE-AND-SEEK! I'LL HIDE AND YOU'LL SEEK!
GRRR
NO, STRAWBERRY! YOU'RE TO WAIT UNTIL I'M WELL-H--
OOOOOOOF!
--HIDDEEEEN!

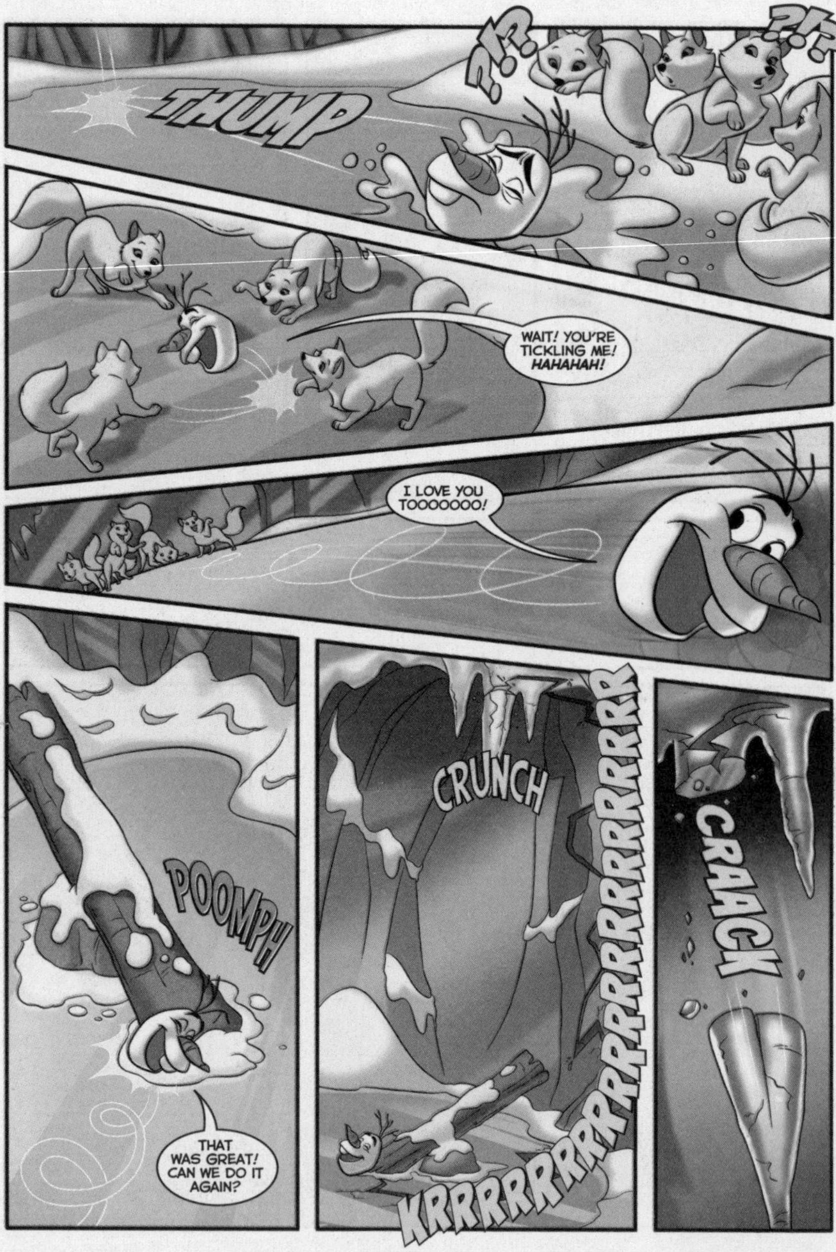
?!?
?!?
THUMP
WAIT! YOU'RE TICKLING ME! HAHAHAH!
I LOVE YOU TOOOOOOO!
POOMPH
THAT WAS GREAT! CAN WE DO IT AGAIN?
CRUNCH
KRRRRRRRRRRRRRRRRRRRRRRRRRR
CRAACK

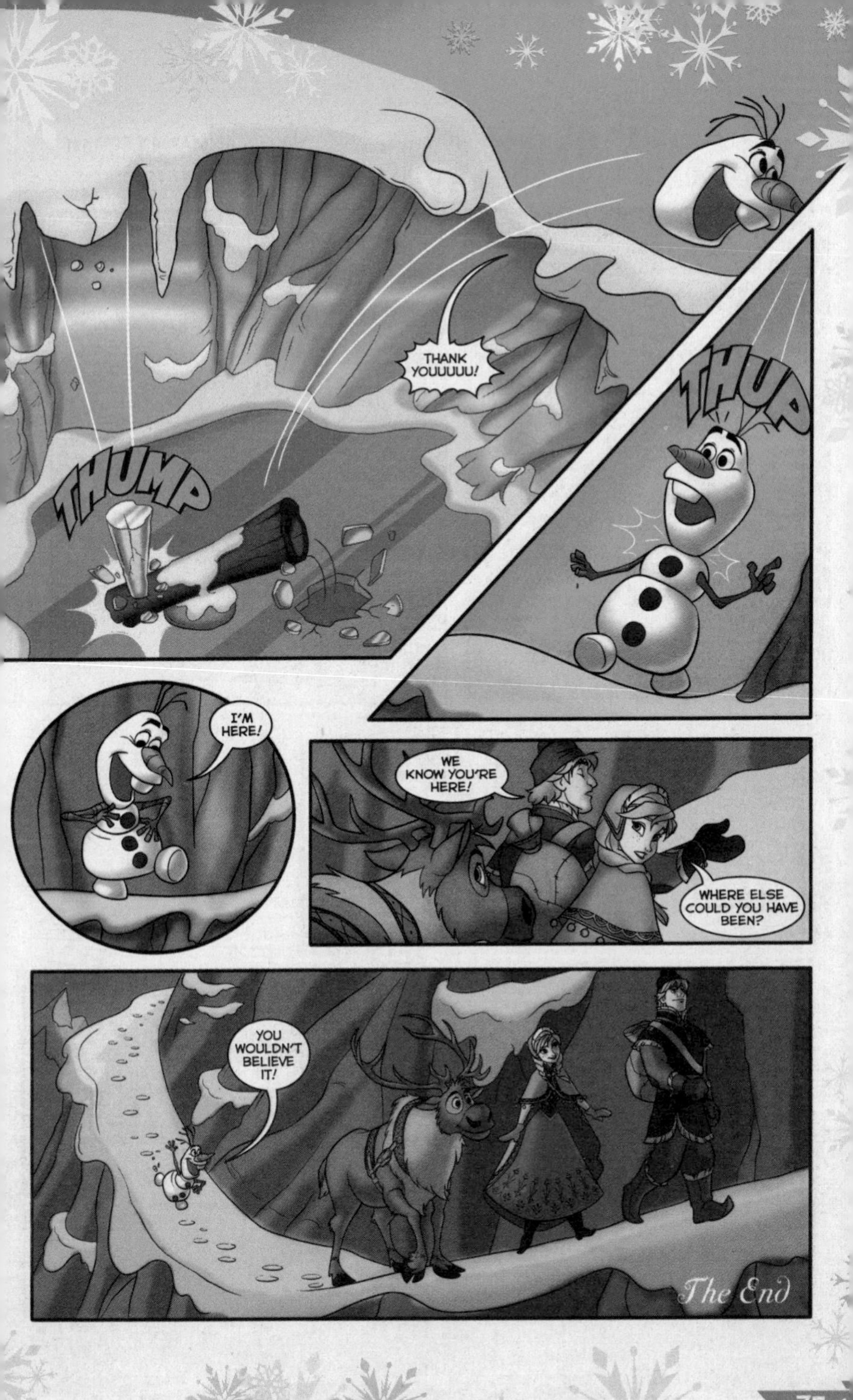
THANK YOUUUUU!
THUMP
THUP
I'M HERE!
WE KNOW YOU'RE HERE!
WHERE ELSE COULD YOU HAVE BEEN?
YOU WOULDN'T BELIEVE IT!
The End

SNOW RECORD

Writer: Alessandro Ferrari
Artist: Iboix Estudi
Colorist: Charles Pickens
Letterer: Patrick Brosseau

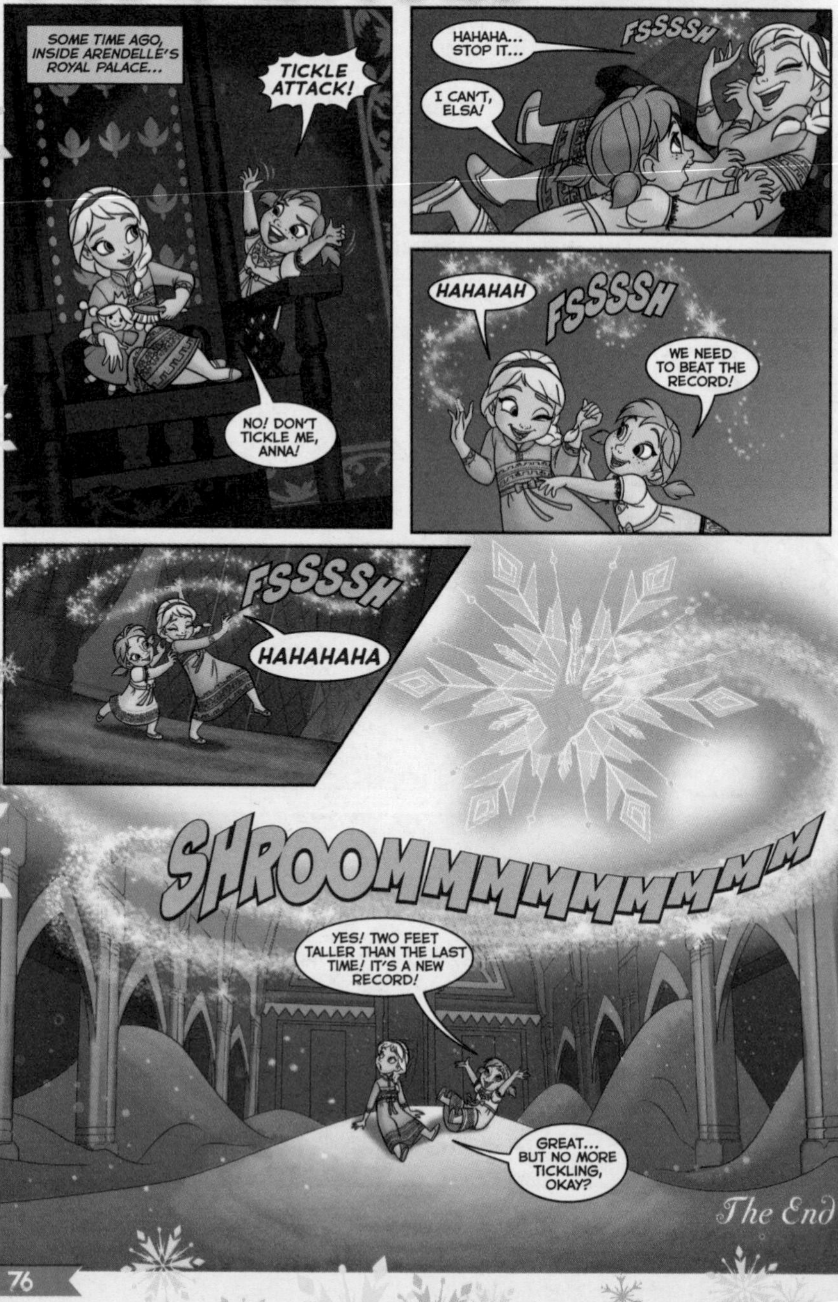

SOME TIME AGO, INSIDE ARENDELLE'S ROYAL PALACE...
TICKLE ATTACK!
NO! DON'T TICKLE ME, ANNA!
HAHAHA... STOP IT...
FSSSSH
I CAN'T, ELSA!
HAHAHAH
FSSSSH
WE NEED TO BEAT THE RECORD!
FSSSSH
HAHAHAHA
SHROOMMMMMMMMMM
YES! TWO FEET TALLER THAN THE LAST TIME! IT'S A NEW RECORD!
GREAT... BUT NO MORE TICKLING, OKAY?
The End

Royal Skating Day

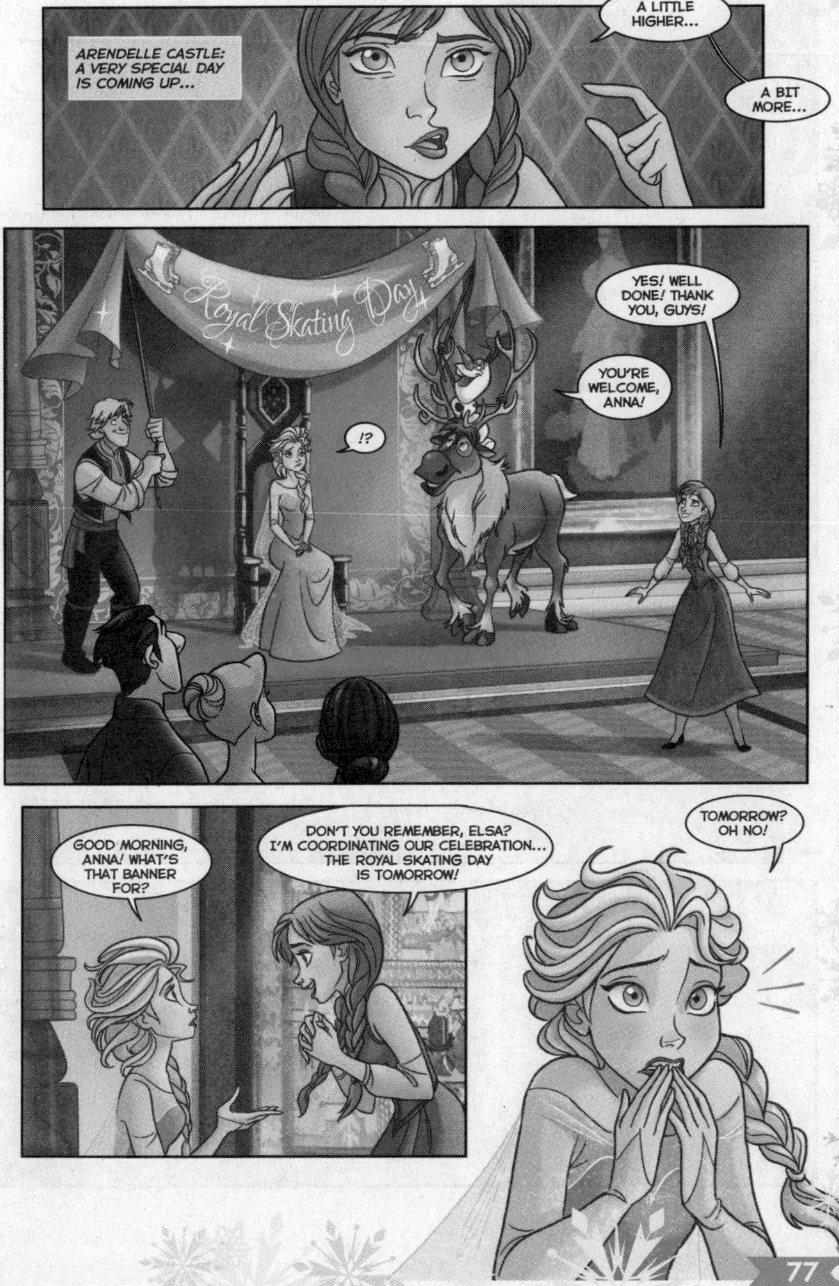

ARENDELLE CASTLE: A VERY SPECIAL DAY IS COMING UP...
A LITTLE HIGHER...
A BIT MORE...
Royal Skating Day
YES! WELL DONE! THANK YOU, GUYS!
YOU'RE WELCOME, ANNA!
!?
GOOD MORNING, ANNA! WHAT'S THAT BANNER FOR?
DON'T YOU REMEMBER, ELSA? I'M COORDINATING OUR CELEBRATION... THE ROYAL SKATING DAY IS TOMORROW!
TOMORROW? OH NO!

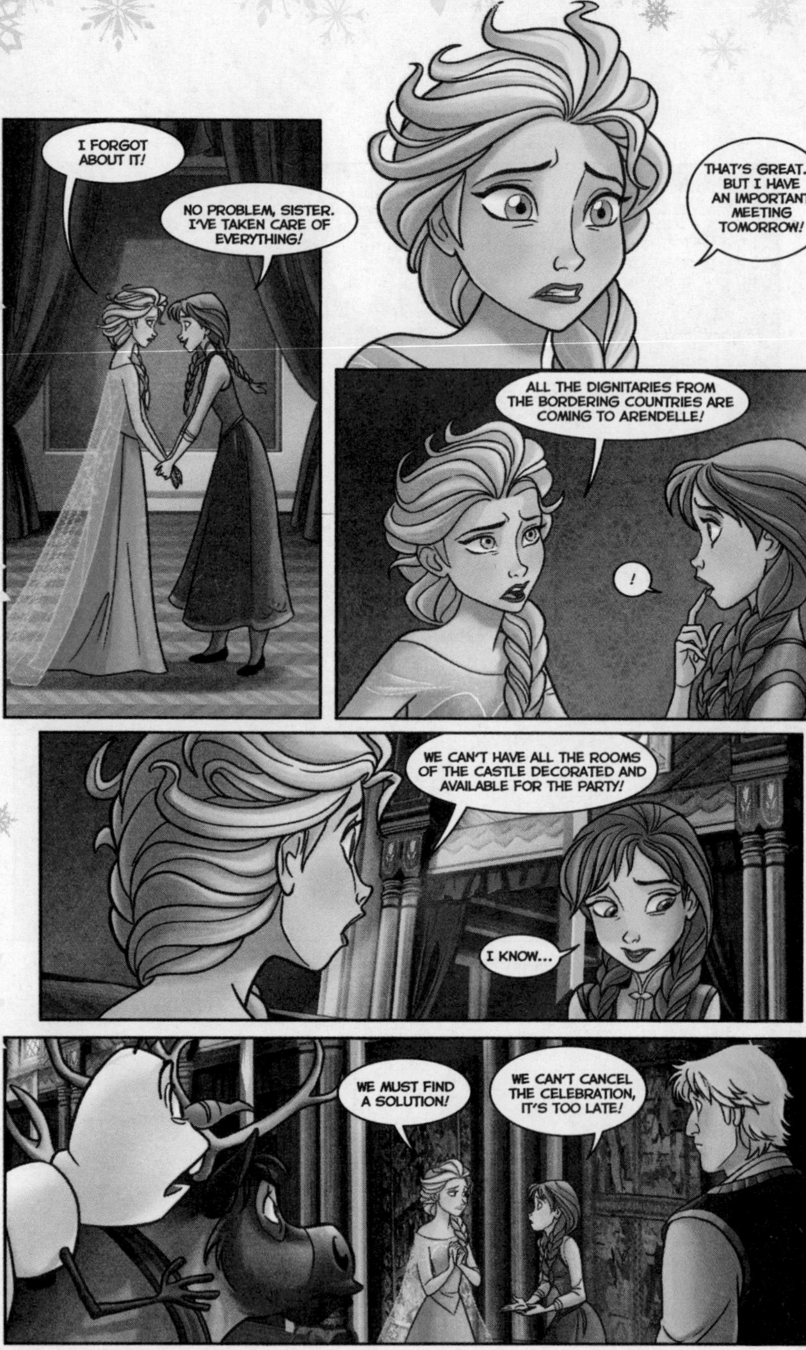
I FORGOT ABOUT IT!
NO PROBLEM, SISTER. I'VE TAKEN CARE OF EVERYTHING!
THAT'S GREAT... BUT I HAVE AN IMPORTANT MEETING TOMORROW!
ALL THE DIGNITARIES FROM THE BORDERING COUNTRIES ARE COMING TO ARENDELLE!
!
WE CAN'T HAVE ALL THE ROOMS OF THE CASTLE DECORATED AND AVAILABLE FOR THE PARTY!
I KNOW...
WE MUST FIND A SOLUTION!
WE CAN'T CANCEL THE CELEBRATION, IT'S TOO LATE!

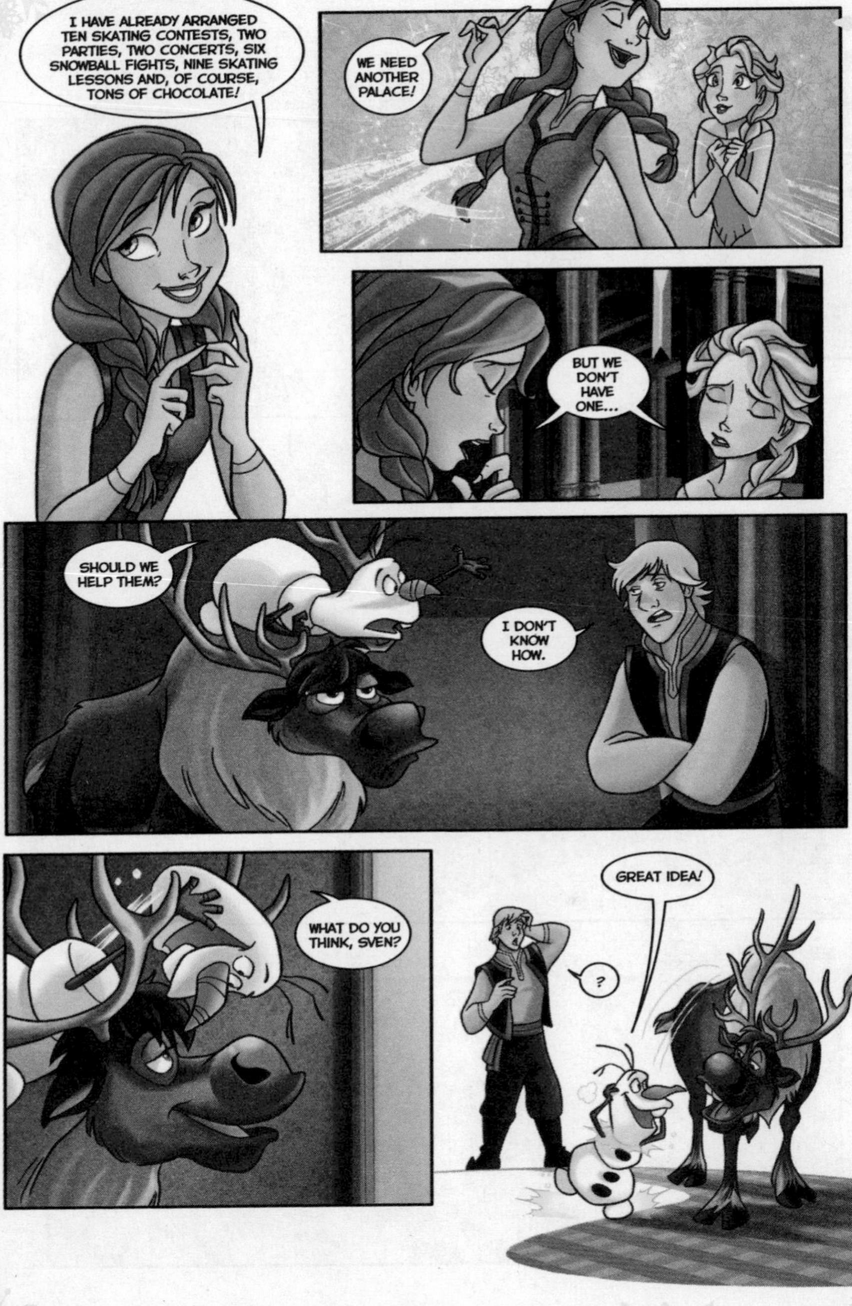
I HAVE ALREADY ARRANGED TEN SKATING CONTESTS, TWO PARTIES, TWO CONCERTS, SIX SNOWBALL FIGHTS, NINE SKATING LESSONS AND, OF COURSE, TONS OF CHOCOLATE!
WE NEED ANOTHER PALACE!
BUT WE DON'T HAVE ONE...
SHOULD WE HELP THEM?
I DON'T KNOW HOW.
WHAT DO YOU THINK, SVEN?
GREAT IDEA!
?

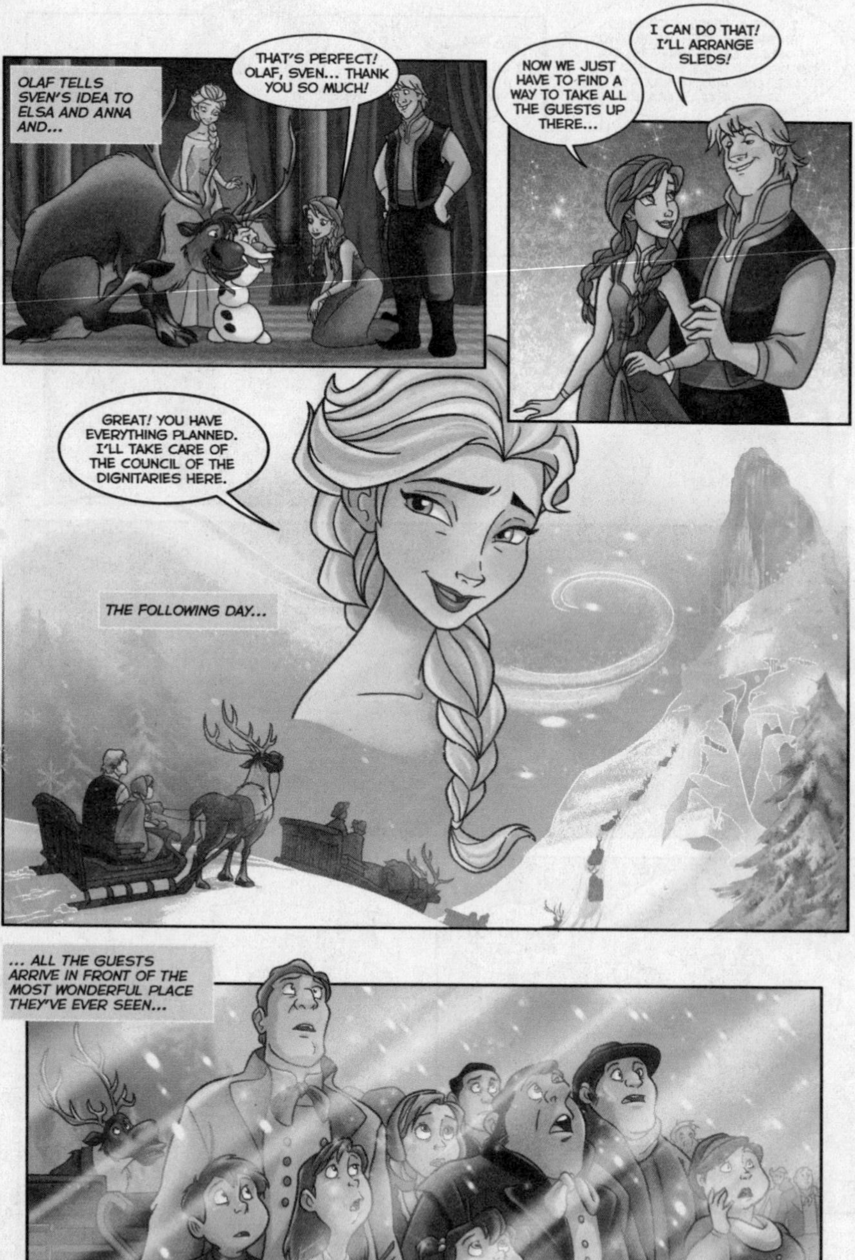
OLAF TELLS SVEN'S IDEA TO ELSA AND ANNA AND...
THAT'S PERFECT! OLAF, SVEN... THANK YOU SO MUCH!
NOW WE JUST HAVE TO FIND A WAY TO TAKE ALL THE GUESTS UP THERE...
I CAN DO THAT! I'LL ARRANGE SLEDS!
GREAT! YOU HAVE EVERYTHING PLANNED. I'LL TAKE CARE OF THE COUNCIL OF THE DIGNITARIES HERE.
THE FOLLOWING DAY...
... ALL THE GUESTS ARRIVE IN FRONT OF THE MOST WONDERFUL PLACE THEY'VE EVER SEEN...

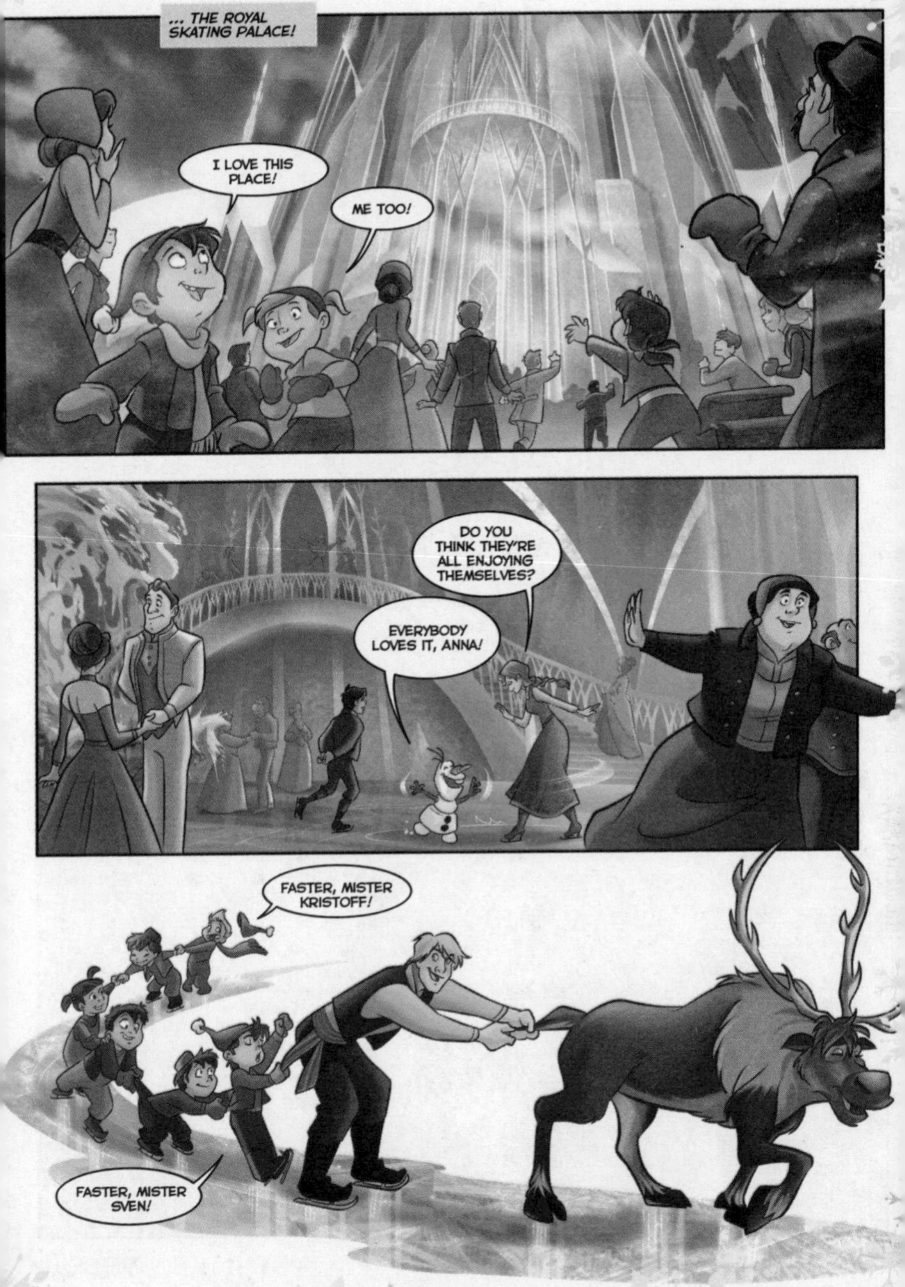
... THE ROYAL SKATING PALACE!
I LOVE THIS PLACE!
ME TOO!
DO YOU THINK THEY'RE ALL ENJOYING THEMSELVES?
EVERYBODY LOVES IT, ANNA!
FASTER, MISTER KRISTOFF!
FASTER, MISTER SVEN!

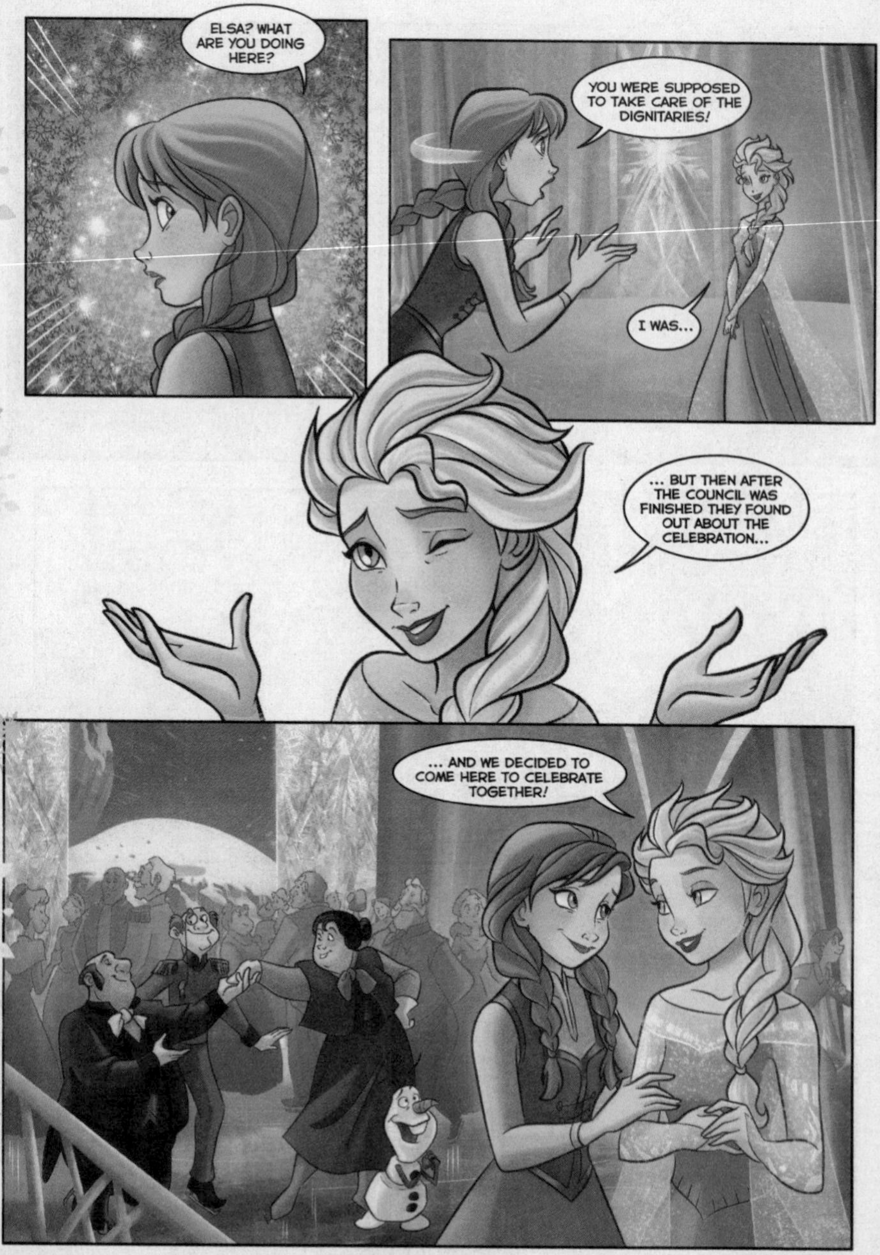
ELSA? WHAT ARE YOU DOING HERE?
YOU WERE SUPPOSED TO TAKE CARE OF THE DIGNITARIES!
I WAS...
... BUT THEN AFTER THE COUNCIL WAS FINISHED THEY FOUND OUT ABOUT THE CELEBRATION...
... AND WE DECIDED TO COME HERE TO CELEBRATE TOGETHER!
The End

The Snow Troll

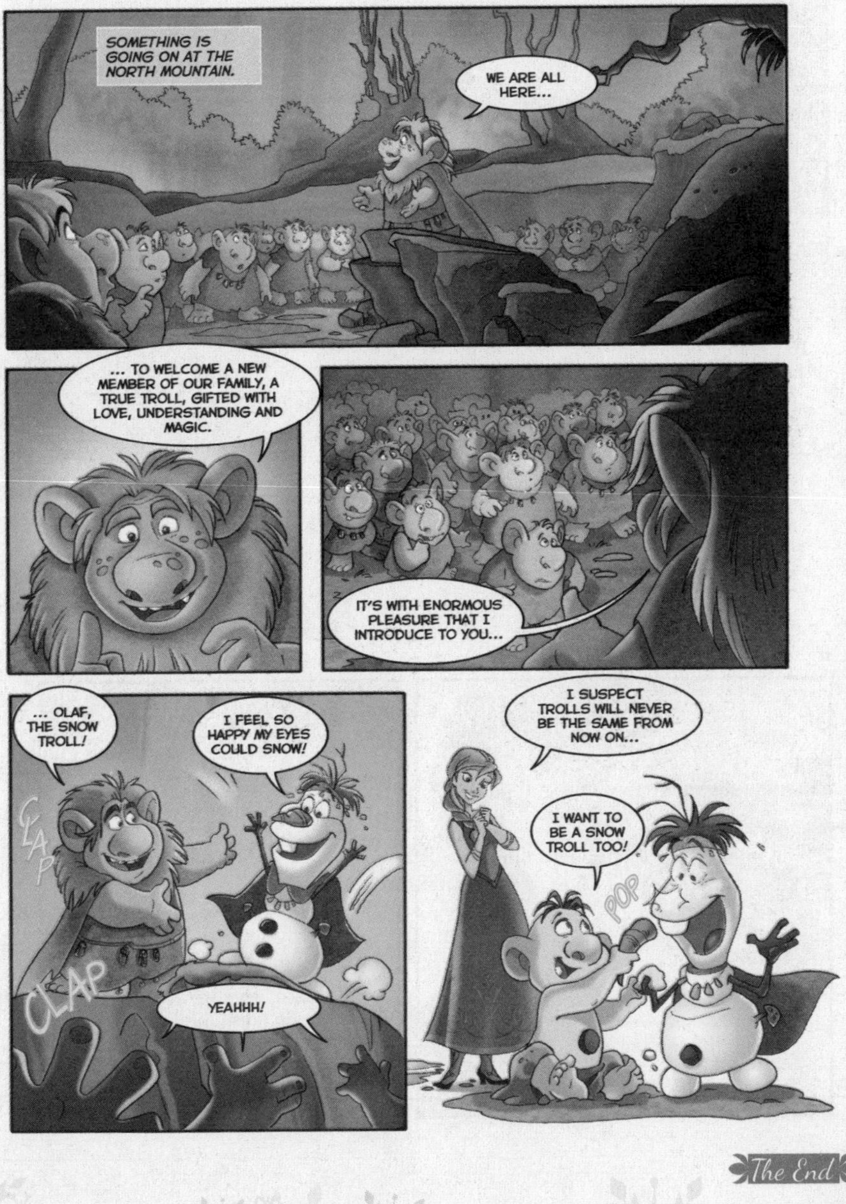
SOMETHING IS GOING ON AT THE NORTH MOUNTAIN.
WE ARE ALL HERE...
... TO WELCOME A NEW MEMBER OF OUR FAMILY, A TRUE TROLL, GIFTED WITH LOVE, UNDERSTANDING AND MAGIC.
IT'S WITH ENORMOUS PLEASURE THAT I INTRODUCE TO YOU...
... OLAF, THE SNOW TROLL!
I FEEL SO HAPPY MY EYES COULD SNOW!
CLAP
CLAP
YEAHHH!
I SUSPECT TROLLS WILL NEVER BE THE SAME FROM NOW ON...
I WANT TO BE A SNOW TROLL TOO!
POP

The End

Open your Eyes

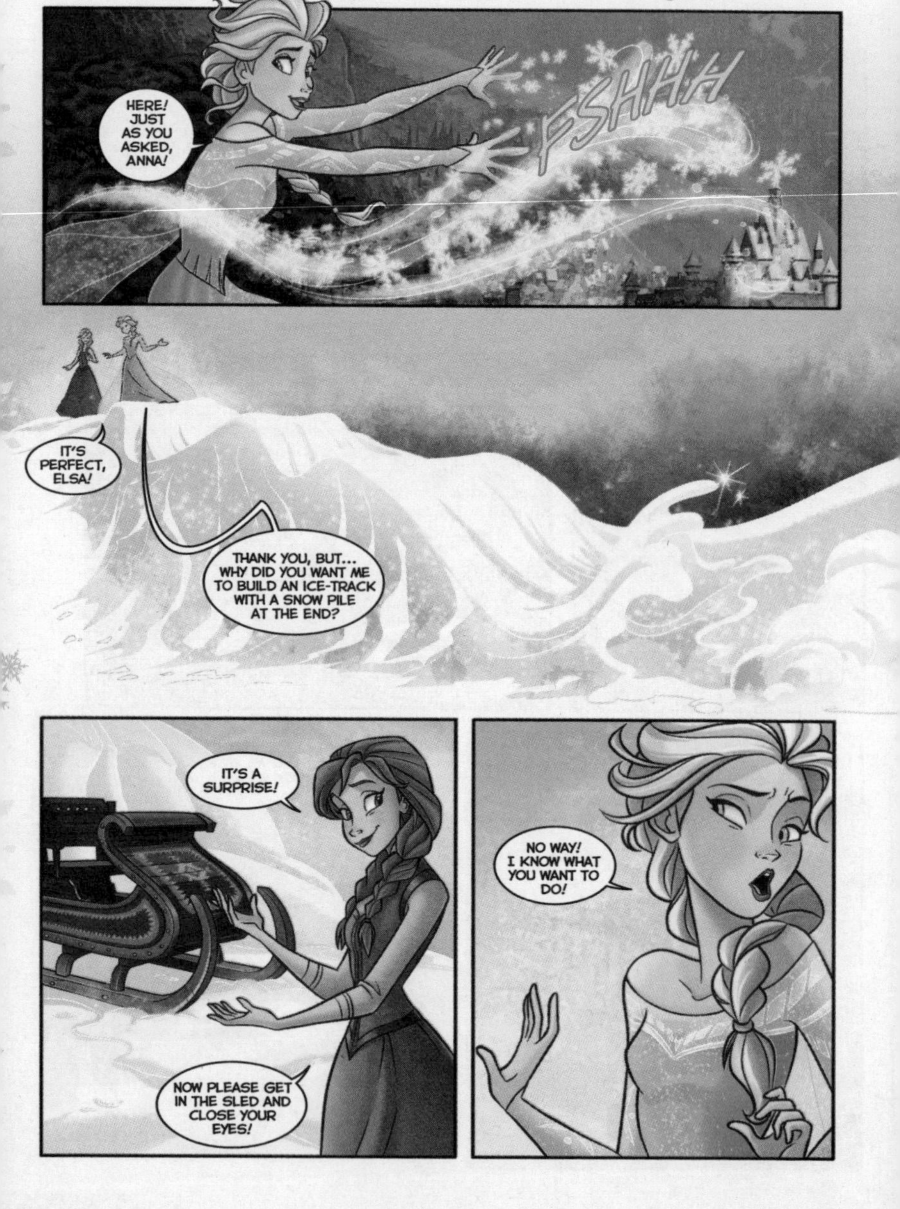
HERE! JUST AS YOU ASKED, ANNA!
FSHHH
IT'S PERFECT, ELSA!
THANK YOU, BUT... WHY DID YOU WANT ME TO BUILD AN ICE-TRACK WITH A SNOW PILE AT THE END?
IT'S A SURPRISE!
NOW PLEASE GET IN THE SLED AND CLOSE YOUR EYES!
NO WAY! I KNOW WHAT YOU WANT TO DO!

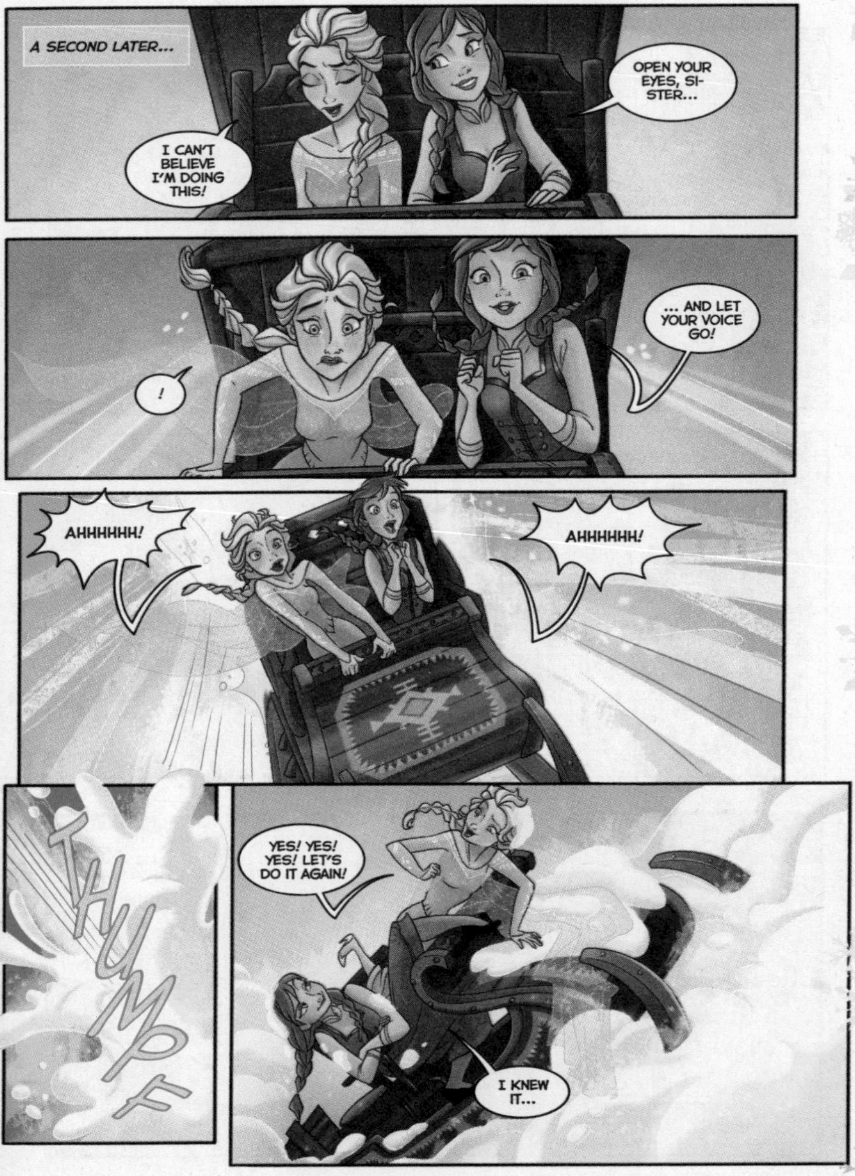

A SECOND LATER...
OPEN YOUR EYES, SI-STER...
I CAN'T BELIEVE I'M DOING THIS!
... AND LET YOUR VOICE GO!
!
AHHHHHH!
AHHHHHH!
THUMPF
YES! YES! YES! LET'S DO IT AGAIN!
I KNEW IT...

The End

Ice Surprise

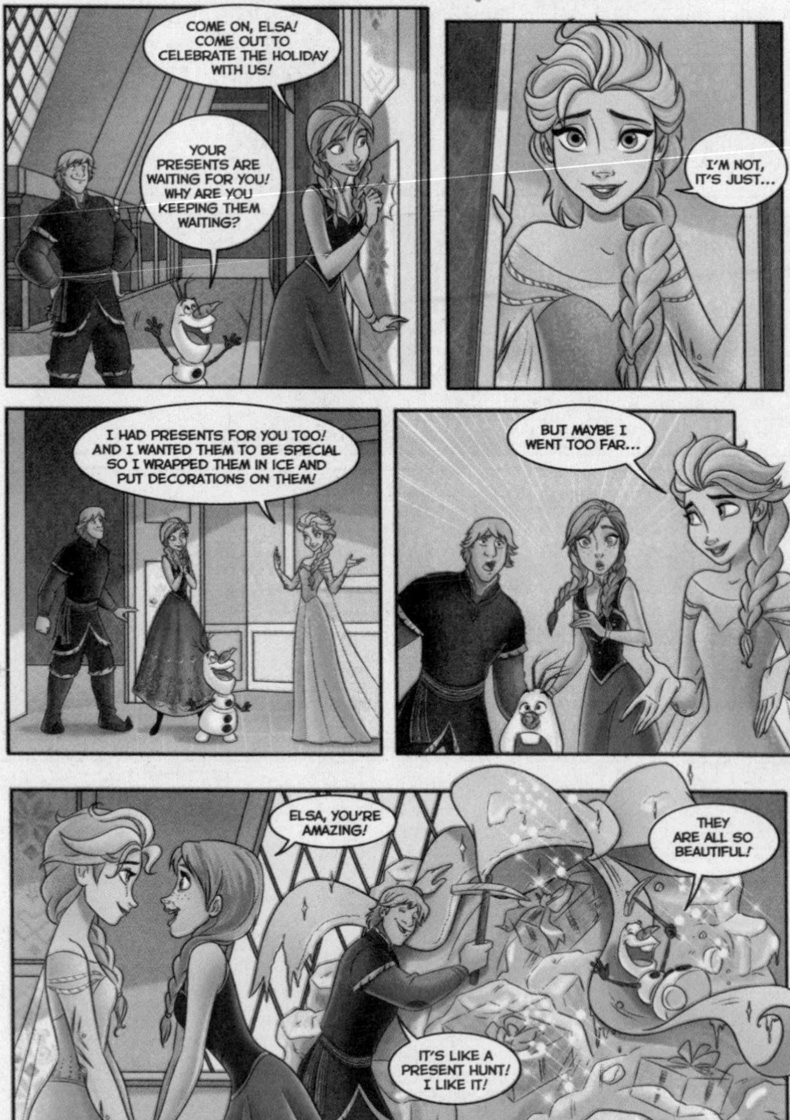
COME ON, ELSA! COME OUT TO CELEBRATE THE HOLIDAY WITH US!
YOUR PRESENTS ARE WAITING FOR YOU! WHY ARE YOU KEEPING THEM WAITING?
I'M NOT, IT'S JUST...
I HAD PRESENTS FOR YOU TOO! AND I WANTED THEM TO BE SPECIAL SO I WRAPPED THEM IN ICE AND PUT DECORATIONS ON THEM!
BUT MAYBE I WENT TOO FAR...
ELSA, YOU'RE AMAZING!
THEY ARE ALL SO BEAUTIFUL!
IT'S LIKE A PRESENT HUNT! I LIKE IT!

The End

The King of Hugs

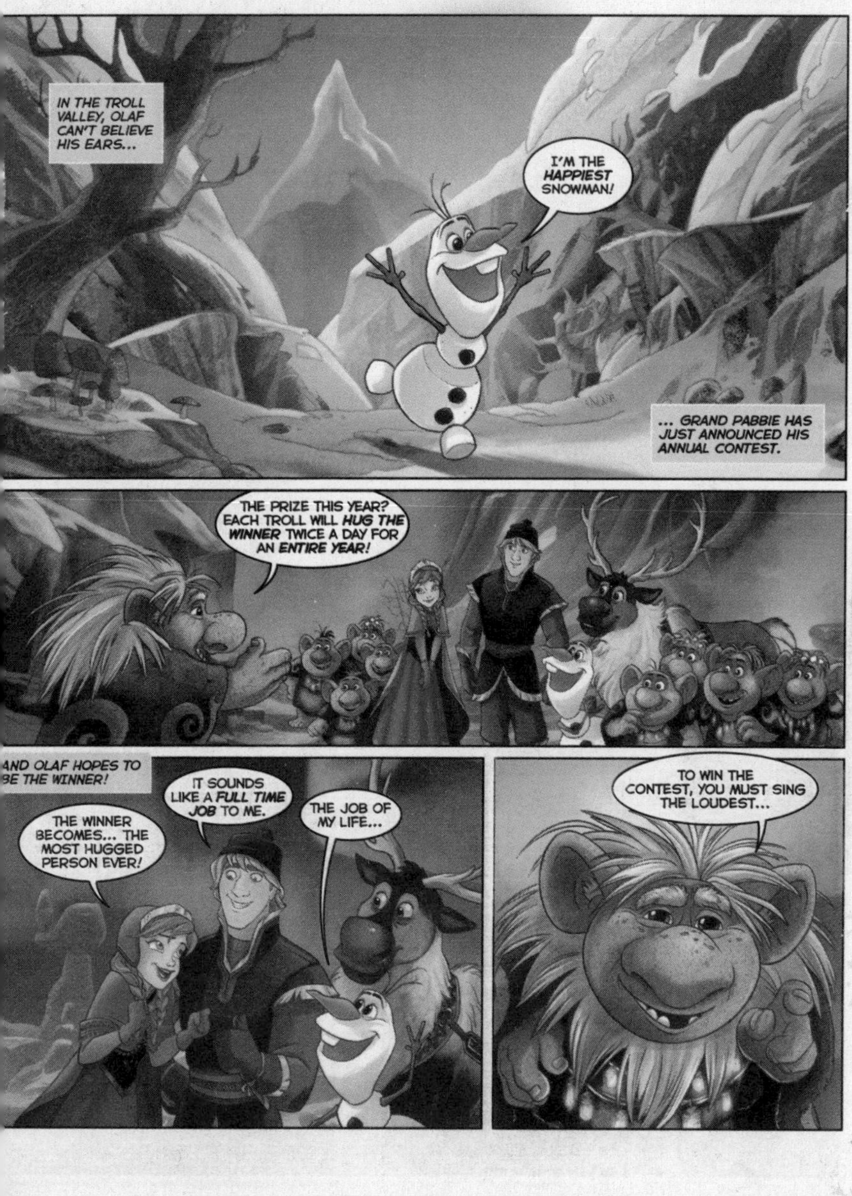
IN THE TROLL VALLEY, OLAF CAN'T BELIEVE HIS EARS...
I'M THE HAPPIEST SNOWMAN!
... GRAND PABBIE HAS JUST ANNOUNCED HIS ANNUAL CONTEST.
THE PRIZE THIS YEAR? EACH TROLL WILL HUG THE WINNER TWICE A DAY FOR AN ENTIRE YEAR!
AND OLAF HOPES TO BE THE WINNER!
THE WINNER BECOMES... THE MOST HUGGED PERSON EVER!
IT SOUNDS LIKE A FULL TIME JOB TO ME.
THE JOB OF MY LIFE...
TO WIN THE CONTEST, YOU MUST SING THE LOUDEST...

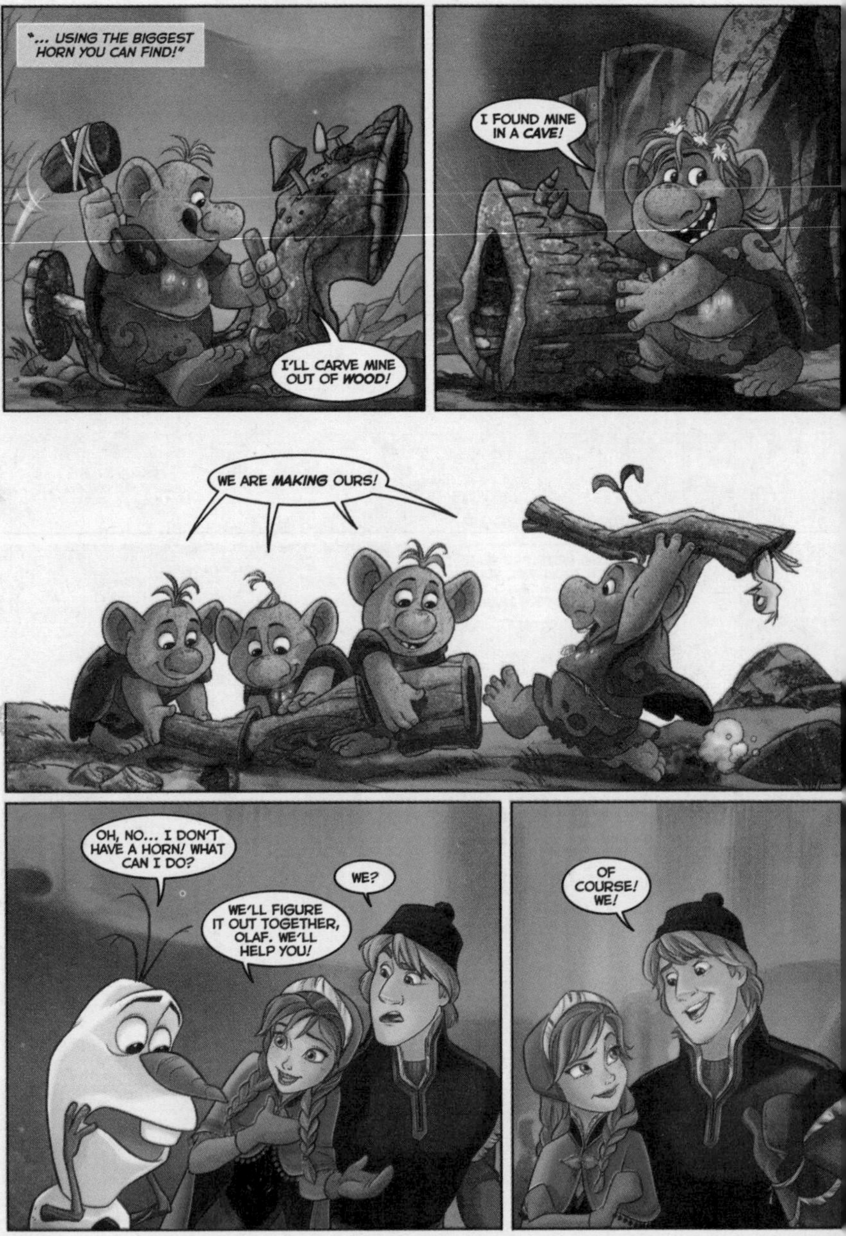
"... USING THE BIGGEST HORN YOU CAN FIND!"
I'LL CARVE MINE OUT OF WOOD!
I FOUND MINE IN A CAVE!
WE ARE MAKING OURS!
OH, NO... I DON'T HAVE A HORN! WHAT CAN I DO?
WE'LL FIGURE IT OUT TOGETHER, OLAF. WE'LL HELP YOU!
WE?
OF COURSE! WE!

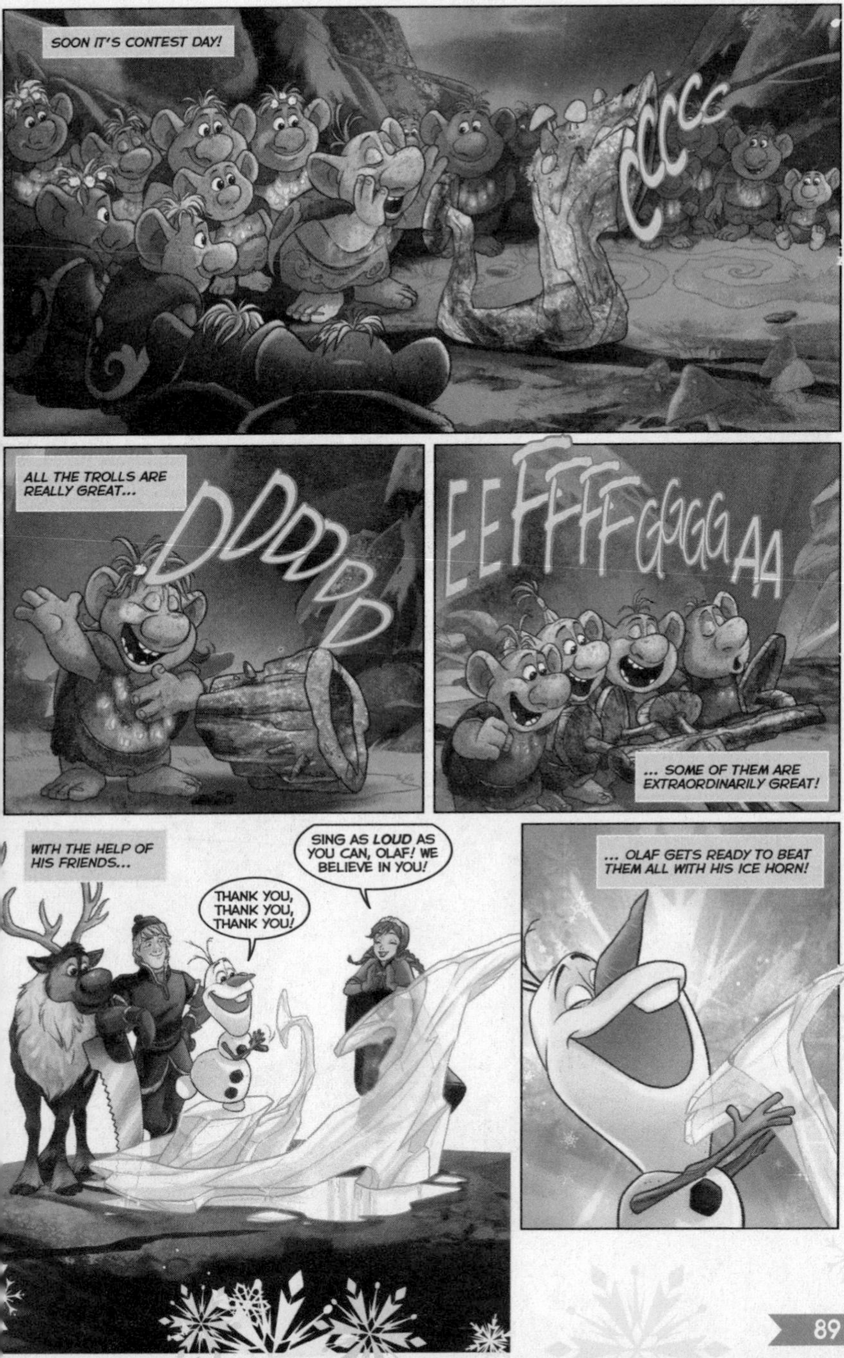
SOON IT'S CONTEST DAY!
CCCCC
ALL THE TROLLS ARE REALLY GREAT...
DDDDDD
EEFFFFGGGGAA
... SOME OF THEM ARE EXTRAORDINARILY GREAT!
WITH THE HELP OF HIS FRIENDS...
SING AS LOUD AS YOU CAN, OLAF! WE BELIEVE IN YOU!
THANK YOU, THANK YOU, THANK YOU!
... OLAF GETS READY TO BEAT THEM ALL WITH HIS ICE HORN!

IT'S TOO LOUD! IT'S DANGEROUS!

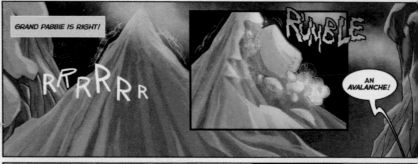

GRAND PABBIE IS RIGHT!

RRRRRr

RUMBLE

AN AVALANCHE!

EVERYBODY RUN!

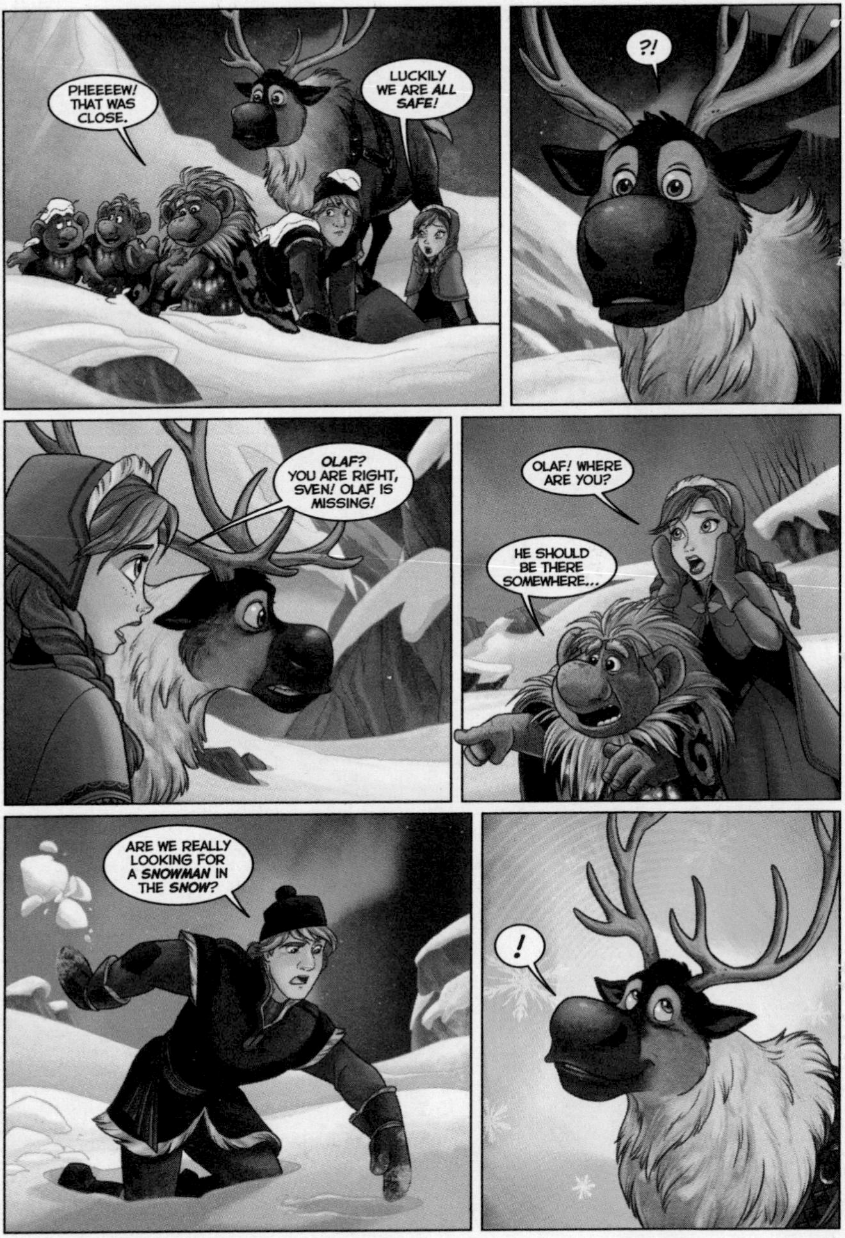
PHEEEEW! THAT WAS CLOSE.
LUCKILY WE ARE ALL SAFE!
?!
OLAF? YOU ARE RIGHT, SVEN! OLAF IS MISSING!
OLAF! WHERE ARE YOU?
HE SHOULD BE THERE SOMEWHERE...
ARE WE REALLY LOOKING FOR A SNOWMAN IN THE SNOW?
!

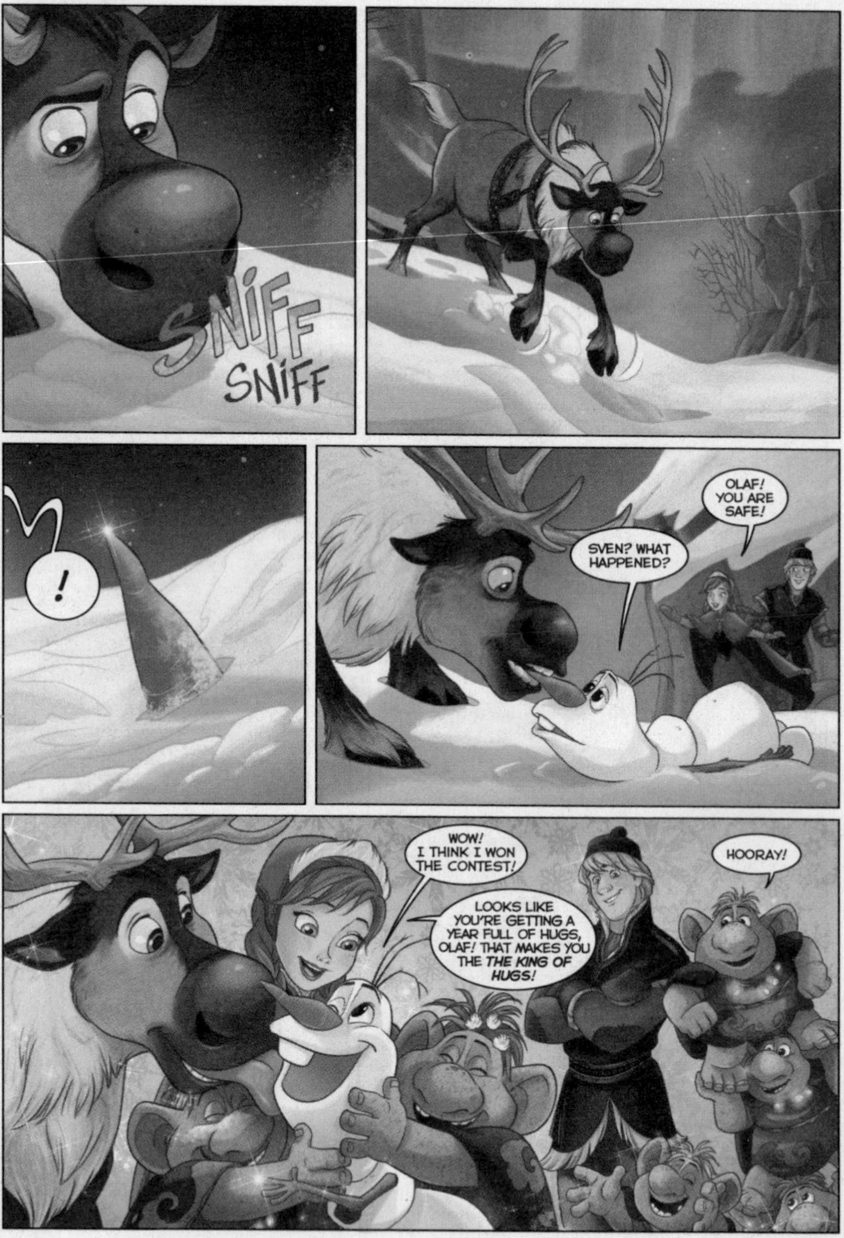
SNIFF
SNIFF
!
SVEN? WHAT HAPPENED?
OLAF! YOU ARE SAFE!
WOW! I THINK I WON THE CONTEST!
LOOKS LIKE YOU'RE GETTING A YEAR FULL OF HUGS, OLAF! THAT MAKES YOU THE *THE KING OF HUGS!*
HOORAY!

The End

A New Hairstyle

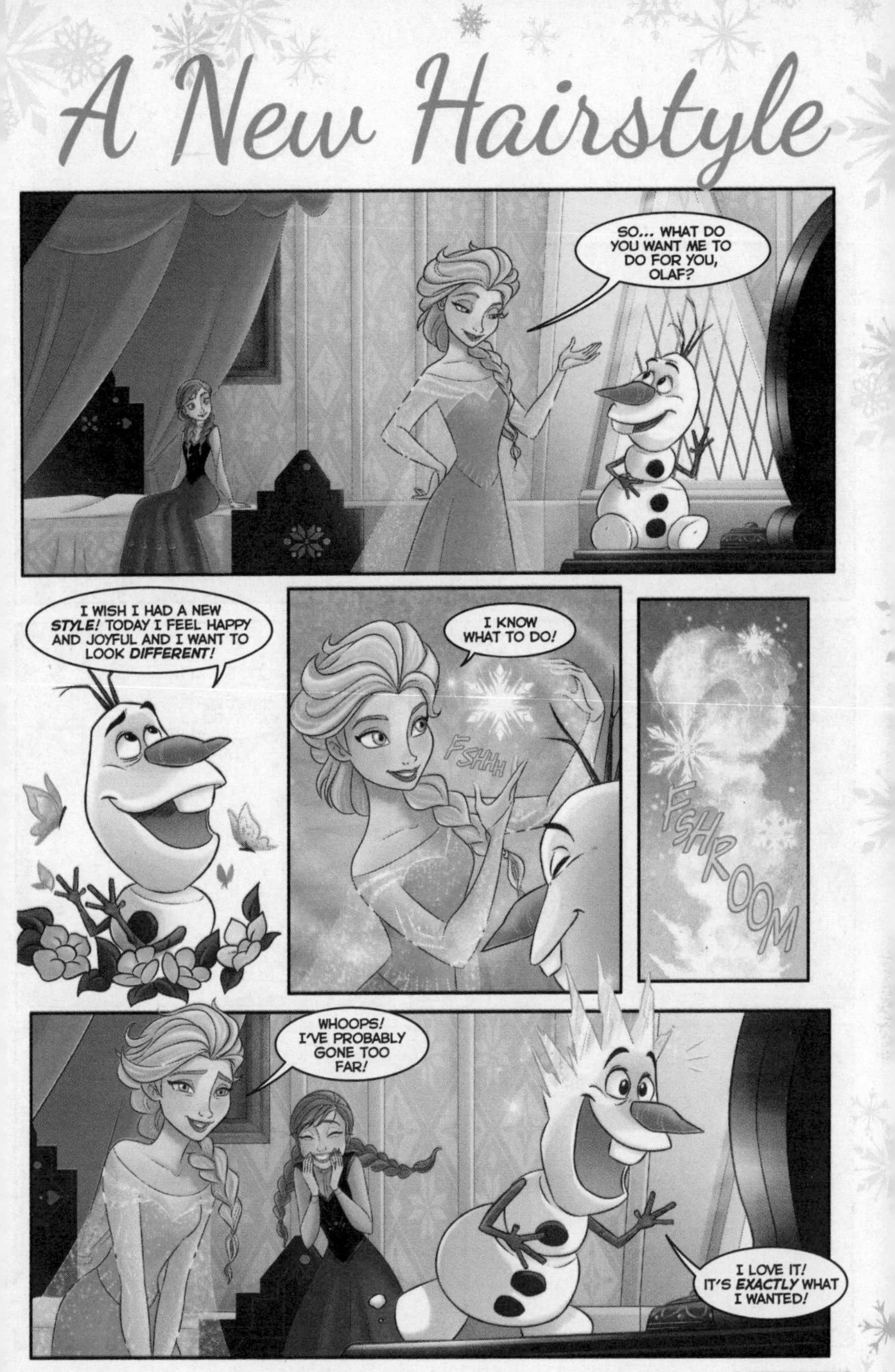

SO... WHAT DO YOU WANT ME TO DO FOR YOU, OLAF?
I WISH I HAD A NEW STYLE! TODAY I FEEL HAPPY AND JOYFUL AND I WANT TO LOOK DIFFERENT!
I KNOW WHAT TO DO!
FSHHH
FSHROOM
WHOOPS! I'VE PROBABLY GONE TOO FAR!
I LOVE IT! IT'S EXACTLY WHAT I WANTED!

The End

Morning Lesson

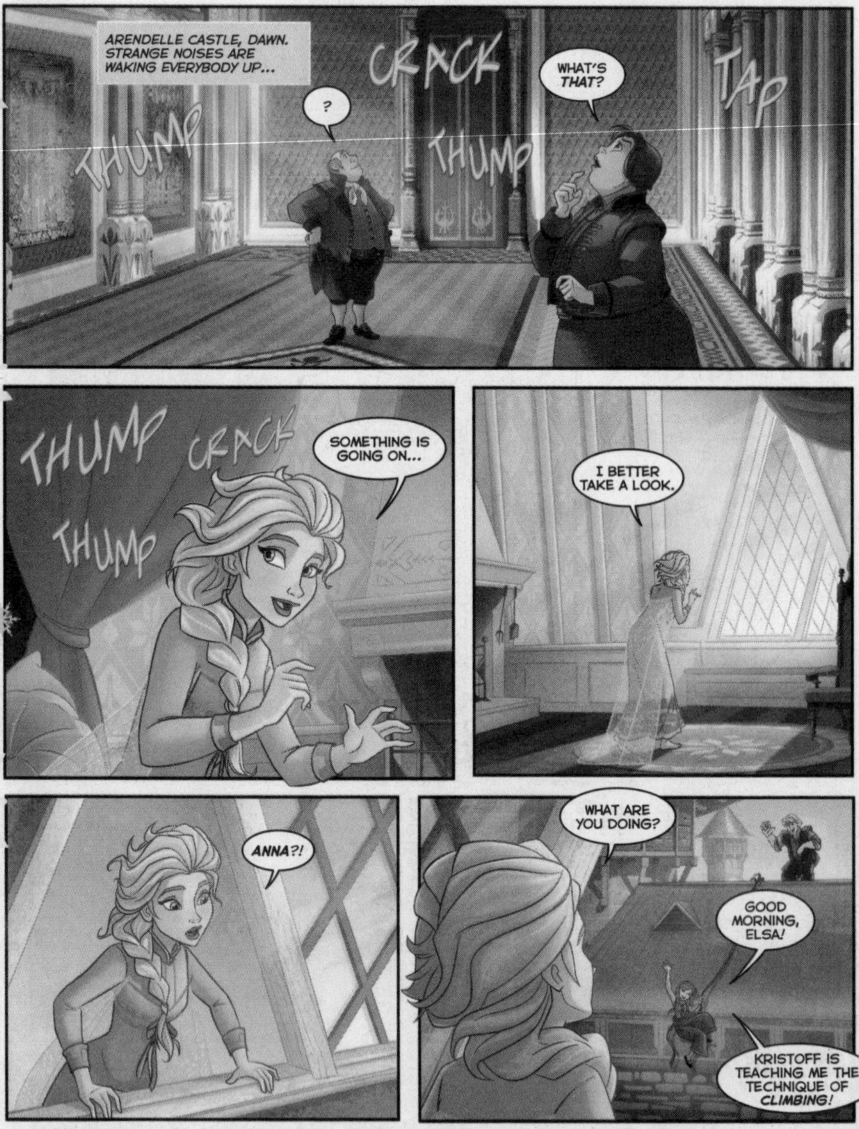

ARENDELLE CASTLE, DAWN. STRANGE NOISES ARE WAKING EVERYBODY UP...
THUMP
?
CRACK
THUMP
WHAT'S *THAT*?
TAP
THUMP
CRACK
THUMP
SOMETHING IS GOING ON...
I BETTER TAKE A LOOK.
ANNA?!
WHAT ARE YOU DOING?
GOOD MORNING, ELSA!
KRISTOFF IS TEACHING ME THE TECHNIQUE OF *CLIMBING!*

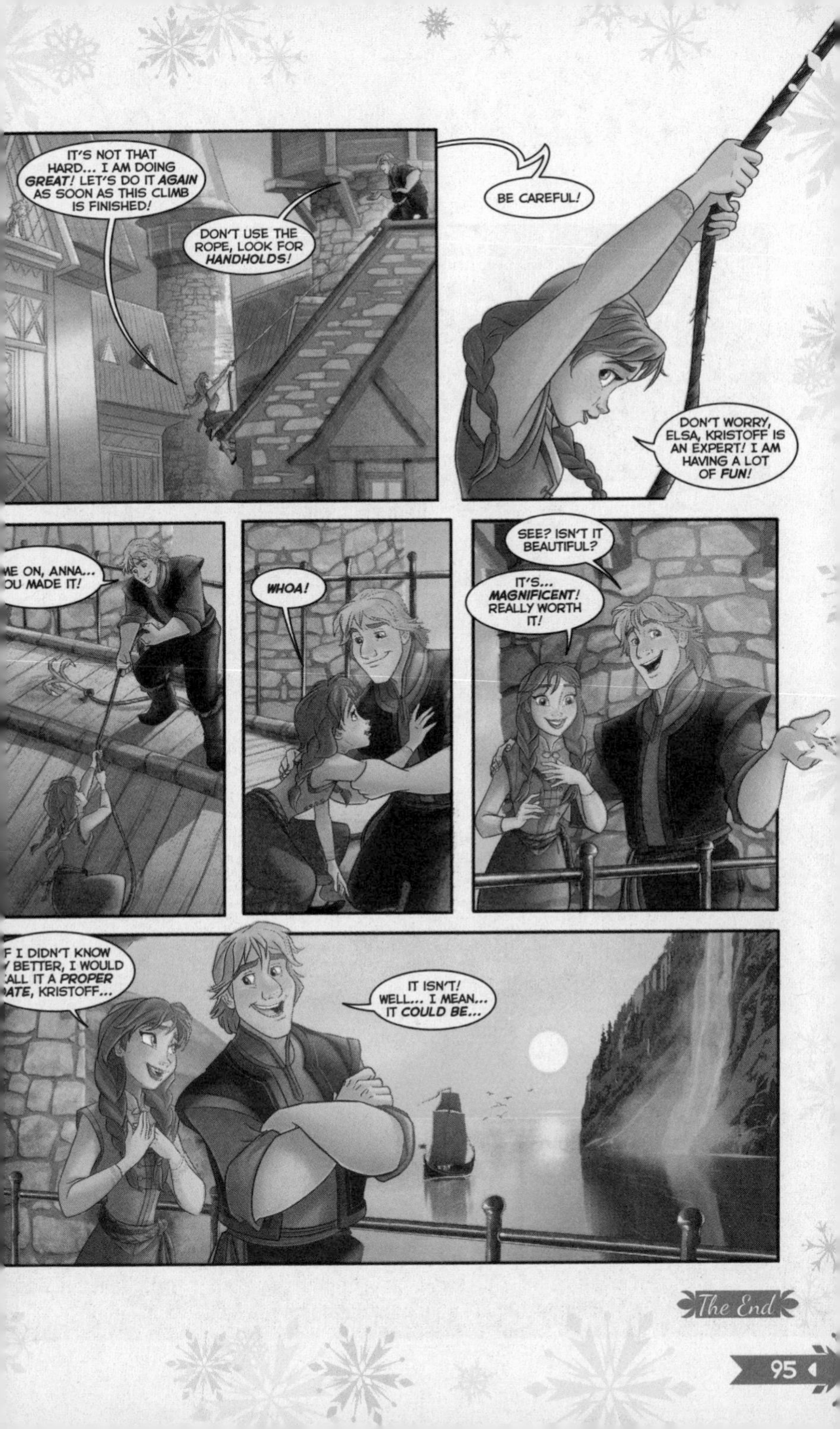

IT'S NOT THAT HARD... I AM DOING GREAT! LET'S DO IT AGAIN AS SOON AS THIS CLIMB IS FINISHED!
DON'T USE THE ROPE, LOOK FOR HANDHOLDS!
BE CAREFUL!
DON'T WORRY, ELSA, KRISTOFF IS AN EXPERT! I AM HAVING A LOT OF FUN!
ME ON, ANNA... OU MADE IT!
WHOA!
SEE? ISN'T IT BEAUTIFUL?
IT'S... MAGNIFICENT! REALLY WORTH IT!
F I DIDN'T KNOW BETTER, I WOULD ALL IT A PROPER ATE, KRISTOFF...
IT ISN'T! WELL... I MEAN... IT COULD BE...
The End

Camping Night

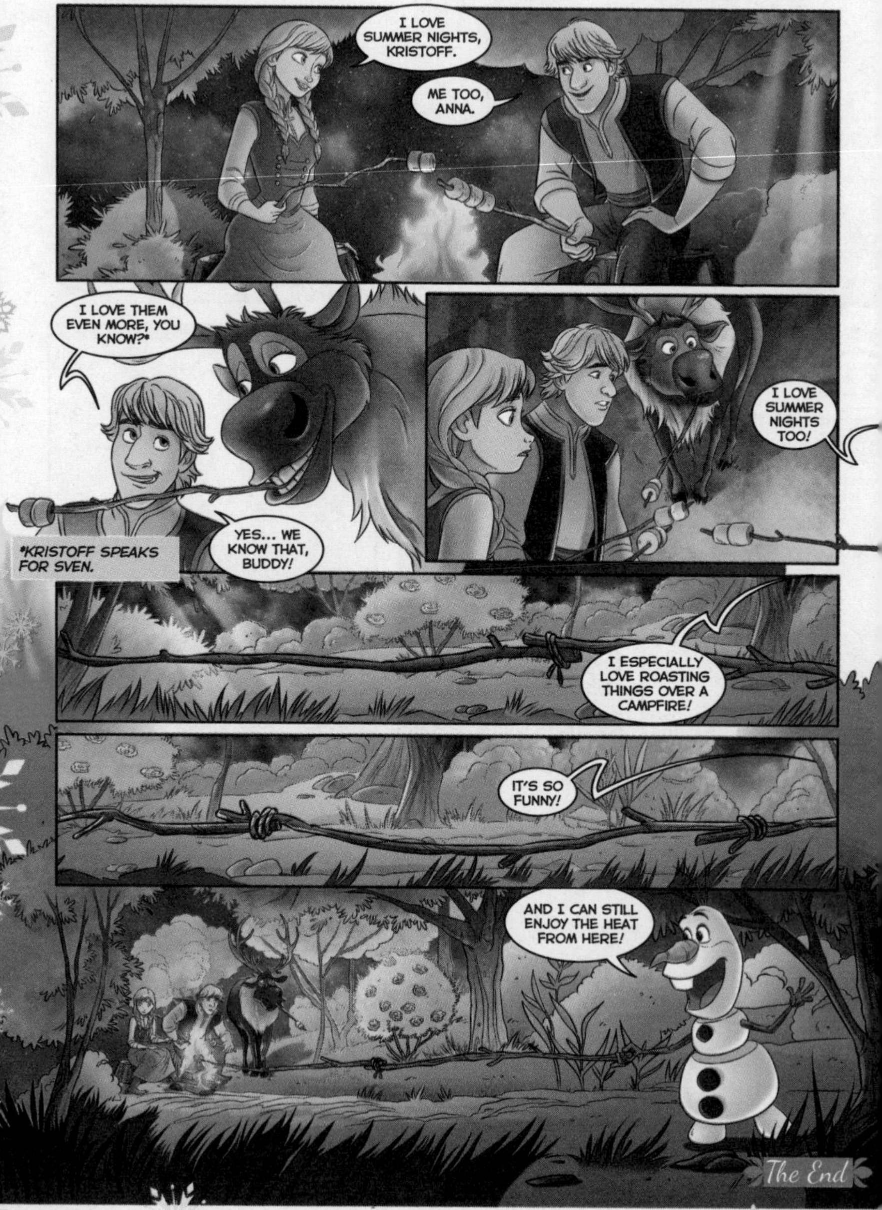
I LOVE SUMMER NIGHTS, KRISTOFF.
ME TOO, ANNA.
I LOVE THEM EVEN MORE, YOU KNOW?*
YES... WE KNOW THAT, BUDDY!
*KRISTOFF SPEAKS FOR SVEN.
I LOVE SUMMER NIGHTS TOO!
I ESPECIALLY LOVE ROASTING THINGS OVER A CAMPFIRE!
IT'S SO FUNNY!
AND I CAN STILL ENJOY THE HEAT FROM HERE!
The End

Sweet Trick

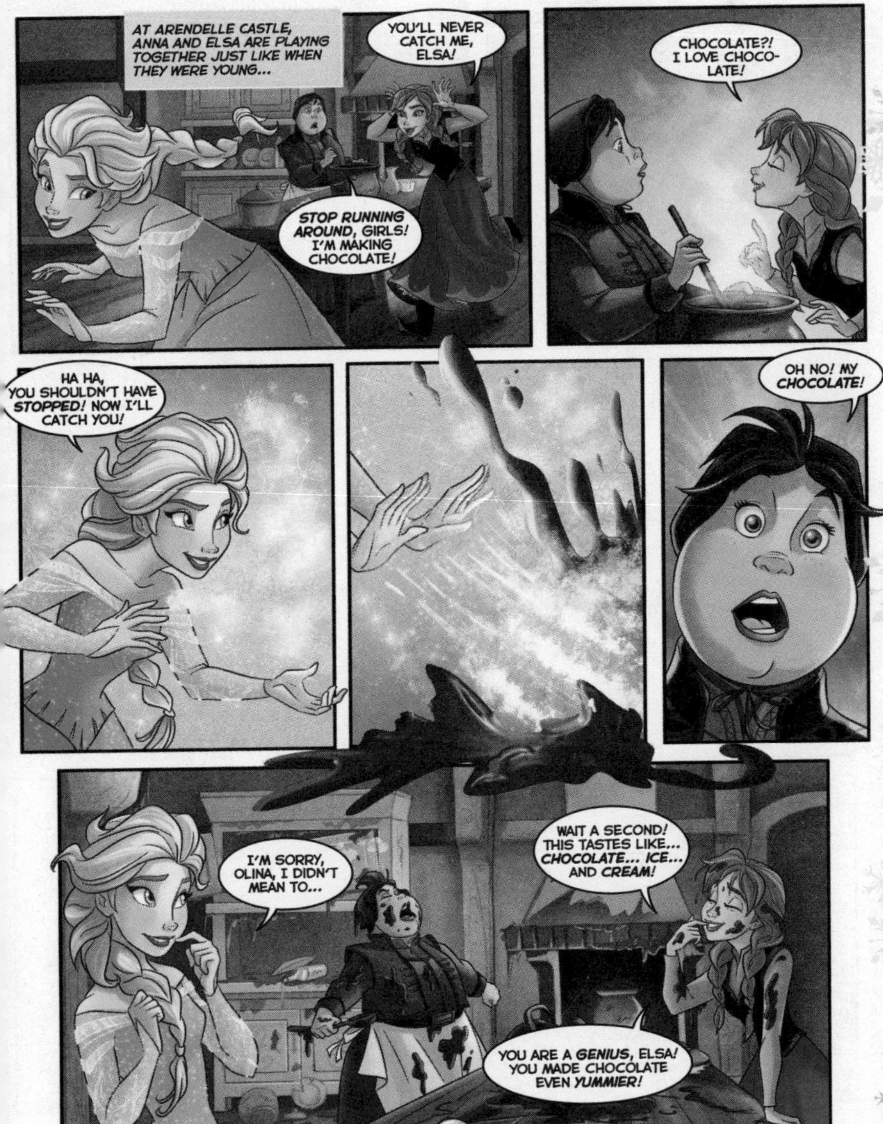

AT ARENDELLE CASTLE, ANNA AND ELSA ARE PLAYING TOGETHER JUST LIKE WHEN THEY WERE YOUNG...
YOU'LL NEVER CATCH ME, ELSA!
STOP RUNNING AROUND, GIRLS! I'M MAKING CHOCOLATE!
CHOCOLATE?! I LOVE CHOCO-LATE!
HA HA, YOU SHOULDN'T HAVE STOPPED! NOW I'LL CATCH YOU!
OH NO! MY CHOCOLATE!
I'M SORRY, OLINA, I DIDN'T MEAN TO...
WAIT A SECOND! THIS TASTES LIKE... CHOCOLATE... ICE... AND CREAM!
YOU ARE A GENIUS, ELSA! YOU MADE CHOCOLATE EVEN YUMMIER!

The End

Swim Dream

Manuscript: Alessandro Ferrari; Layout: Elisabetta ...elarani; Clea... p: Arianna R... ...ederica Salfo; Ink: Michela Frare, Cristina Stella; Co...: Dario Calabria

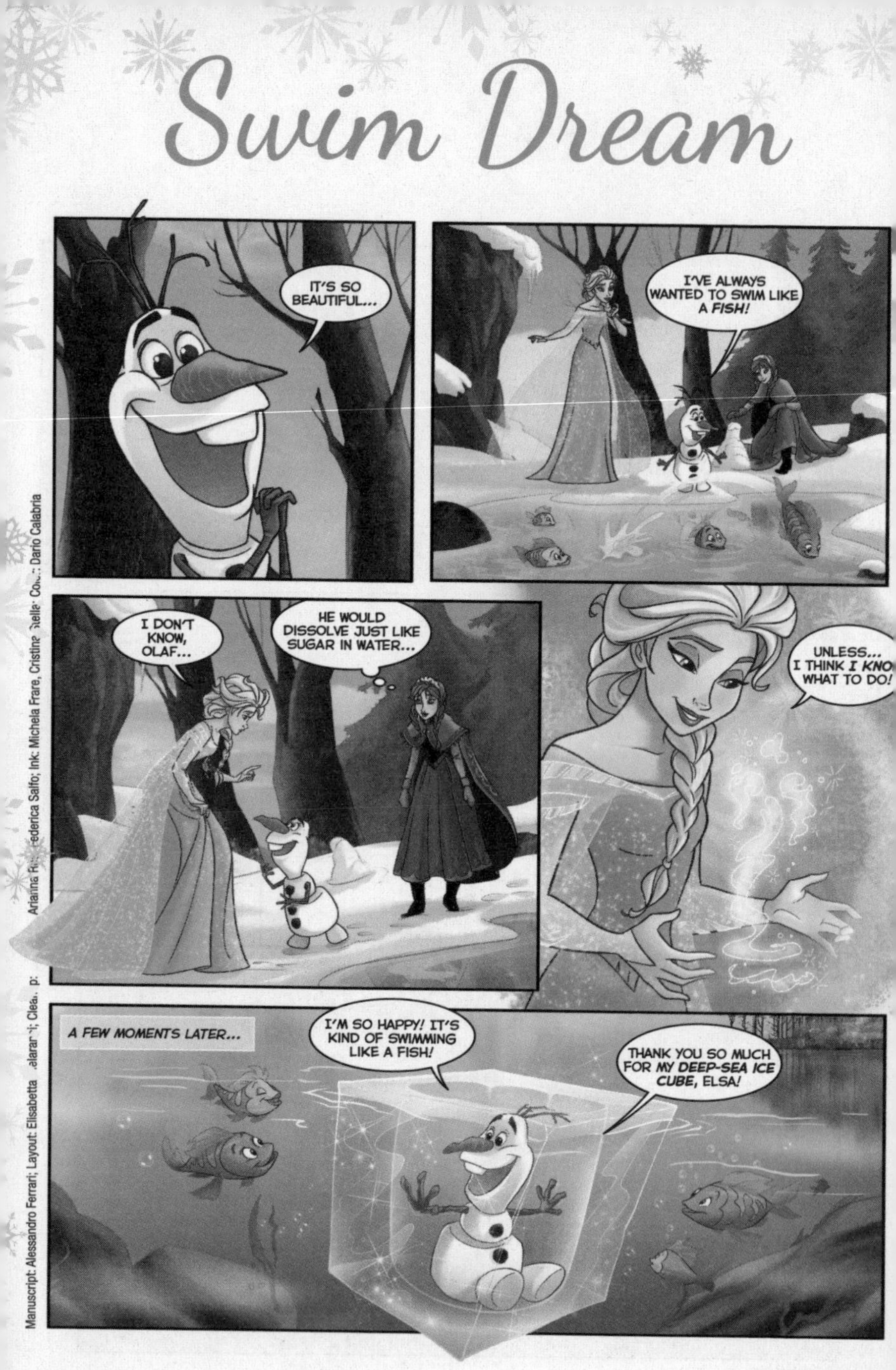

IT'S SO BEAUTIFUL...
I'VE ALWAYS WANTED TO SWIM LIKE A *FISH!*
I DON'T KNOW, OLAF...
HE WOULD DISSOLVE JUST LIKE SUGAR IN WATER...
UNLESS... I THINK *I KNO* WHAT TO DO!
A FEW MOMENTS LATER...
I'M SO HAPPY! IT'S KIND OF SWIMMING LIKE A FISH!
THANK YOU SO MUCH FOR MY *DEEP-SEA ICE CUBE*, ELSA!

The End

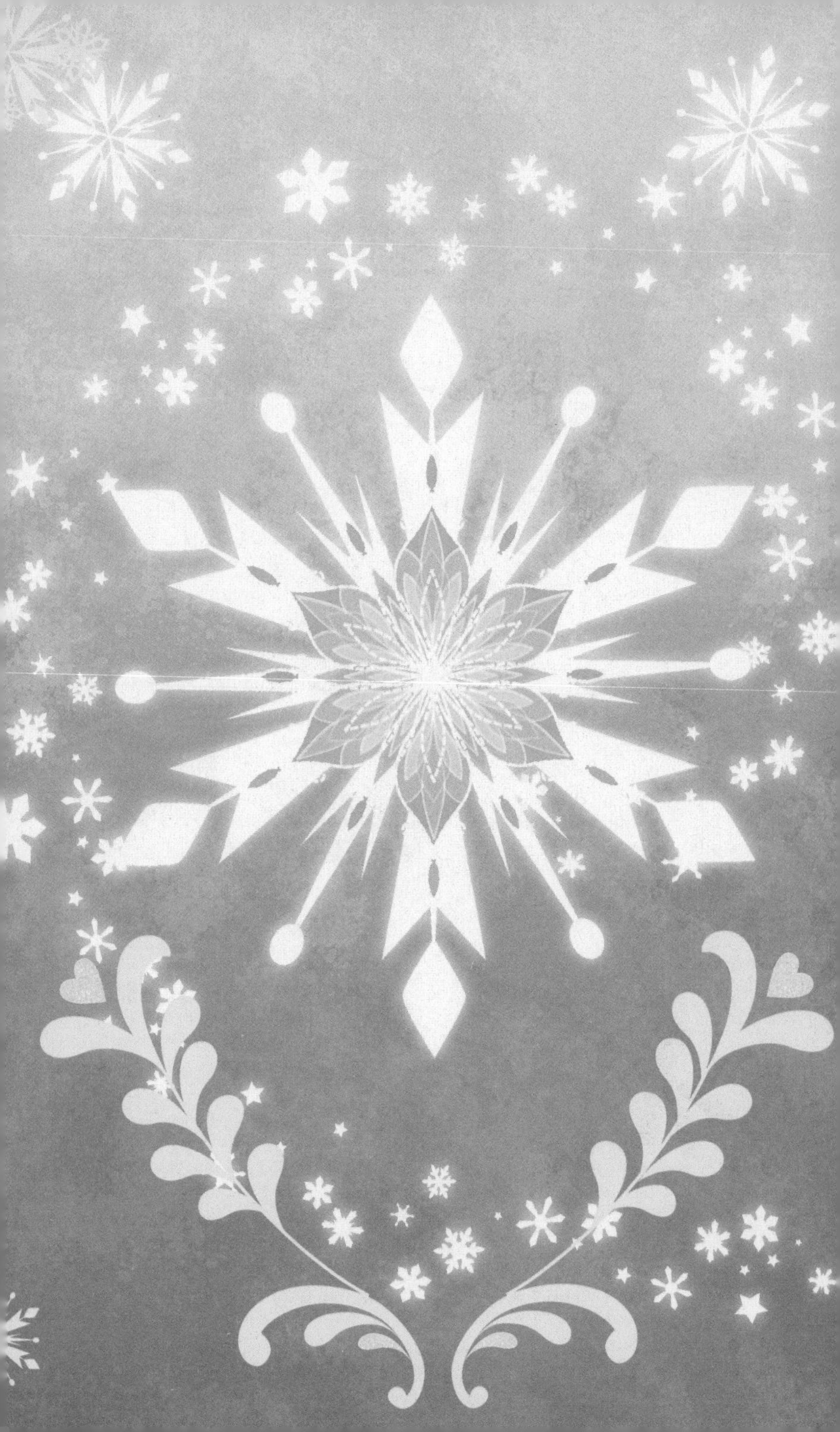

Disney

FROZEN Activities

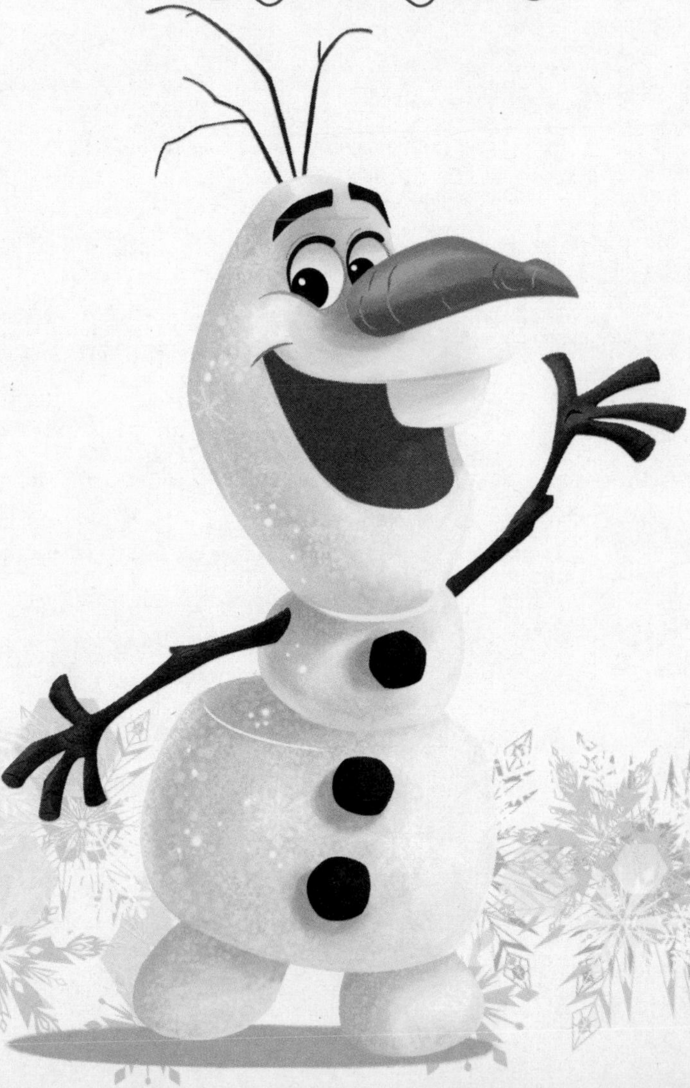

OLAF'S ACTIVITY CORNER!

Olaf loves to dream about summer. He doesn't seem to realize what might happen if he spends too much time under the warm sun! See if you can finish each of these puzzles in one minute each, and keep Olaf on his feet. (Or head!)

EACH DAY

Can you spot all 7 differences between these two pictures before Olaf melts? Go!

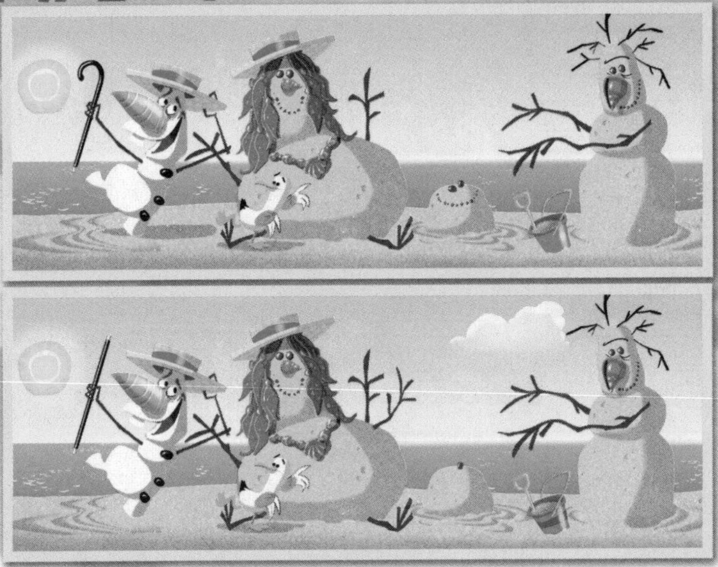

WHAT'S WRONG?

Can you figure out the one thing that is wrong with each of these Olafs?

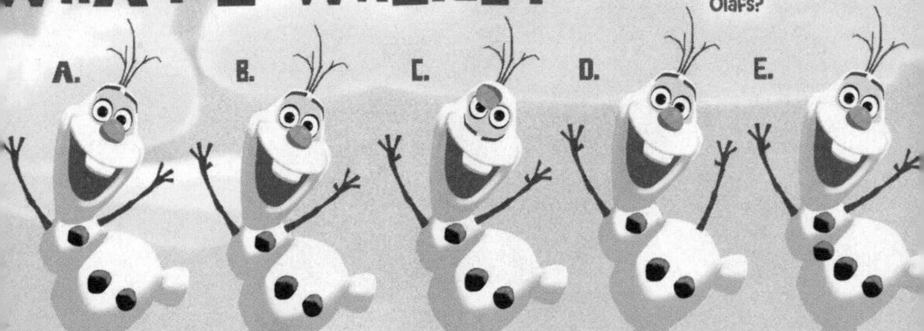
A.
B.
C.
D.
E.

SUMMER GETAWAY

See if you can find this picture of Olaf somewhere else in this magazine.

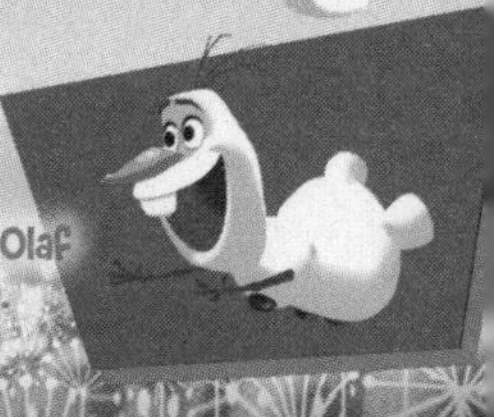

Fjord-Hopping with Sven!

Sven sees some carrots across the fjord, and he wants them! Which path is the shortest route for him to take?

HINT: He needs to choose the path with the fewest pieces of ice.

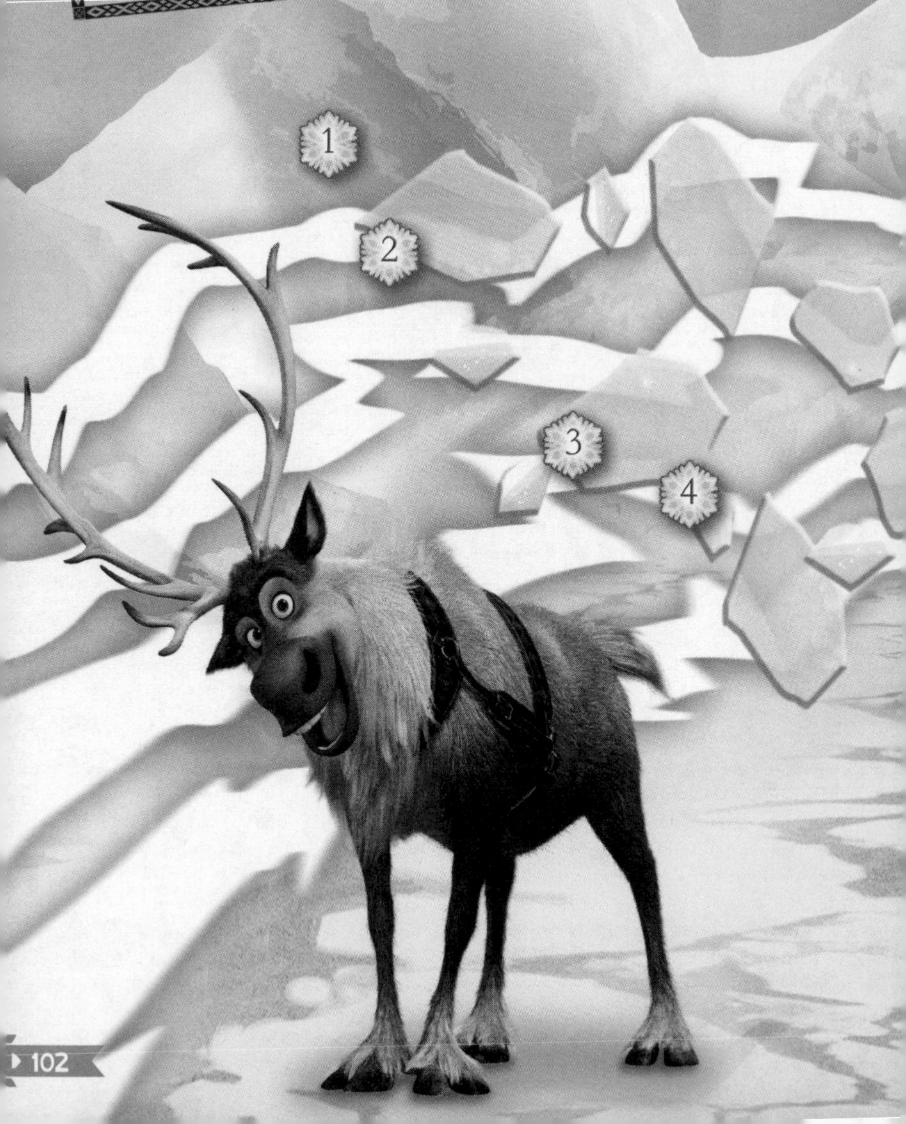

1
2
3
4

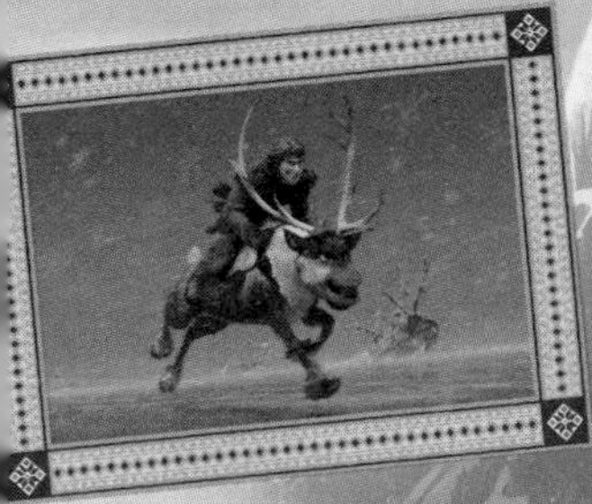

Reindeer Mix-Up!

Where do each of the missing puzzle pieces belong?

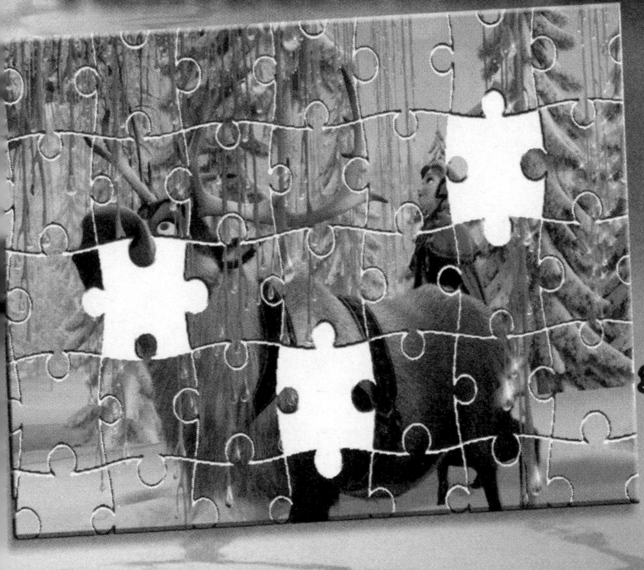

1.

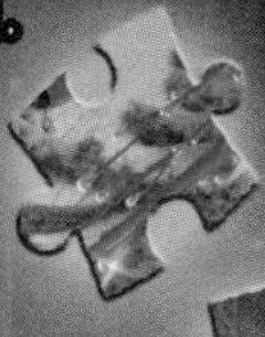

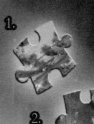

2.

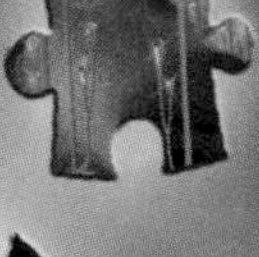

3.

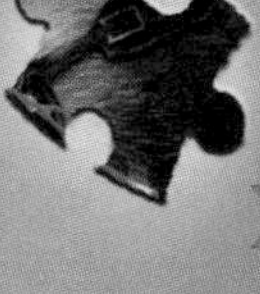

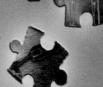

REACH ELSA!

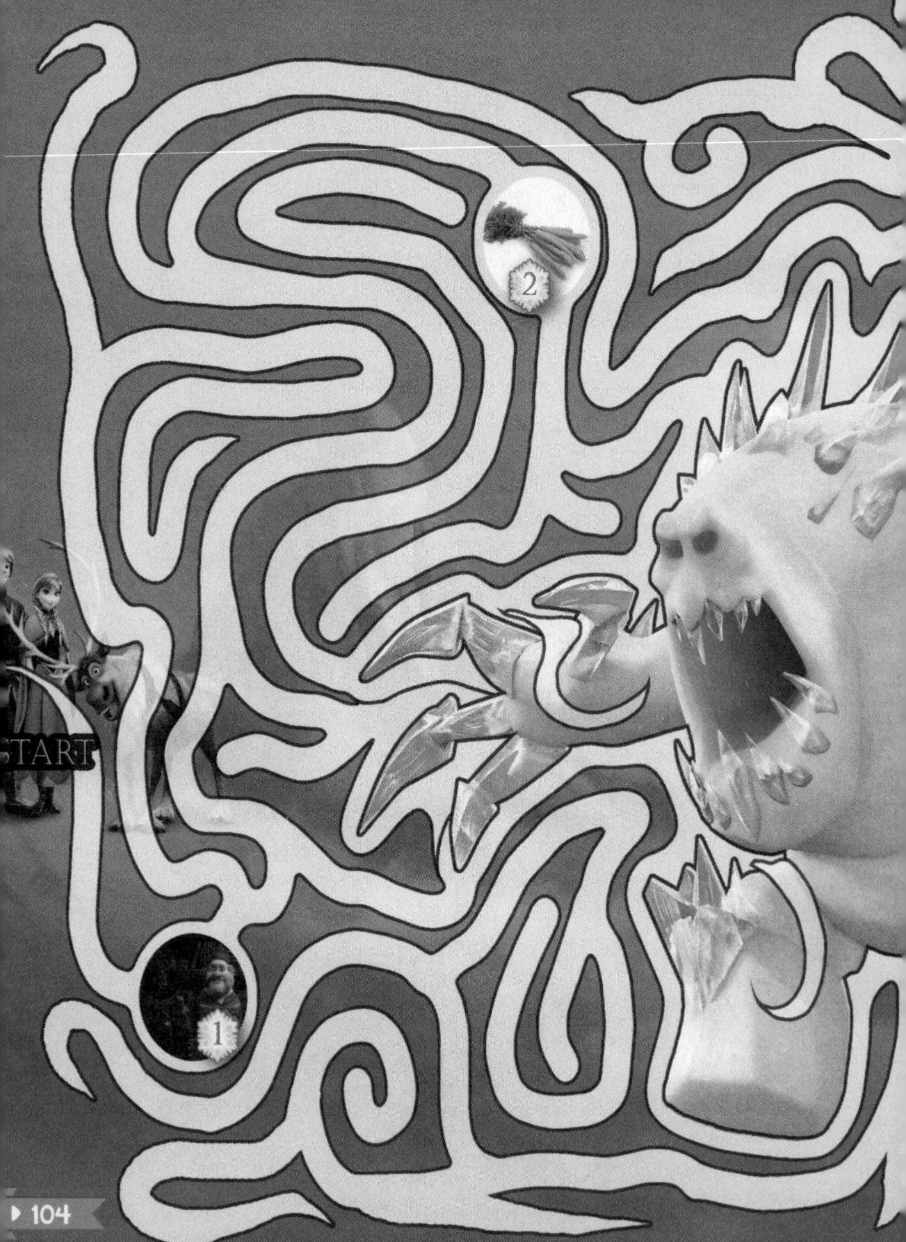
START
2
1

Anna, Kristoff, and Sven are trying to get to Elsa's ice palace, but they keep running into obstacles. Help them avoid Marshmallow so they can reach the palace!

Along the way, they need to make a few stops. Hint: Be sure to make these stops in the order they appear in this list.

1. *Stop at Oaken's Trading Post for dry clothes.*
2. *Pick up a snack for Sven.*
3. *Chat with the trolls.*

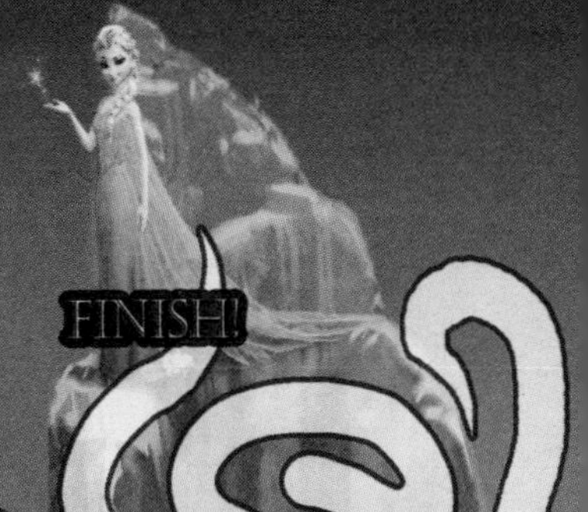
FINISH!

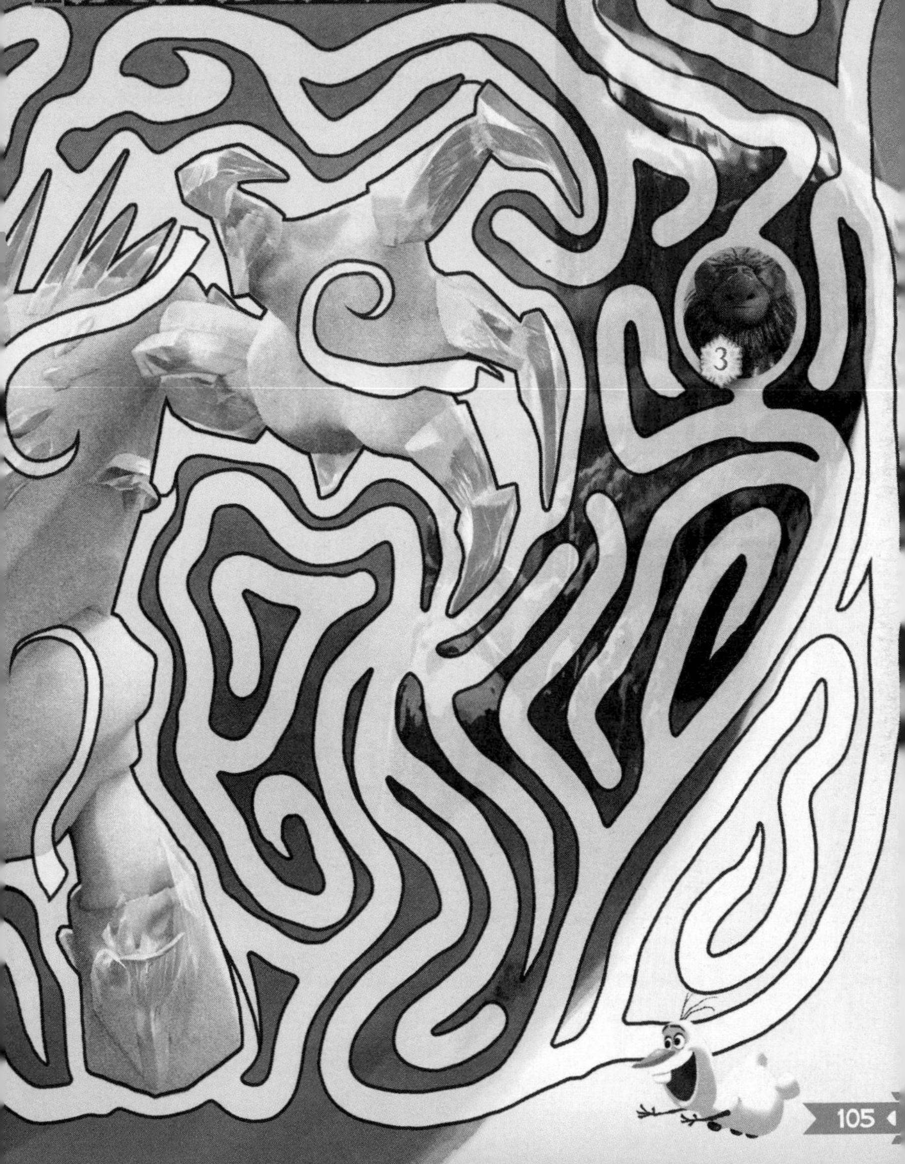
3

Sisters: They Have Their Differences!

Which pictures of Elsa and Anna below match the originals above?

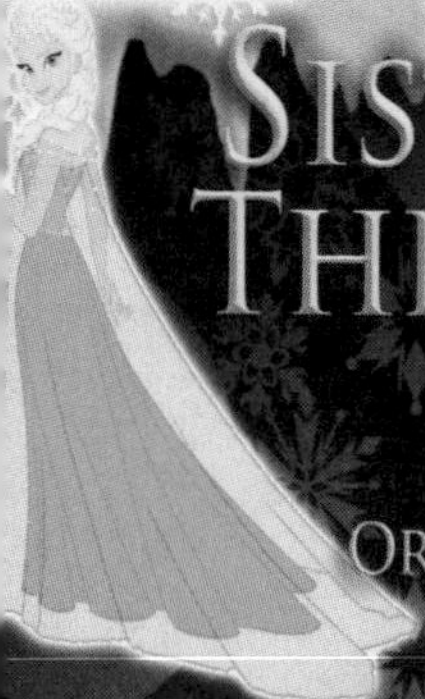

Original

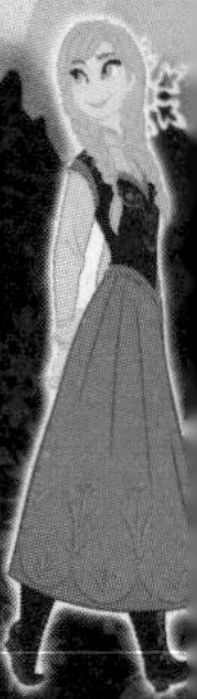

Original

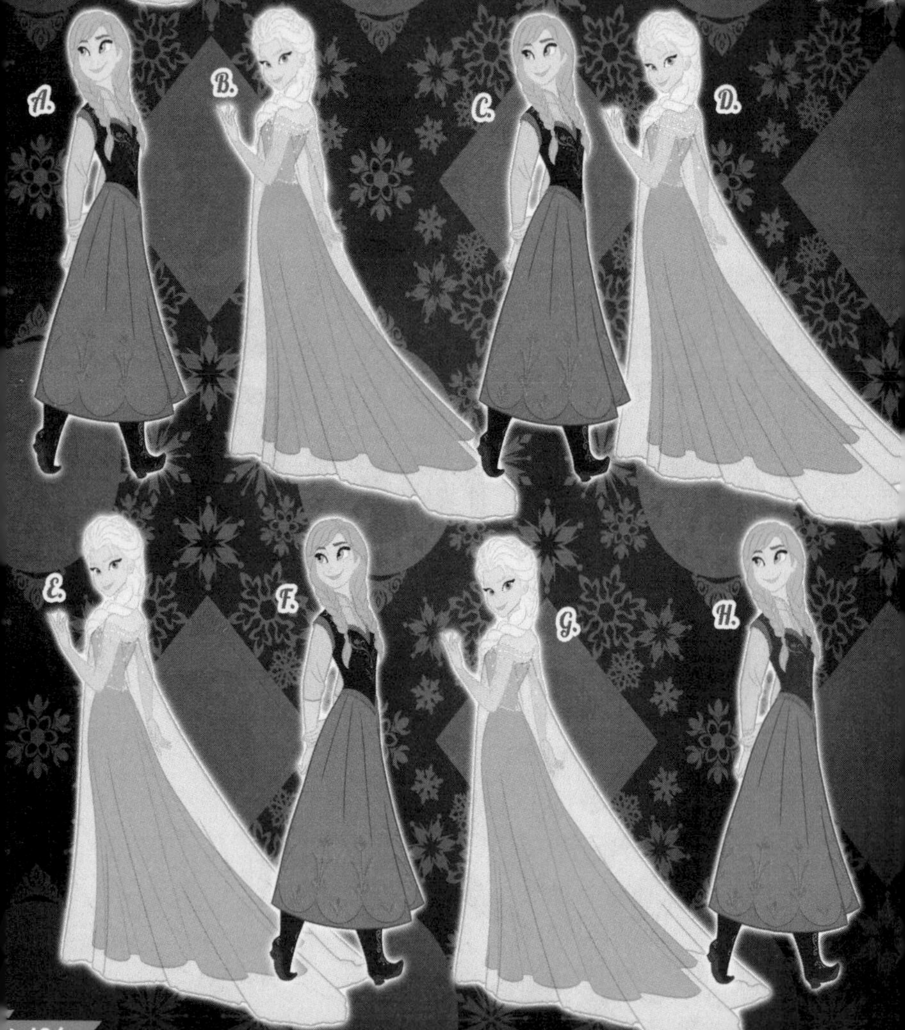
A.
B.
C.
D.
E.
F.
G.
H.

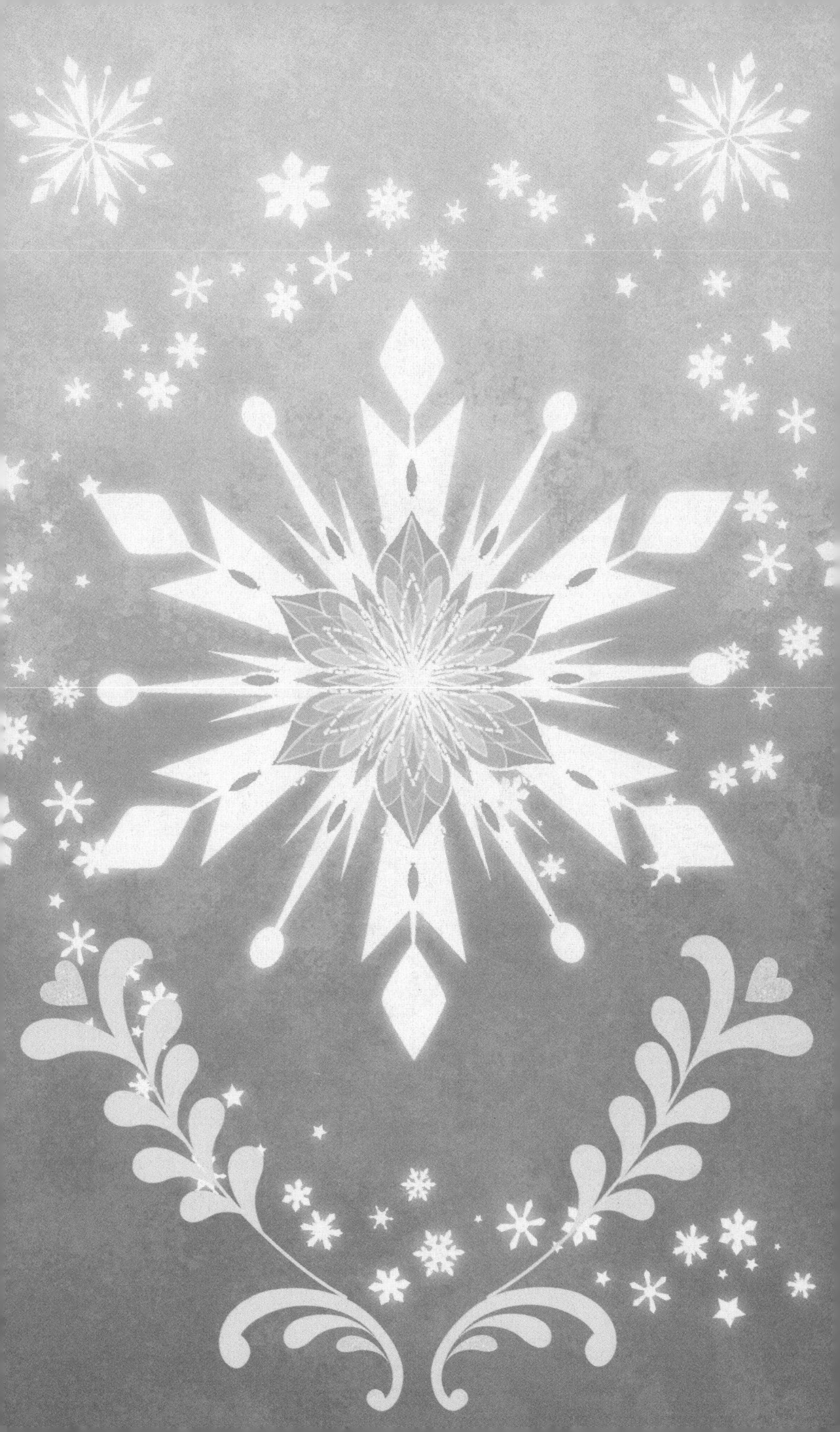

Welcome to A

Enter the fabulous world of *Frozen* and experience the magic of ice! Meet Elsa, Anna and all the wonderful characters of the Kingdom of Arendelle: They will be your guides throughout the pages!

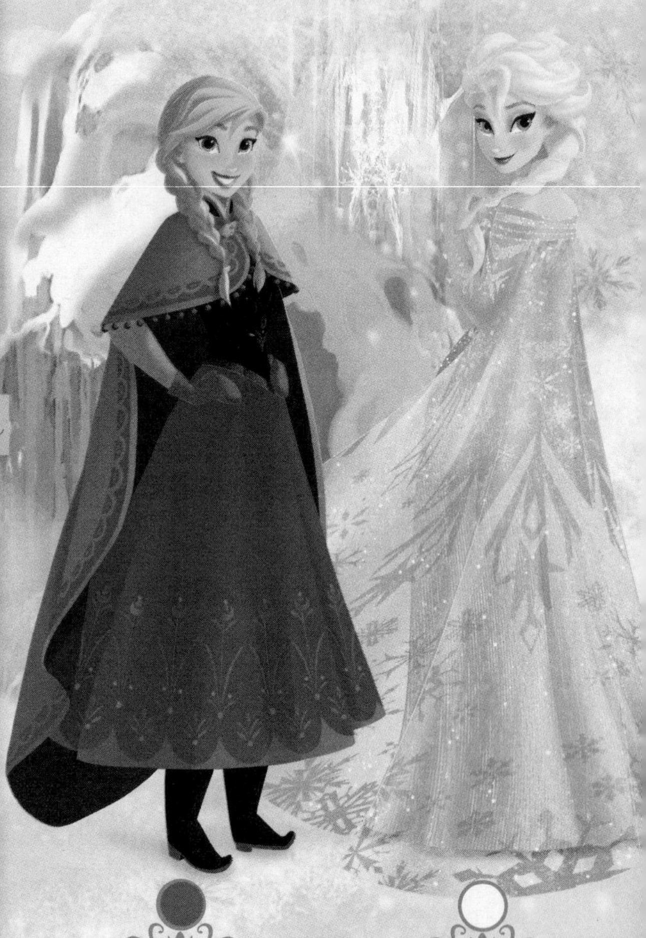

Find the Details

Look at these details below and match them to the characters they belong to by coloring the dots.

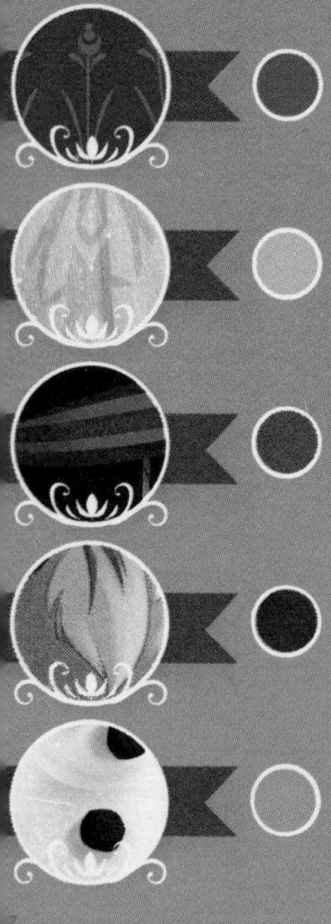

Anna

Anna is generous, optimistic and always starts her day with a smile. She's also caring, brave and always active!

Elsa

Elsa is the elegant first-born child in the royal family of Arendelle and Anna's older sister. She has the magic power to control ice and snow.

endelle!

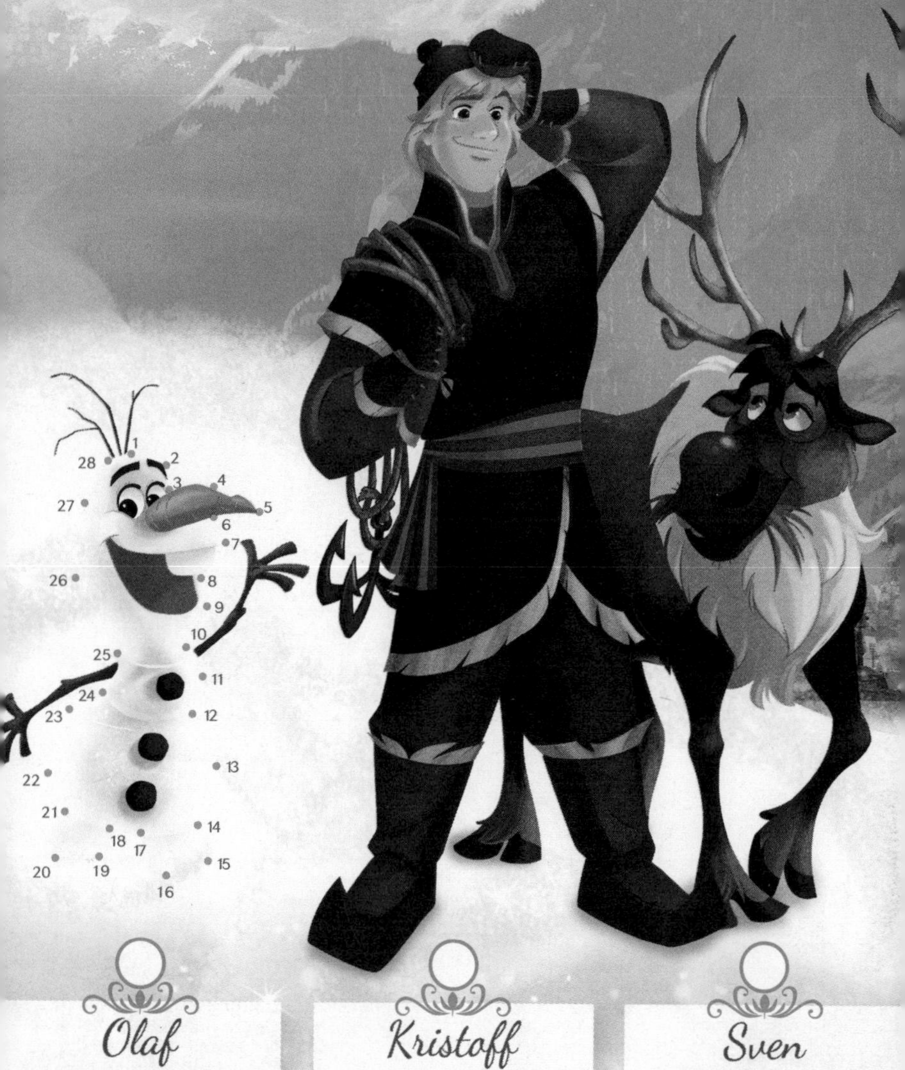

Olaf

Connect the dots to reveal Olaf, the funny snowman created by Elsa's magic. He loves warm hugs and summer, even though he's never experienced it!

Kristoff

Kristoff loves the cold and the snow as he grew up in the mountains. Solitary and independent, he carries blocks of ice with his sled.

Sven

Sven is a strong, friendly reindeer who likes carrots. He's Kristoff's best friend, and is always ready to face danger when it comes to helping his friends.

Snowflakes Path

Olaf and Sven had a great idea: Celebrate Royal Skating Day at the ice palace! Enter the maze and guide them to reach the palace by following the highlighted snowflakes.

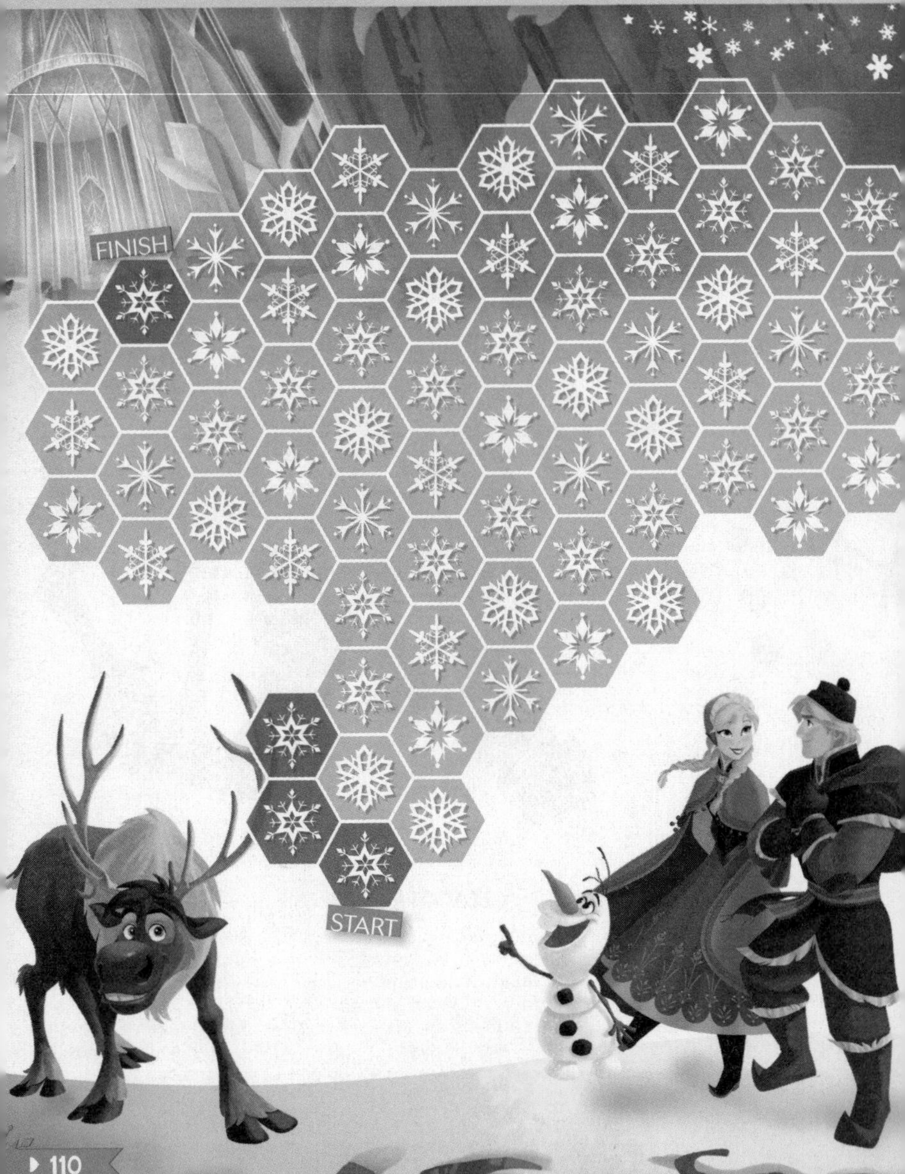
FINISH
START

Hide-and-Seek

Olaf, Anna and Sven are strolling in the North Mountain forest... but where are the trolls? Play hide-and-seek with them: Look at the scene and find where they are hiding!

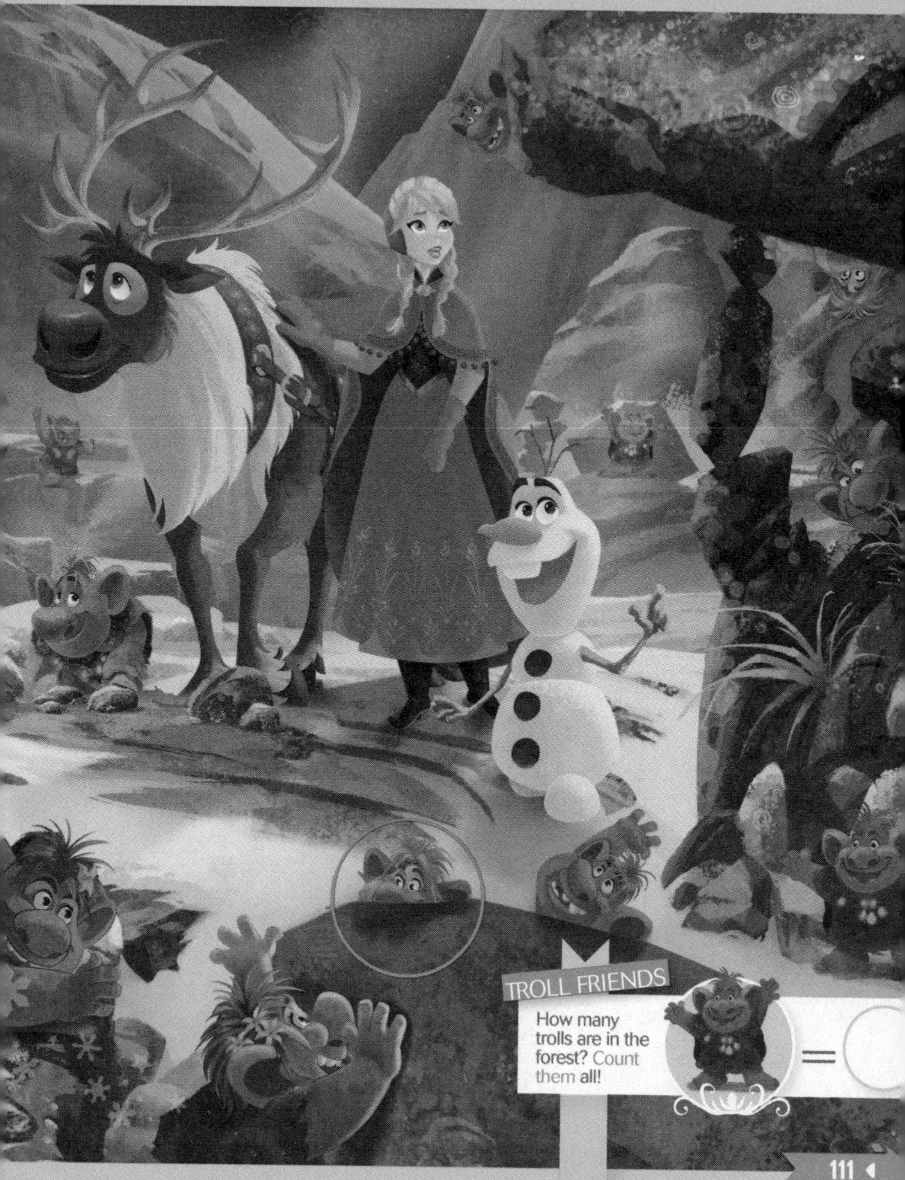

TROLL FRIENDS

How many trolls are in the forest? Count them all!

=

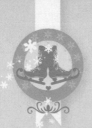

Olaf's Dreams

Olaf loves summer even though he has never lived it. Join the dots from 1 to 16 to find out what he's dreaming about. Then complete the puzzle of his dream vacation by writing the correct sequence of the pieces.

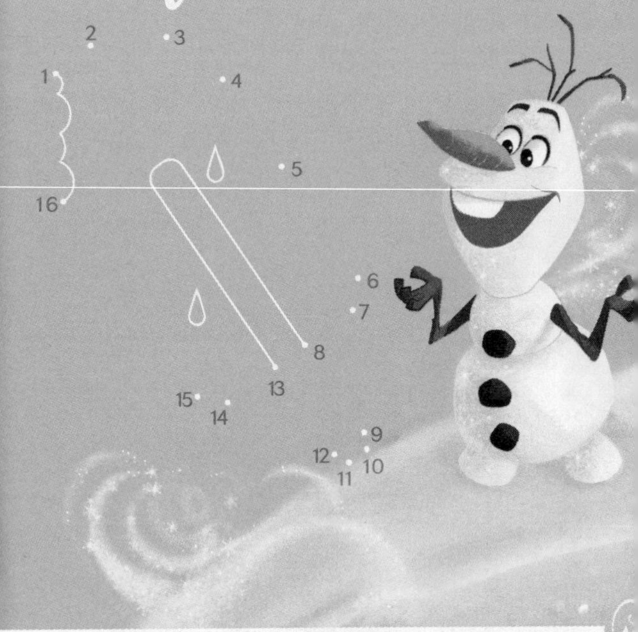

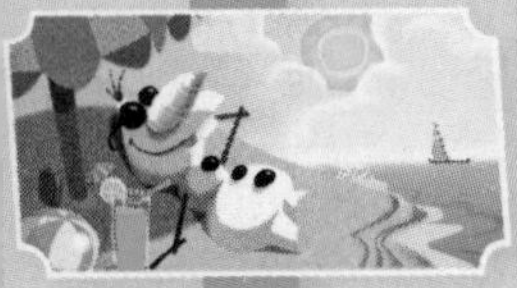

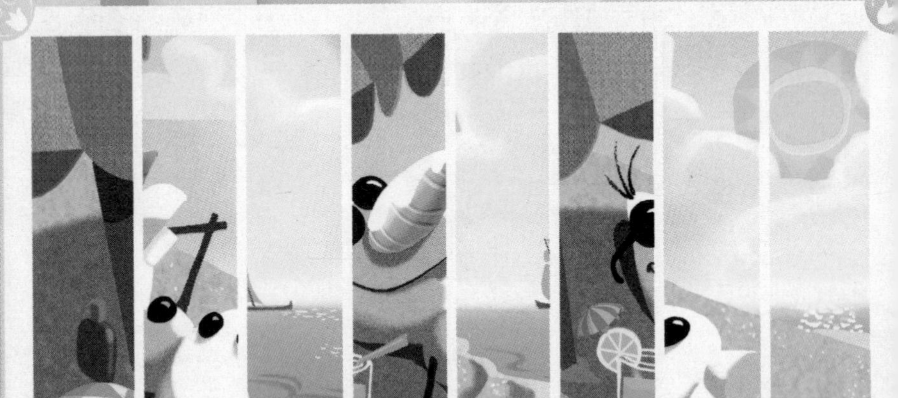
1

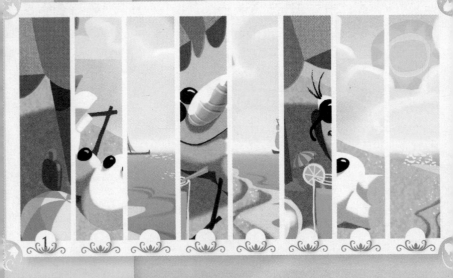

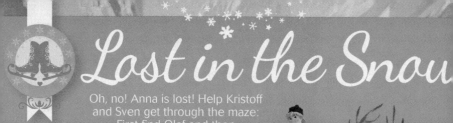

Lost in the Snow

Oh, no! Anna is lost! Help Kristoff and Sven get through the maze: First find Olaf and then guide them to find and save Anna.

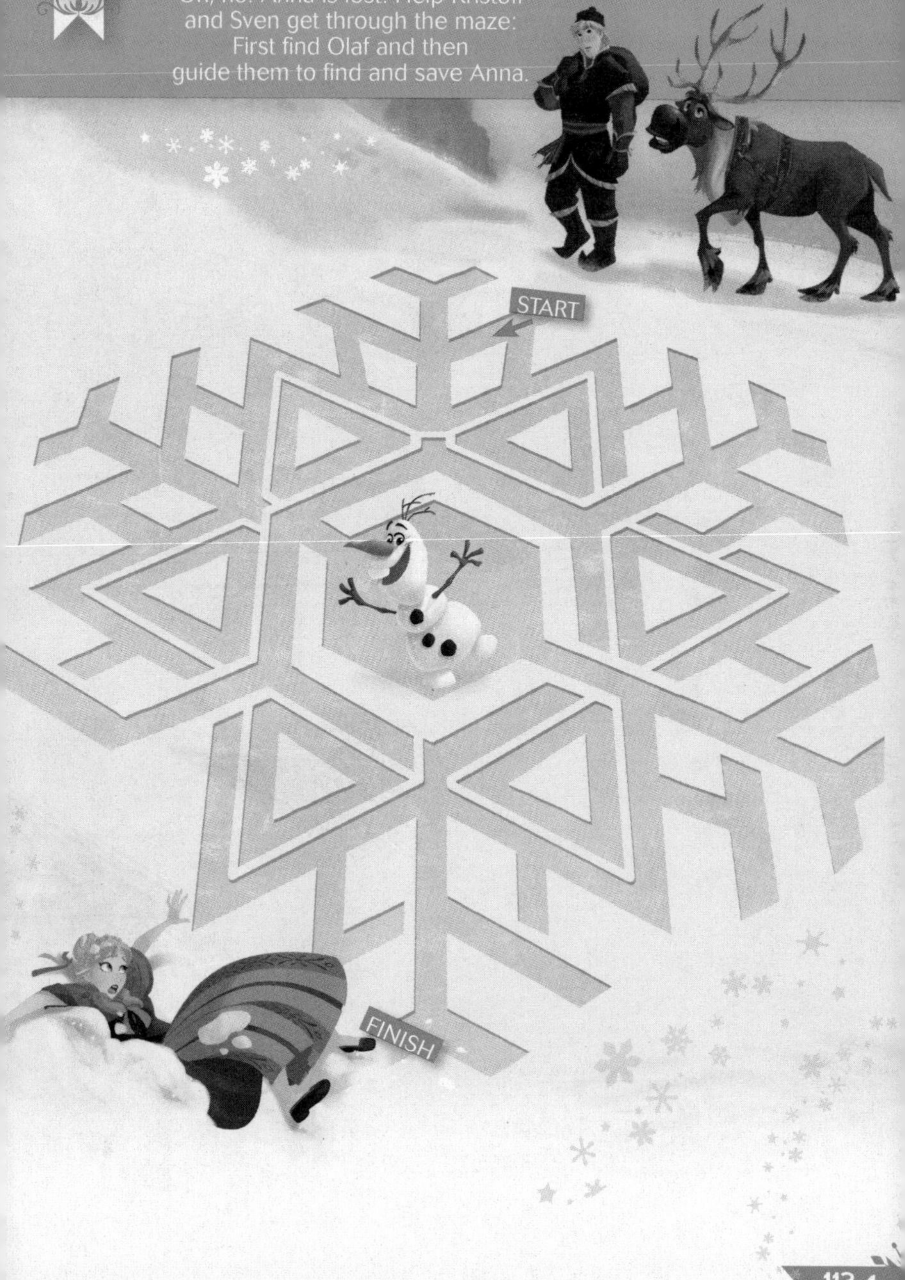
START
FINISH

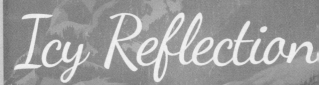

Icy Reflection

What's happened? The ice seems magical! Look at the scene below, then find and circle 20 small differences in the reflection!

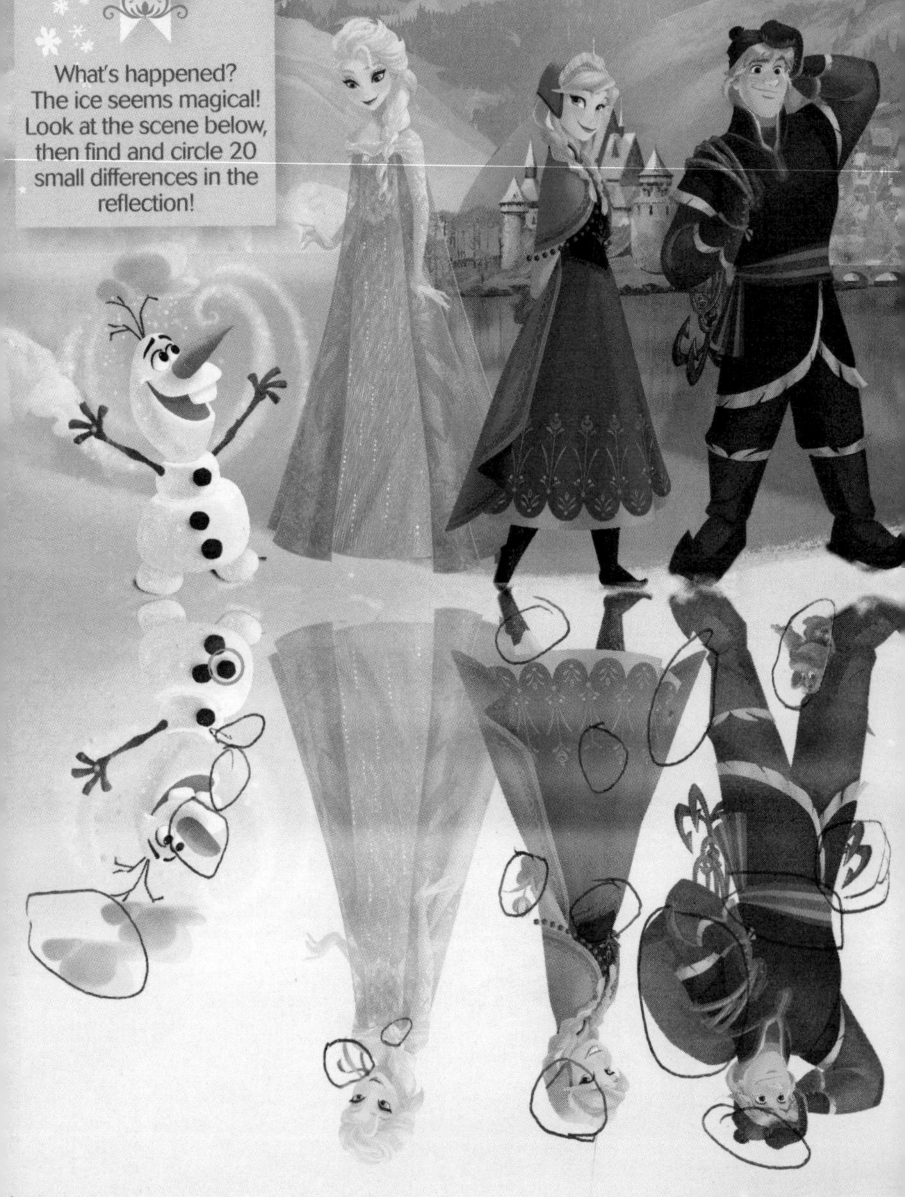

Marshmallow's Chase

The giant snowman created by Elsa is chasing Anna and Kristoff. Try to stop him by hitting the target with a snowball. Only one of these 3 shots will score a direct hit!

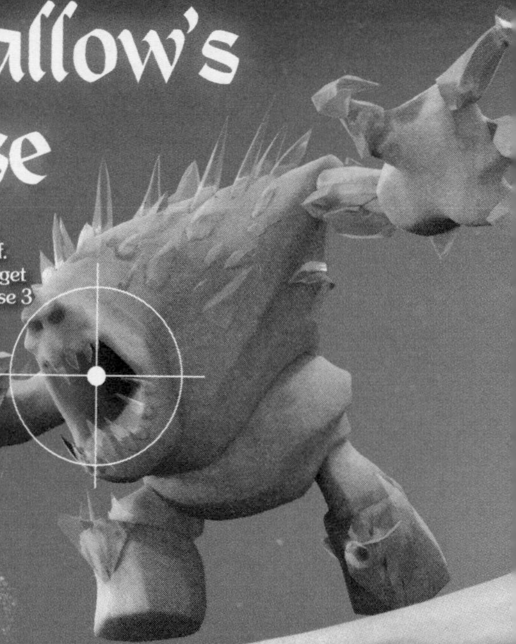

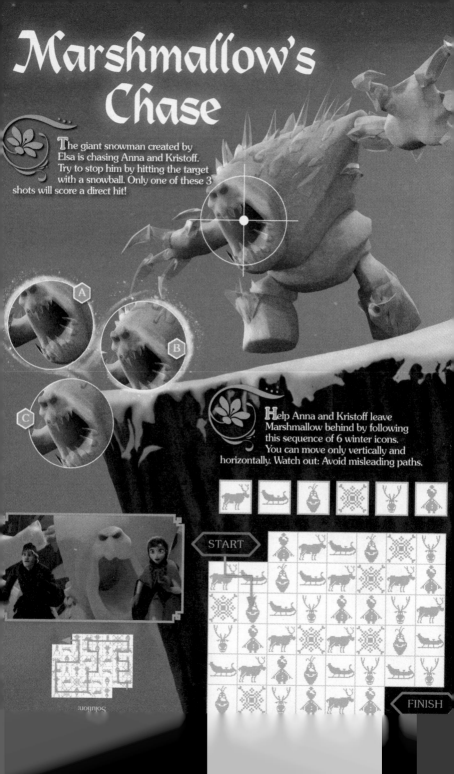

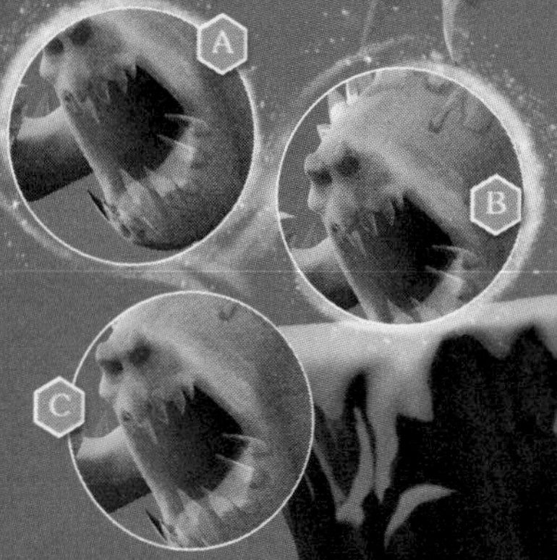
A
B
C

Help Anna and Kristoff leave Marshmallow behind by following this sequence of 6 winter icons. You can move only vertically and horizontally. Watch out: Avoid misleading paths.

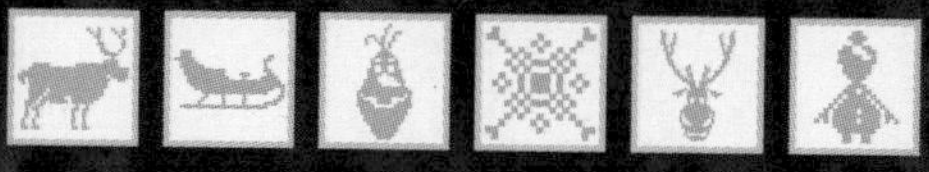

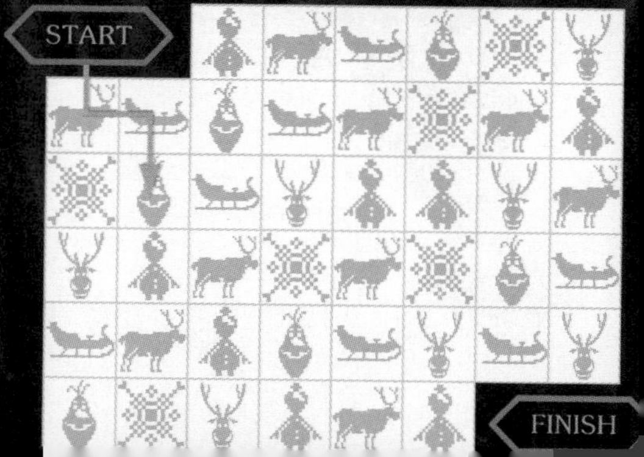
START
FINISH

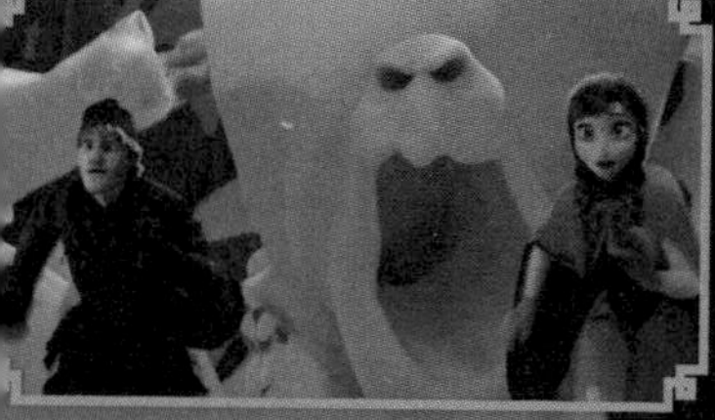

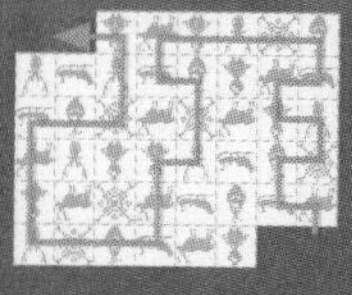

Solution:

Ice Harvesters

Ice harvesters are strong and hearty men, which are used to accompany their hard work with ancient songs. Kristoff, one of them, has cut a nice shape made of the ice blocks in the box below. Color them in the load at the bottom and find out Kristoff's ice sculpture.

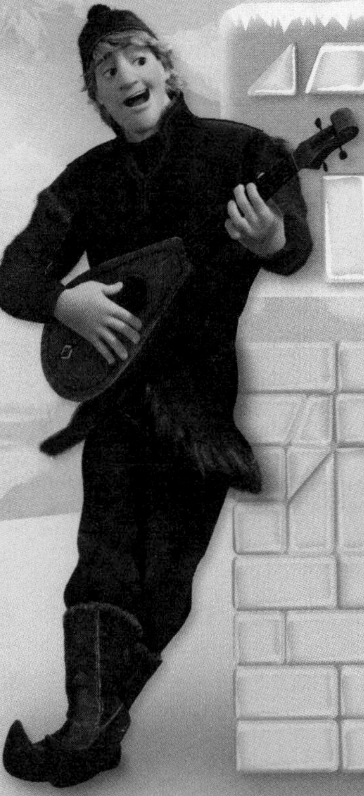

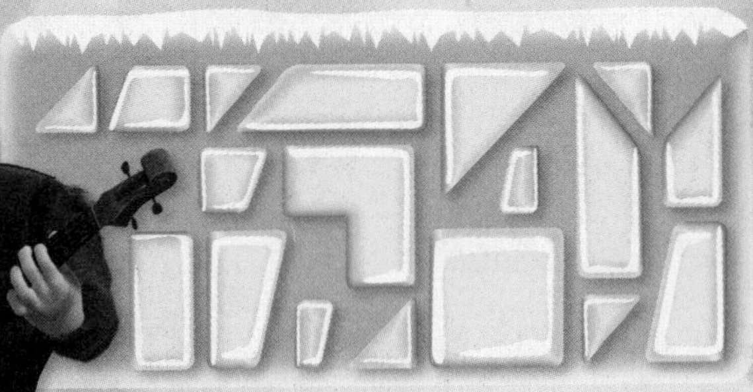

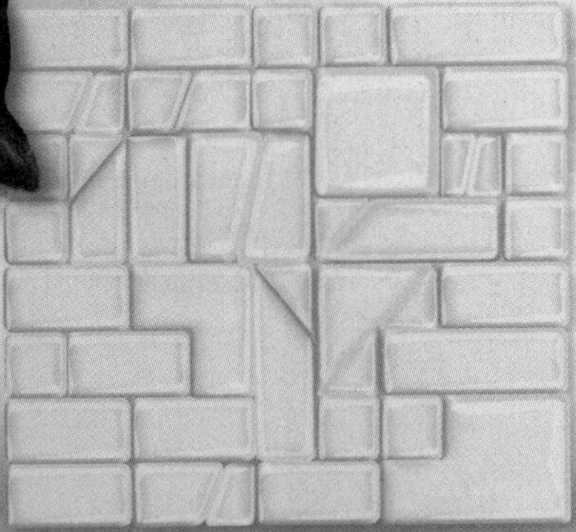

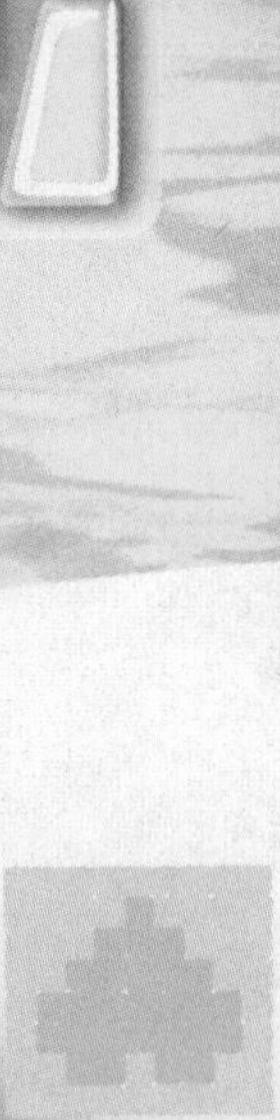

Answer: An heart.

Each of the three sleighs at the bottom of this page is ready to bring its load to Arendelle. Which of them is on the right track?

....

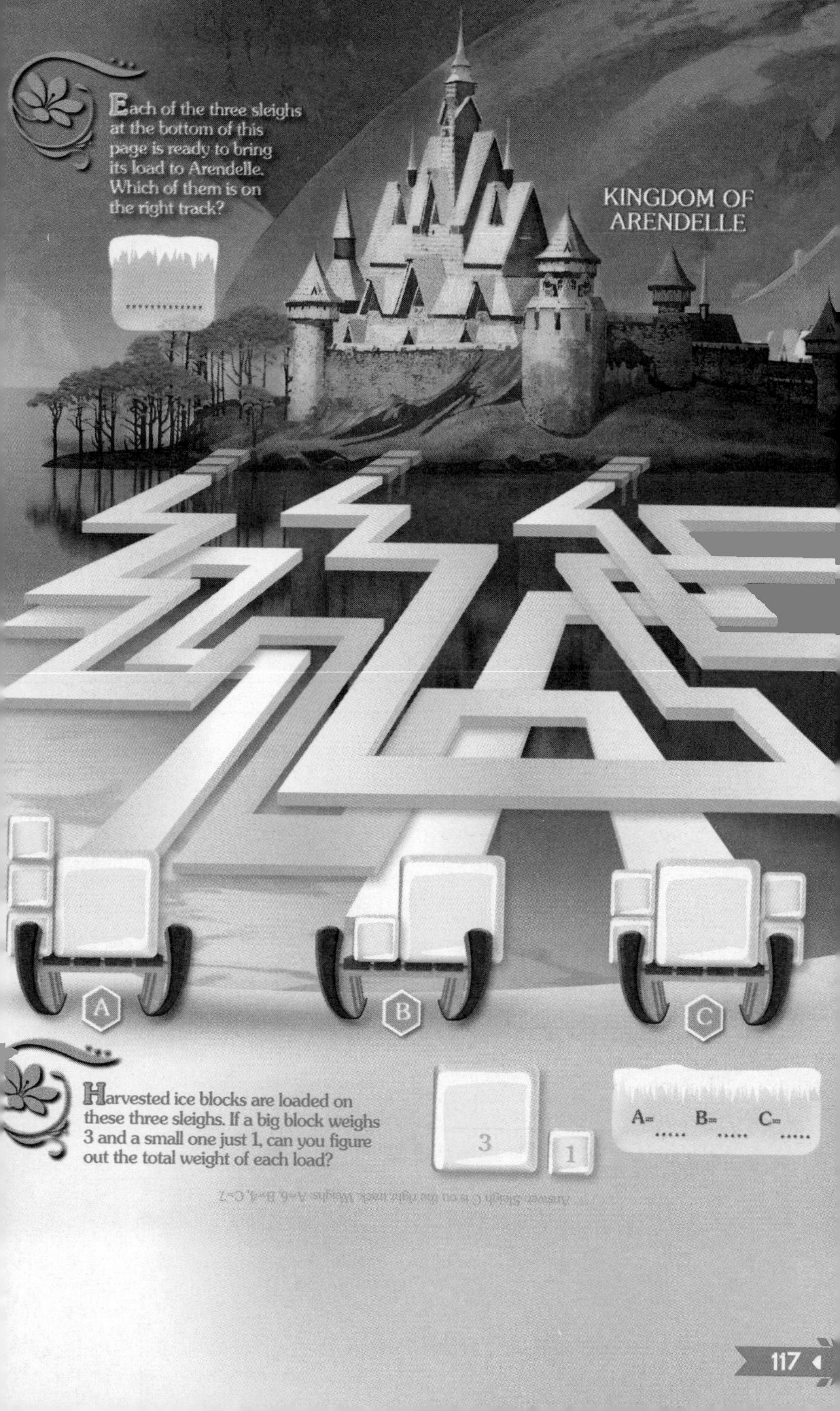

KINGDOM OF ARENDELLE
A
B
C

Harvested ice blocks are loaded on these three sleighs. If a big block weighs 3 and a small one just 1, can you figure out the total weight of each load?

3

1

A= ..... B= ..... C= .....

Answer: Sleigh C is on the right track. Weighs: A=6, B=4, C=7

Elsa's Amazing Power

When ice spirals shooting from Elsa's hands hit something, it freezes up and becomes covered by frost. Can you guess which parts of the scene below got frozen by Elsa's magic?

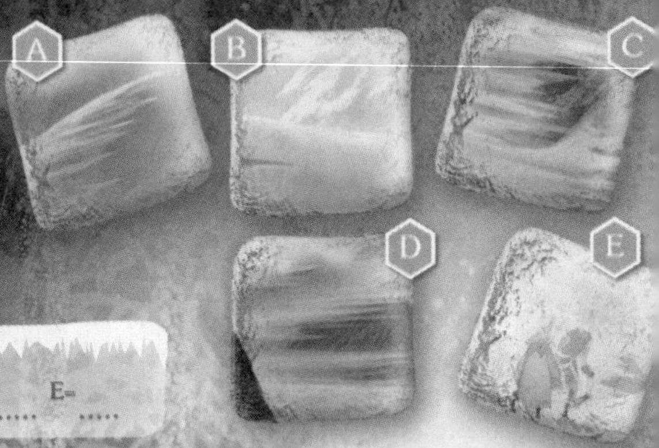

A
B
C
D
E

A= 1 B= B C= ...... D= ...... E= ......

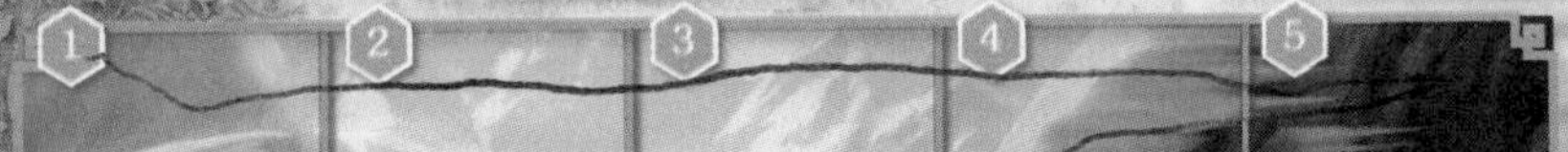

1
2
3
4
5
6
7
8
9
10
11
12
13
14
15

Answer: A-1, B-3, C-10, D-12, E-14.

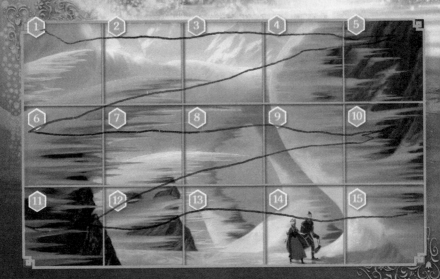

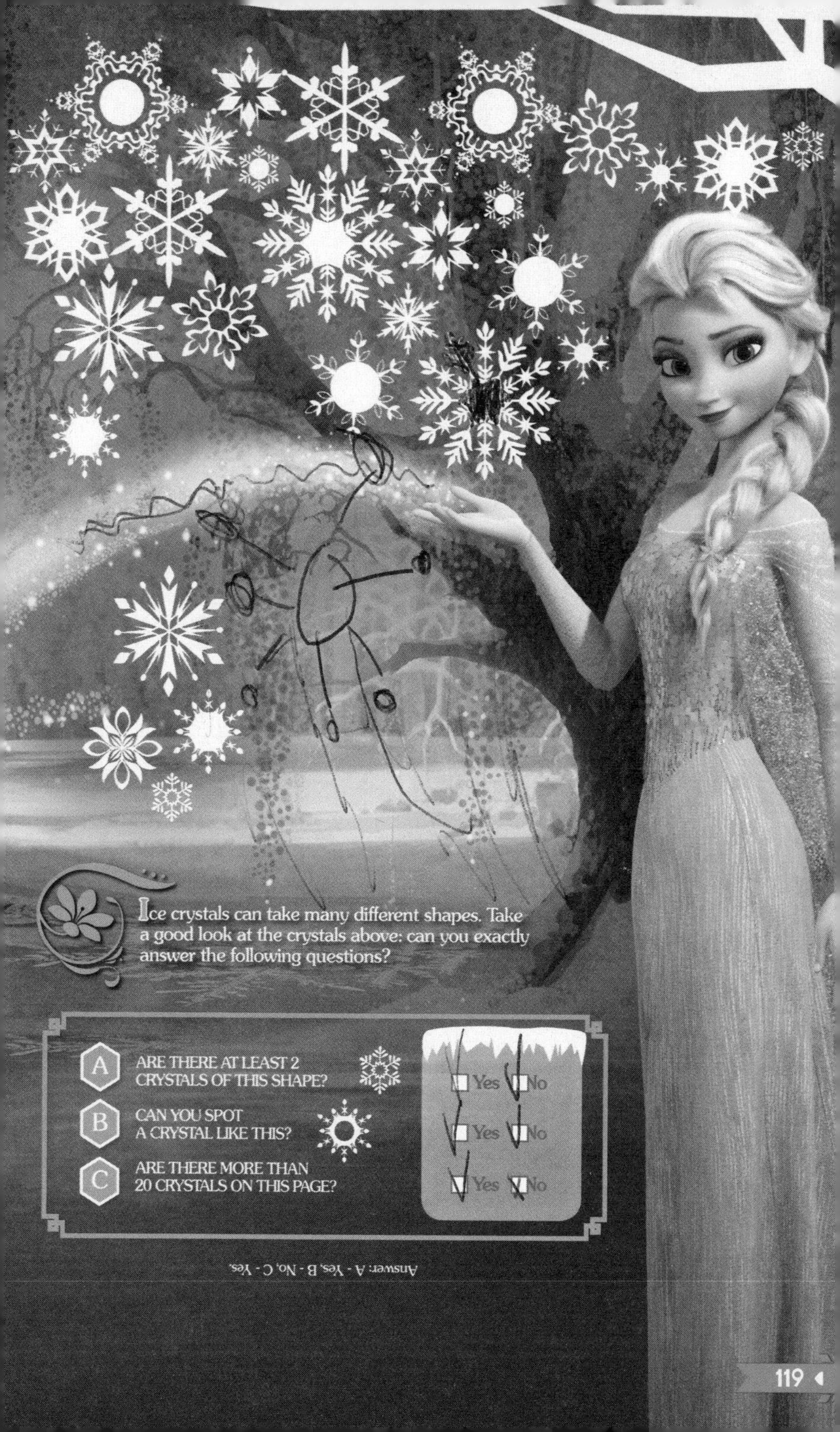

Ice crystals can take many different shapes. Take a good look at the crystals above: can you exactly answer the following questions?

A	ARE THERE AT LEAST 2 CRYSTALS OF THIS SHAPE?	☐ Yes ☐ No
B	CAN YOU SPOT A CRYSTAL LIKE THIS?	☐ Yes ☐ No
C	ARE THERE MORE THAN 20 CRYSTALS ON THIS PAGE?	☐ Yes ☐ No

Answer: A - Yes, B - No, C - Yes.

Let's Build a Snowman!

Olaf is a magic snowman whose body parts can come off and come back together. Can you guess which of Olaf's parts below don't belong to this picture of him?

....

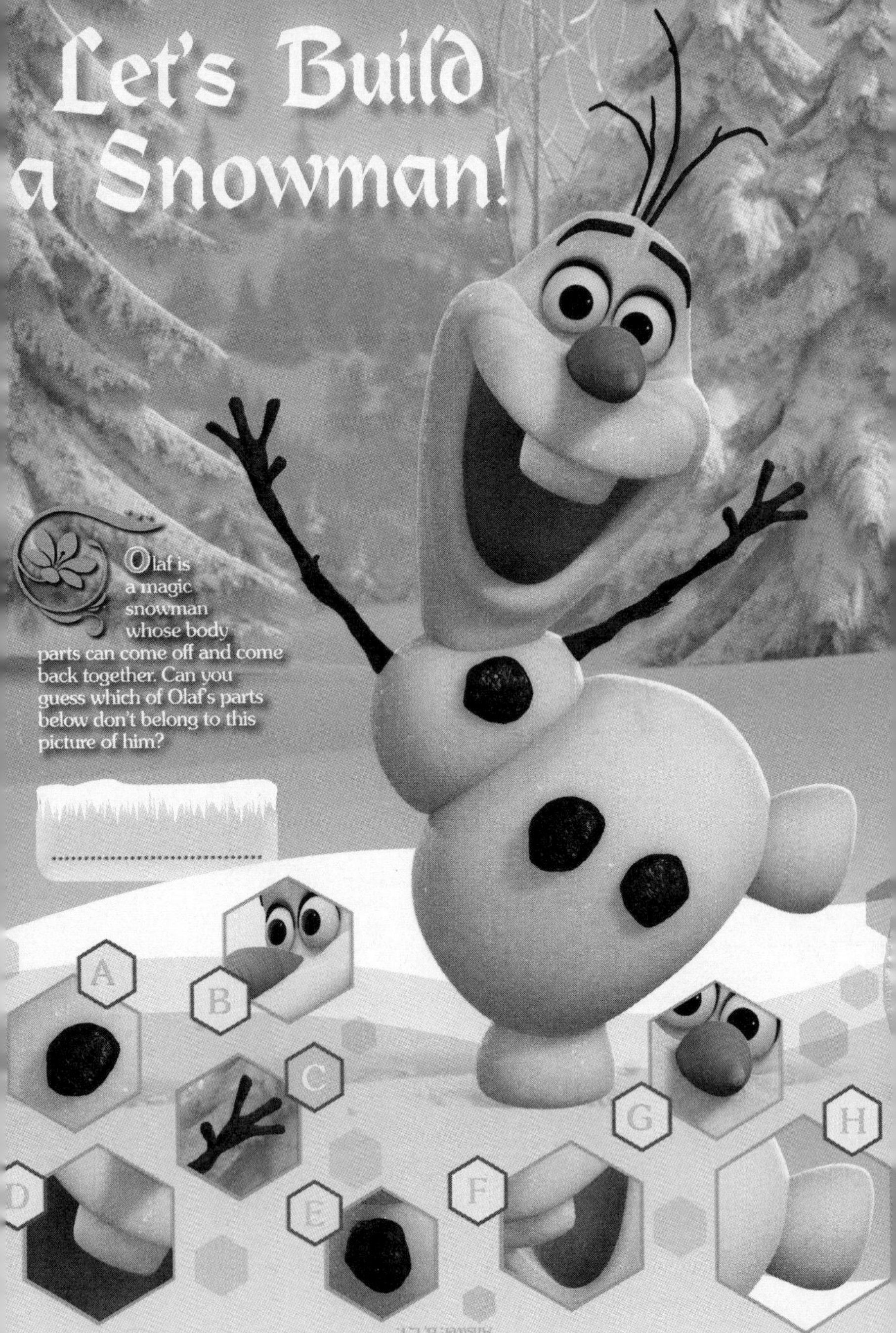
A
B
C
D
E
F
G
H

Answer: B, E, F

If you want to build a snowman, play this game! You just need to fill all empty squares so that all the elements (head, body, arm, scarf) appear exactly once in each row, column and box.

Oops! It's happened again. Olaf's body parts are lying around! Can you find the 5 differences among these two white silhouettes?

A B

Differences in silhouette B: Missing branch on the head, missing finger in hand on the right, missing hole in upper part of the body, mirrored arm on the right, left foot moved on the left.

Sudoku's solution:

Elsa Flees...

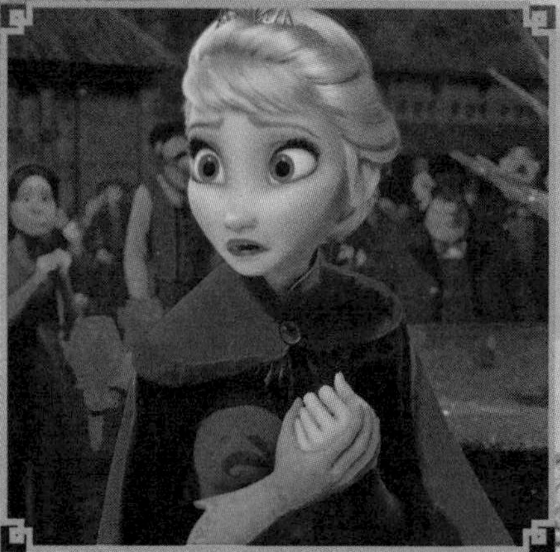

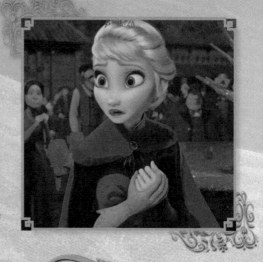

After Anna pulls off Elsa's glove, magic shoots out from the queen's bare hand. Everything she touches turns to ice! Can you spot Elsa's missing glove hidden on this page?

The citizens of Arendelle are startled by Elsa's powers. She can't control herself and, afraid of hurting innocent people, she runs away, toward the fjord. But as Elsa steps into the water it starts freezing under her feet. She runs across the ice until she reaches the mountain on the other side. Help Elsa escape by choosing the right path made of iced tiles like the one at the start.

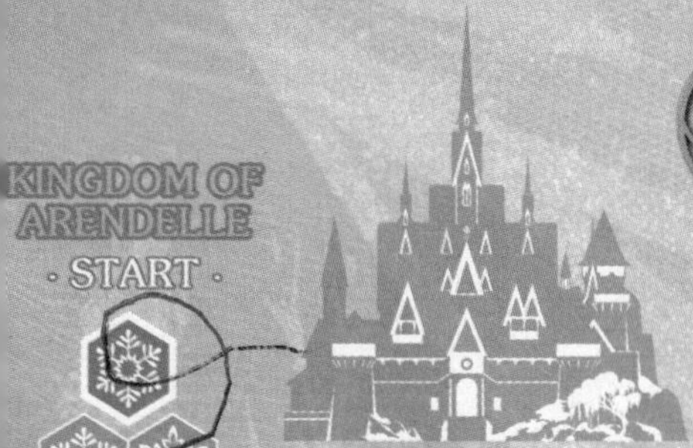
KINGDOM OF
ARENDELLE
· START ·

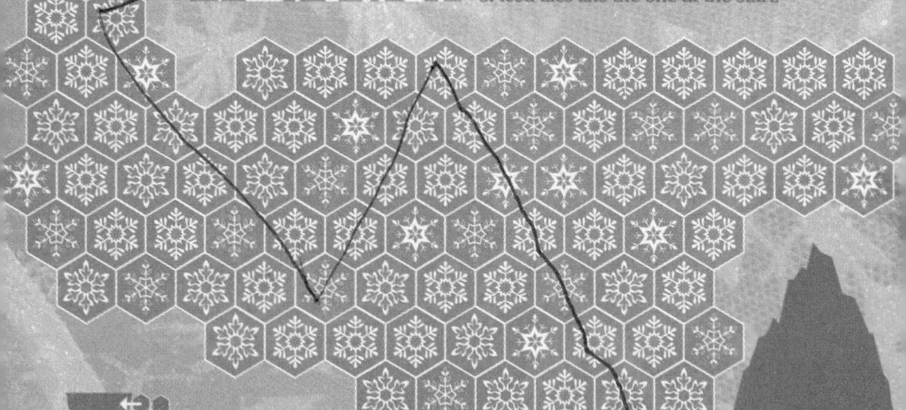
THE NORTH
MOUNTAIN
· FINISH ·

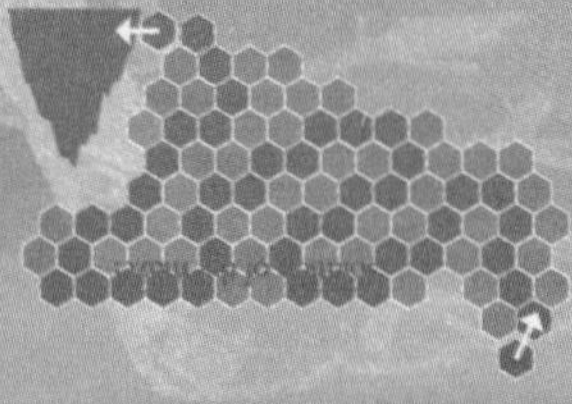

Answer: The glove is next to the top of the mountain.

...Anna Pursues!

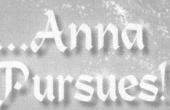

Anna wants to reach her sister, who's hidden somewhere in the mountains. Help the princess follow Elsa's path by putting each section of the path in the correct order.

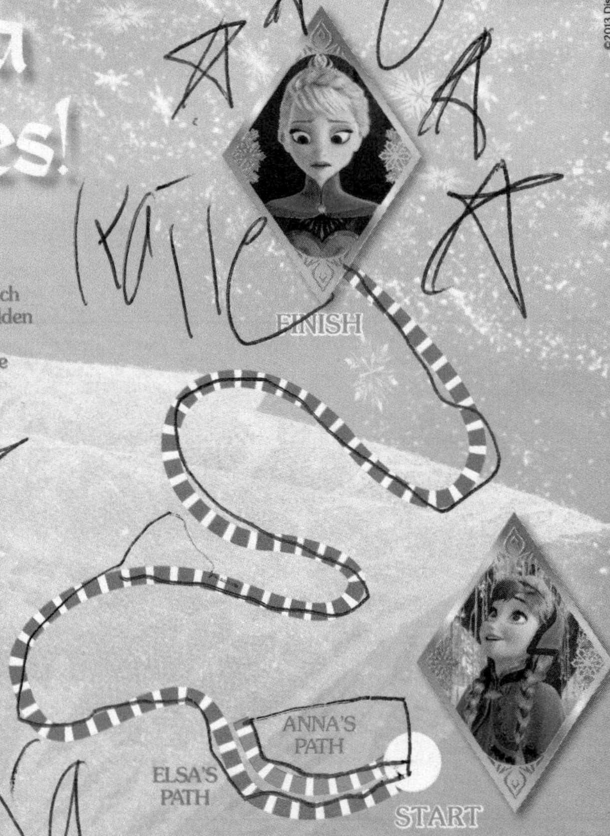
FINISH
ANNA'S PATH
ELSA'S PATH
START

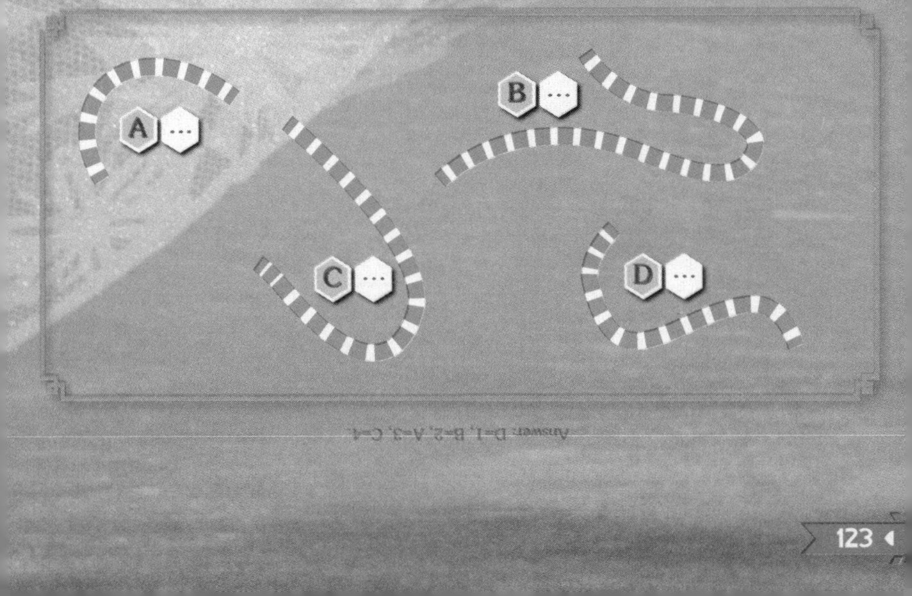
A ...
B ...
C ...
D ...

Answer: D=1, B=2, A=3, C=4

True Friends

Kristoff knows he can rely on his reindeer, Sven, no matter what happens. Place the eight tiles below into the frame to complete the two paths of tracks that lead the loyal friends to each other.

1

2

3

4

5

6

7

8

		A	B
C		D	E
F		G	
	H		

Sven adores carrots! He could eat tons of them, or at least as many as he can find. Just one carrot is forbidden: Olaf's nose! Help Sven collect carrots as he moves along the maze. Each time he meets the snowman, he must turn around and find another way!

Count the carrots as you help Sven along the correct path. How many carrots does he find?

START

FINISH

Solution of the maze:

On the right path Sven finds 24 carrots.

125

The Ice Palace

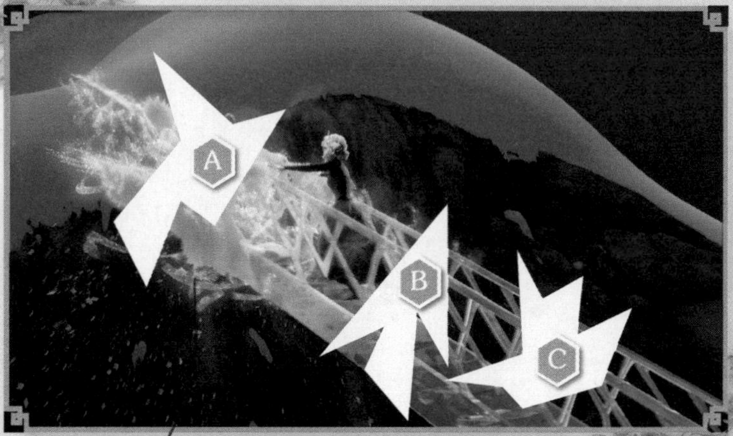
A
B
C

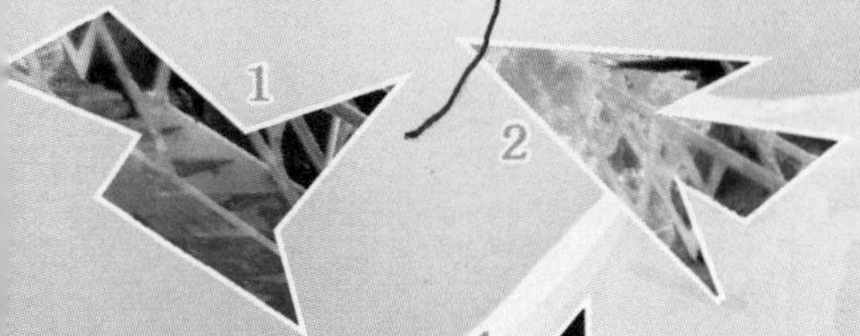
1
2

Trudging through the snow, Elsa reaches the top of the North Mountain. That's where, using her magic, she'll build a new ice palace. Help her create a staircase out of ice by finding the three missing parts that belong to it.

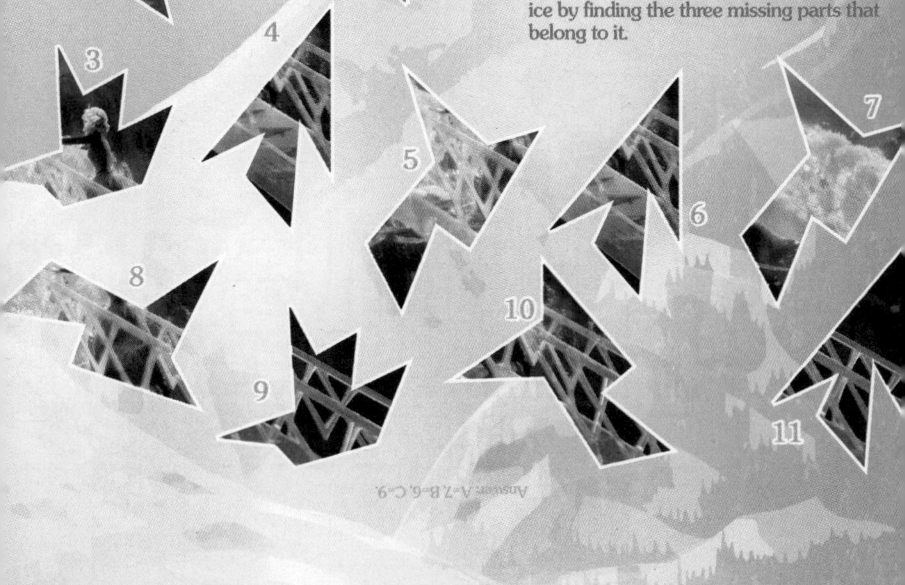
3
4
5
6
7
8
9
10
11

Answer: A=7, B=6, C=9.

Using her powers, Elsa builds an ice palace near the peak of the North Mountain. Which of the small images on the left matches Elsa's palace?

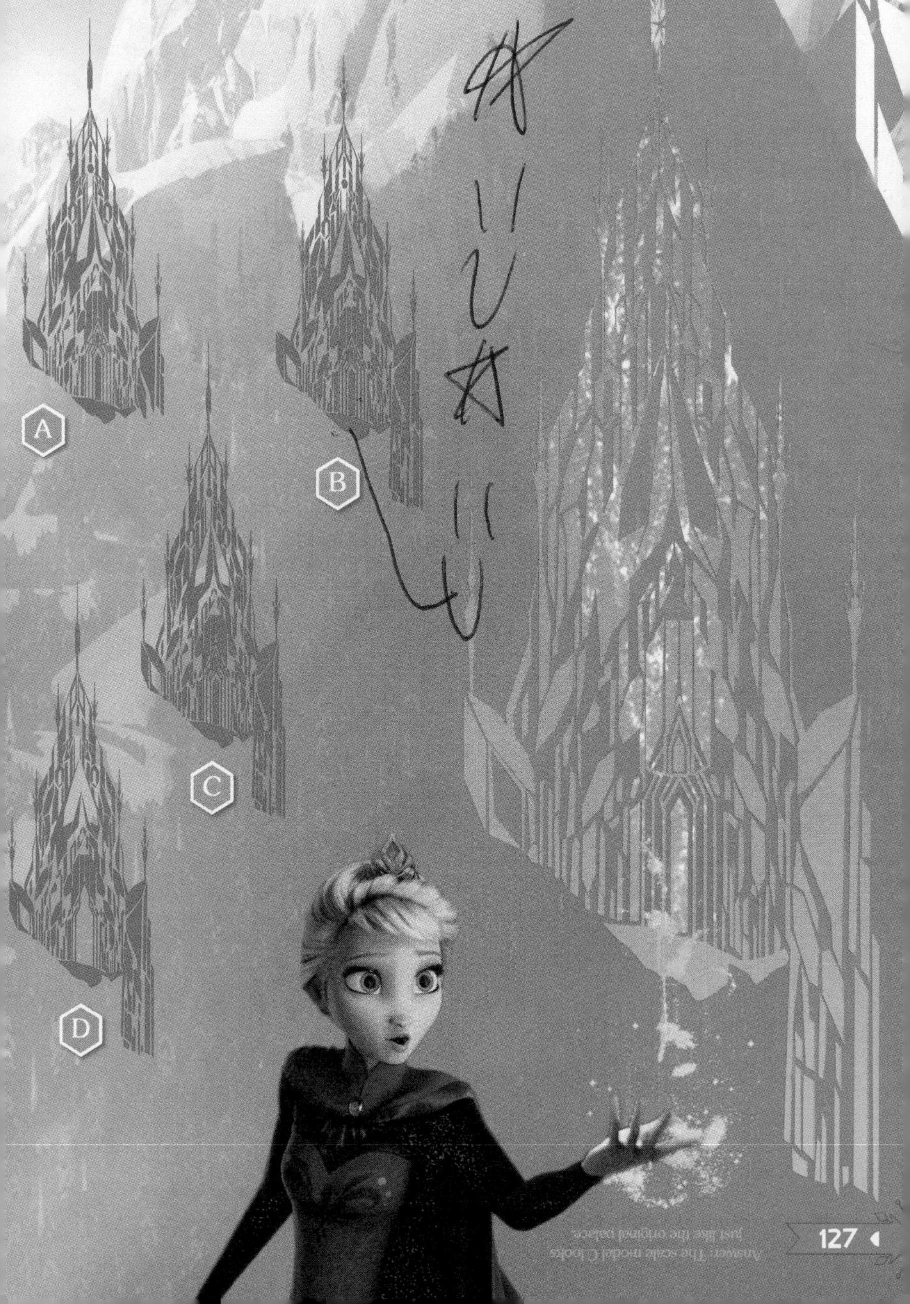
A
B
C
D

Answer: The scale model C looks just like the original palace.

Sisters' Match

Sisters can be quite different from each oth
but still feel a close bond. Do you think you
personality is closer to Anna
or Elsa? Answer the questions below
and find out!

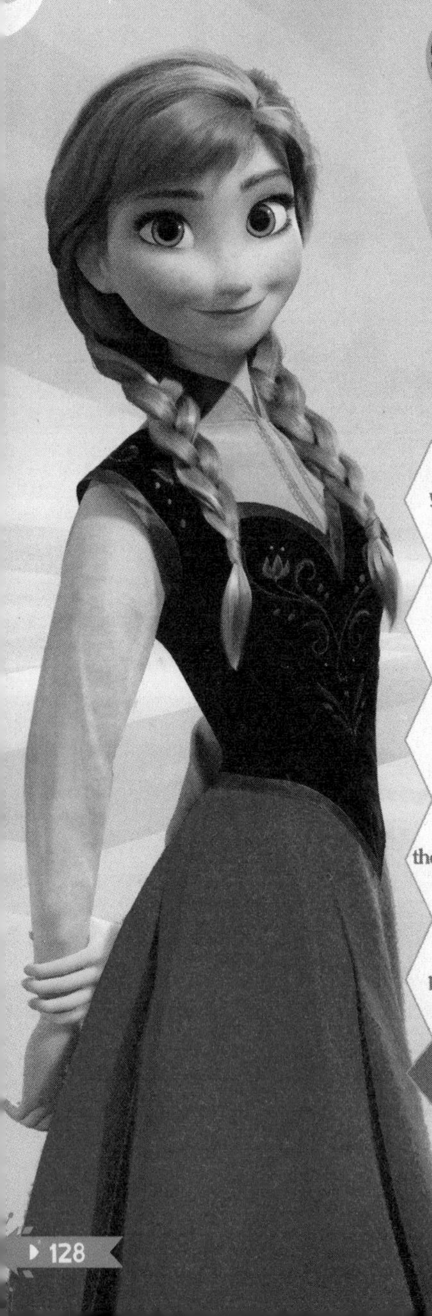

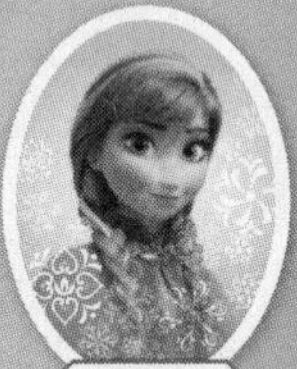

ANNA

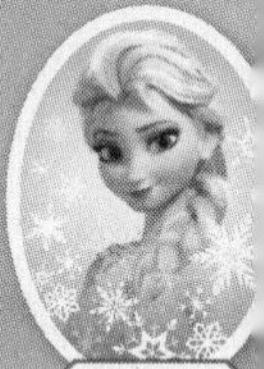

ELSA

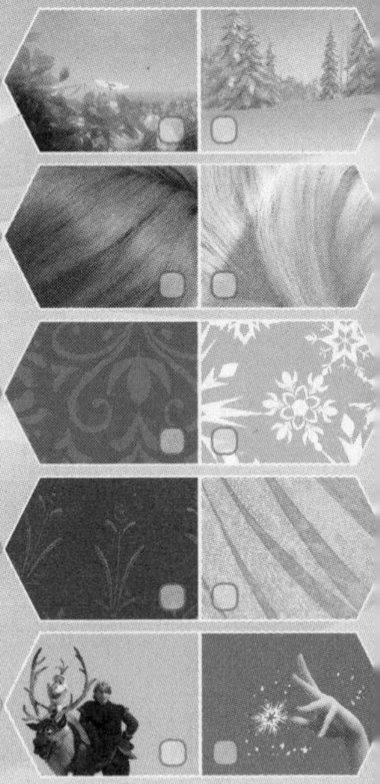

Which season do you prefer between spring and winter?

Which hair color do you like more, red or blonde?

Which of these patterns do you like?

Which of these fabrics would you choose?

What is more powerful, friendship or magic?

TOTAL ....

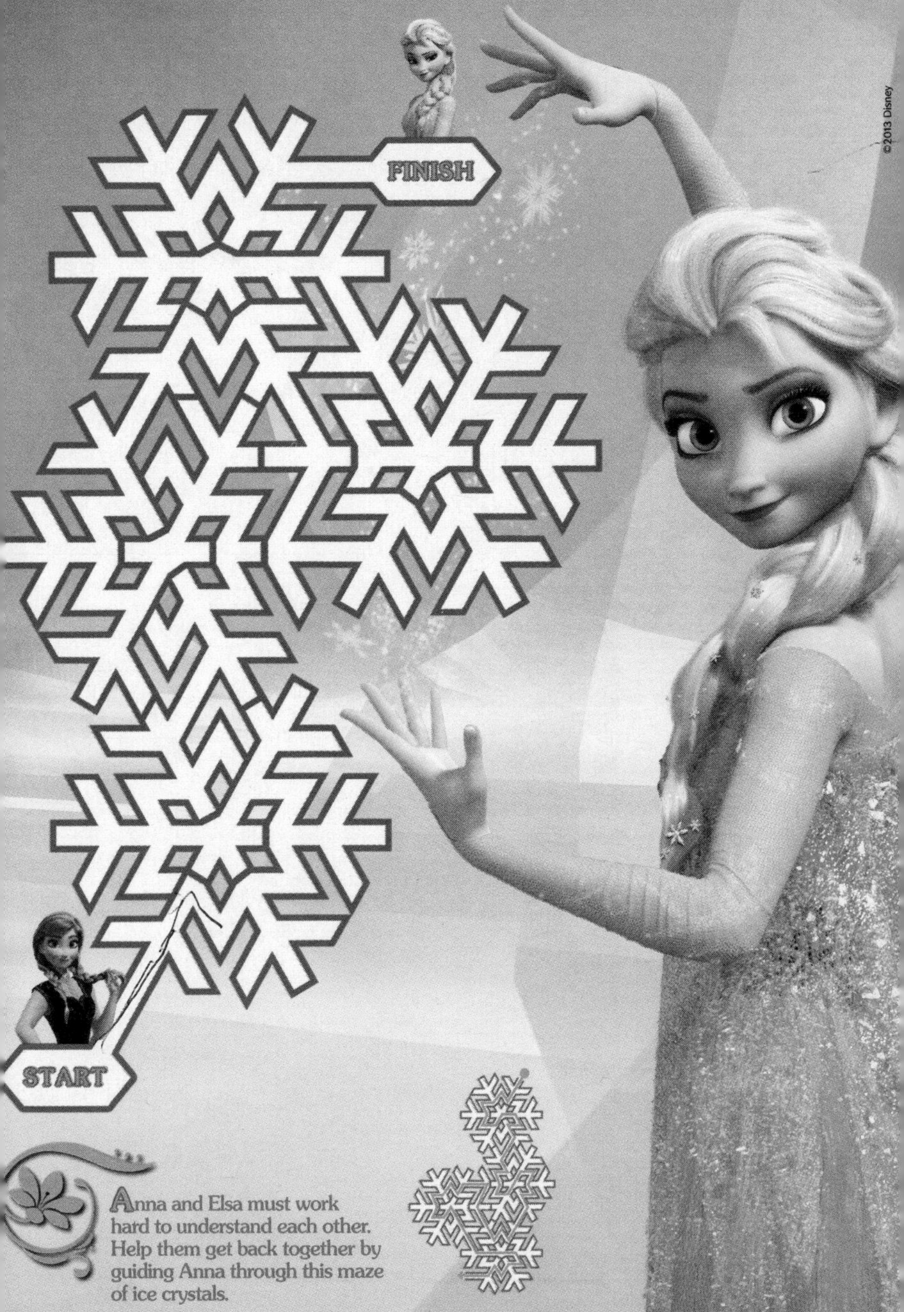
FINISH
START

Anna and Elsa must work hard to understand each other. Help them get back together by guiding Anna through this maze of ice crystals.

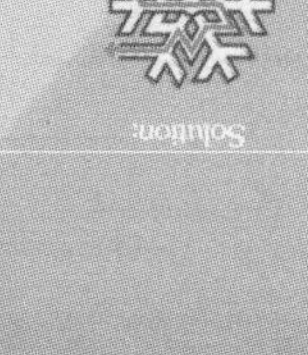

Solution:

Party Preps

Anna and Elsa are ready for a celebration at the palace. Look at the ice sculpture Elsa has created with her magic, and check off its correct shadow on the right. Then, use the picture code below to find out the name of the dessert Anna has just baked.

Flower Code

Use the visual key below and write the name of Anna's treat in the blanks.

A	C
E	H
K	L
O	T

Glacial Shadows

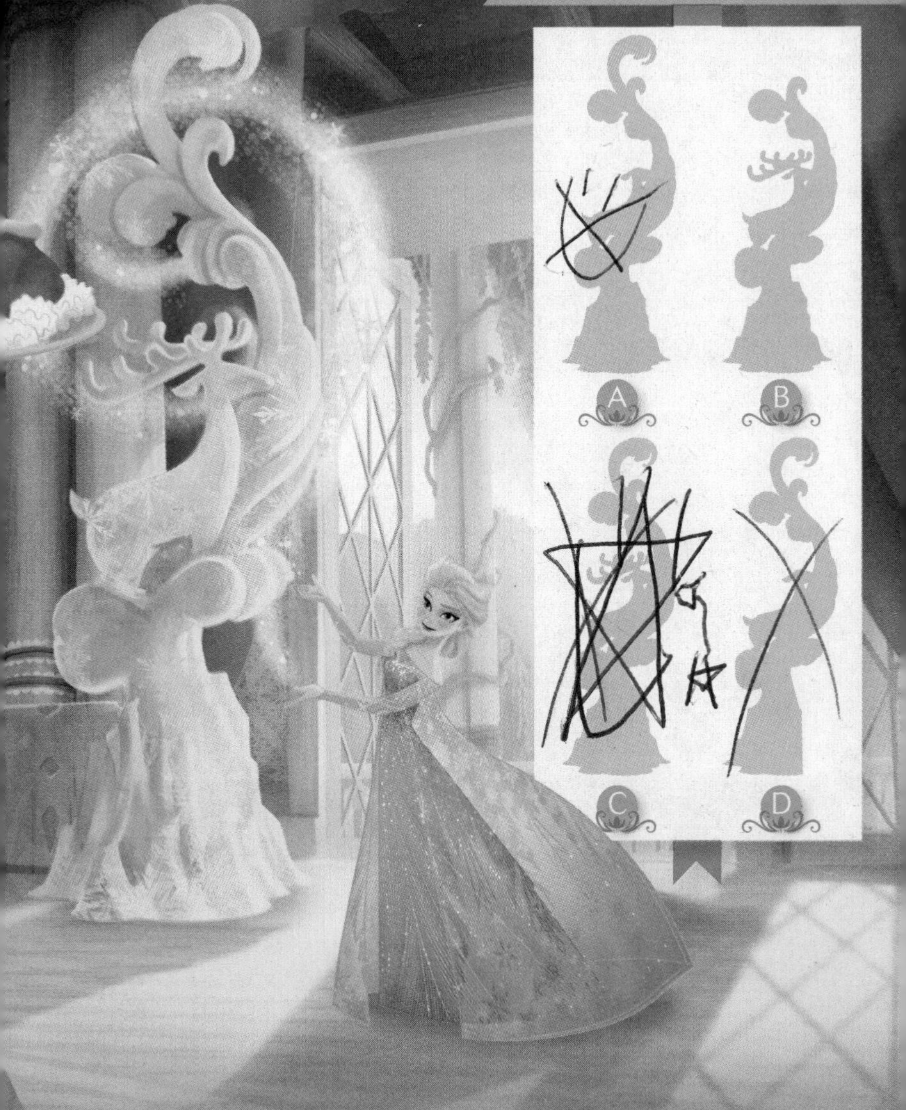
A
B
C
D

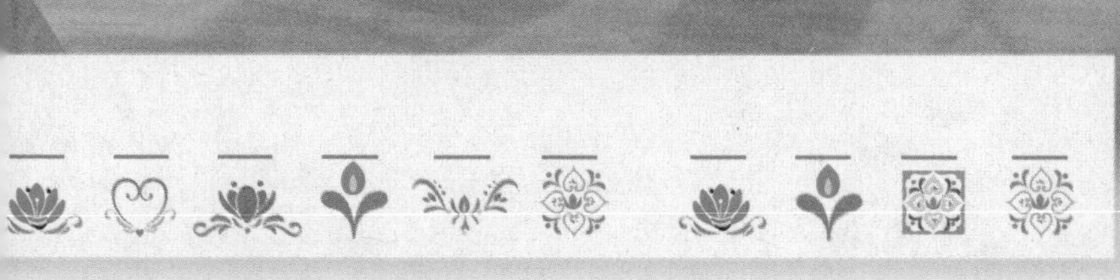

Noble Portraits

Anna and Elsa have posed in front of the court painter, but there's something missing. Look at their portraits: Each pair has 6 different details. Can you spot them all?

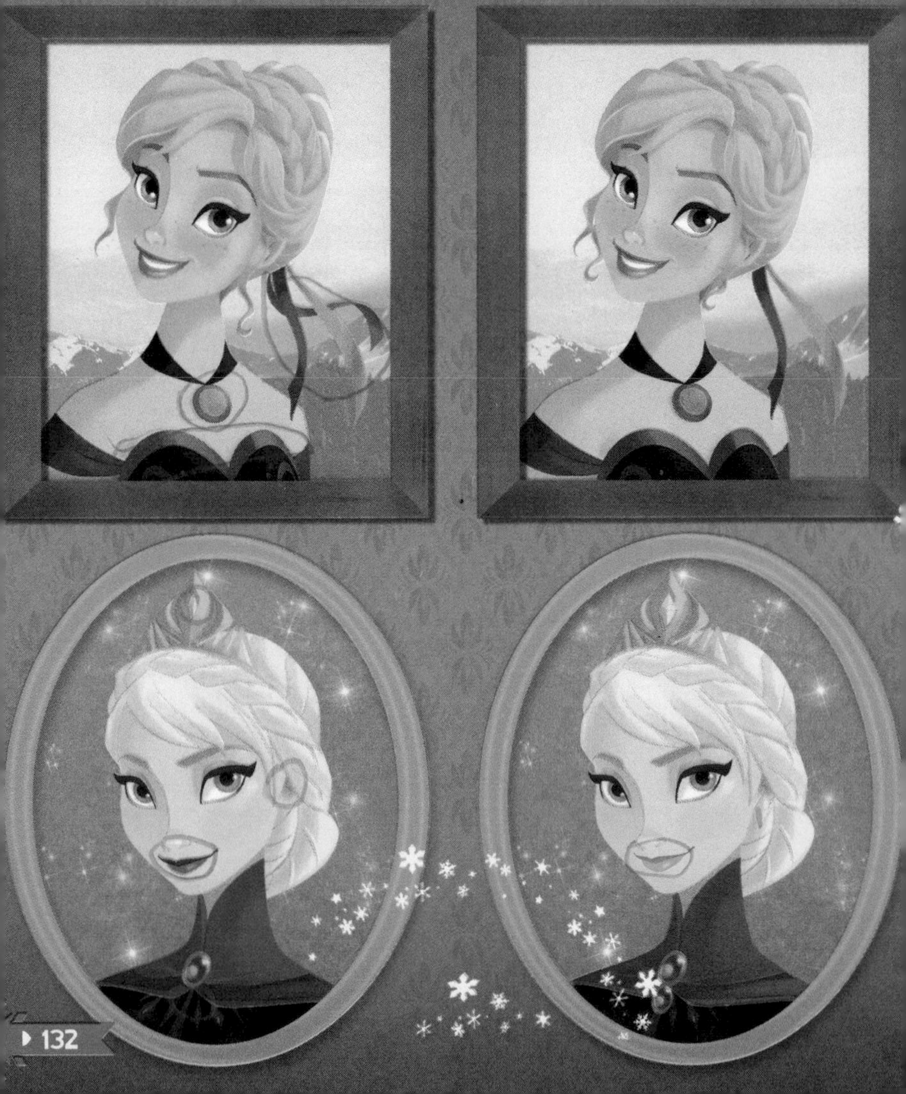

To a Secret Place

Olaf and his friends need to reach the trolls' realm to enjoy Grand Pabbie's annual contest. Guide them down the right path!

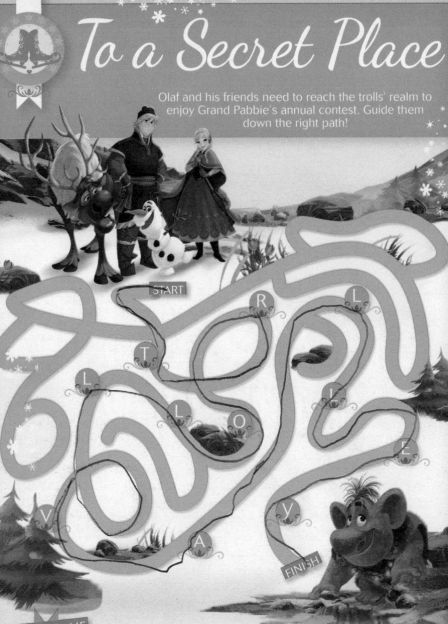

START

FINISH

HIDDEN NAME

Write **the letters you encounter on the blanks** to discover where our magic friends live.

T _ _ _ _ _

_ _ _ _ _ _

Scenes from the

DISNEP

FROZEN

Cinestory Comic

Cinestory Scene #1
"Kristoff's Boyhood Dream"

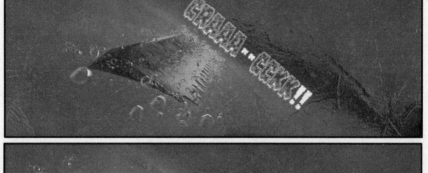

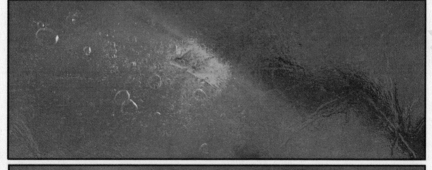

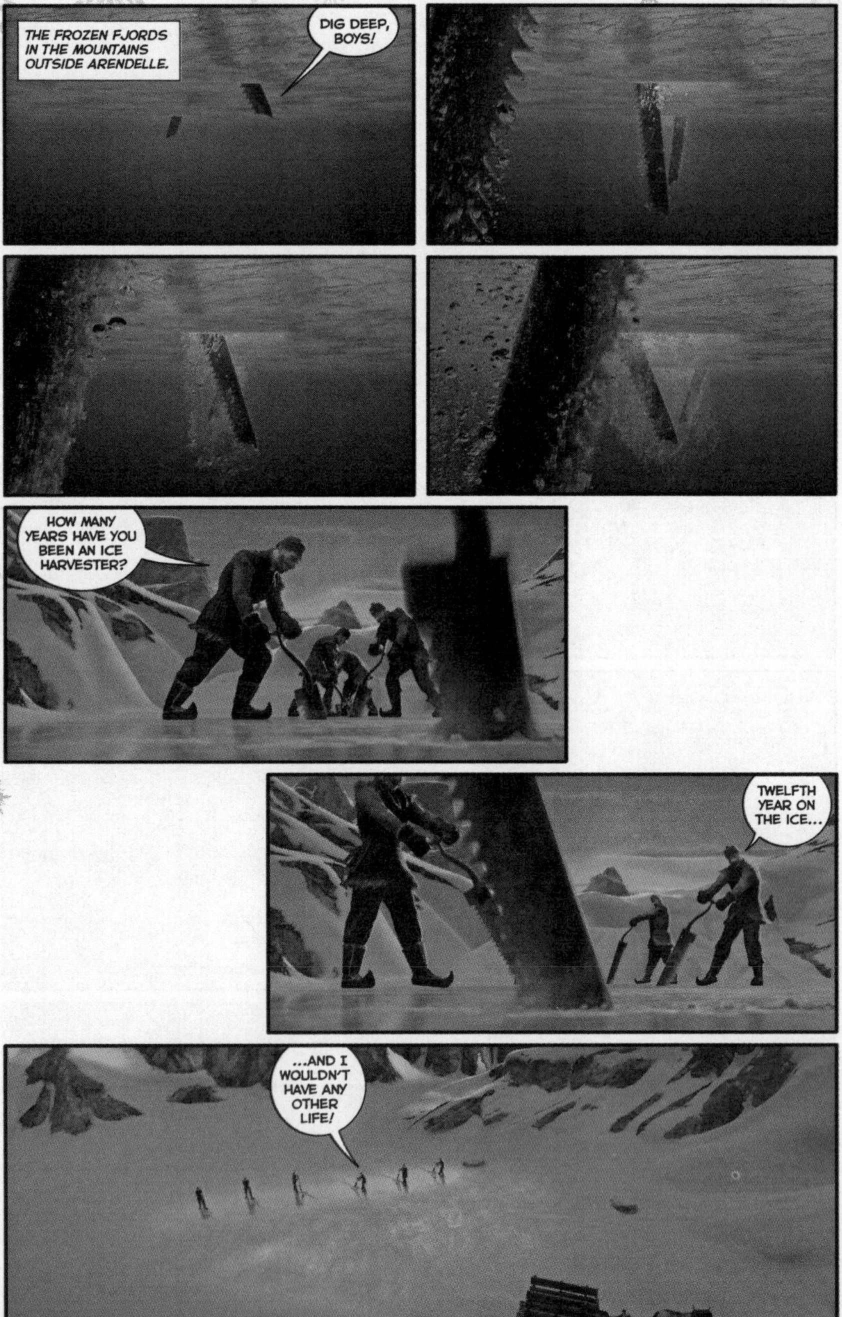
THE FROZEN FJORDS IN THE MOUNTAINS OUTSIDE ARENDELLE.
DIG DEEP, BOYS!
HOW MANY YEARS HAVE YOU BEEN AN ICE HARVESTER?
TWELFTH YEAR ON THE ICE...
...AND I WOULDN'T HAVE ANY OTHER LIFE!

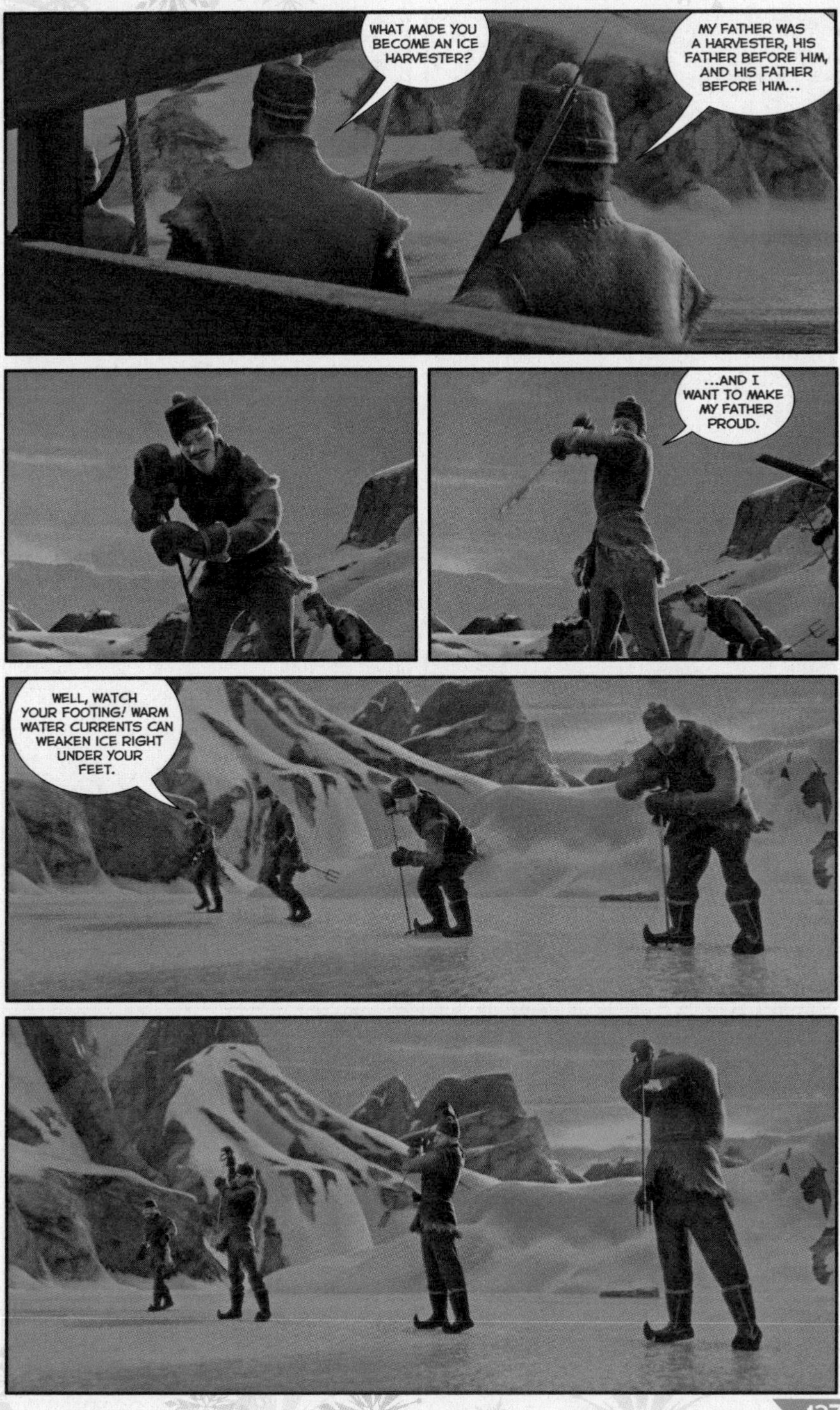
WHAT MADE YOU BECOME AN ICE HARVESTER?
MY FATHER WAS A HARVESTER, HIS FATHER BEFORE HIM, AND HIS FATHER BEFORE HIM...
...AND I WANT TO MAKE MY FATHER PROUD.
WELL, WATCH YOUR FOOTING! WARM WATER CURRENTS CAN WEAKEN ICE RIGHT UNDER YOUR FEET.

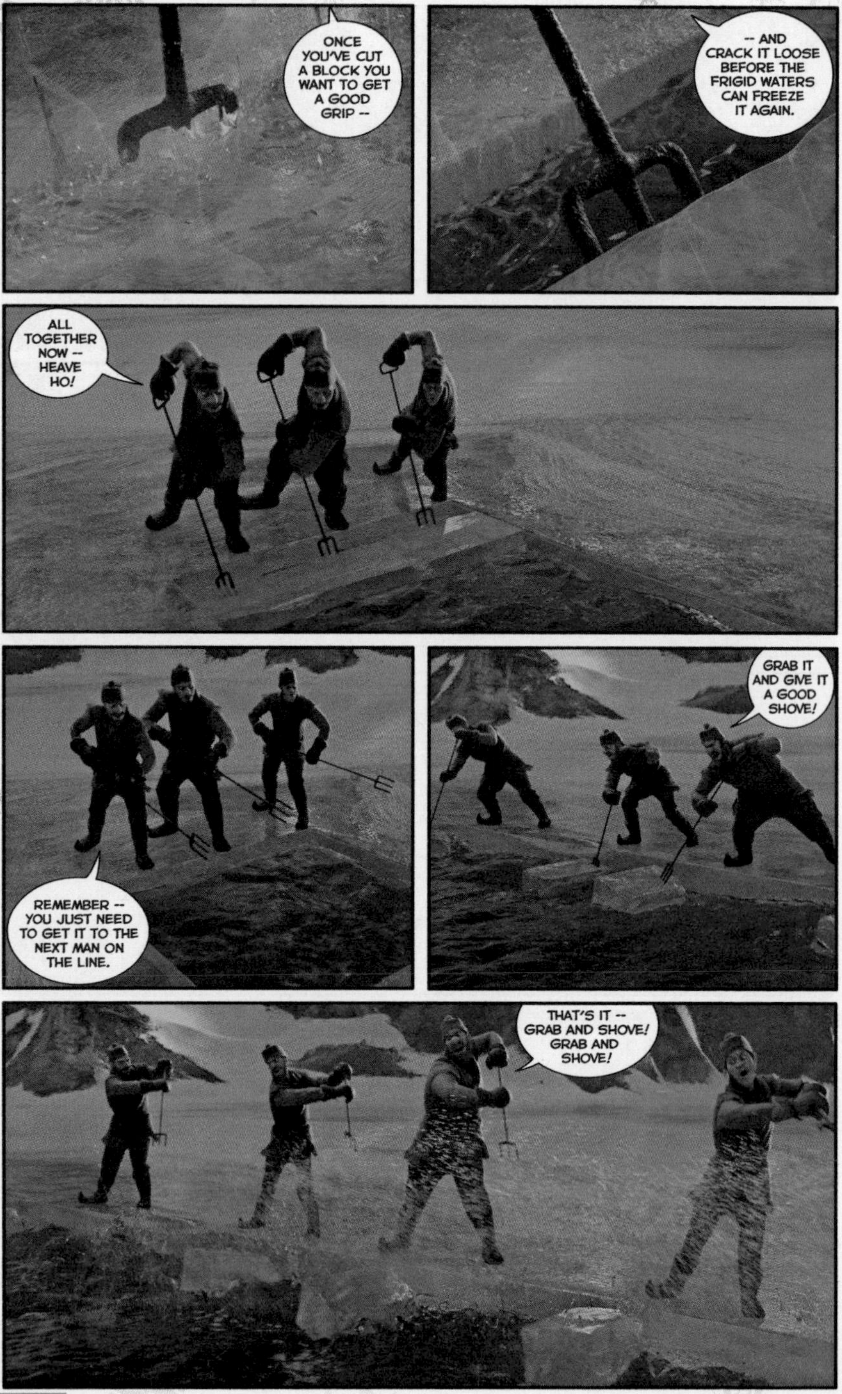
ONCE YOU'VE CUT A BLOCK YOU WANT TO GET A GOOD GRIP --
-- AND CRACK IT LOOSE BEFORE THE FRIGID WATERS CAN FREEZE IT AGAIN.
ALL TOGETHER NOW -- HEAVE HO!
REMEMBER -- YOU JUST NEED TO GET IT TO THE NEXT MAN ON THE LINE.
GRAB IT AND GIVE IT A GOOD SHOVE!
THAT'S IT -- GRAB AND SHOVE! GRAB AND SHOVE!

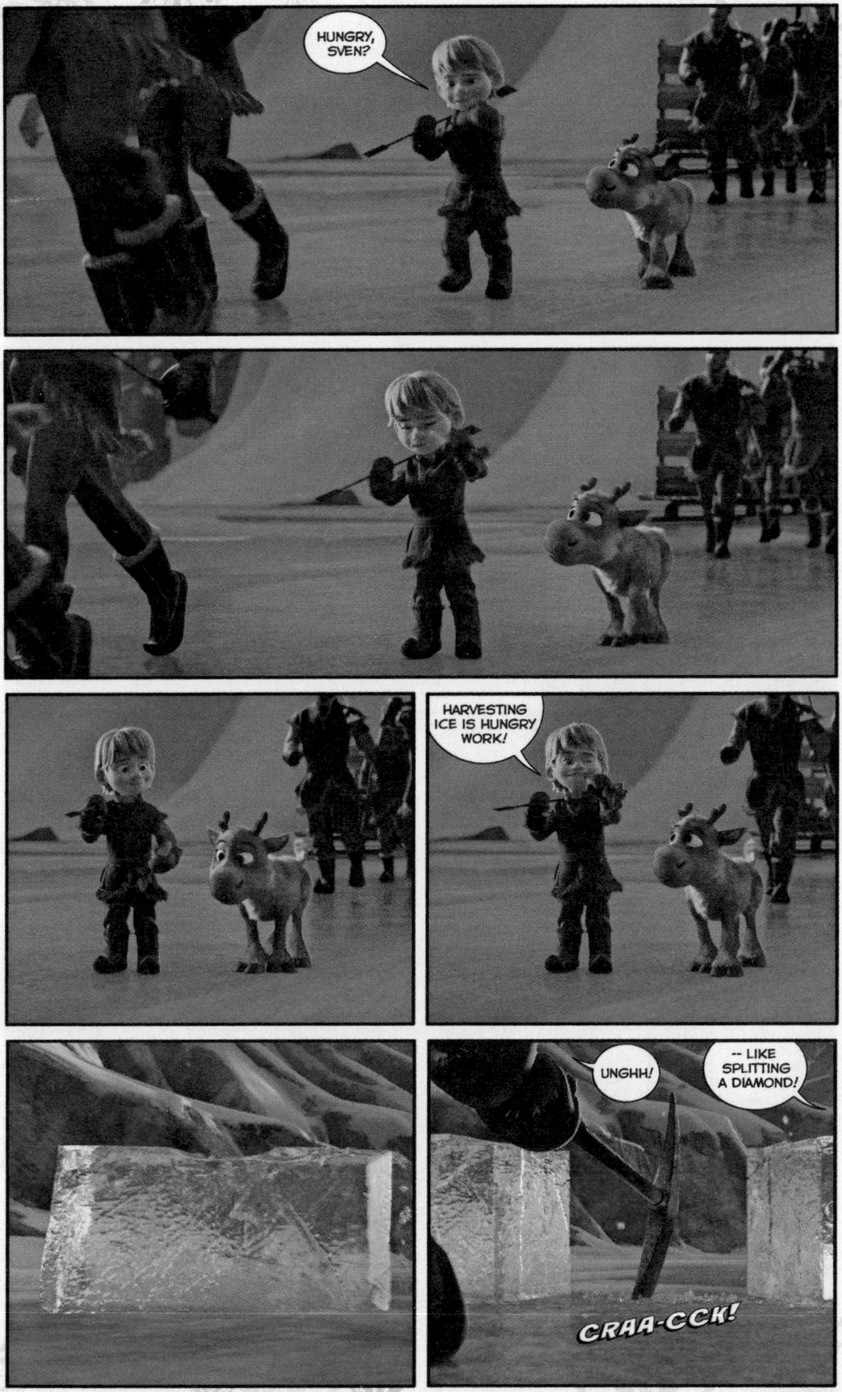
HUNGRY, SVEN?
HARVESTING ICE IS HUNGRY WORK!
UNGHH!
-- LIKE SPLITTING A DIAMOND!
CRAA-CCK!

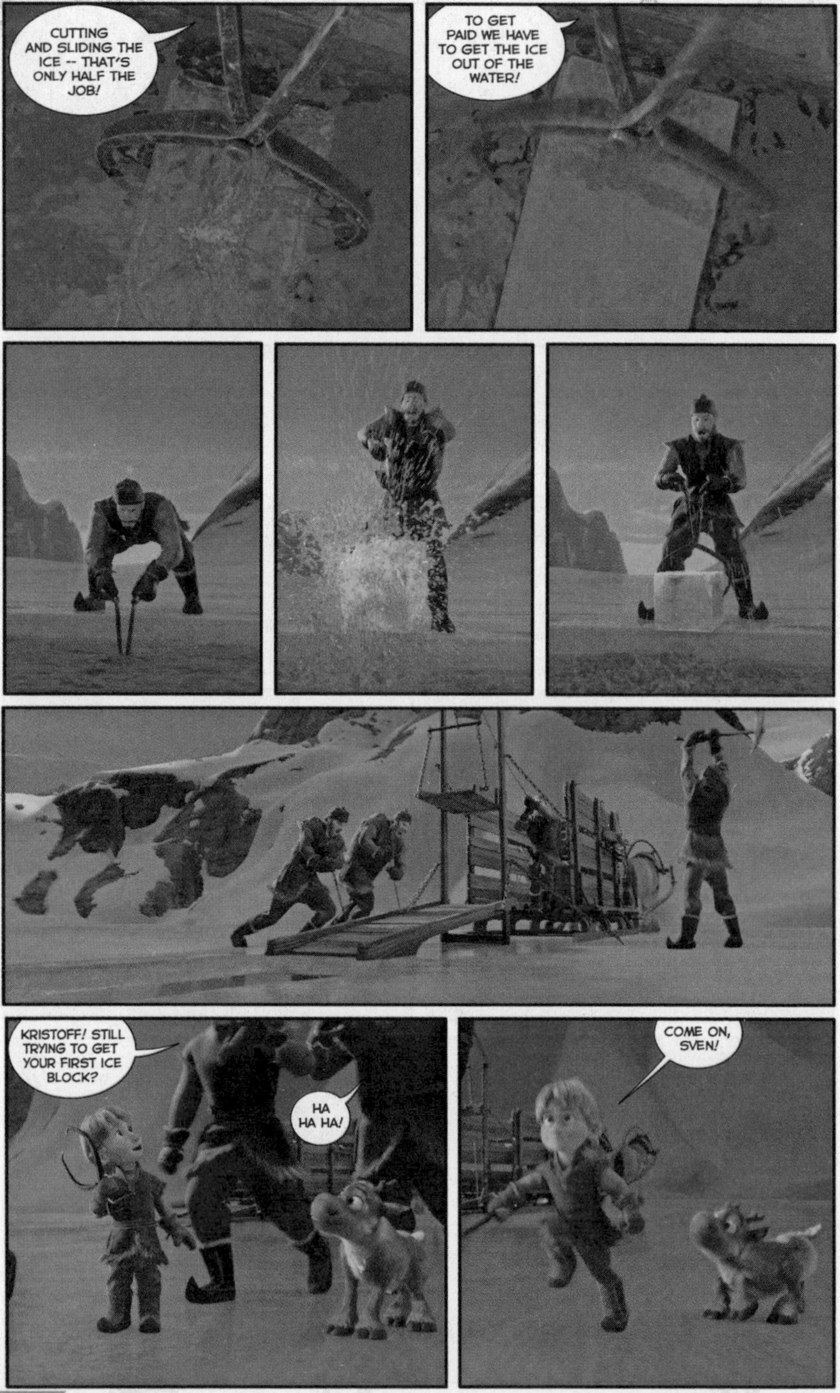
CUTTING AND SLIDING THE ICE -- THAT'S ONLY HALF THE JOB!
TO GET PAID WE HAVE TO GET THE ICE OUT OF THE WATER!
KRISTOFF! STILL TRYING TO GET YOUR FIRST ICE BLOCK?
HA HA HA!
COME ON, SVEN!

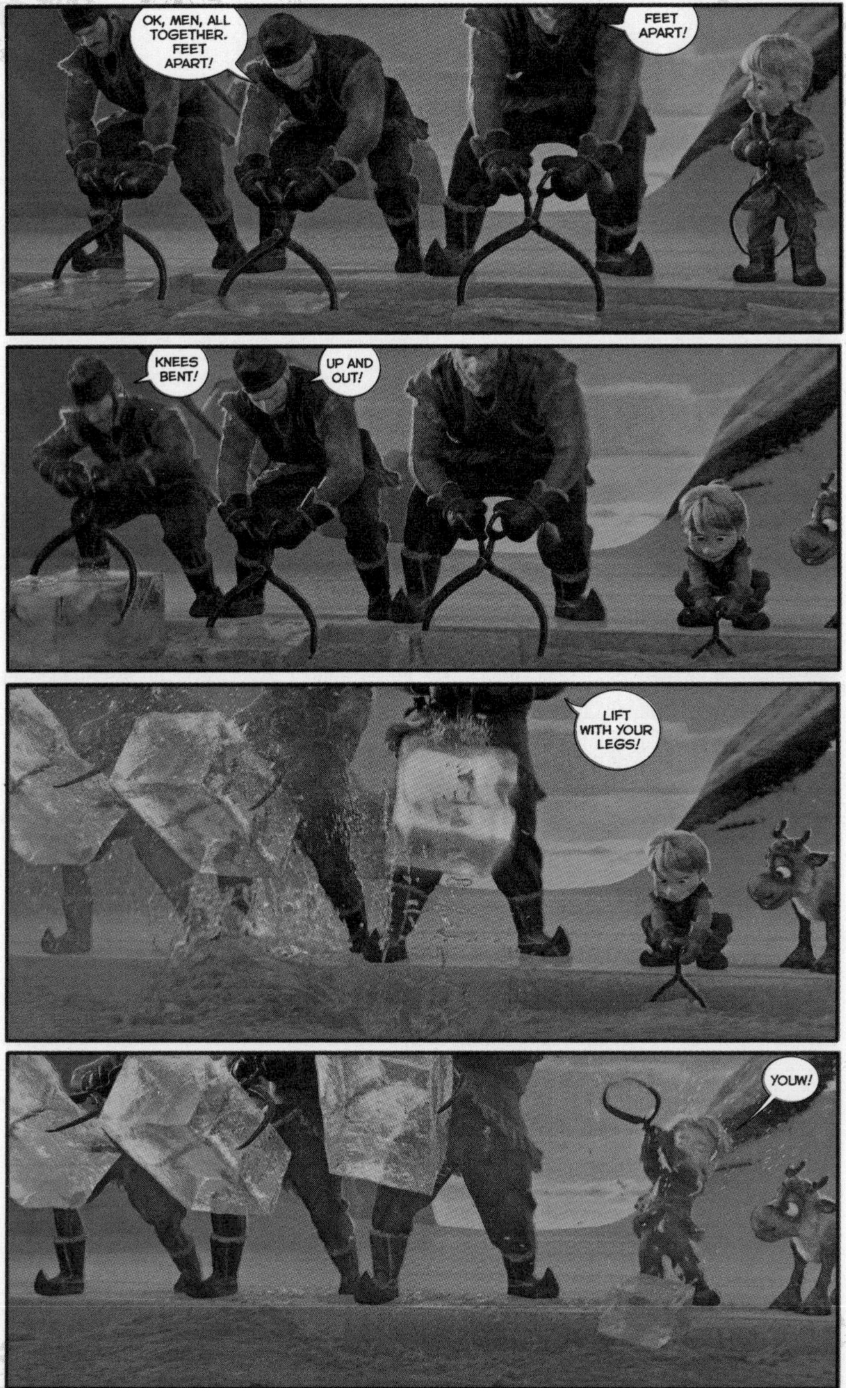

OK, MEN, ALL TOGETHER. FEET APART!
FEET APART!
KNEES BENT!
UP AND OUT!
LIFT WITH YOUR LEGS!
YOUW!

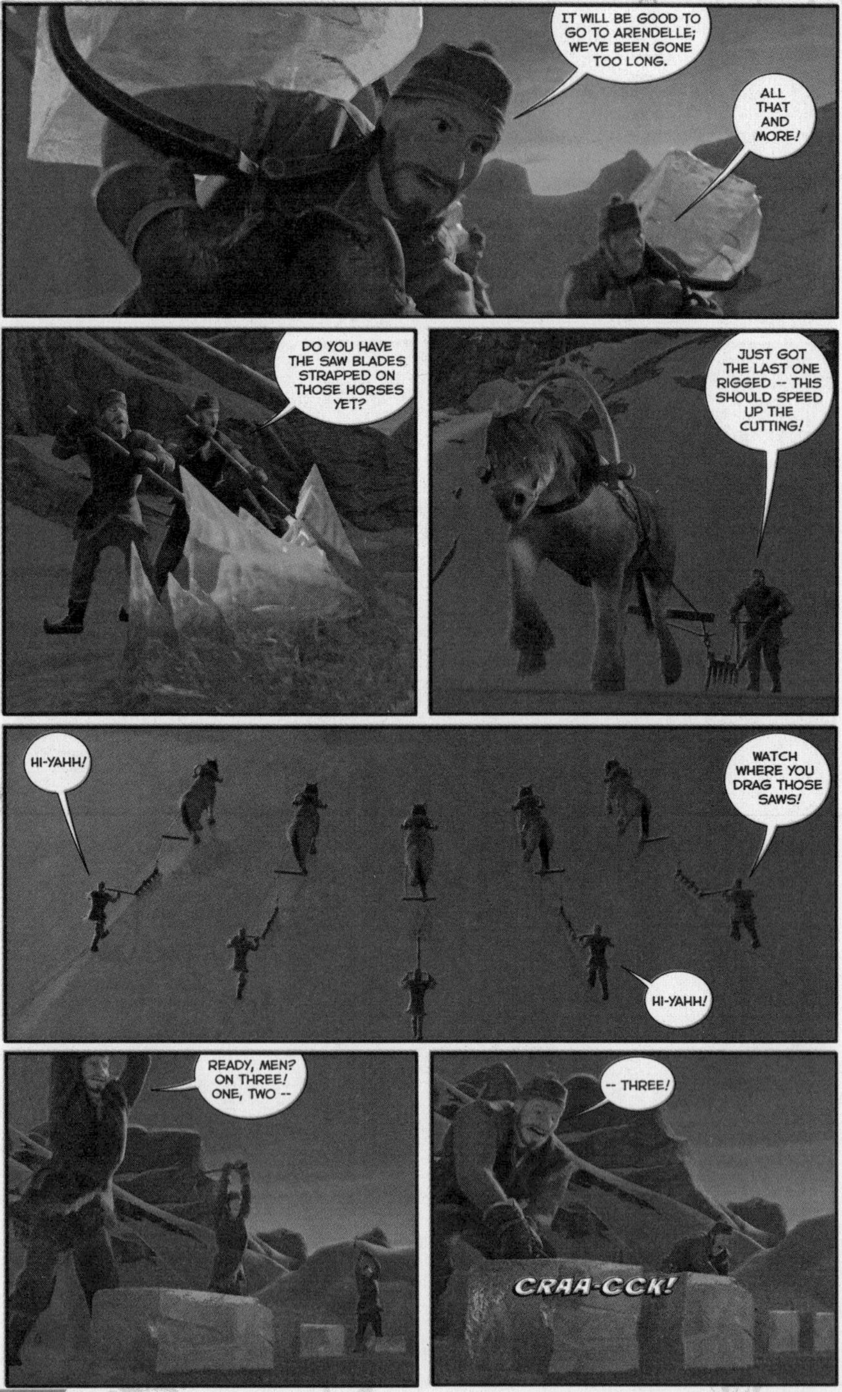
IT WILL BE GOOD TO GO TO ARENDELLE; WE'VE BEEN GONE TOO LONG.
ALL THAT AND MORE!
DO YOU HAVE THE SAW BLADES STRAPPED ON THOSE HORSES YET?
JUST GOT THE LAST ONE RIGGED -- THIS SHOULD SPEED UP THE CUTTING!
HI-YAHH!
WATCH WHERE YOU DRAG THOSE SAWS!
HI-YAHH!
READY, MEN? ON THREE! ONE, TWO --
-- THREE!
CRAA-CCK!

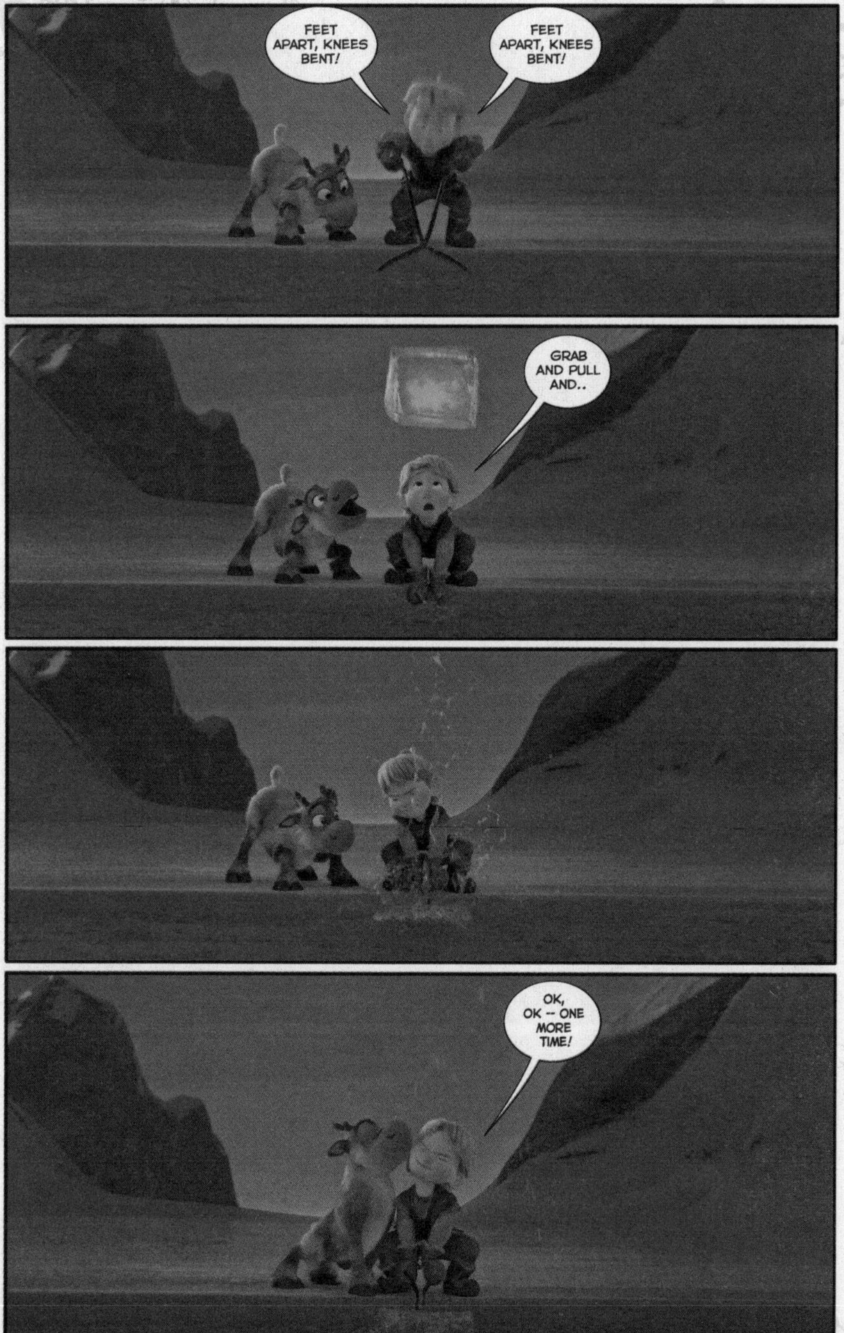
FEET APART, KNEES BENT!
FEET APART, KNEES BENT!
GRAB AND PULL AND..
OK, OK -- ONE MORE TIME!

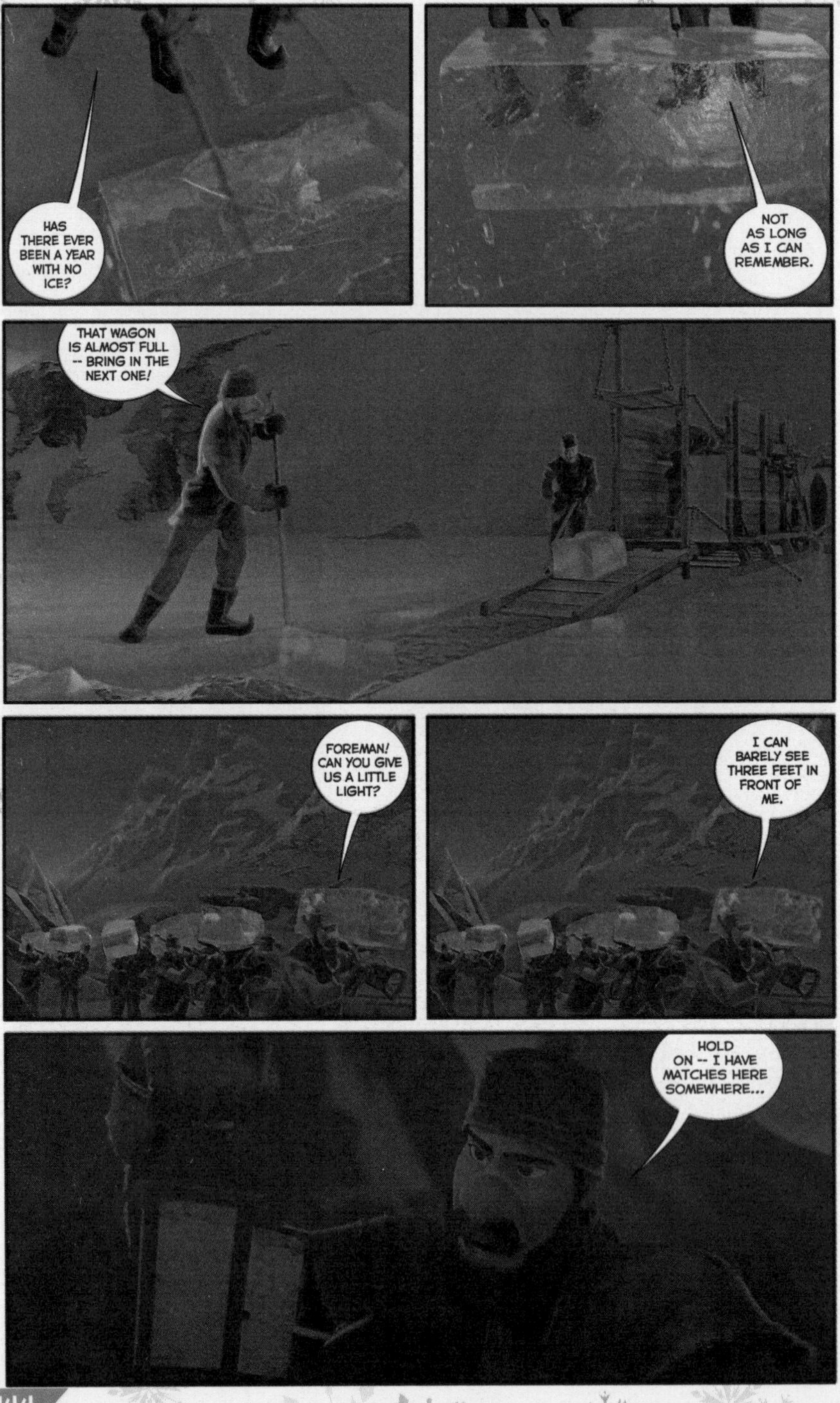
HAS THERE EVER BEEN A YEAR WITH NO ICE?
NOT AS LONG AS I CAN REMEMBER.
THAT WAGON IS ALMOST FULL -- BRING IN THE NEXT ONE!
FOREMAN! CAN YOU GIVE US A LITTLE LIGHT?
I CAN BARELY SEE THREE FEET IN FRONT OF ME.
HOLD ON -- I HAVE MATCHES HERE SOMEWHERE...

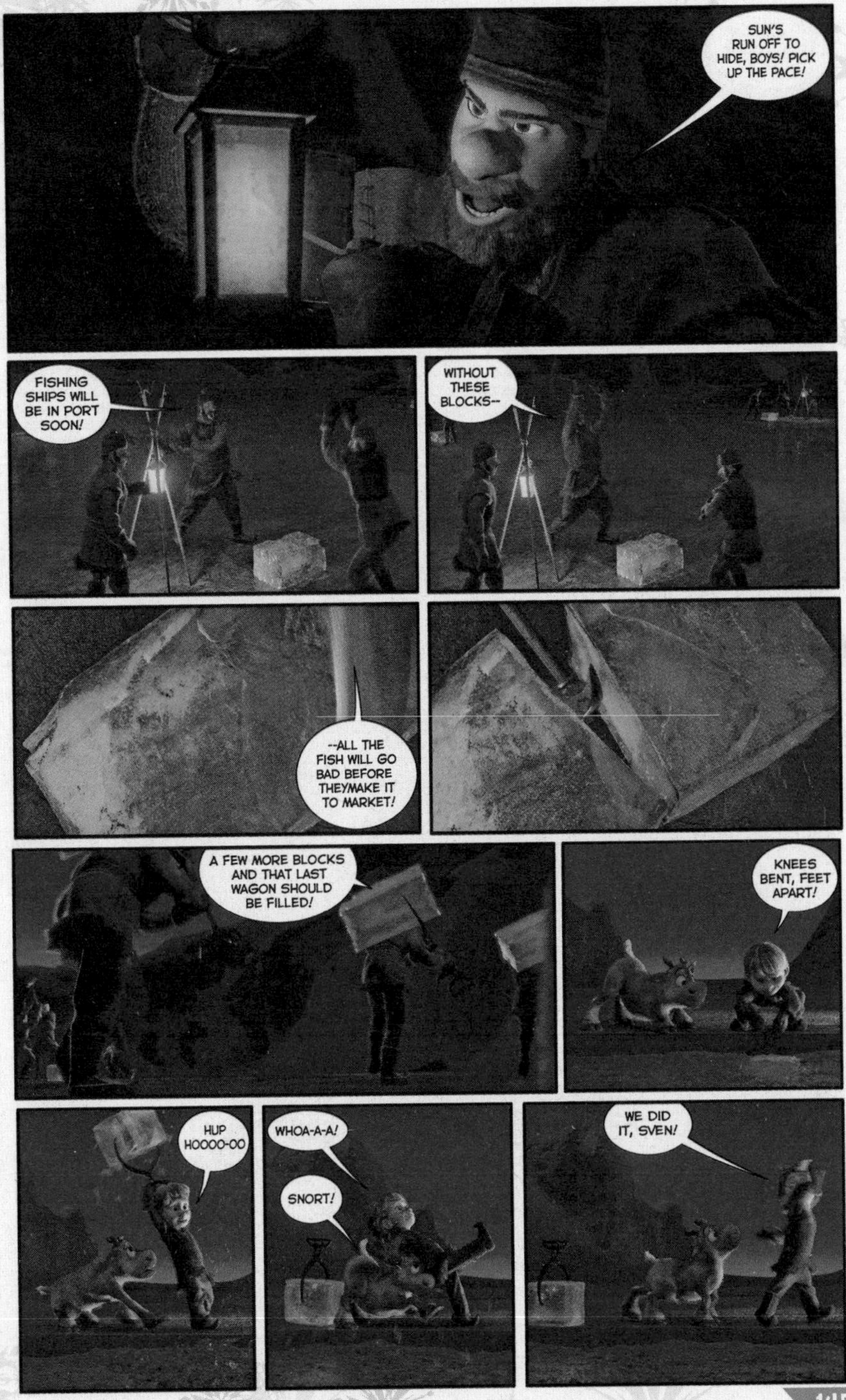
SUN'S RUN OFF TO HIDE, BOYS! PICK UP THE PACE!
FISHING SHIPS WILL BE IN PORT SOON!
WITHOUT THESE BLOCKS--
--ALL THE FISH WILL GO BAD BEFORE THEYMAKE IT TO MARKET!
A FEW MORE BLOCKS AND THAT LAST WAGON SHOULD BE FILLED!
KNEES BENT, FEET APART!
HUP HOOOO-OO
WHOA-A-A!
SNORT!
WE DID IT, SVEN!

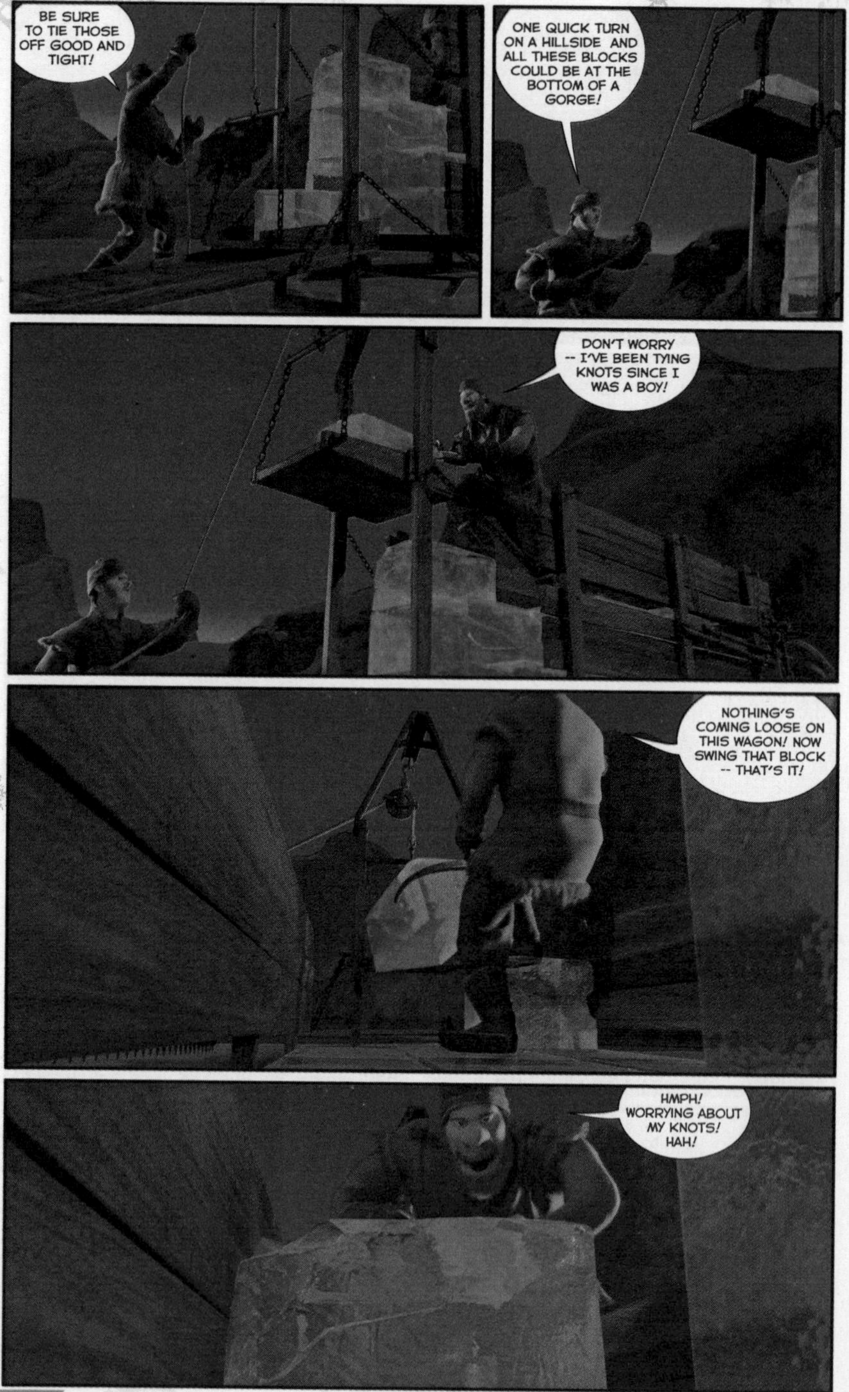
BE SURE TO TIE THOSE OFF GOOD AND TIGHT!
ONE QUICK TURN ON A HILLSIDE AND ALL THESE BLOCKS COULD BE AT THE BOTTOM OF A GORGE!
DON'T WORRY -- I'VE BEEN TYING KNOTS SINCE I WAS A BOY!
NOTHING'S COMING LOOSE ON THIS WAGON! NOW SWING THAT BLOCK -- THAT'S IT!
HMPH! WORRYING ABOUT MY KNOTS! HAH!

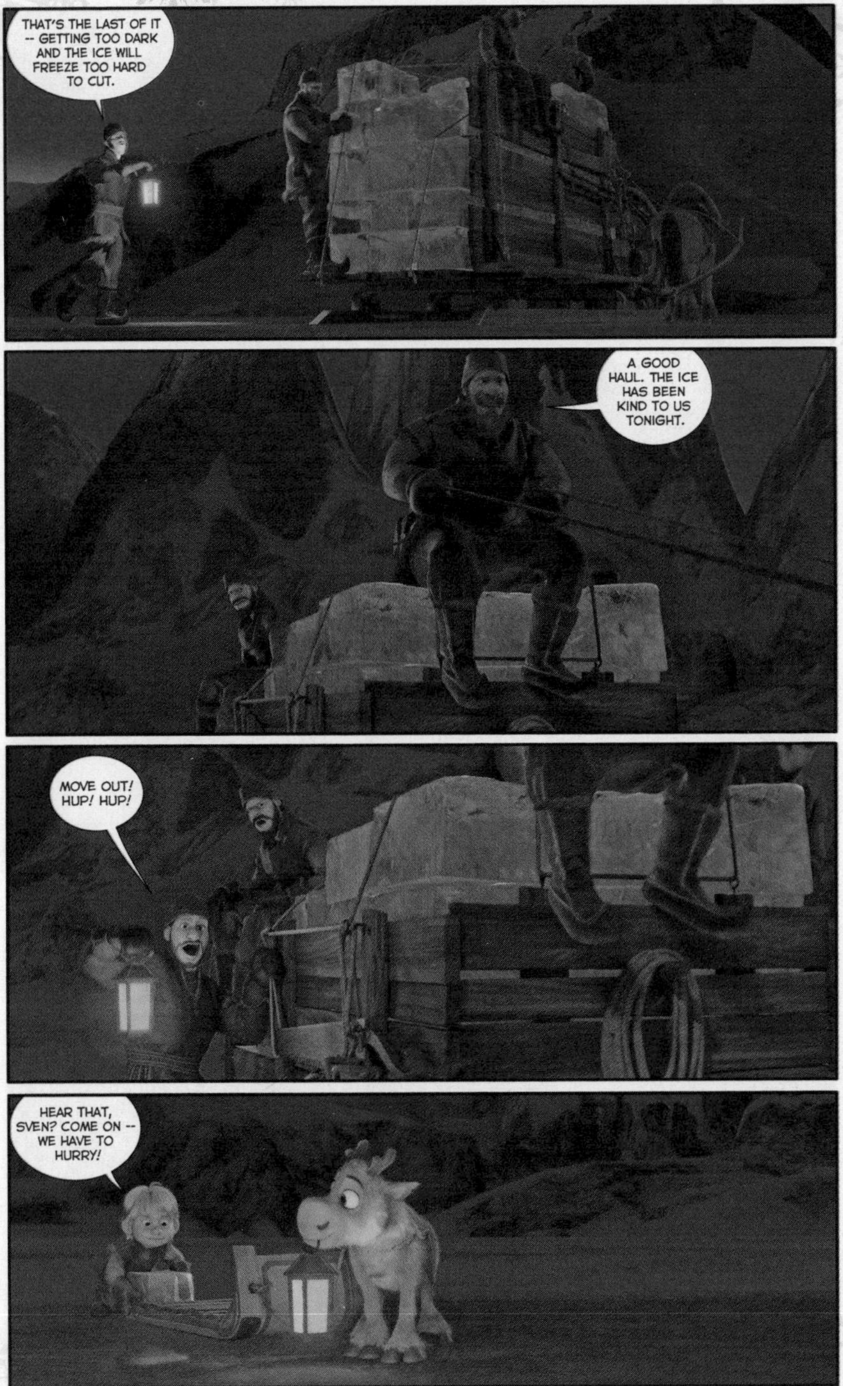
THAT'S THE LAST OF IT -- GETTING TOO DARK AND THE ICE WILL FREEZE TOO HARD TO CUT.
A GOOD HAUL. THE ICE HAS BEEN KIND TO US TONIGHT.
MOVE OUT! HUP! HUP!
HEAR THAT, SVEN? COME ON -- WE HAVE TO HURRY!

WE'LL SHOW THEM, SVEN--

-- SOMEDAY WE'LL BE THE GREATEST ICE HARVESTERS EVER!

WAIT FOR US! WE'RE COMING!

HII-YAAH! NEXT STOP: ARENDELLE!

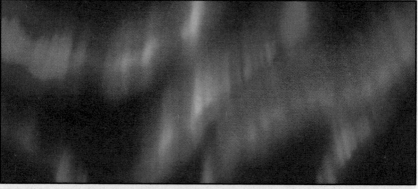

THE ICE FARMER'S SONG CARRIES ACROSS THE HILLS AND MOUNTAINS, THROUGH THE NIGHT ON THE WINDS OF THE NORTHERN LIGHTS.

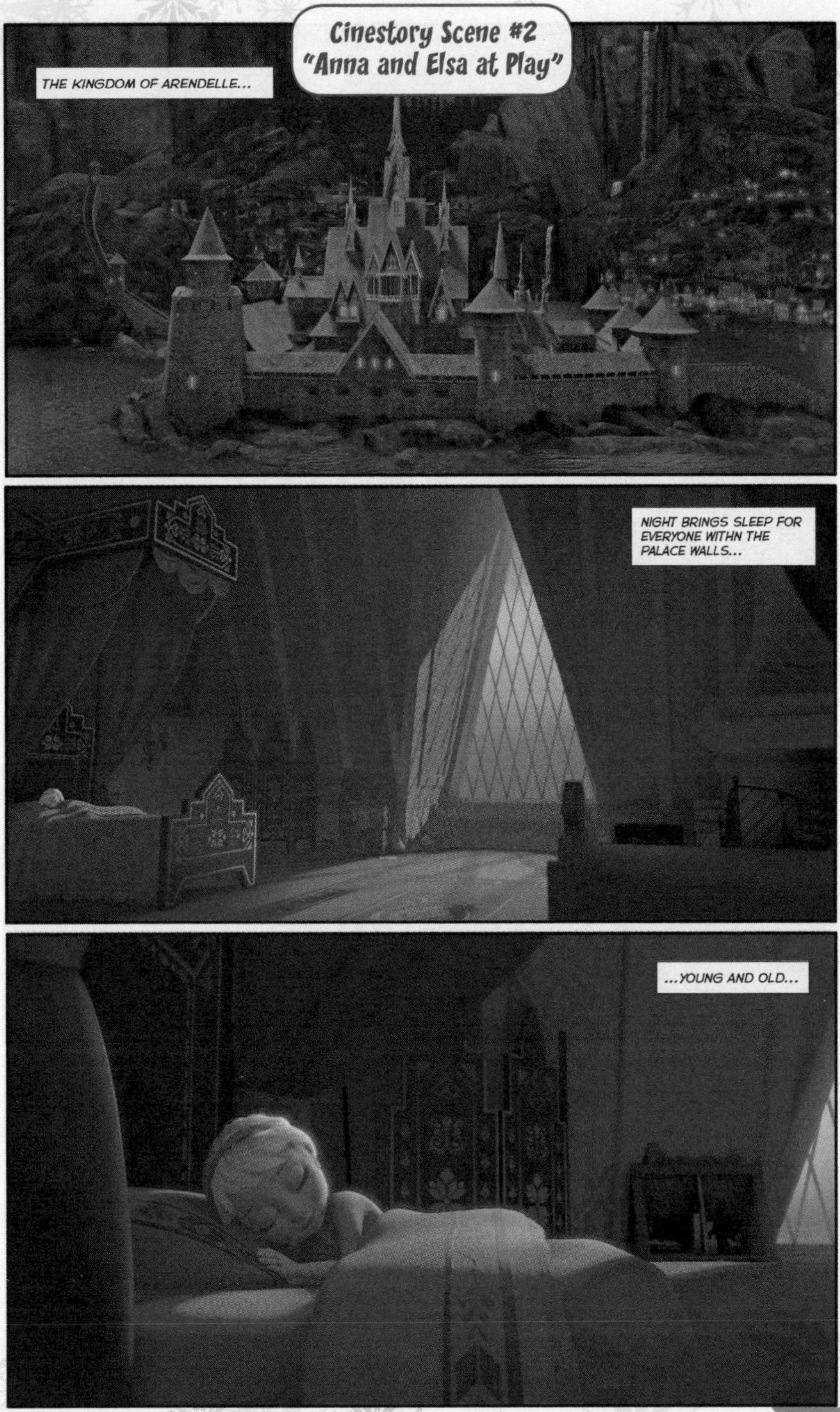
Cinestory Scene #2
"Anna and Elsa at Play"
THE KINGDOM OF ARENDELLE...
NIGHT BRINGS SLEEP FOR EVERYONE WITHN THE PALACE WALLS...
...YOUNG AND OLD...

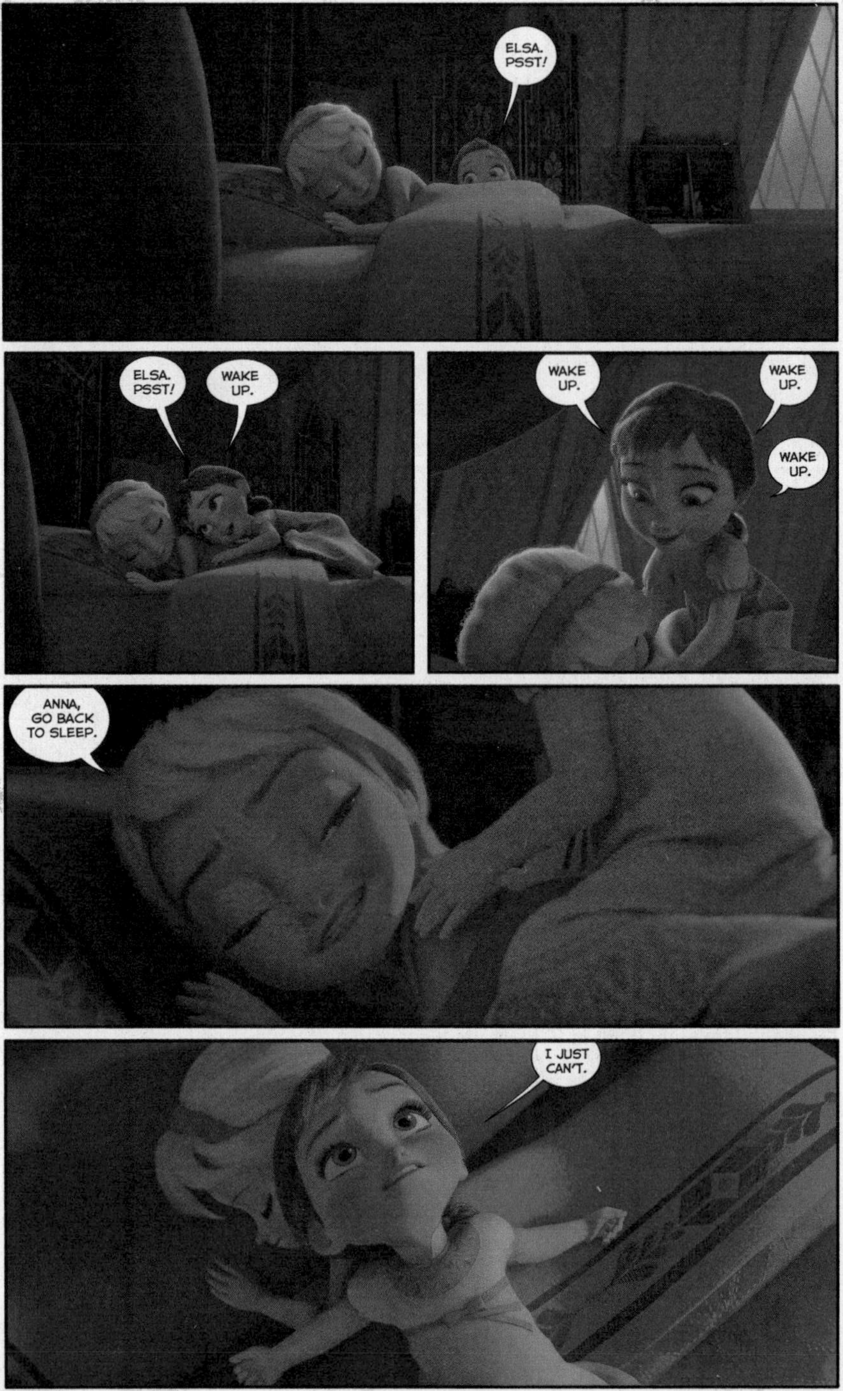
ELSA. PSST!
ELSA. PSST!
WAKE UP.
WAKE UP.
WAKE UP.
WAKE UP.
ANNA, GO BACK TO SLEEP.
I JUST CAN'T.

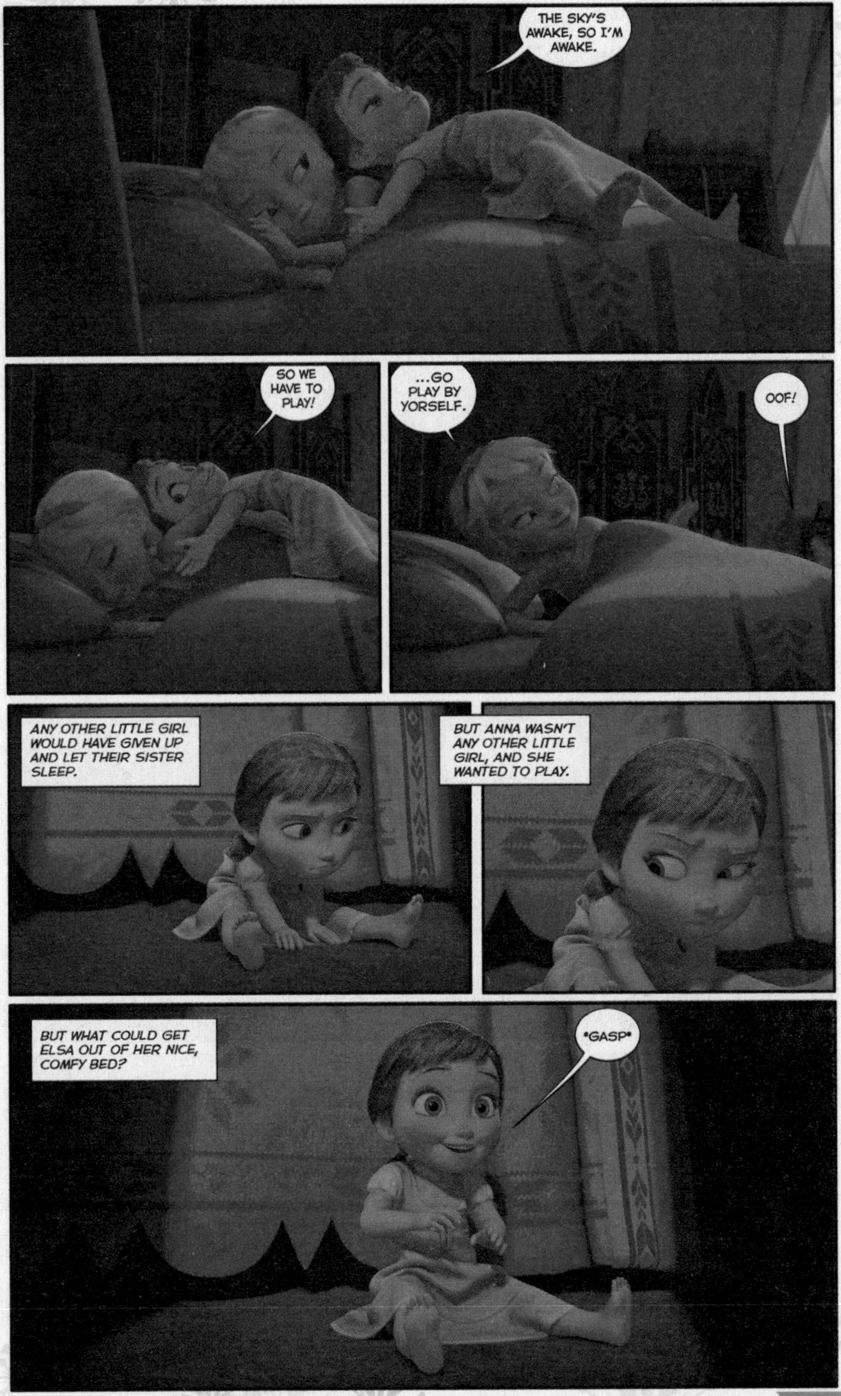
THE SKY'S AWAKE, SO I'M AWAKE.
SO WE HAVE TO PLAY!
...GO PLAY BY YORSELF.
OOF!
ANY OTHER LITTLE GIRL WOULD HAVE GIVEN UP AND LET THEIR SISTER SLEEP.
BUT ANNA WASN'T ANY OTHER LITTLE GIRL, AND SHE WANTED TO PLAY.
BUT WHAT COULD GET ELSA OUT OF HER NICE, COMFY BED?
GASP

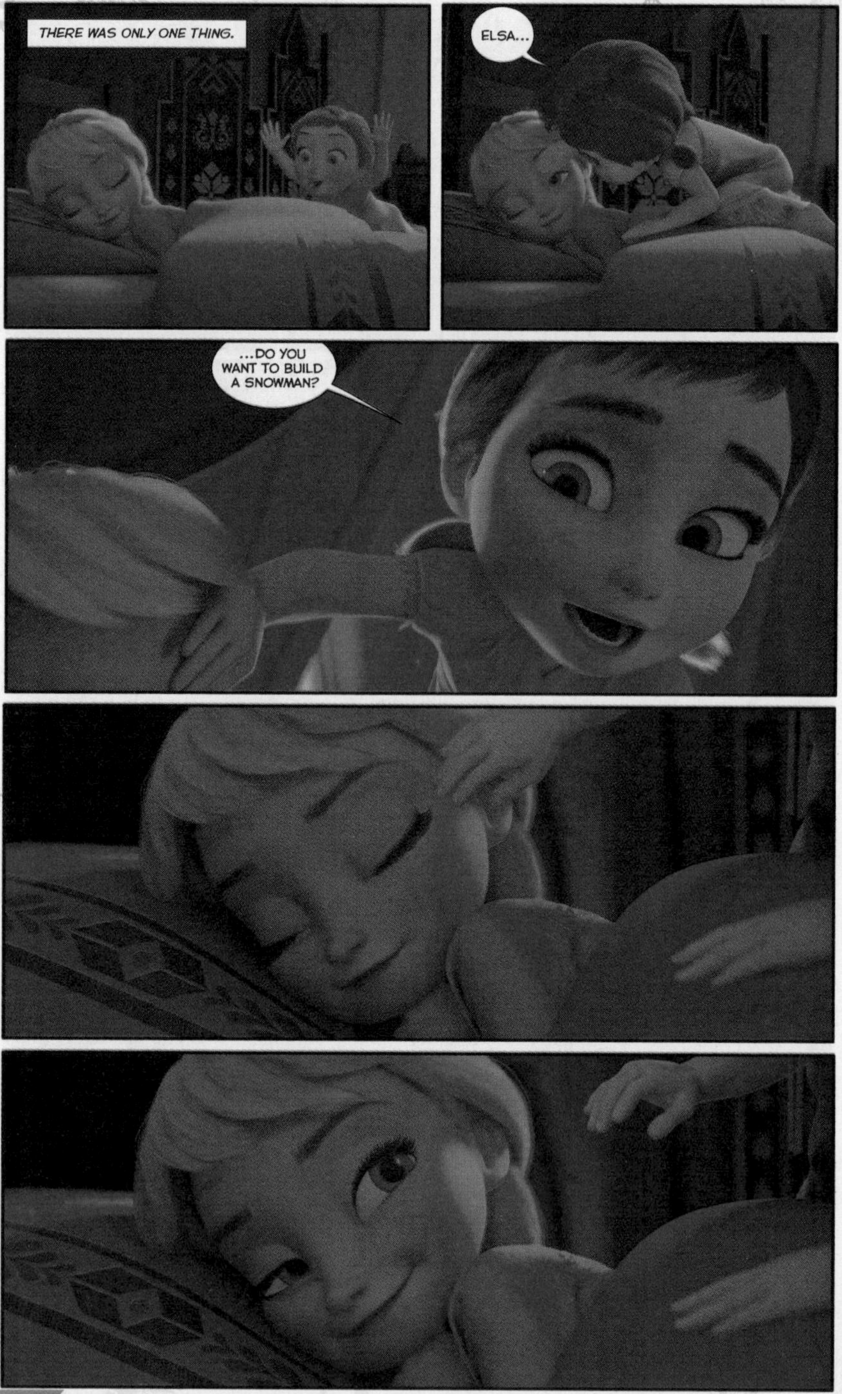
THERE WAS ONLY ONE THING.
ELSA...
...DO YOU WANT TO BUILD A SNOWMAN?

COME ON!
COME ON!
COME ON!

SHHH!

COME ON!

THE GIRLS RACE THROUGH THE CASTLE, GIGGLING AS QUIETLY AS THEY CAN...

...UNTIL THEY REACH THE GRAND BALLROOM, ONE OF THE BIGGEST ROOMS IN THE WHOLE CASTLE.

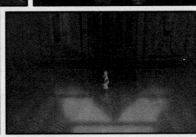

HEEHEE!

HAH!

AND THEY DID IT WITHOUT WAKING UP THEIR PARENTS!

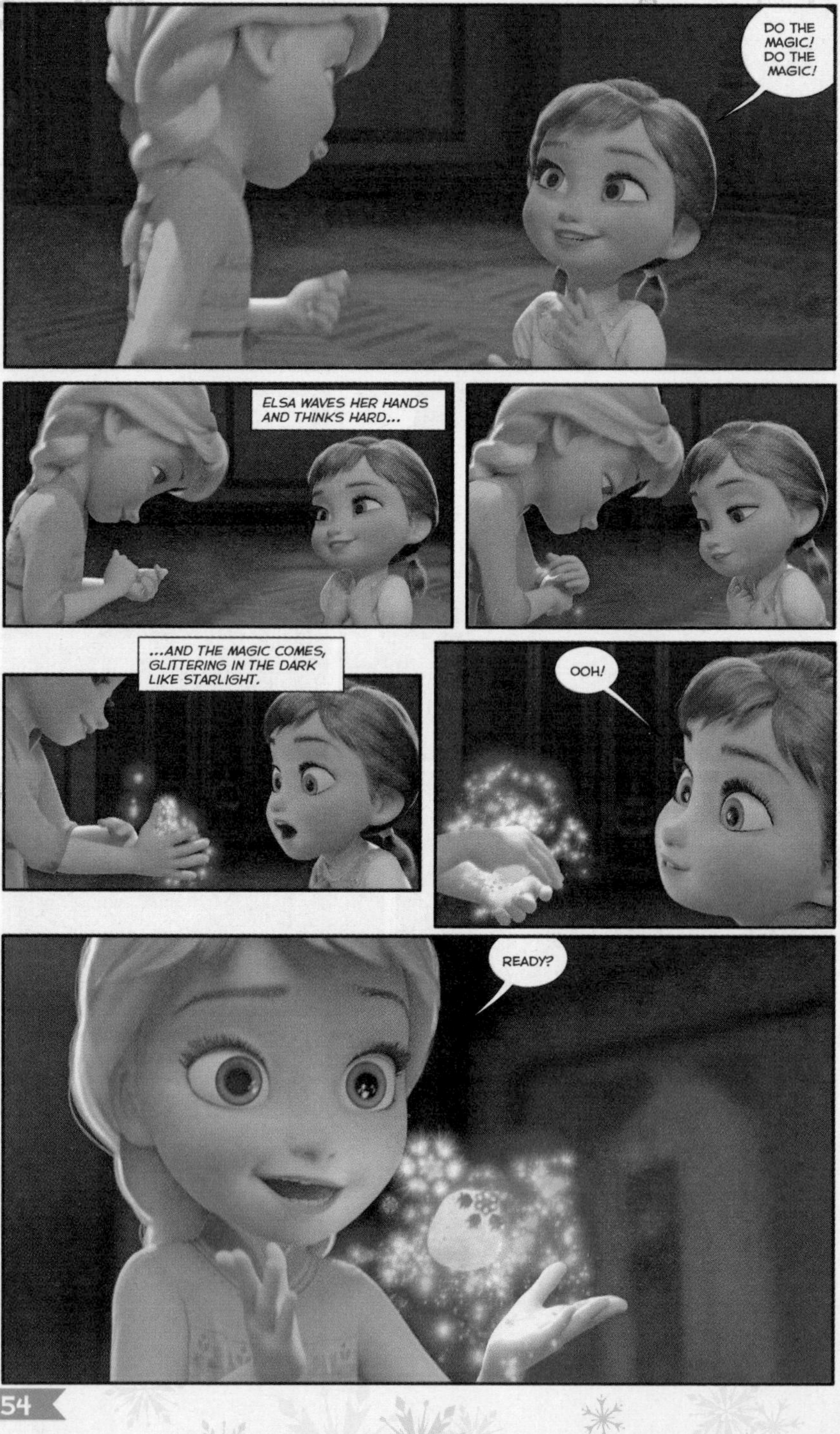
DO THE MAGIC! DO THE MAGIC!
ELSA WAVES HER HANDS AND THINKS HARD...
...AND THE MAGIC COMES, GLITTERING IN THE DARK LIKE STARLIGHT.
OOH!
READY?

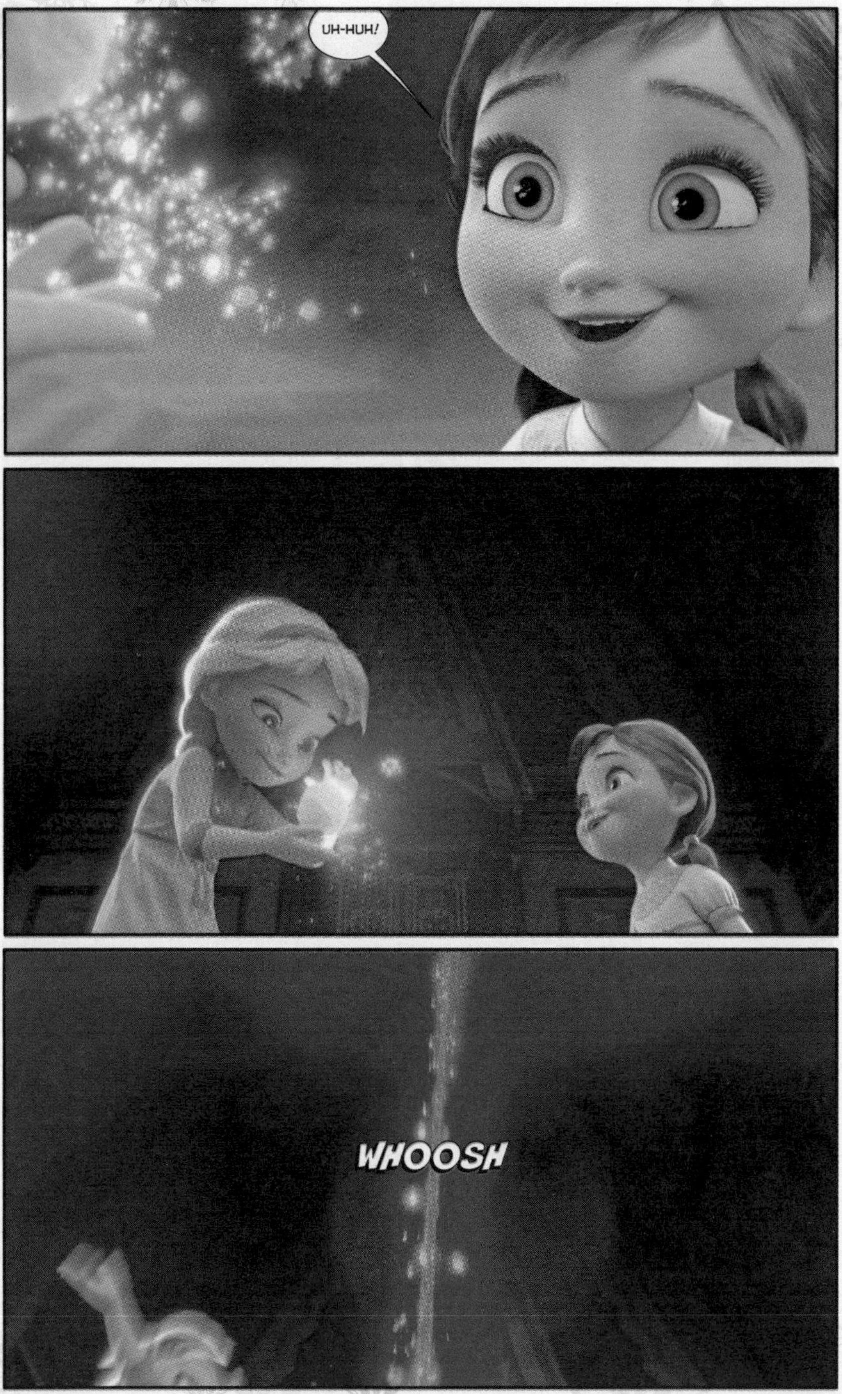
UH-HUH!
WHOOSH

ANNA'S MAGIC FLEW TO THE HIGHEST POINT IN THE GRAND HALL...

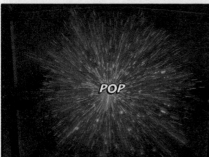

POP

...AND BECAME A GENTLE SNOWFALL.

THIS IS AMAZING!

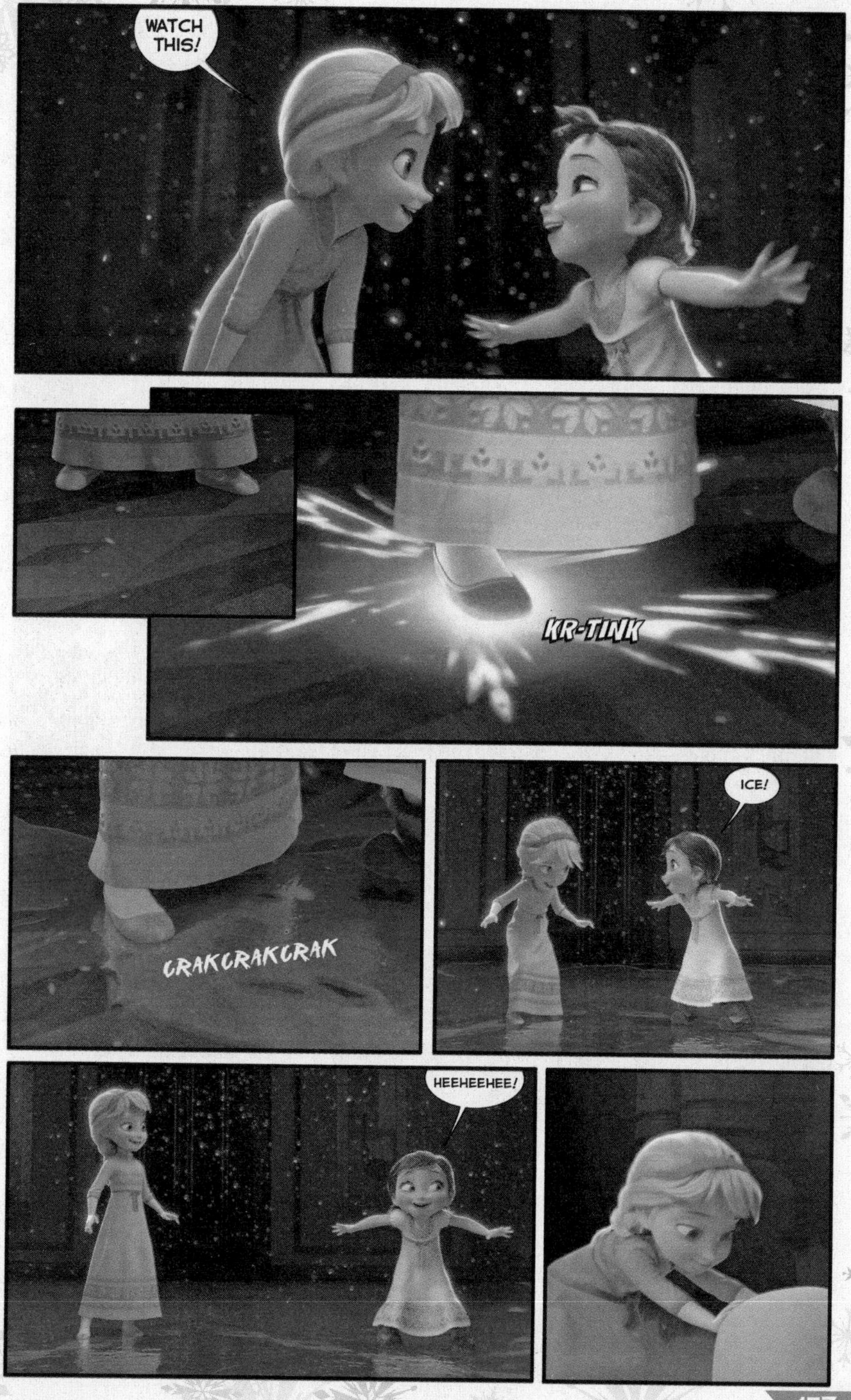

WATCH THIS!
KR-TINK
CRAKCRAKCRAK
ICE!
HEEHEEHEE!

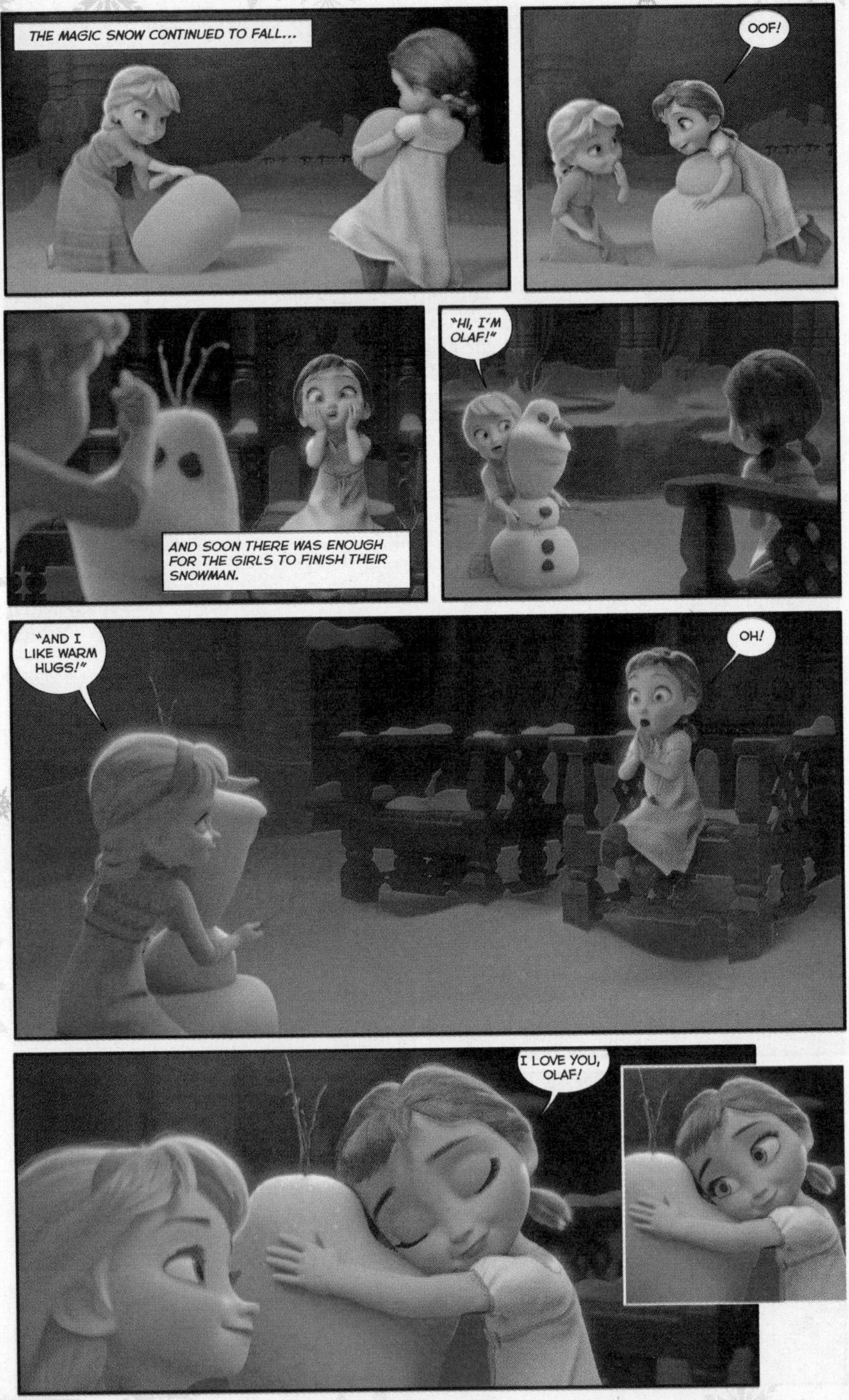

THE MAGIC SNOW CONTINUED TO FALL...
OOF!
AND SOON THERE WAS ENOUGH FOR THE GIRLS TO FINISH THEIR SNOWMAN.
"HI, I'M OLAF!"
"AND I LIKE WARM HUGS!"
OH!
I LOVE YOU, OLAF!

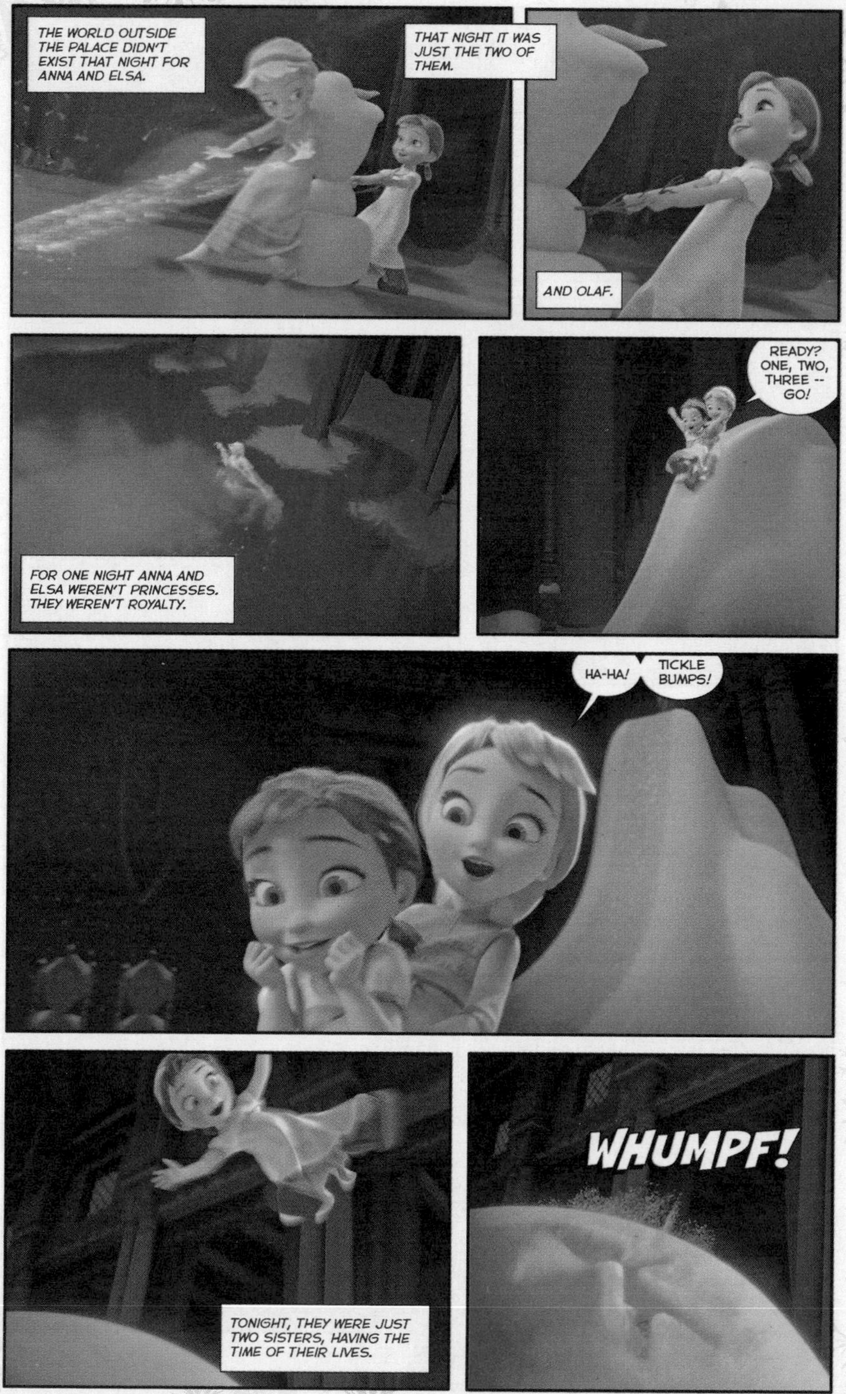
THE WORLD OUTSIDE THE PALACE DIDN'T EXIST THAT NIGHT FOR ANNA AND ELSA.
THAT NIGHT IT WAS JUST THE TWO OF THEM.
AND OLAF.
FOR ONE NIGHT ANNA AND ELSA WEREN'T PRINCESSES. THEY WEREN'T ROYALTY.
READY? ONE, TWO, THREE -- GO!
HA-HA!
TICKLE BUMPS!
TONIGHT, THEY WERE JUST TWO SISTERS, HAVING THE TIME OF THEIR LIVES.
WHUMPF!

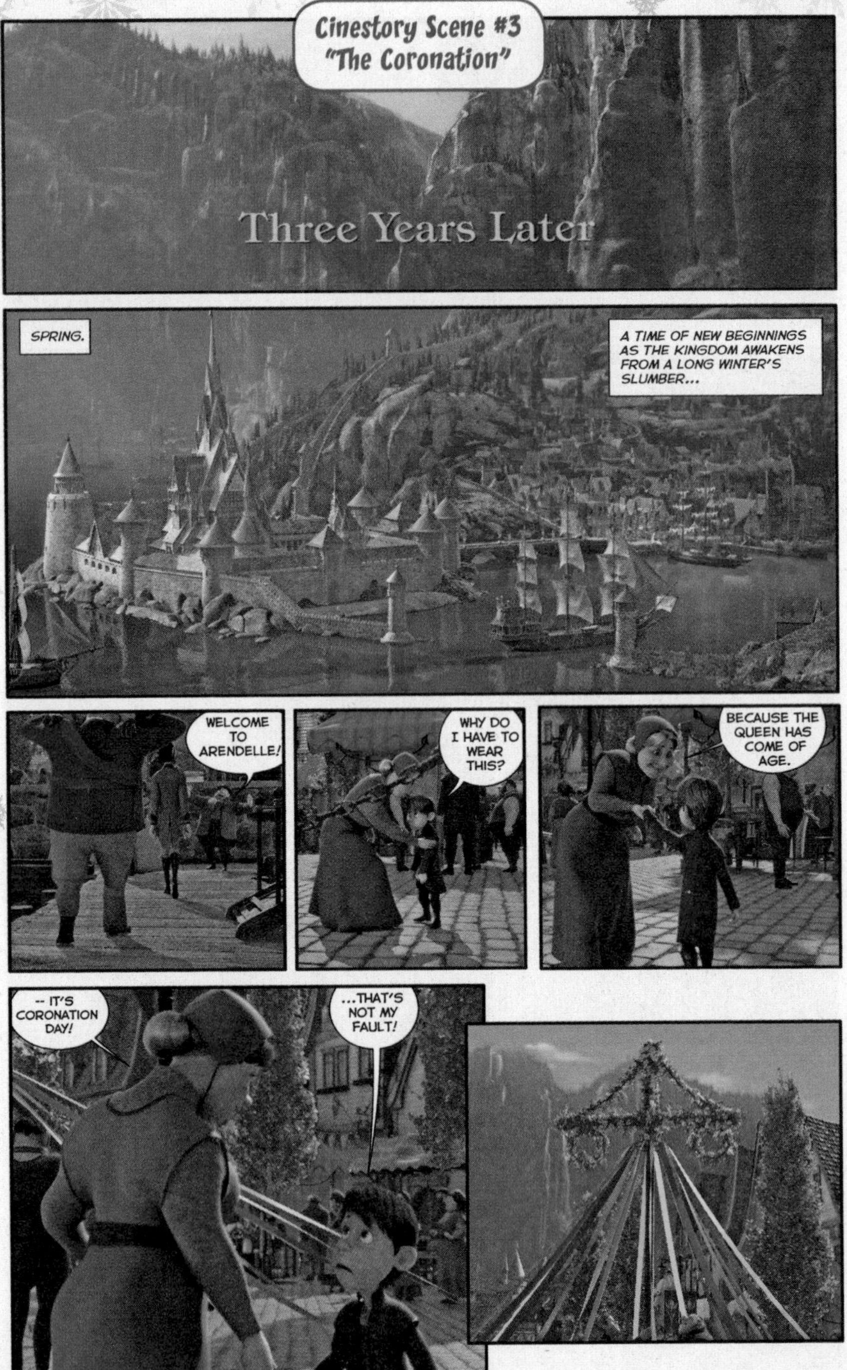
Cinestory Scene #3
"The Coronation"
Three Years Later
SPRING.
A TIME OF NEW BEGINNINGS AS THE KINGDOM AWAKENS FROM A LONG WINTER'S SLUMBER...
WELCOME TO ARENDELLE!
WHY DO I HAVE TO WEAR THIS?
BECAUSE THE QUEEN HAS COME OF AGE.
-- IT'S CORONATION DAY!
...THAT'S NOT MY FAULT!

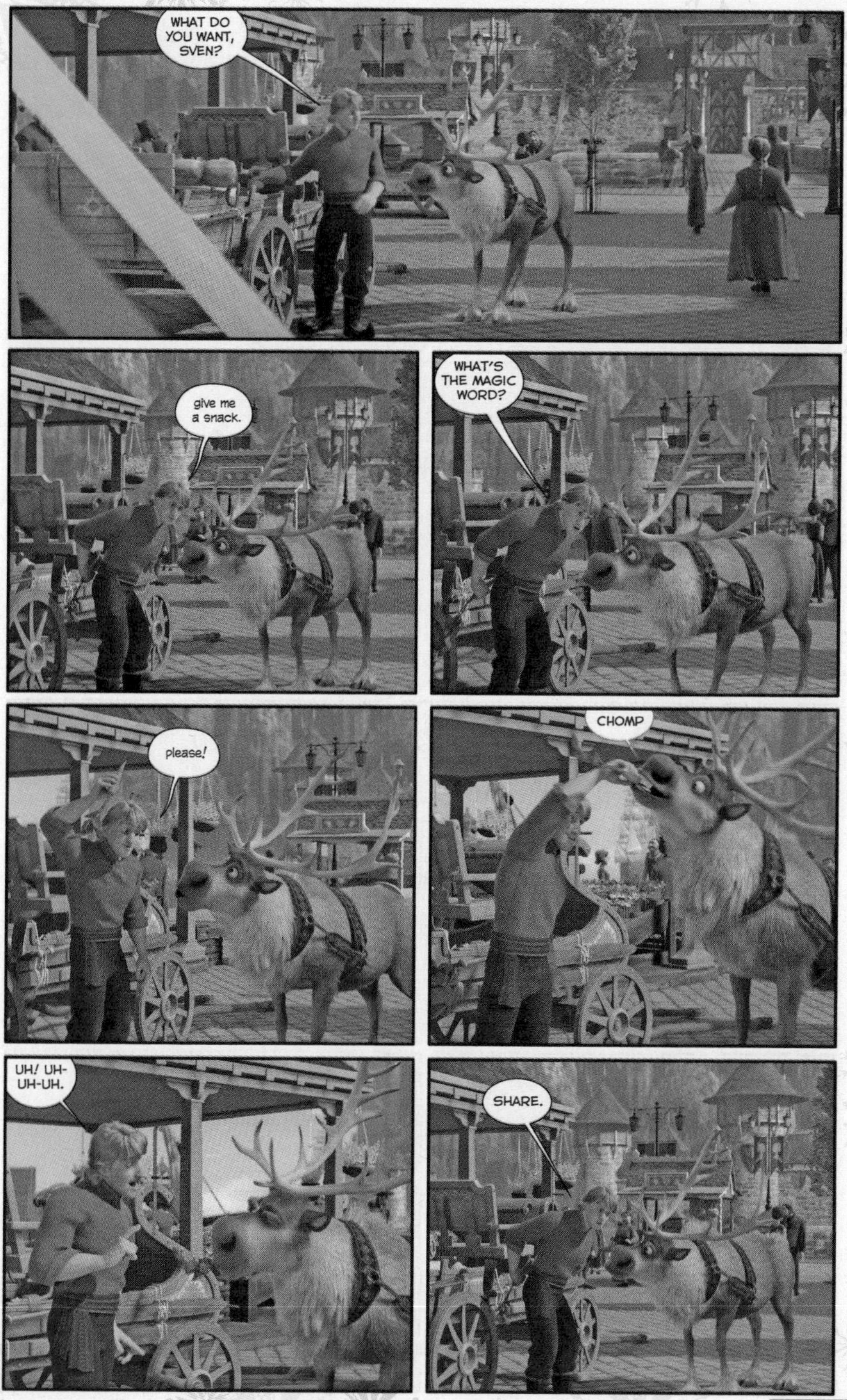
WHAT DO YOU WANT, SVEN?
give me a snack.
WHAT'S THE MAGIC WORD?
please!
CHOMP
UH! UH-UH-UH.
SHARE.

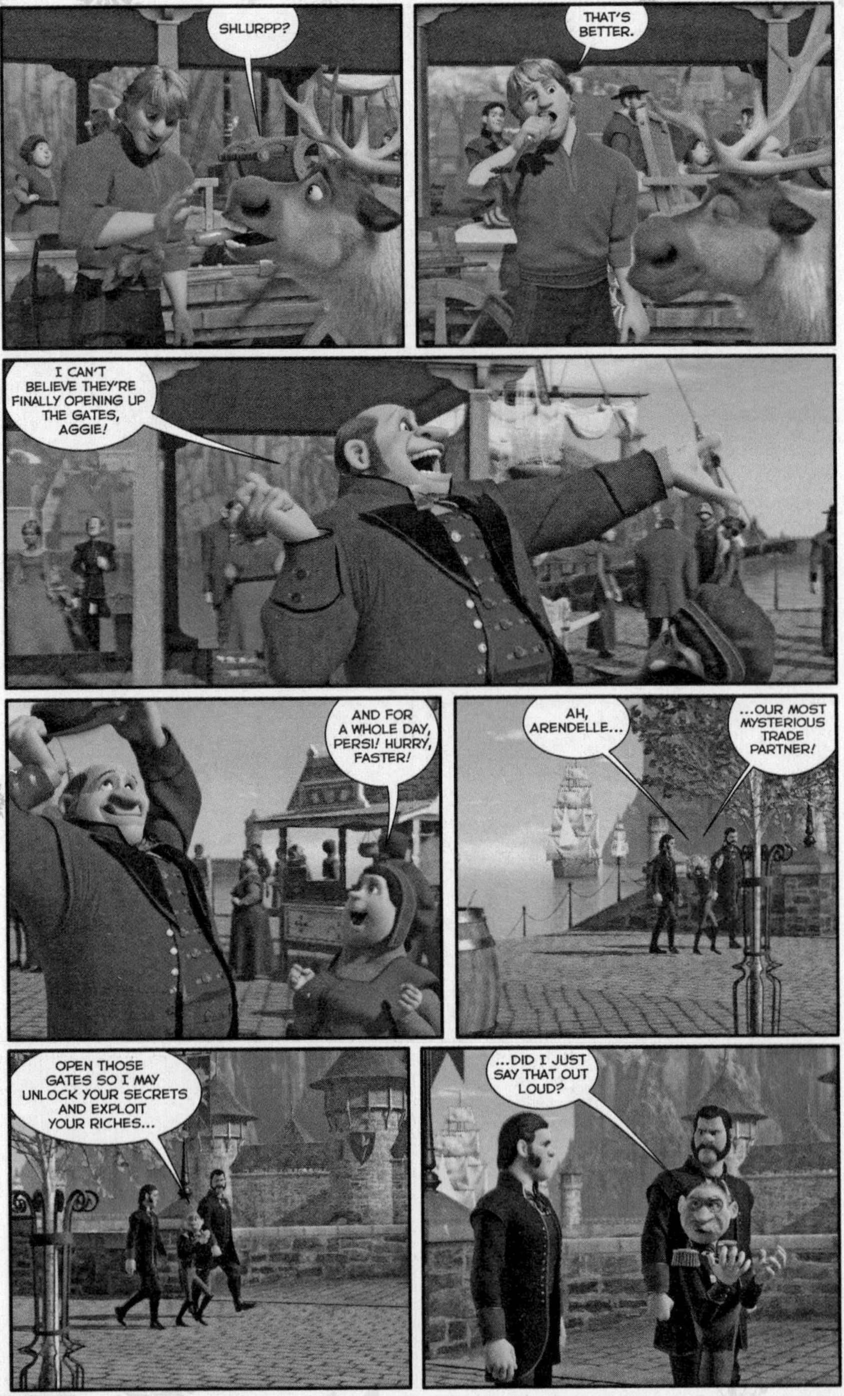
SHLURPP?
THAT'S BETTER.
I CAN'T BELIEVE THEY'RE FINALLY OPENING UP THE GATES, AGGIE!
AND FOR A WHOLE DAY, PERSI! HURRY, FASTER!
AH, ARENDELLE...
...OUR MOST MYSTERIOUS TRADE PARTNER!
OPEN THOSE GATES SO I MAY UNLOCK YOUR SECRETS AND EXPLOIT YOUR RICHES...
...DID I JUST SAY THAT OUT LOUD?

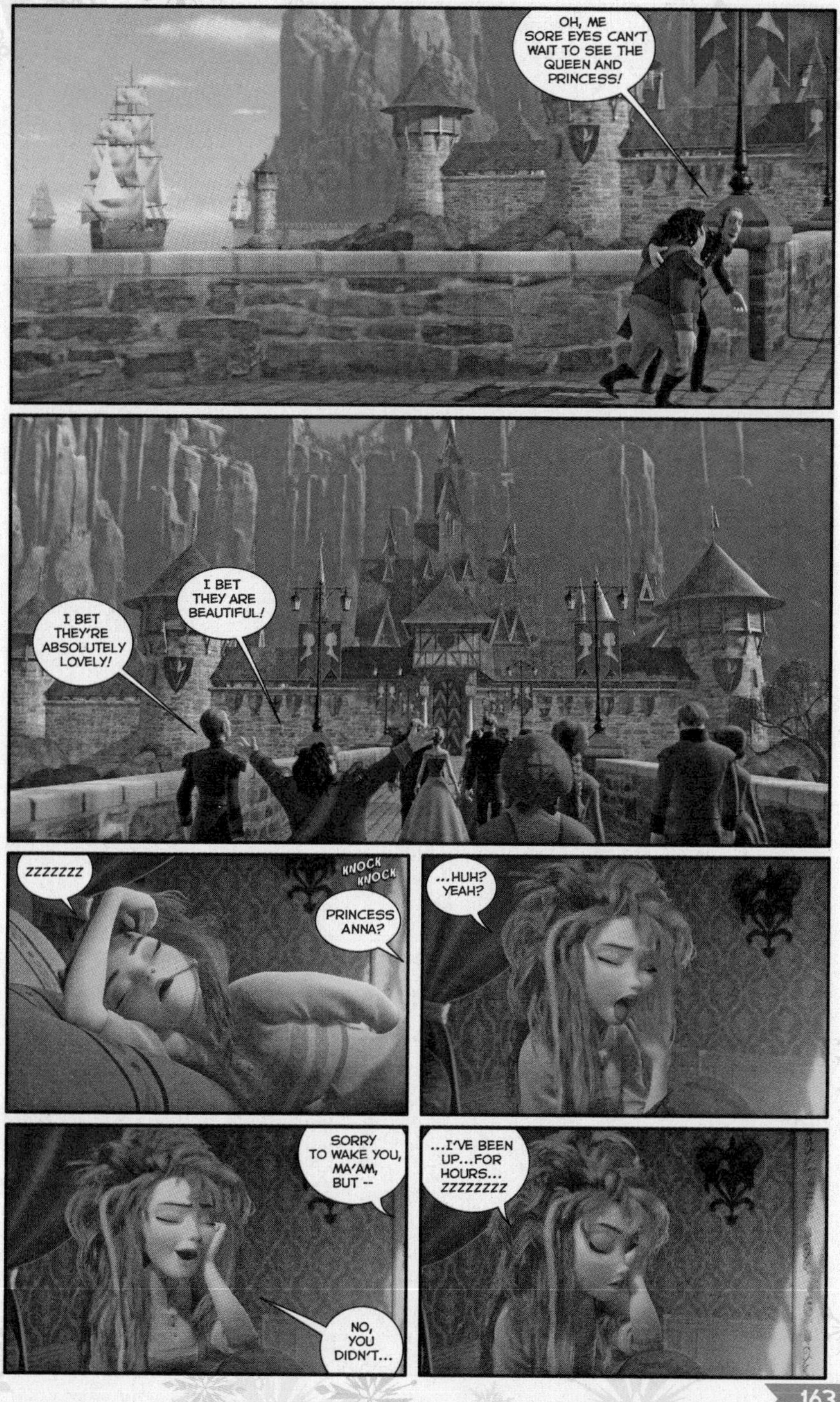
OH, ME SORE EYES CAN'T WAIT TO SEE THE QUEEN AND PRINCESS!
I BET THEY'RE ABSOLUTELY LOVELY!
I BET THEY ARE BEAUTIFUL!
ZZZZZZZ
KNOCK KNOCK
PRINCESS ANNA?
...HUH? YEAH?
SORRY TO WAKE YOU, MA'AM, BUT --
NO, YOU DIDN'T...
...I'VE BEEN UP...FOR HOURS... ZZZZZZZZ

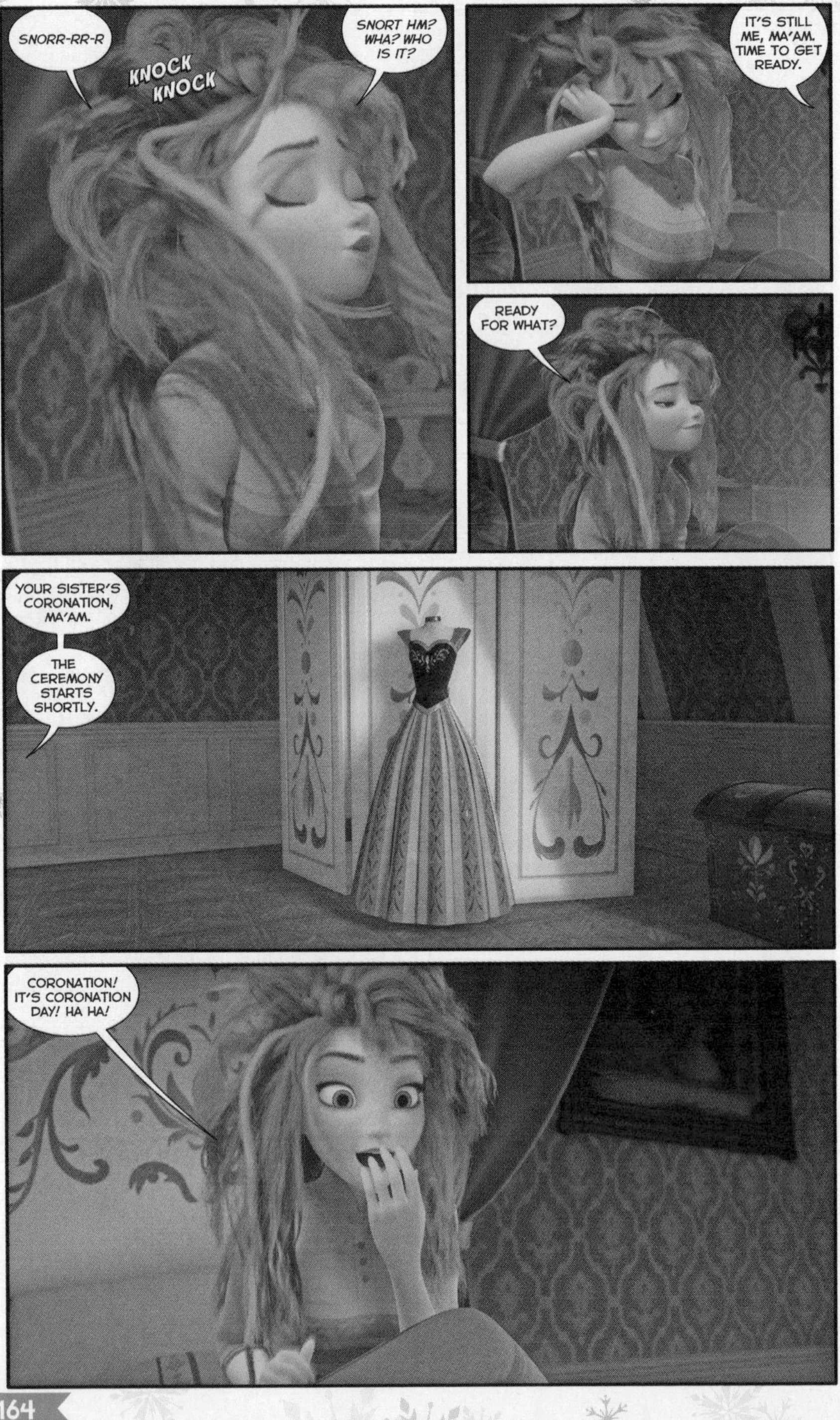
SNORR-RR-R
KNOCK KNOCK
SNORT HM? WHA? WHO IS IT?
IT'S STILL ME, MA'AM. TIME TO GET READY.
READY FOR WHAT?
YOUR SISTER'S CORONATION, MA'AM.
THE CEREMONY STARTS SHORTLY.
CORONATION! IT'S CORONATION DAY! HA HA!

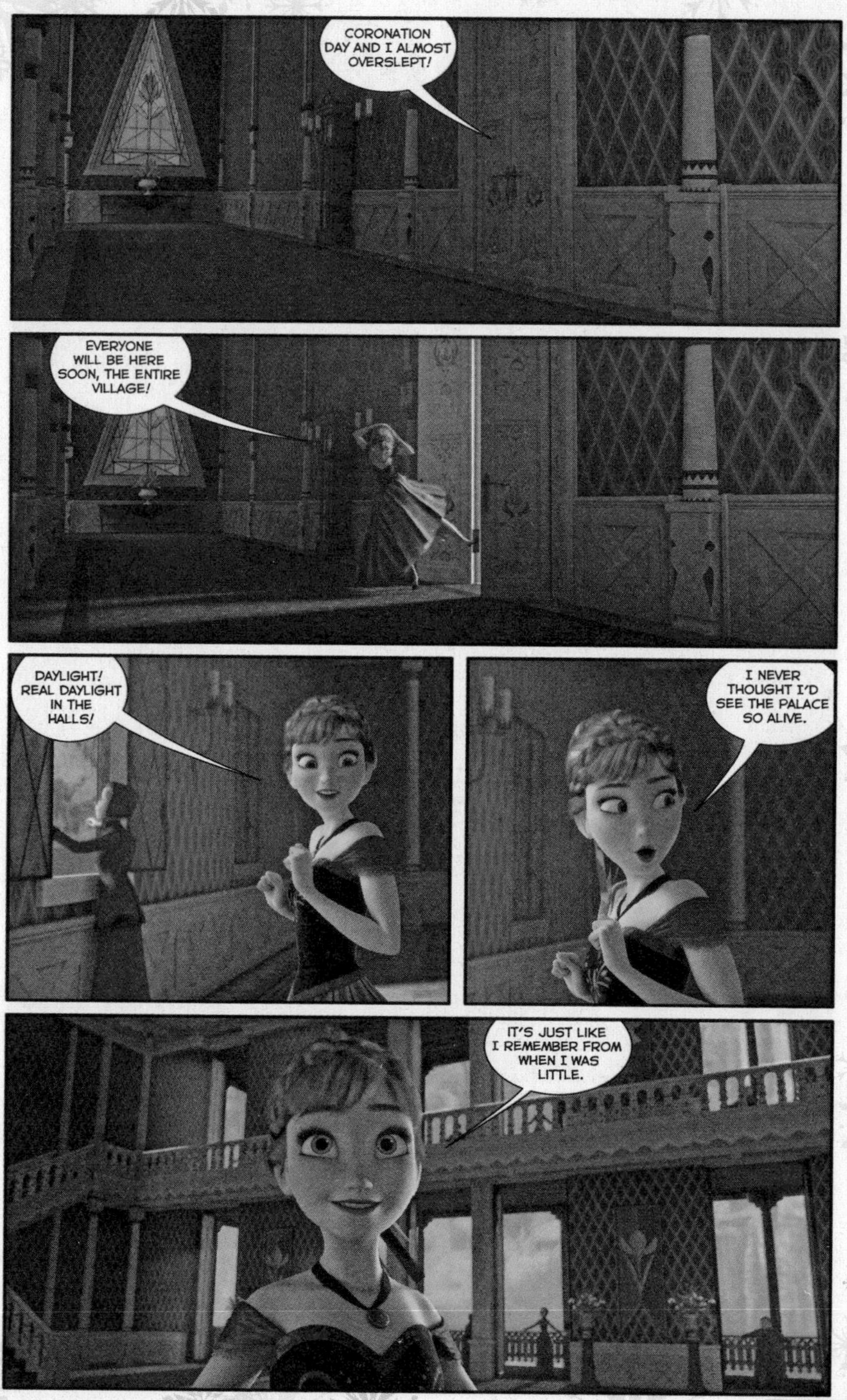
CORONATION DAY AND I ALMOST OVERSLEPT!
EVERYONE WILL BE HERE SOON, THE ENTIRE VILLAGE!
DAYLIGHT! REAL DAYLIGHT IN THE HALLS!
I NEVER THOUGHT I'D SEE THE PALACE SO ALIVE.
IT'S JUST LIKE I REMEMBER FROM WHEN I WAS LITTLE.

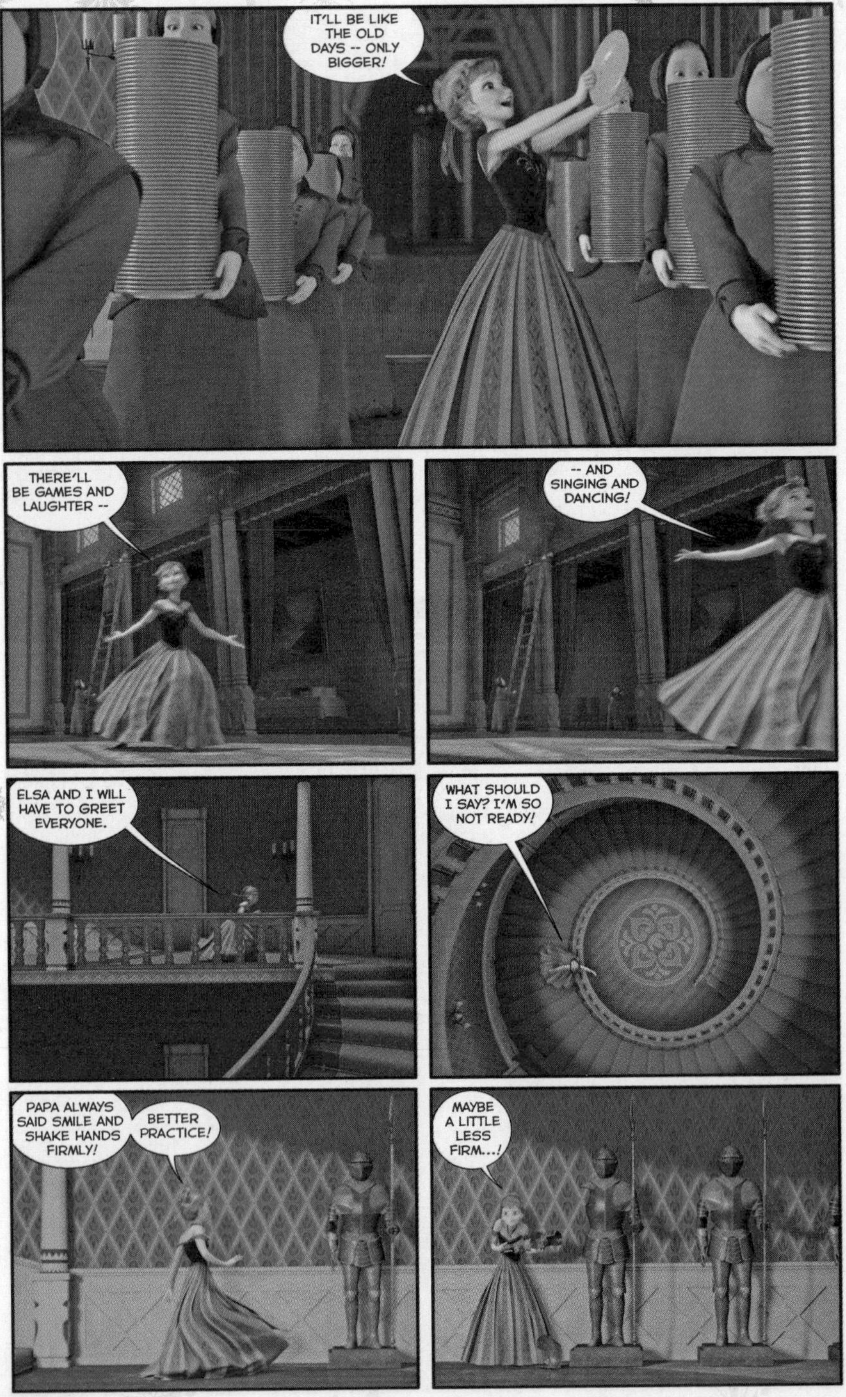
IT'LL BE LIKE THE OLD DAYS -- ONLY BIGGER!
THERE'LL BE GAMES AND LAUGHTER --
-- AND SINGING AND DANCING!
ELSA AND I WILL HAVE TO GREET EVERYONE.
WHAT SHOULD I SAY? I'M SO NOT READY!
PAPA ALWAYS SAID SMILE AND SHAKE HANDS FIRMLY!
BETTER PRACTICE!
MAYBE A LITTLE LESS FIRM...!

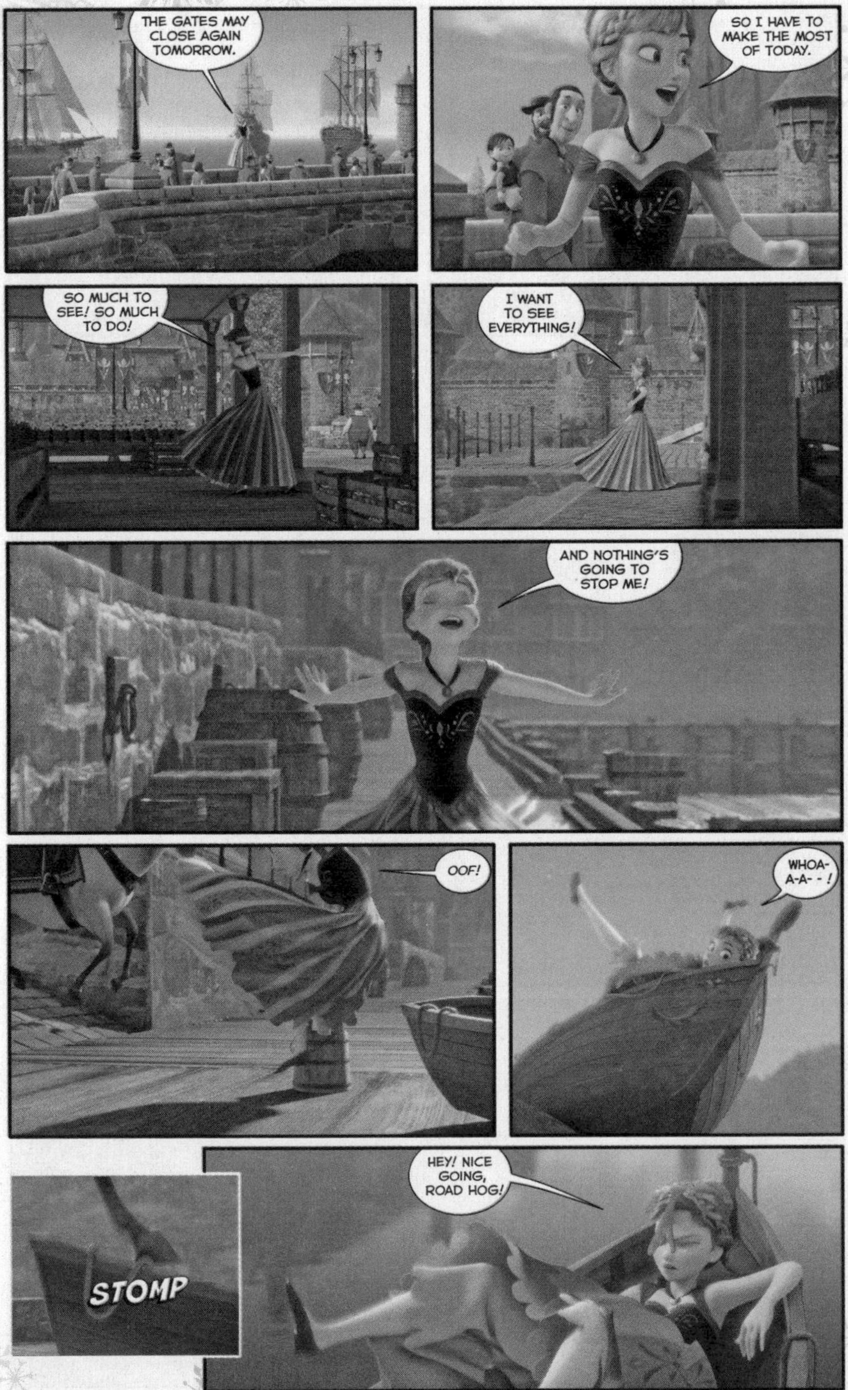
THE GATES MAY CLOSE AGAIN TOMORROW.
SO I HAVE TO MAKE THE MOST OF TODAY.
SO MUCH TO SEE! SO MUCH TO DO!
I WANT TO SEE EVERYTHING!
AND NOTHING'S GOING TO STOP ME!
OOF!
WHOA-A-A- - !
STOMP
HEY! NICE GOING, ROAD HOG!

I SHOULD --

I'M SO SORRY. ARE YOU HURT?

HEY. I-YA, NO. NO. I'M OKAY.

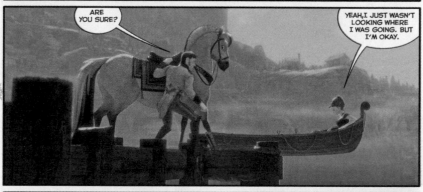

ARE YOU SURE?

YEAH, I JUST WASN'T LOOKING WHERE I WAS GOING. BUT I'M OKAY.

I'M GREAT, ACTUALLY.

OH, THANK GOODNESS.

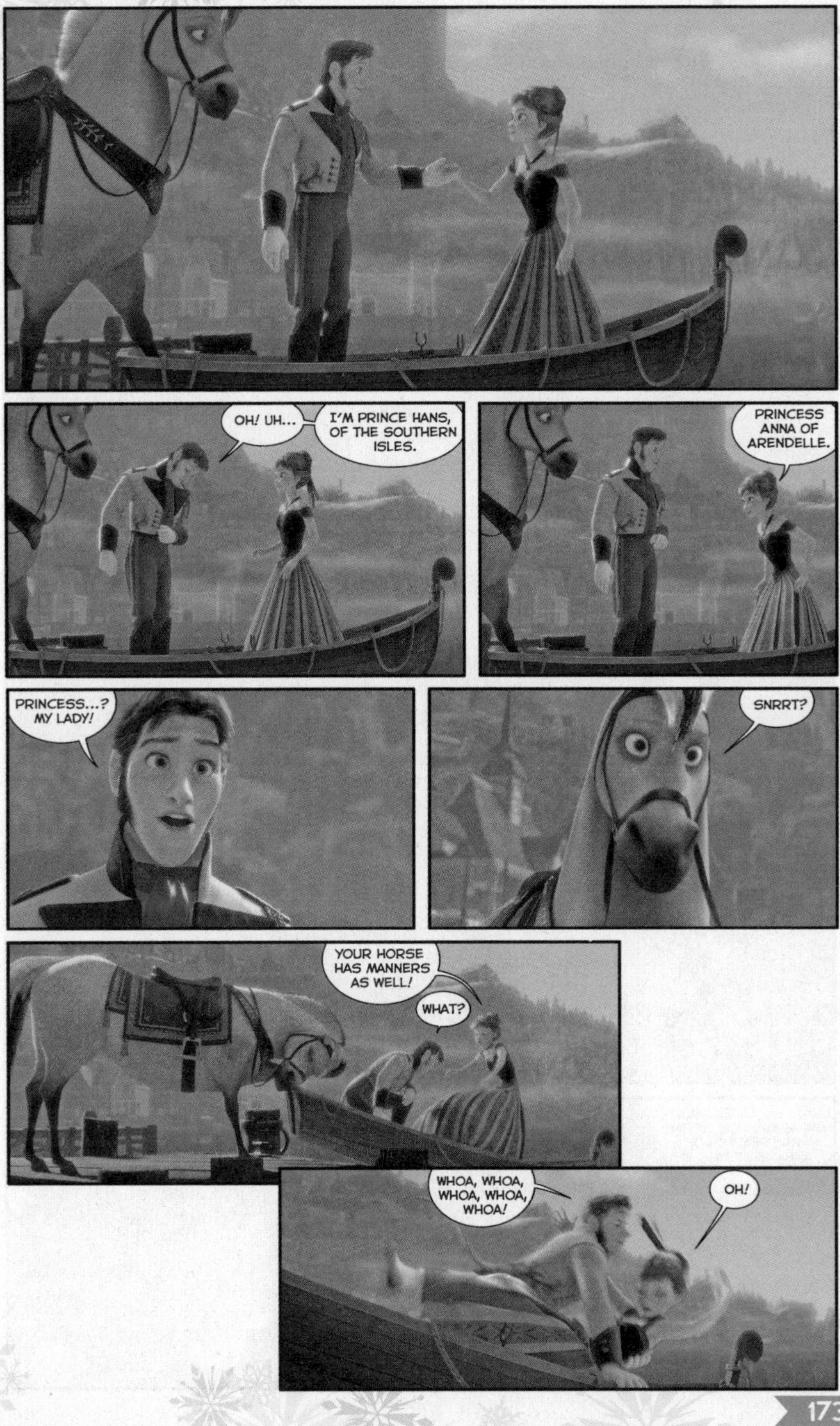
OH! UH...
I'M PRINCE HANS, OF THE SOUTHERN ISLES.
PRINCESS ANNA OF ARENDELLE.
PRINCESS...? MY LADY!
SNRRT?
YOUR HORSE HAS MANNERS AS WELL!
WHAT?
WHOA, WHOA, WHOA, WHOA, WHOA!
OH!

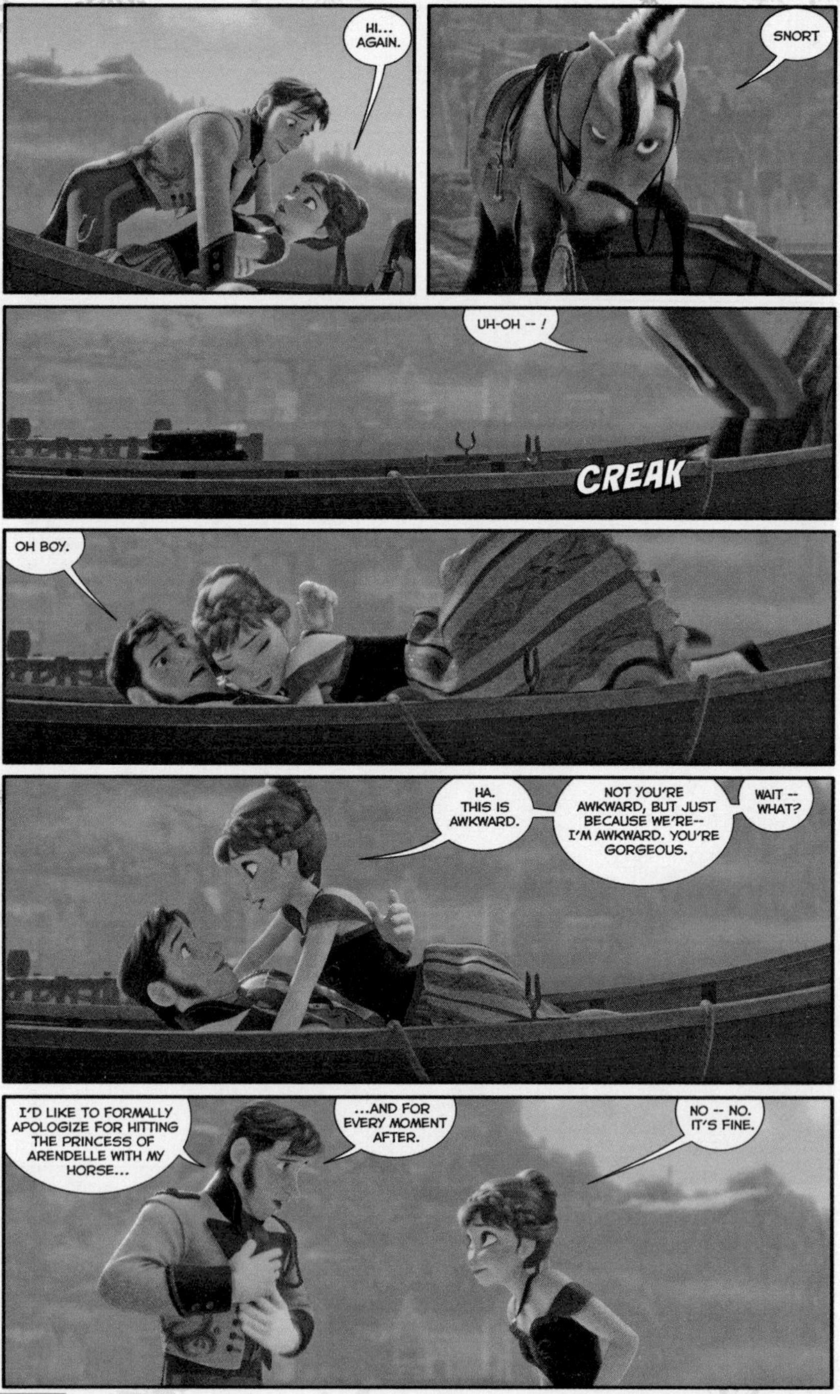
HI... AGAIN.
SNORT
UH-OH -- !
CREAK
OH BOY.
HA. THIS IS AWKWARD.
NOT YOU'RE AWKWARD, BUT JUST BECAUSE WE'RE-- I'M AWKWARD. YOU'RE GORGEOUS.
WAIT -- WHAT?
I'D LIKE TO FORMALLY APOLOGIZE FOR HITTING THE PRINCESS OF ARENDELLE WITH MY HORSE...
...AND FOR EVERY MOMENT AFTER.
NO -- NO. IT'S FINE.

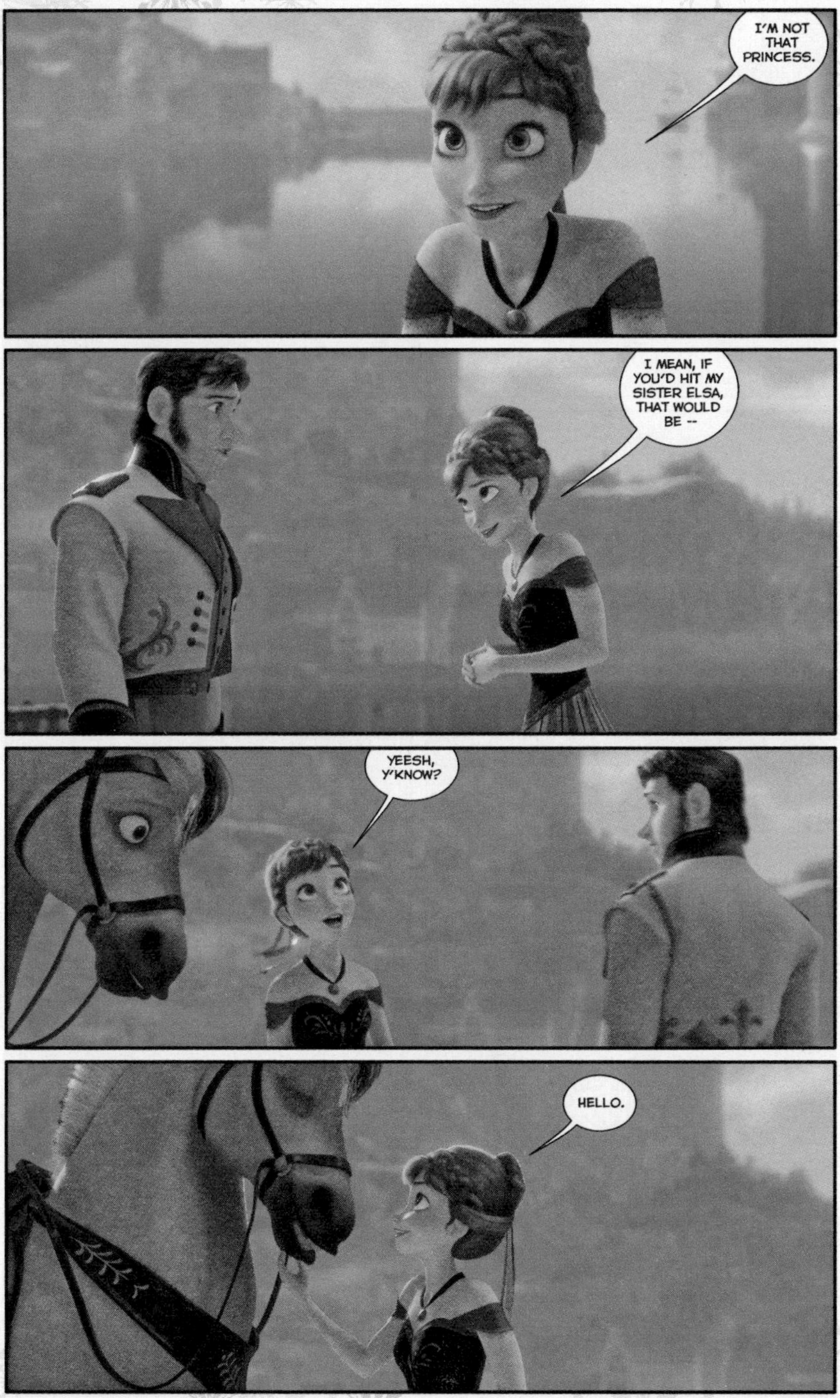
I'M NOT THAT PRINCESS.
I MEAN, IF YOU'D HIT MY SISTER ELSA, THAT WOULD BE --
YEESH, Y'KNOW?
HELLO.

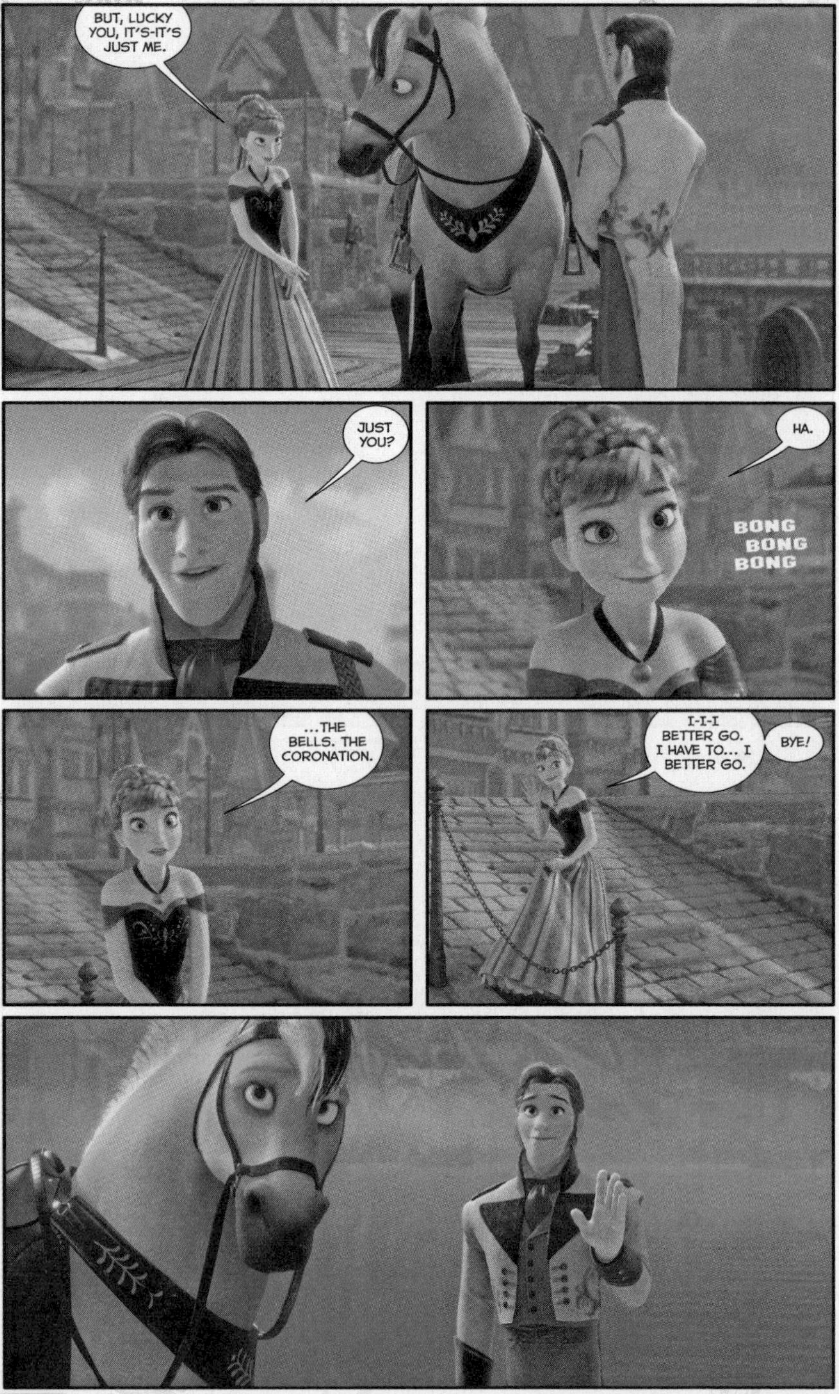
BUT, LUCKY YOU, IT'S-IT'S JUST ME.
JUST YOU?
HA.
BONG BONG BONG
...THE BELLS. THE CORONATION.
I-I-I BETTER GO. I HAVE TO... I BETTER GO.
BYE!

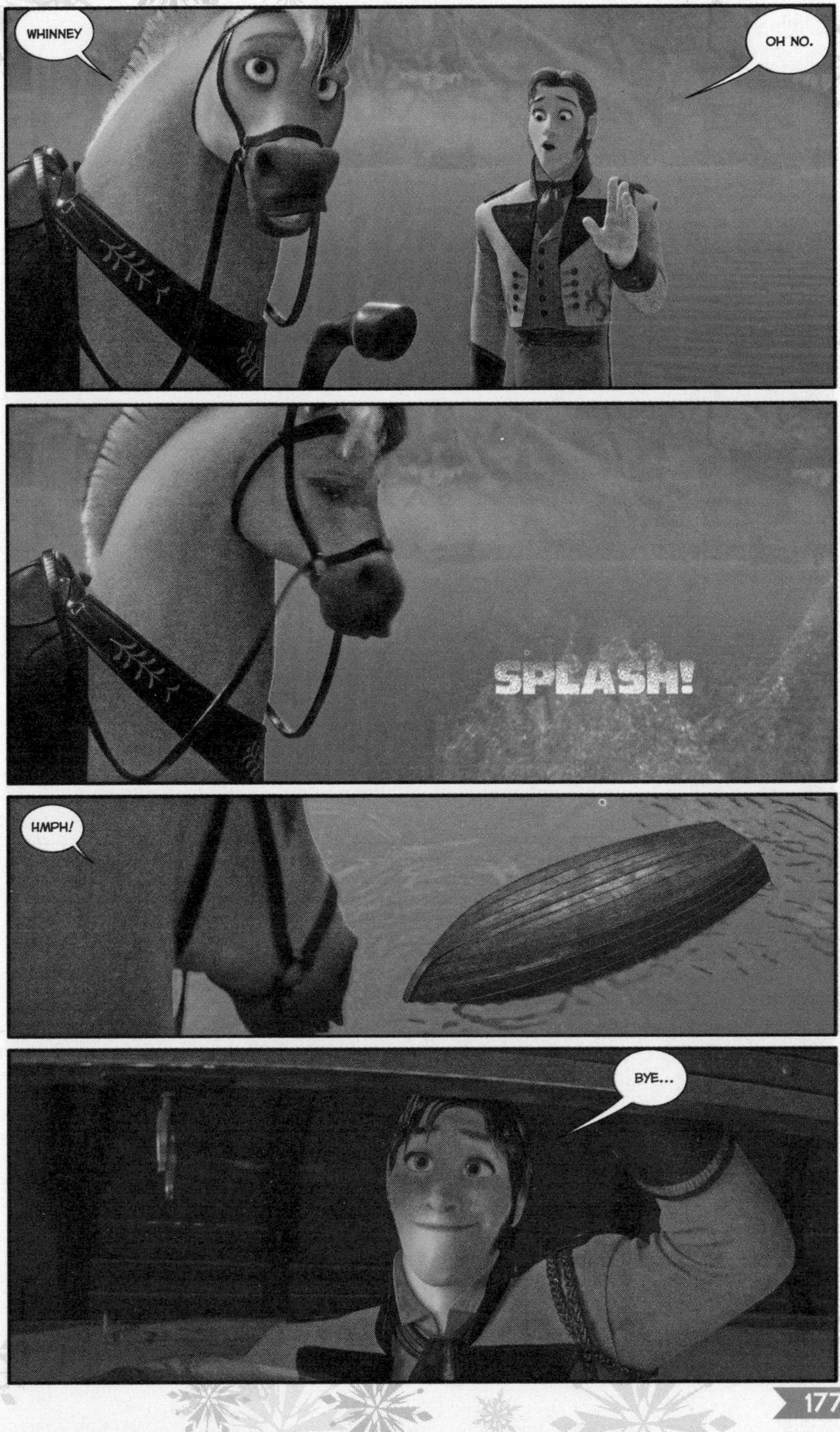
WHINNEY
OH NO.
SPLASH!
HMPH!
BYE...

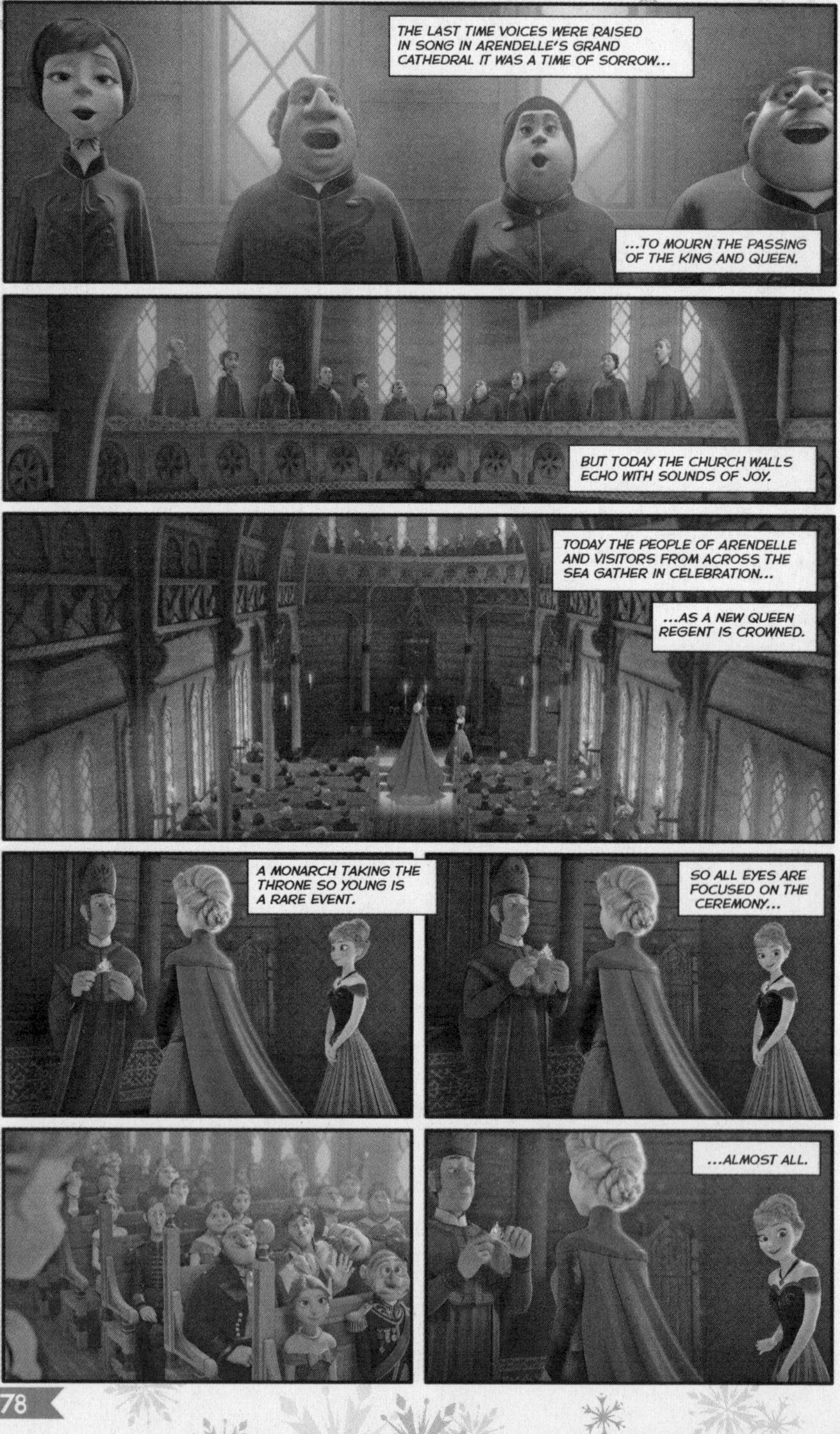
THE LAST TIME VOICES WERE RAISED IN SONG IN ARENDELLE'S GRAND CATHEDRAL IT WAS A TIME OF SORROW...
...TO MOURN THE PASSING OF THE KING AND QUEEN.
BUT TODAY THE CHURCH WALLS ECHO WITH SOUNDS OF JOY.
TODAY THE PEOPLE OF ARENDELLE AND VISITORS FROM ACROSS THE SEA GATHER IN CELEBRATION...
...AS A NEW QUEEN REGENT IS CROWNED.
A MONARCH TAKING THE THRONE SO YOUNG IS A RARE EVENT.
SO ALL EYES ARE FOCUSED ON THE CEREMONY...
...ALMOST ALL.

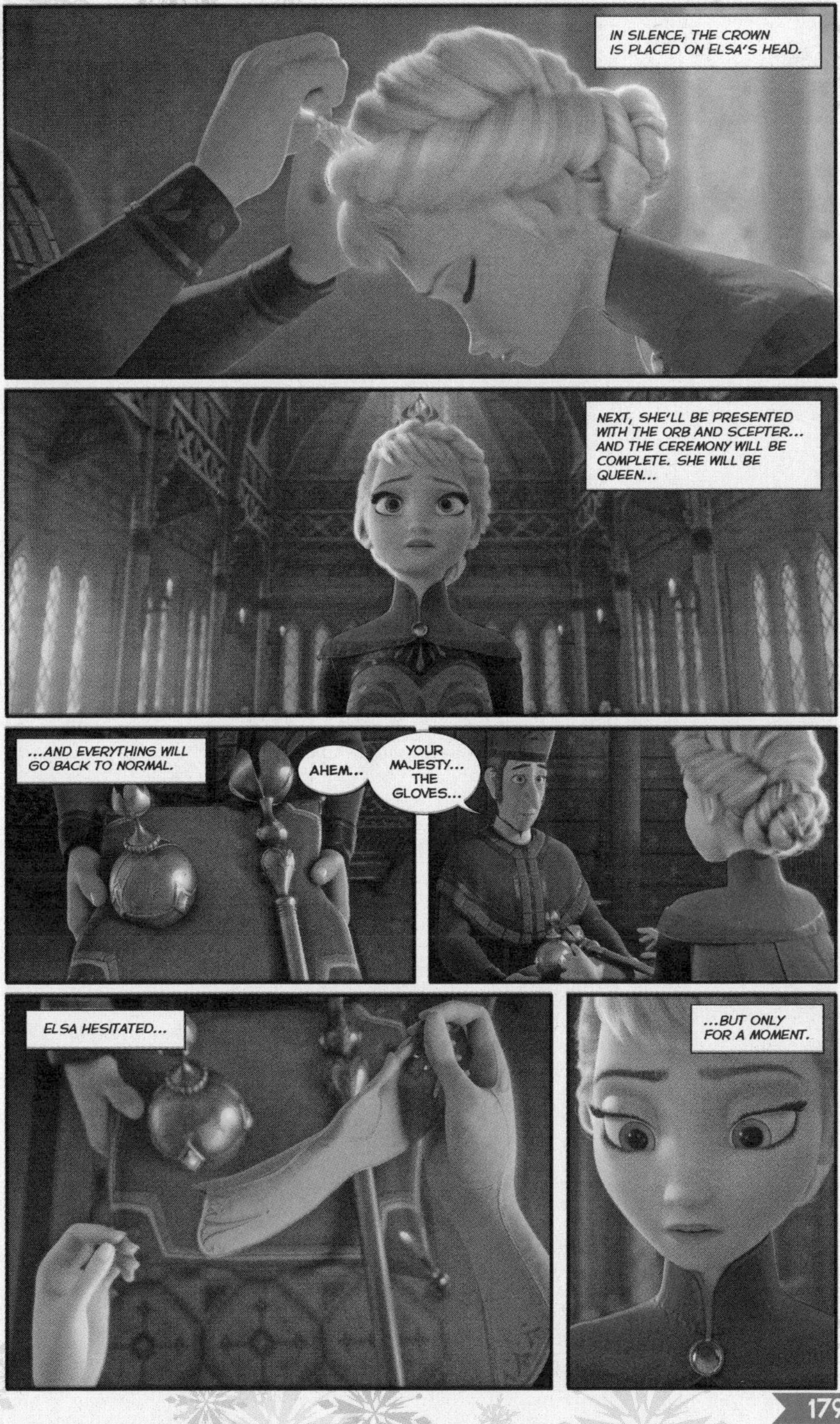
IN SILENCE, THE CROWN IS PLACED ON ELSA'S HEAD.
NEXT, SHE'LL BE PRESENTED WITH THE ORB AND SCEPTER... AND THE CEREMONY WILL BE COMPLETE. SHE WILL BE QUEEN...
...AND EVERYTHING WILL GO BACK TO NORMAL.
AHEM...
YOUR MAJESTY... THE GLOVES...
ELSA HESITATED...
...BUT ONLY FOR A MOMENT.

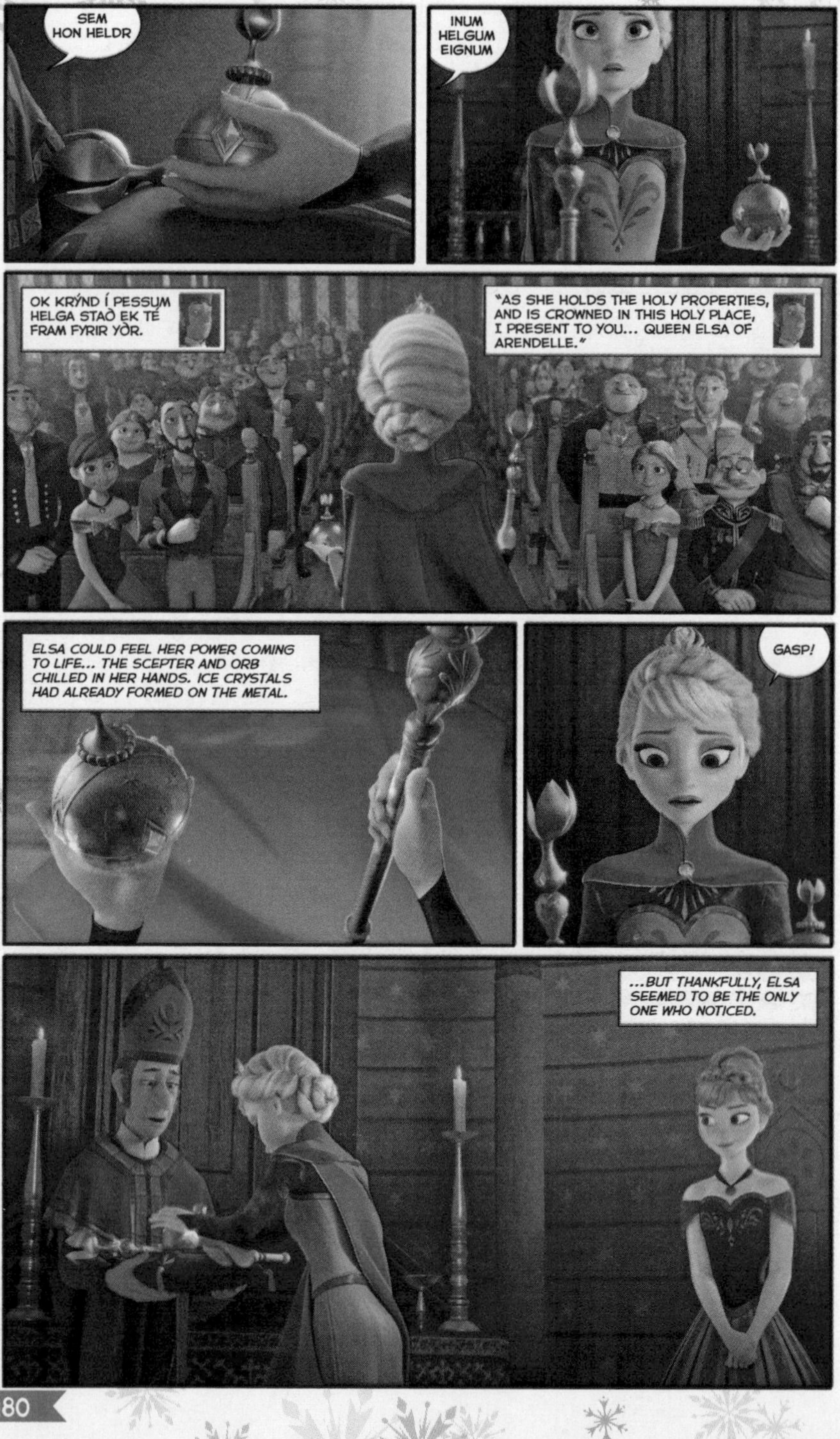
SEM HON HELDR
INUM HELGUM EIGNUM
OK KRÝND Í PESSUM HELGA STAÐ EK TÉ FRAM FYRIR YÐR.
"AS SHE HOLDS THE HOLY PROPERTIES, AND IS CROWNED IN THIS HOLY PLACE, I PRESENT TO YOU... QUEEN ELSA OF ARENDELLE."
ELSA COULD FEEL HER POWER COMING TO LIFE... THE SCEPTER AND ORB CHILLED IN HER HANDS. ICE CRYSTALS HAD ALREADY FORMED ON THE METAL.
GASP!
...BUT THANKFULLY, ELSA SEEMED TO BE THE ONLY ONE WHO NOTICED.

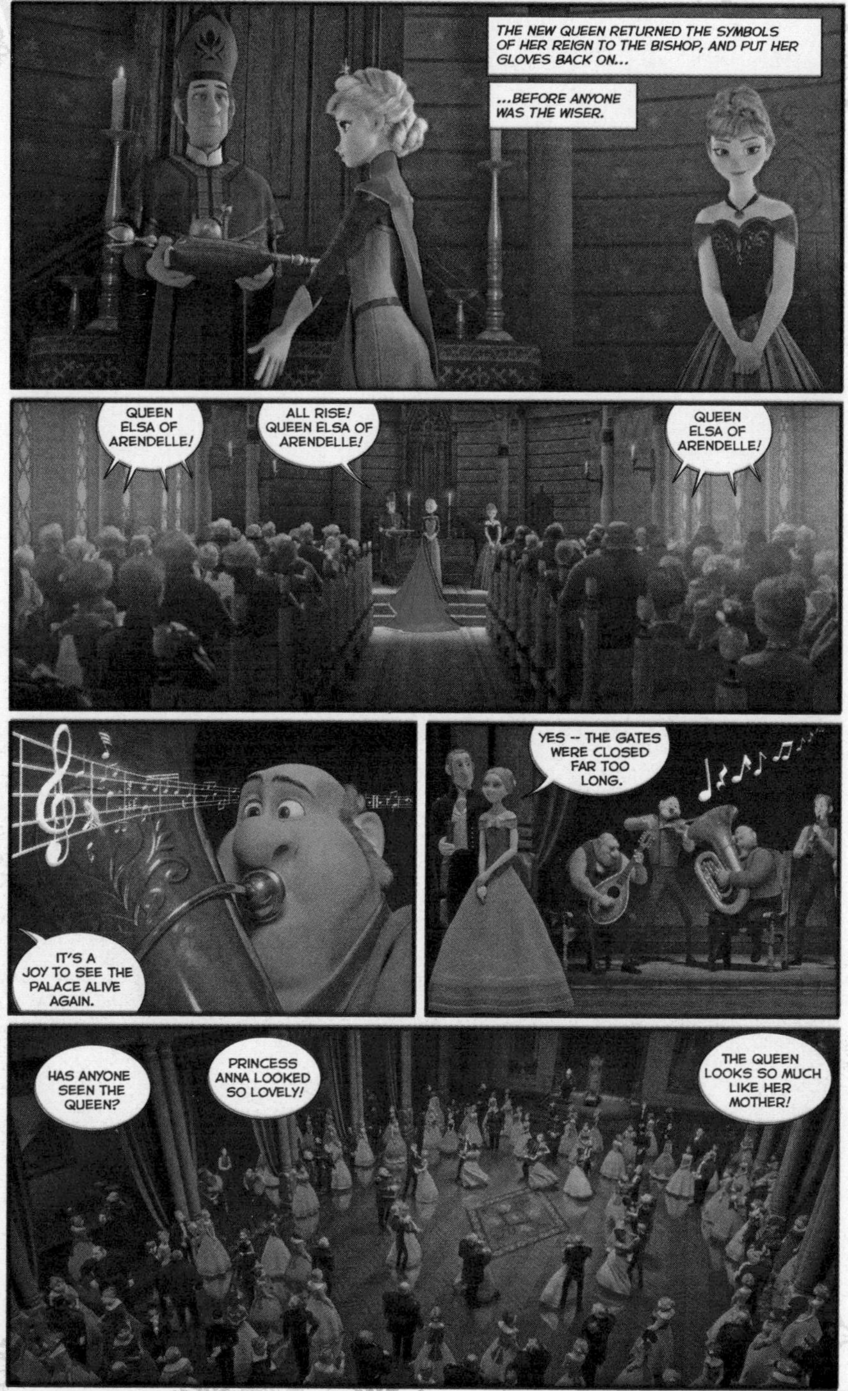
THE NEW QUEEN RETURNED THE SYMBOLS OF HER REIGN TO THE BISHOP, AND PUT HER GLOVES BACK ON...
...BEFORE ANYONE WAS THE WISER.
QUEEN ELSA OF ARENDELLE!
ALL RISE! QUEEN ELSA OF ARENDELLE!
QUEEN ELSA OF ARENDELLE!
IT'S A JOY TO SEE THE PALACE ALIVE AGAIN.
YES -- THE GATES WERE CLOSED FAR TOO LONG.
HAS ANYONE SEEN THE QUEEN?
PRINCESS ANNA LOOKED SO LOVELY!
THE QUEEN LOOKS SO MUCH LIKE HER MOTHER!

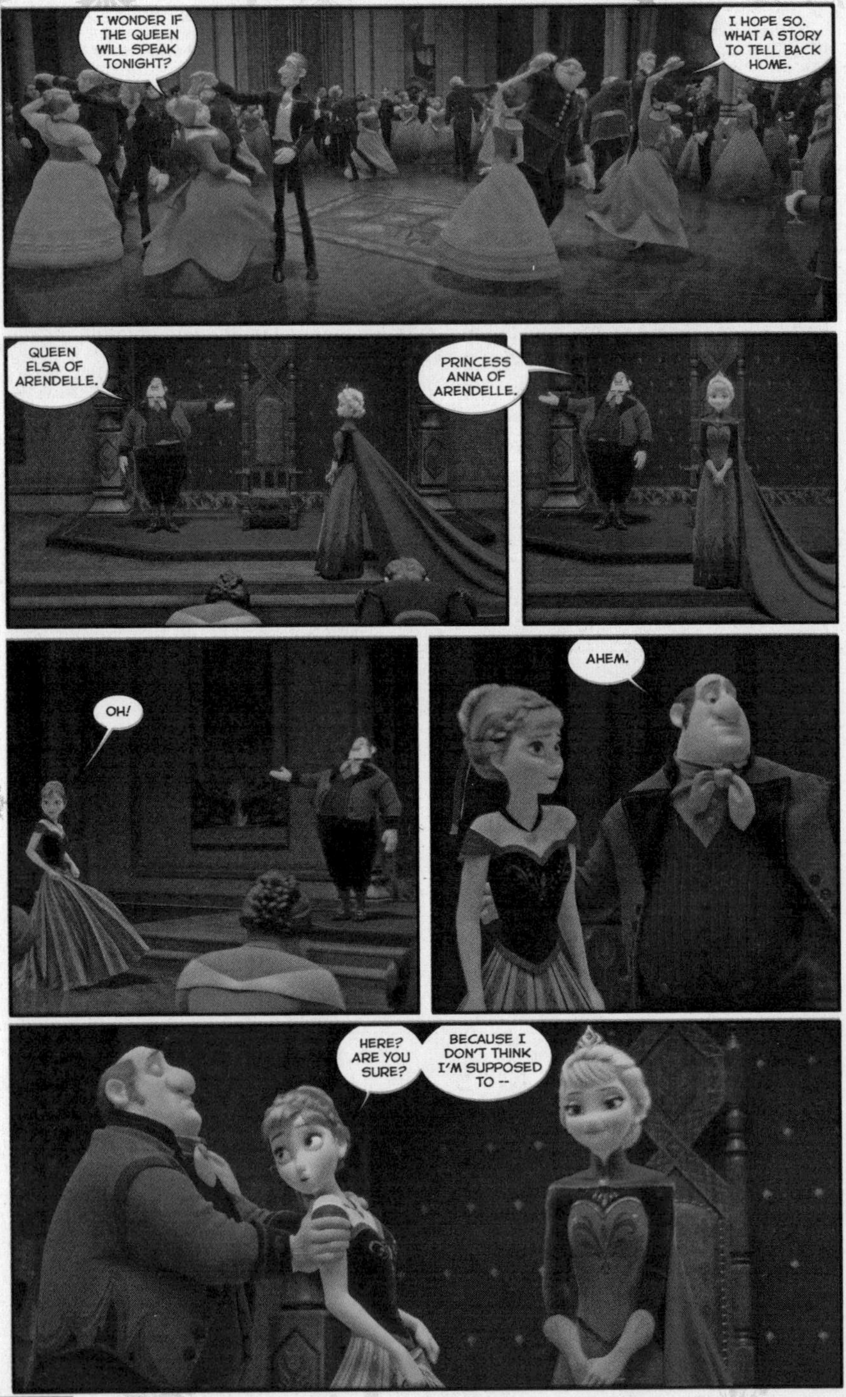
I WONDER IF THE QUEEN WILL SPEAK TONIGHT?
I HOPE SO. WHAT A STORY TO TELL BACK HOME.
QUEEN ELSA OF ARENDELLE.
PRINCESS ANNA OF ARENDELLE.
OH!
AHEM.
HERE? ARE YOU SURE?
BECAUSE I DON'T THINK I'M SUPPOSED TO --

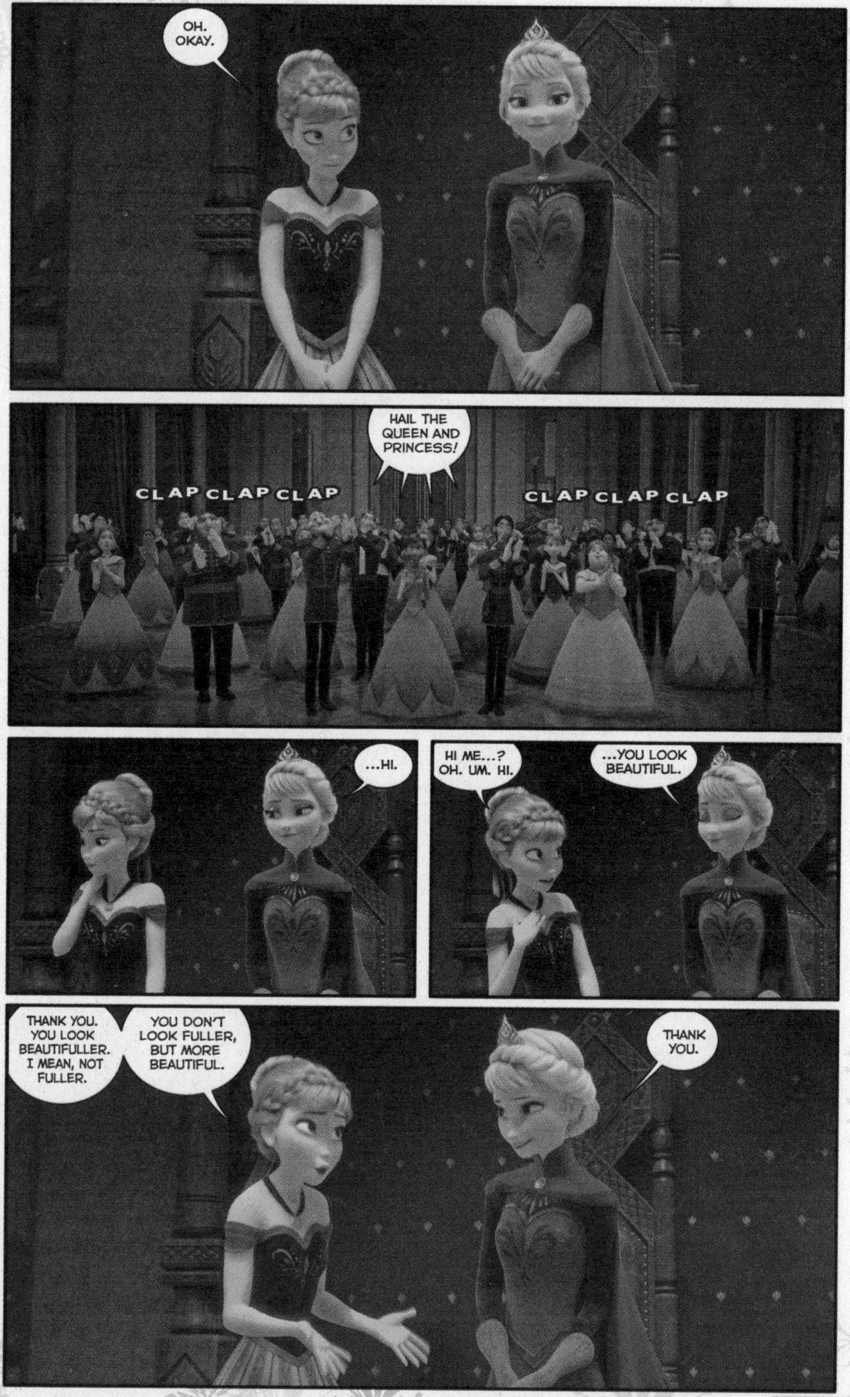
OH. OKAY.
HAIL THE QUEEN AND PRINCESS!
CLAP CLAP CLAP
CLAP CLAP CLAP
...HI.
HI ME...? OH. UM. HI.
...YOU LOOK BEAUTIFUL.
THANK YOU. YOU LOOK BEAUTIFULLER. I MEAN, NOT FULLER.
YOU DON'T LOOK FULLER, BUT MORE BEAUTIFUL.
THANK YOU.

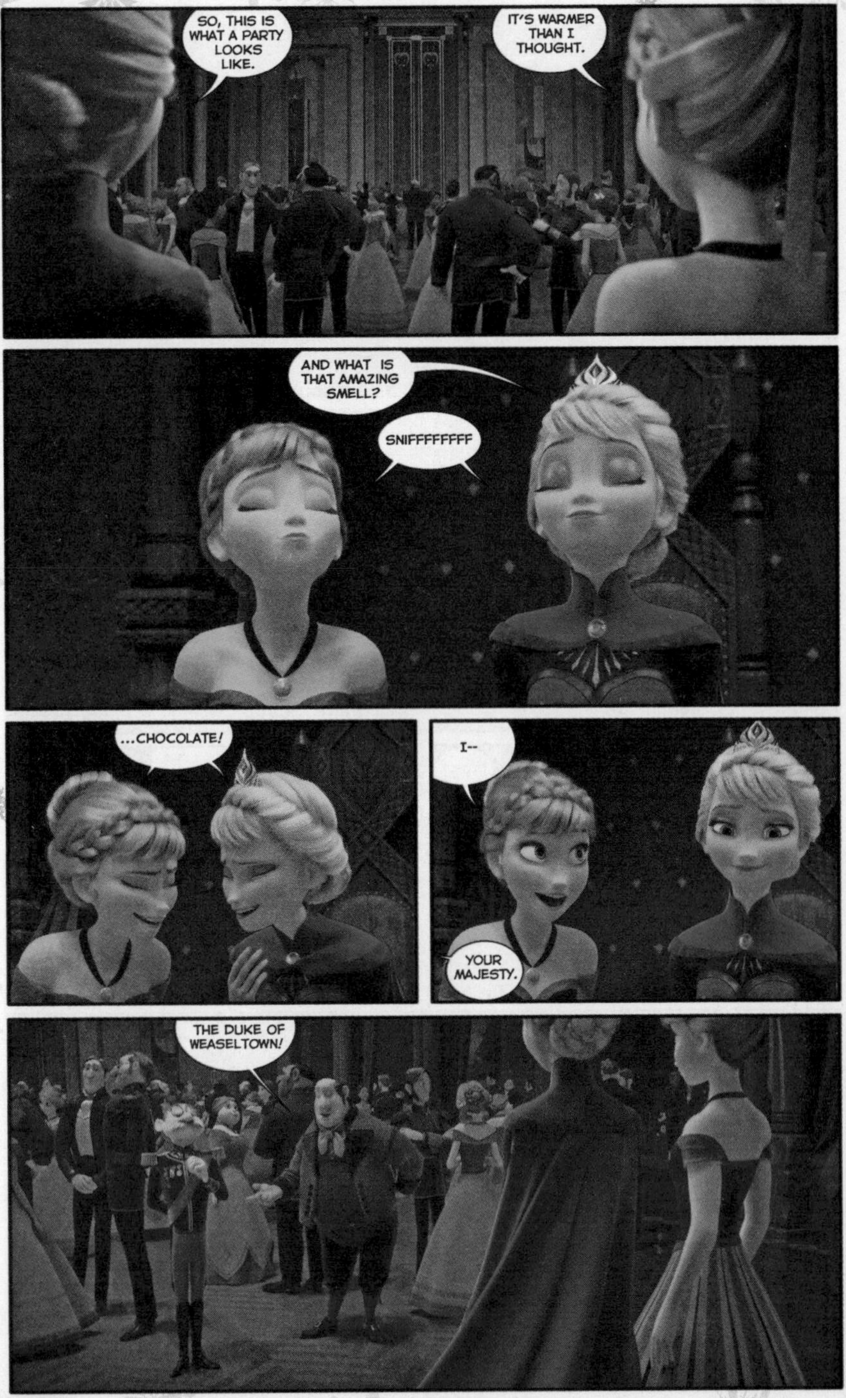
SO, THIS IS WHAT A PARTY LOOKS LIKE.
IT'S WARMER THAN I THOUGHT.
AND WHAT IS THAT AMAZING SMELL?
SNIFFFFFFFF
...CHOCOLATE!
I--
YOUR MAJESTY.
THE DUKE OF WEASELTOWN!

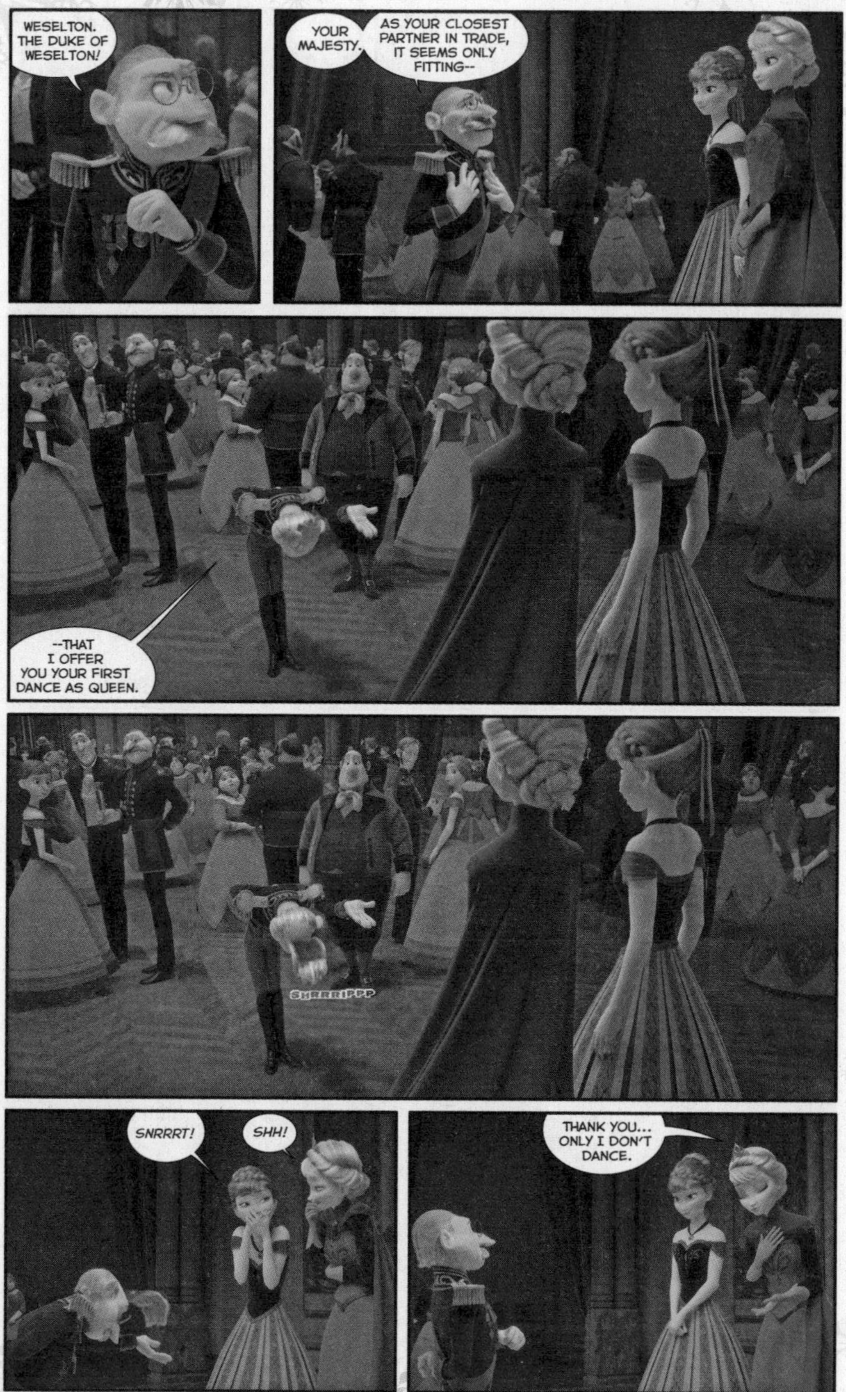
WESELTON. THE DUKE OF WESELTON!
YOUR MAJESTY.
AS YOUR CLOSEST PARTNER IN TRADE, IT SEEMS ONLY FITTING--
--THAT I OFFER YOU YOUR FIRST DANCE AS QUEEN.
SHRRRIPPP
SNRRRT!
SHH!
THANK YOU... ONLY I DON'T DANCE.

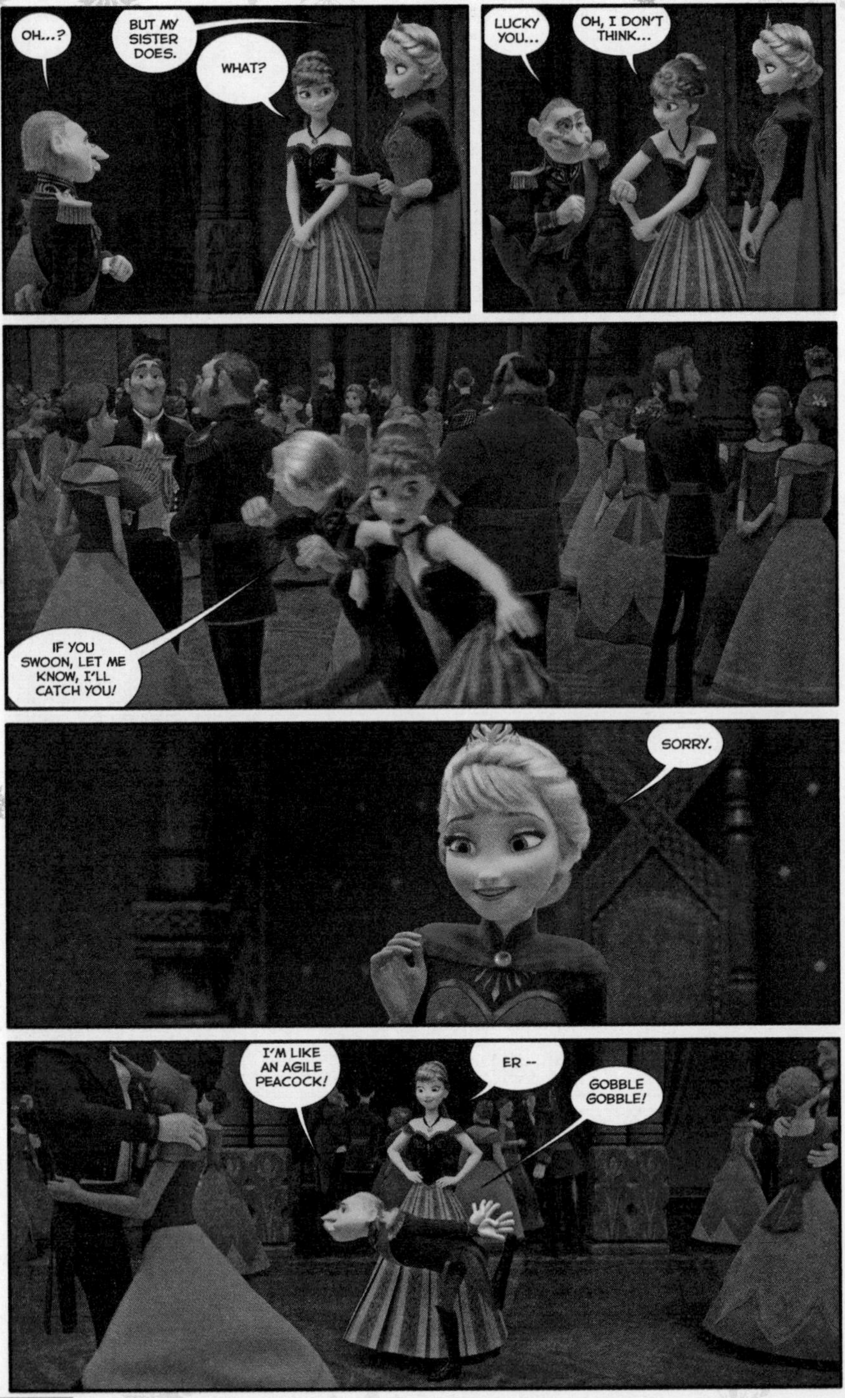
OH...?
BUT MY SISTER DOES.
WHAT?
LUCKY YOU...
OH, I DON'T THINK...
IF YOU SWOON, LET ME KNOW, I'LL CATCH YOU!
SORRY.
I'M LIKE AN AGILE PEACOCK!
ER --
GOBBLE GOBBLE!

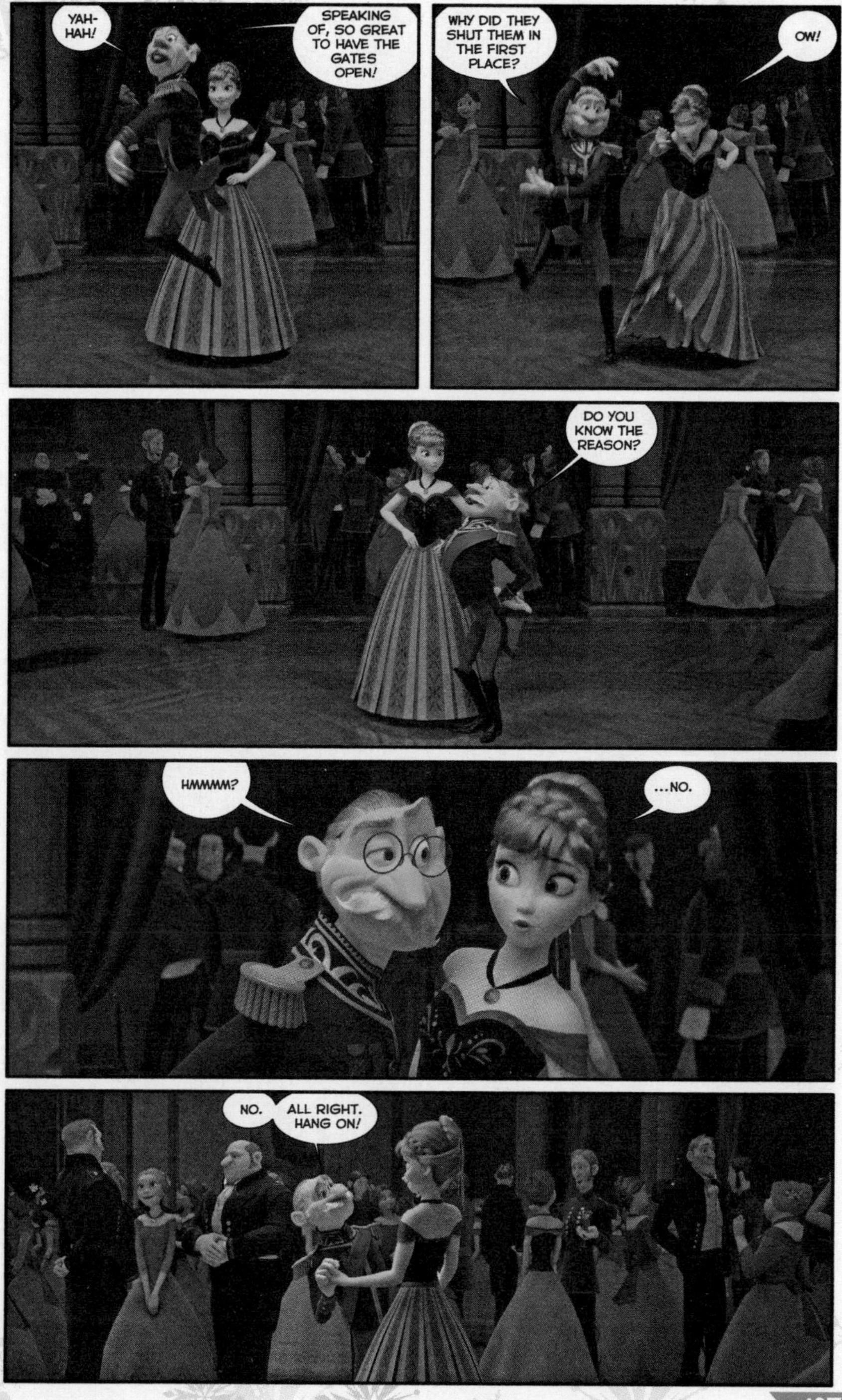
YAH-HAH!
SPEAKING OF, SO GREAT TO HAVE THE GATES OPEN!
WHY DID THEY SHUT THEM IN THE FIRST PLACE?
OW!
DO YOU KNOW THE REASON?
HMMMM?
...NO.
NO.
ALL RIGHT. HANG ON!

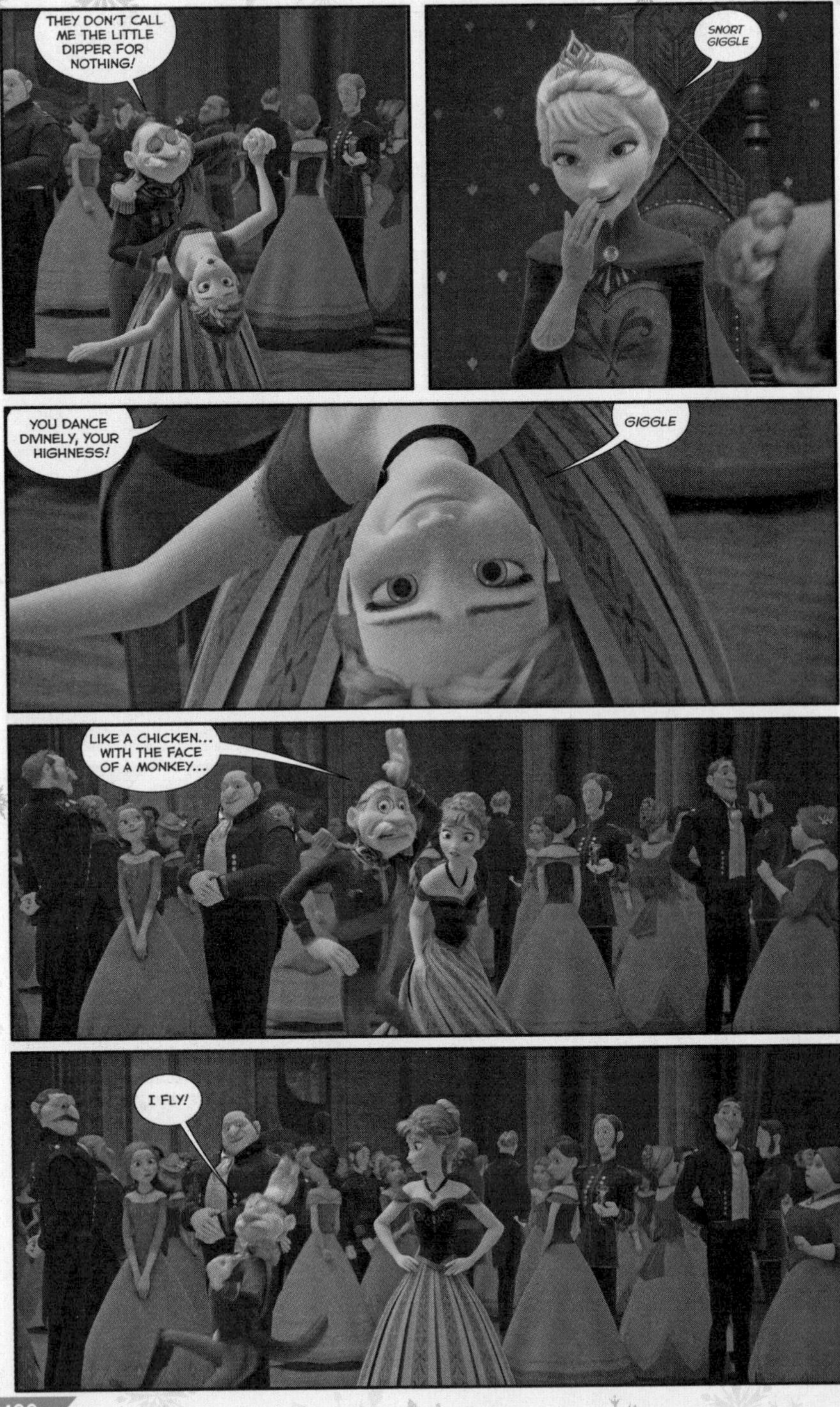
THEY DON'T CALL ME THE LITTLE DIPPER FOR NOTHING!
SNORT GIGGLE
YOU DANCE DIVINELY, YOUR HIGHNESS!
GIGGLE
LIKE A CHICKEN... WITH THE FACE OF A MONKEY...
I FLY!

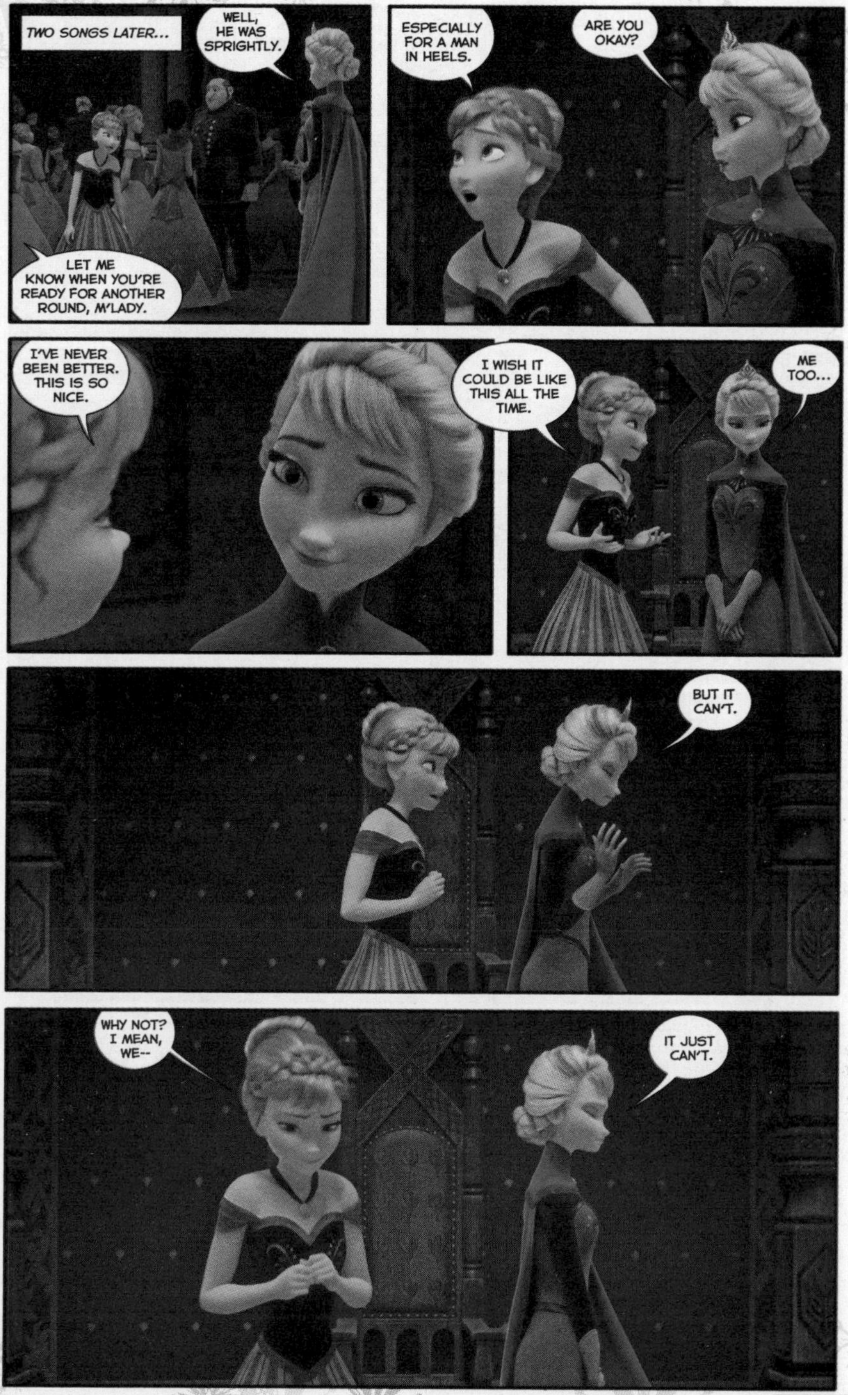
TWO SONGS LATER...
WELL, HE WAS SPRIGHTLY.
LET ME KNOW WHEN YOU'RE READY FOR ANOTHER ROUND, M'LADY.
ESPECIALLY FOR A MAN IN HEELS.
ARE YOU OKAY?
I'VE NEVER BEEN BETTER. THIS IS SO NICE.
I WISH IT COULD BE LIKE THIS ALL THE TIME.
ME TOO...
BUT IT CAN'T.
WHY NOT? I MEAN, WE--
IT JUST CAN'T.

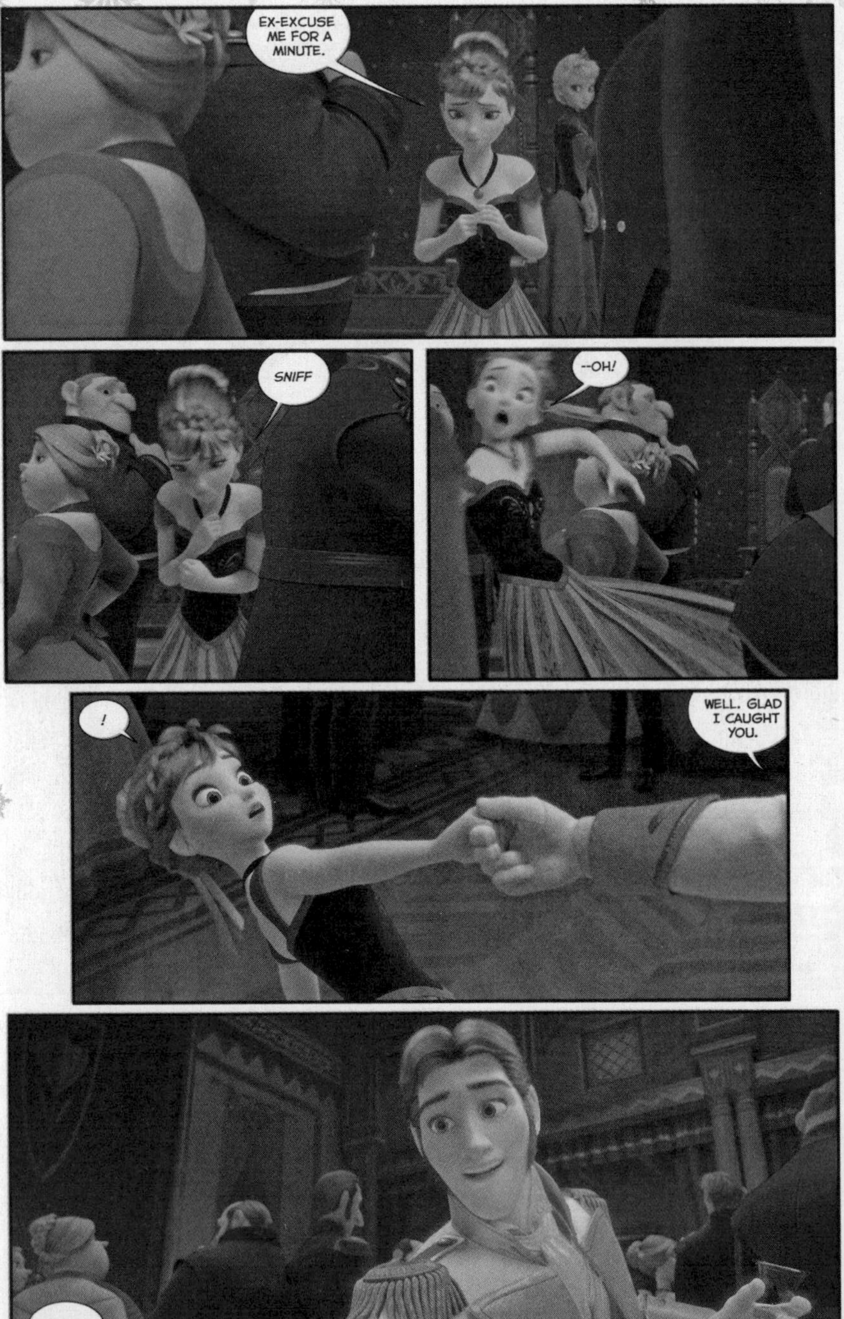
EX-EXCUSE ME FOR A MINUTE.
SNIFF
--OH!
!
WELL. GLAD I CAUGHT YOU.
HANS!

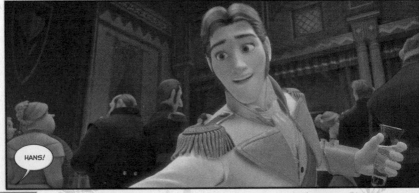

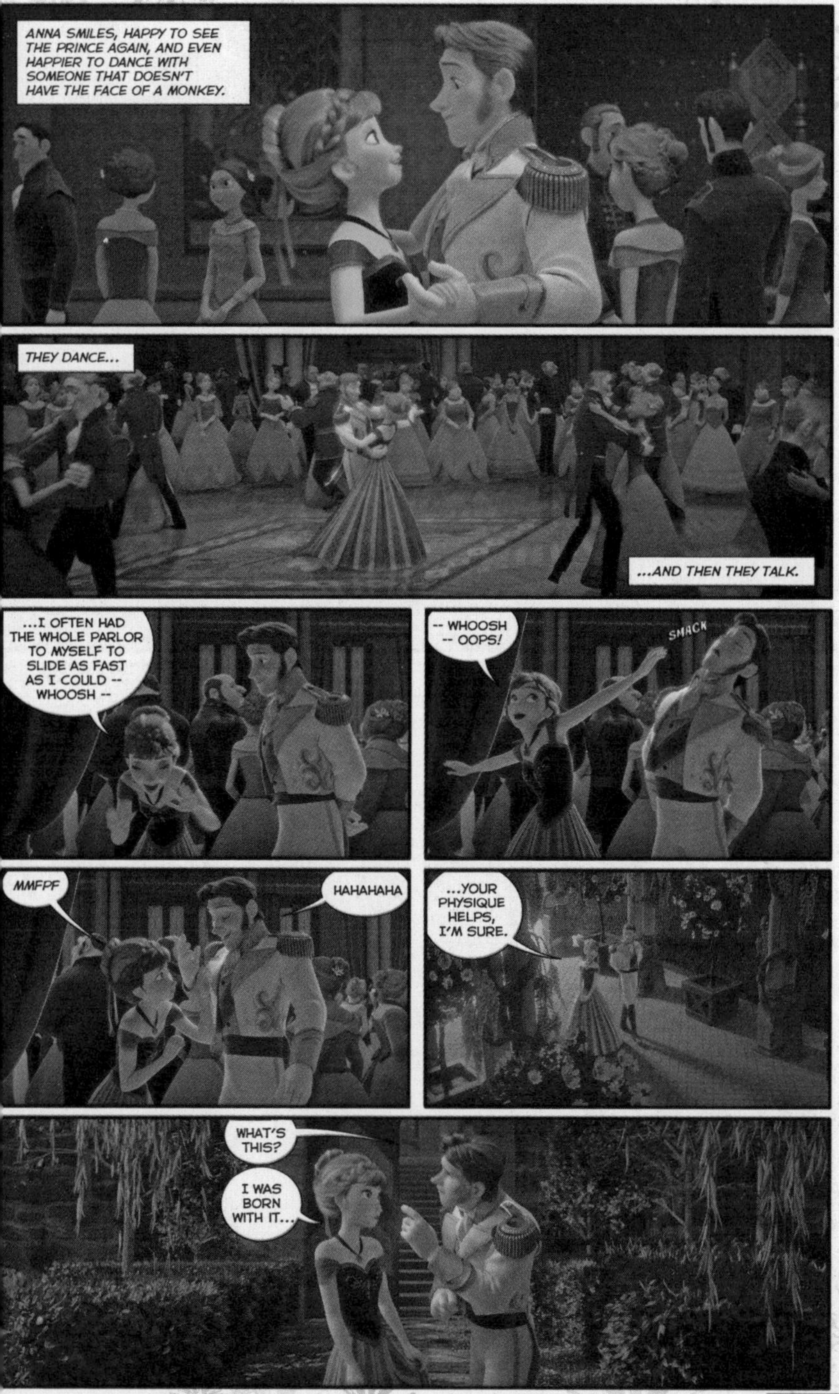
ANNA SMILES, HAPPY TO SEE THE PRINCE AGAIN, AND EVEN HAPPIER TO DANCE WITH SOMEONE THAT DOESN'T HAVE THE FACE OF A MONKEY.
THEY DANCE...
...AND THEN THEY TALK.
...I OFTEN HAD THE WHOLE PARLOR TO MYSELF TO SLIDE AS FAST AS I COULD -- WHOOSH --
-- WHOOSH -- OOPS!
SMACK
MMFPF
HAHAHAHA
...YOUR PHYSIQUE HELPS, I'M SURE.
WHAT'S THIS?
I WAS BORN WITH IT...

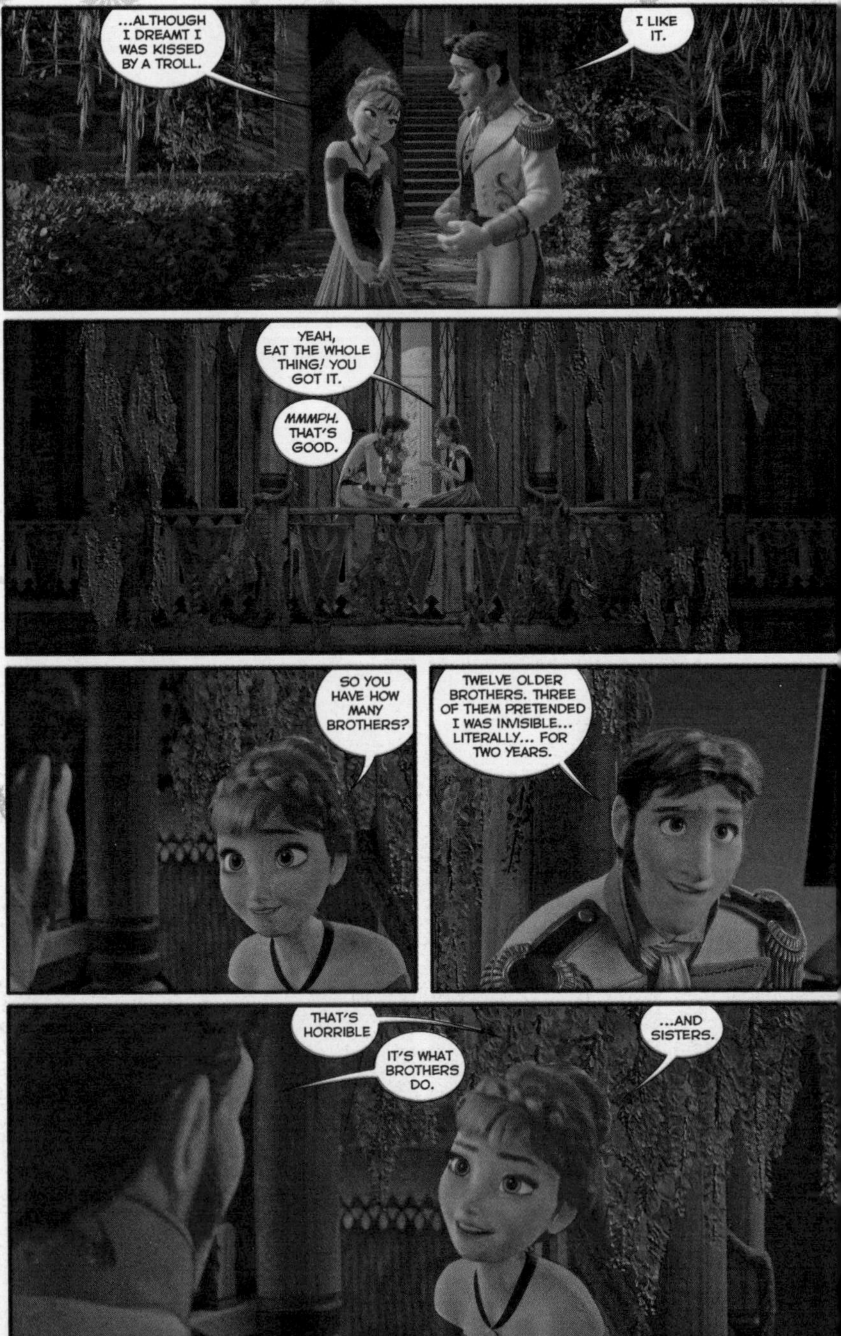
...ALTHOUGH I DREAMT I WAS KISSED BY A TROLL.
I LIKE IT.
YEAH, EAT THE WHOLE THING! YOU GOT IT.
MMMPH. THAT'S GOOD.
SO YOU HAVE HOW MANY BROTHERS?
TWELVE OLDER BROTHERS. THREE OF THEM PRETENDED I WAS INVISIBLE... LITERALLY... FOR TWO YEARS.
THAT'S HORRIBLE
IT'S WHAT BROTHERS DO.
...AND SISTERS.

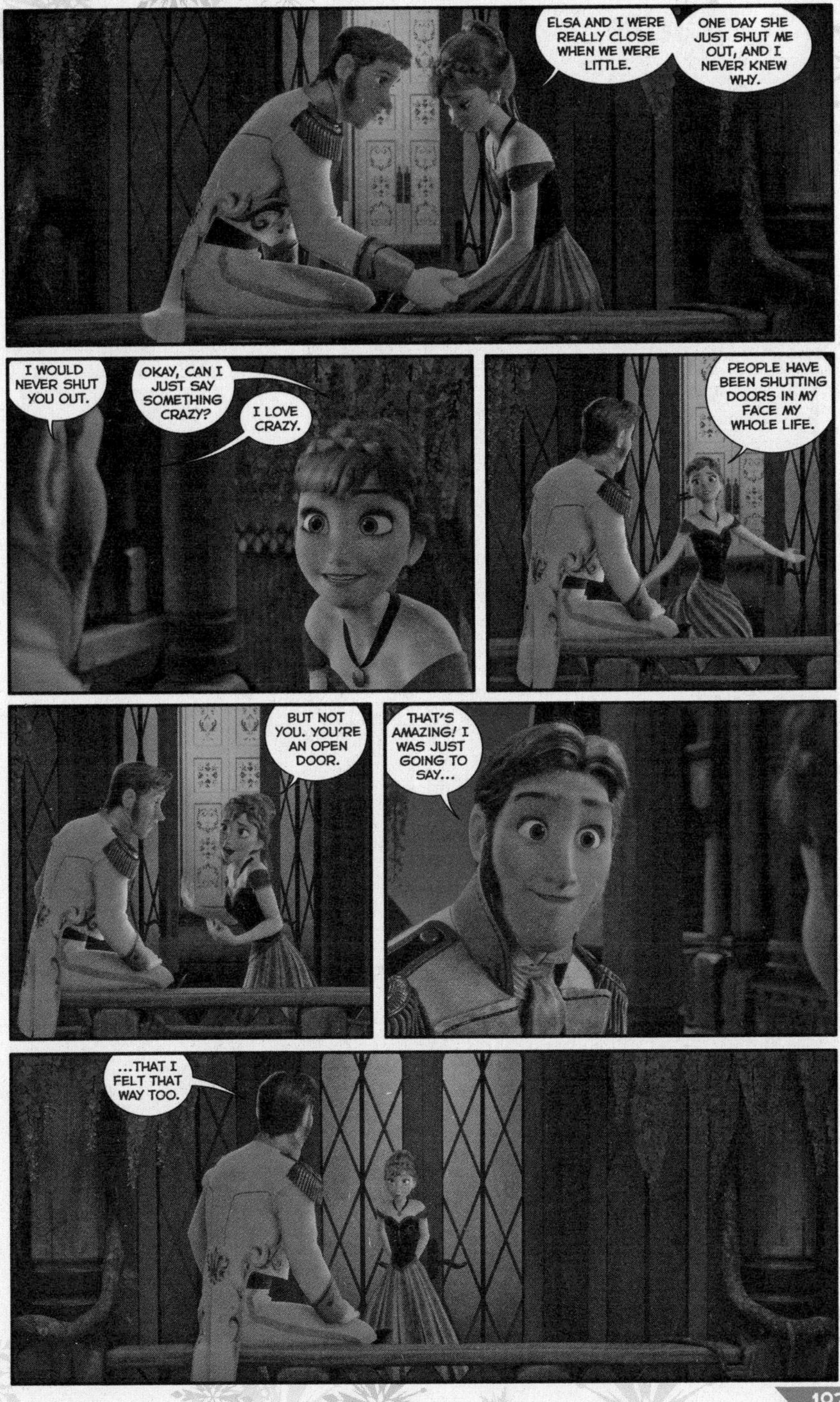
ELSA AND I WERE REALLY CLOSE WHEN WE WERE LITTLE.
ONE DAY SHE JUST SHUT ME OUT, AND I NEVER KNEW WHY.
I WOULD NEVER SHUT YOU OUT.
OKAY, CAN I JUST SAY SOMETHING CRAZY?
I LOVE CRAZY.
PEOPLE HAVE BEEN SHUTTING DOORS IN MY FACE MY WHOLE LIFE.
BUT NOT YOU. YOU'RE AN OPEN DOOR.
THAT'S AMAZING! I WAS JUST GOING TO SAY...
...THAT I FELT THAT WAY TOO.

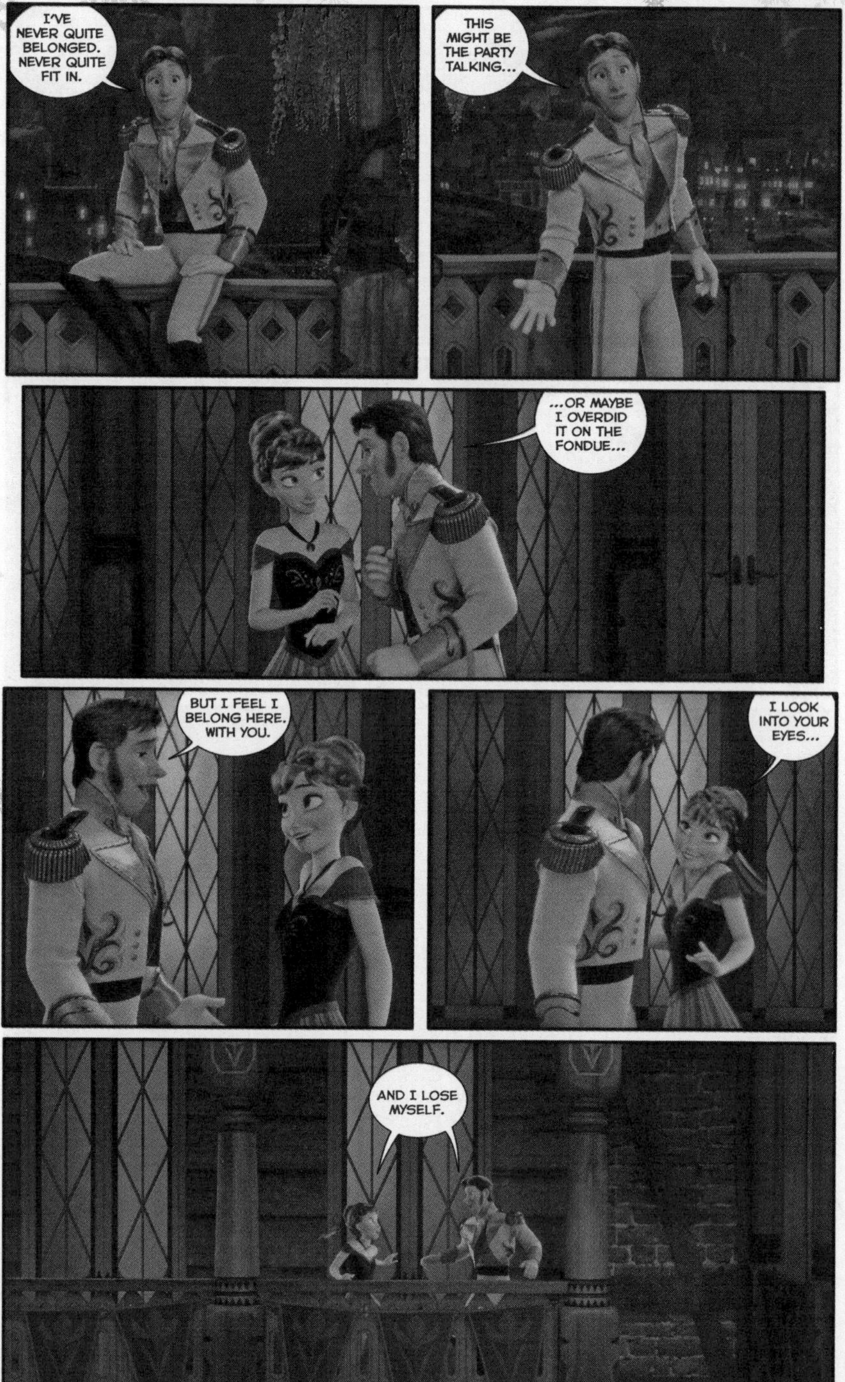
I'VE NEVER QUITE BELONGED. NEVER QUITE FIT IN.
THIS MIGHT BE THE PARTY TALKING...
...OR MAYBE I OVERDID IT ON THE FONDUE...
BUT I FEEL I BELONG HERE. WITH YOU.
I LOOK INTO YOUR EYES...
AND I LOSE MYSELF.

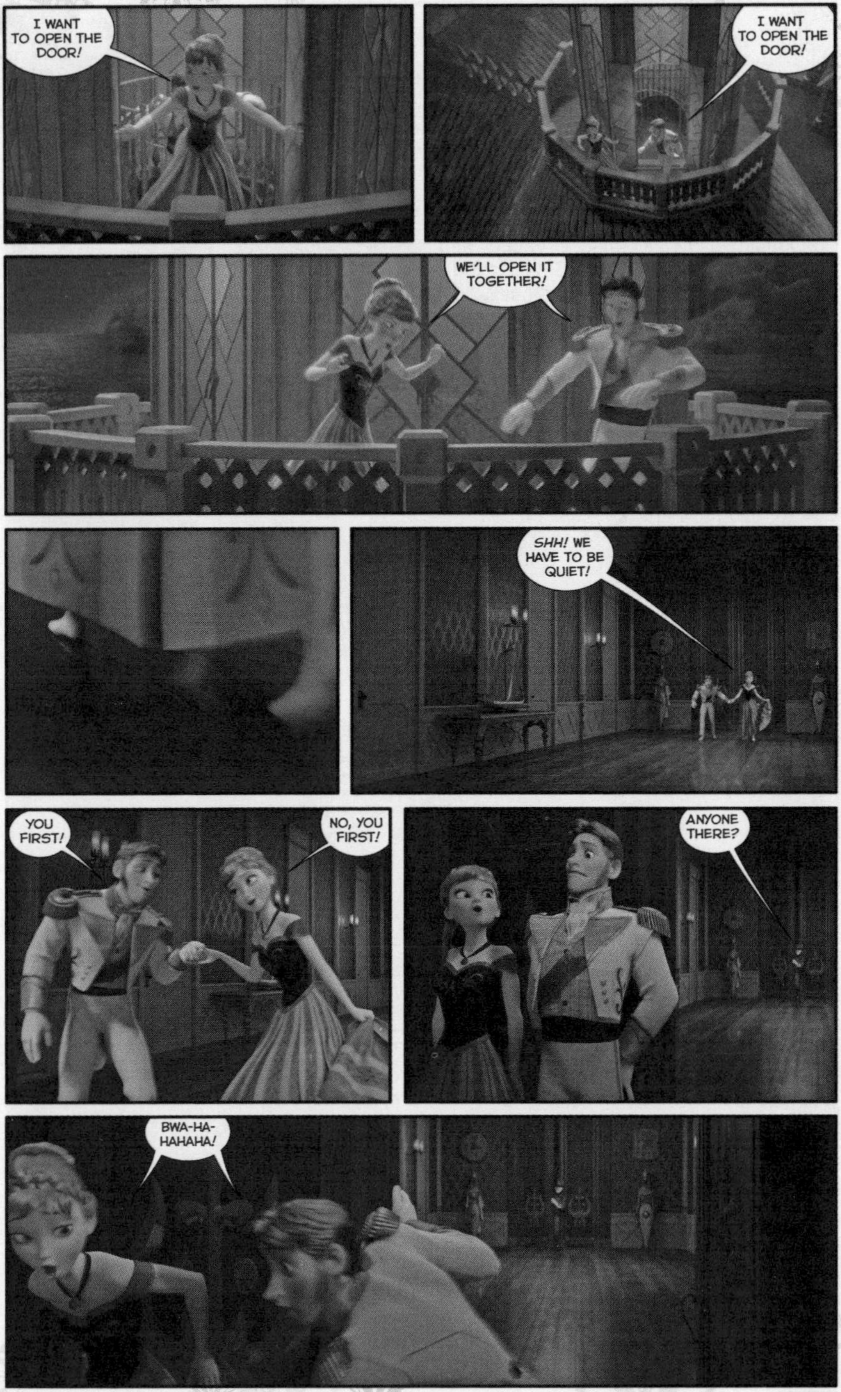
I WANT TO OPEN THE DOOR!
I WANT TO OPEN THE DOOR!
WE'LL OPEN IT TOGETHER!
SHH! WE HAVE TO BE QUIET!
YOU FIRST!
NO, YOU FIRST!
ANYONE THERE?
BWA-HA-HAHAHA!

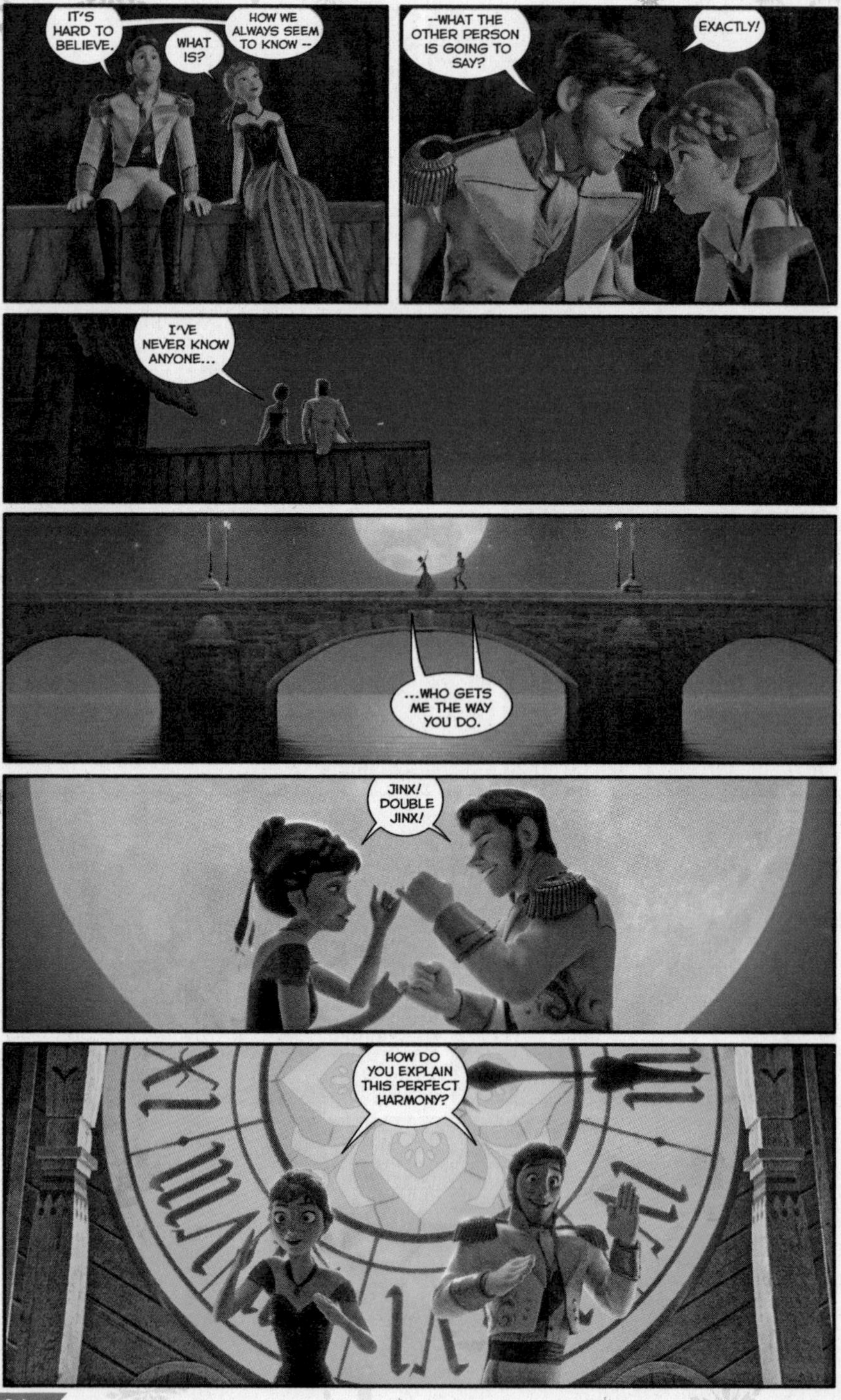
IT'S HARD TO BELIEVE.
WHAT IS?
HOW WE ALWAYS SEEM TO KNOW --
--WHAT THE OTHER PERSON IS GOING TO SAY?
EXACTLY!
I'VE NEVER KNOW ANYONE...
...WHO GETS ME THE WAY YOU DO.
JINX! DOUBLE JINX!
HOW DO YOU EXPLAIN THIS PERFECT HARMONY?

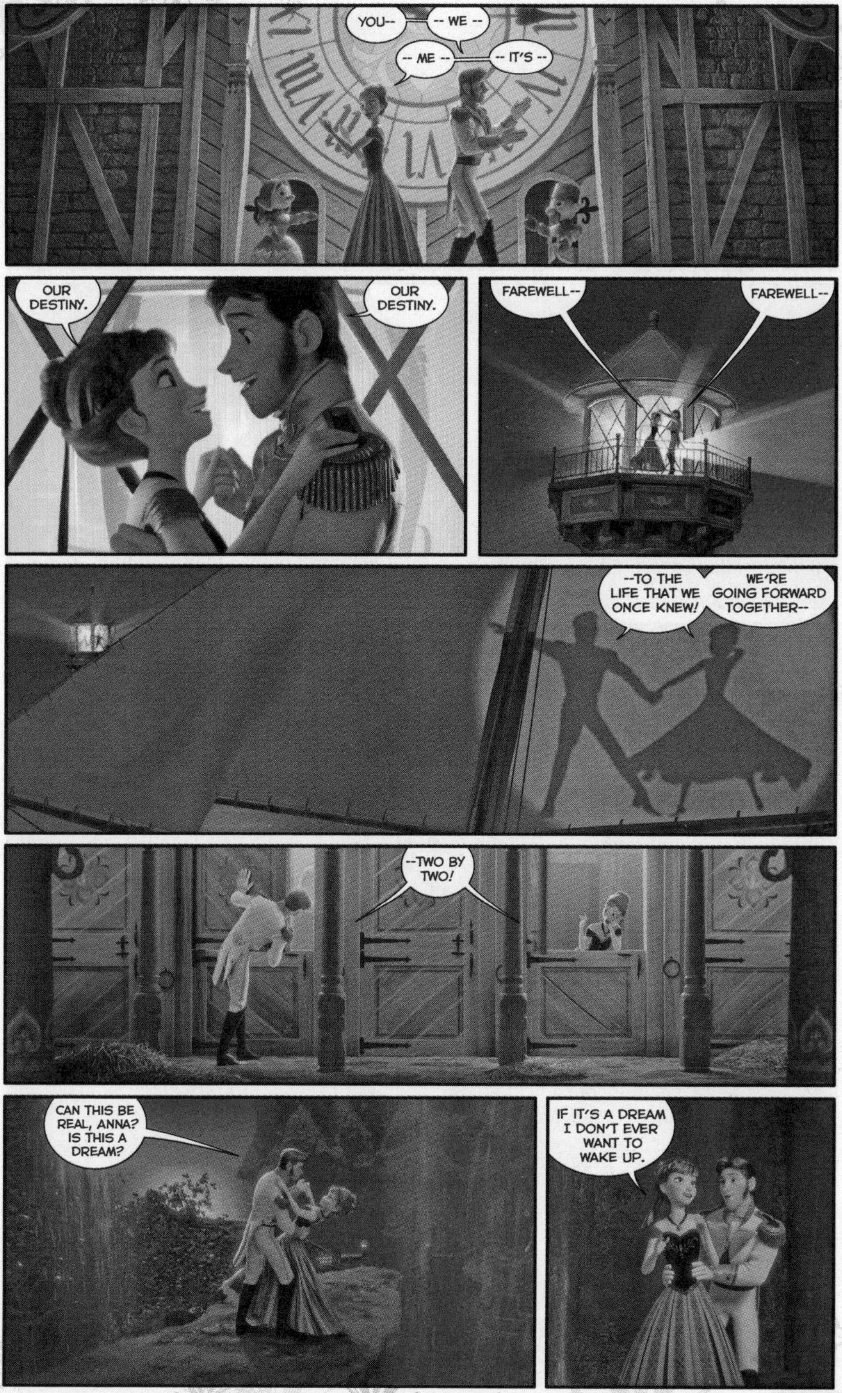
YOU--
-- WE --
-- ME --
-- IT'S --
OUR DESTINY.
OUR DESTINY.
FAREWELL--
FAREWELL--
WE'RE GOING FORWARD TOGETHER--
--TO THE LIFE THAT WE ONCE KNEW!
--TWO BY TWO!
CAN THIS BE REAL, ANNA? IS THIS A DREAM?
IF IT'S A DREAM I DON'T EVER WANT TO WAKE UP.

MY LIFE IS SO MUCH BETTER --

SINCE...

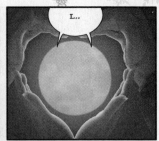

I...

...MET YOU!

SO THIS IS WHAT LOVE IS?

YEAH, I THINK SO.

CAN I SAY SOMETHING CRAZY...?

WILL YOU MARRY ME?

CAN I JUST SAY SOMETHING EVEN CRAZIER?

YES.

Cinestory Scene #4 "Elsa Finds Herself"

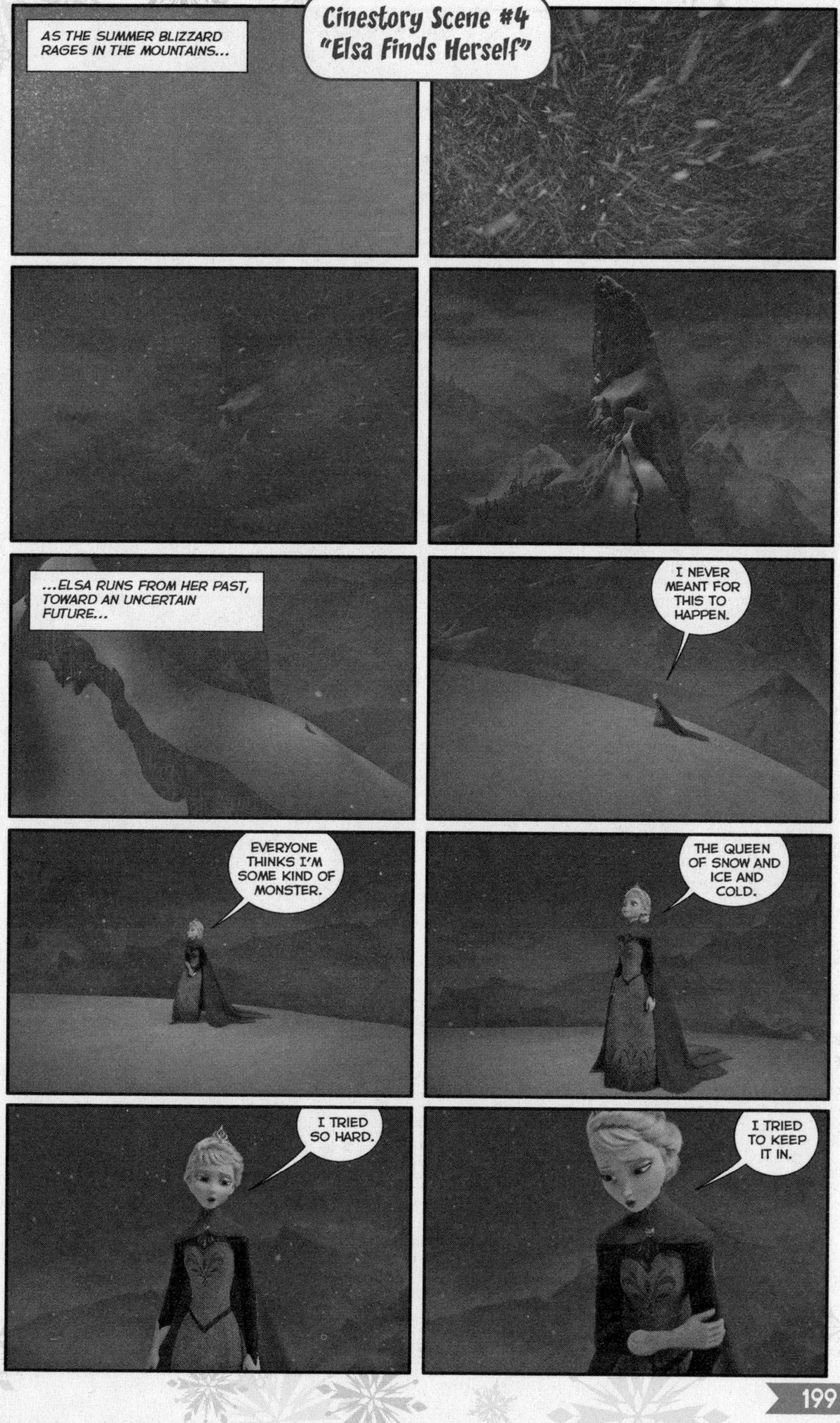
AS THE SUMMER BLIZZARD RAGES IN THE MOUNTAINS...
...ELSA RUNS FROM HER PAST, TOWARD AN UNCERTAIN FUTURE...
I NEVER MEANT FOR THIS TO HAPPEN.
EVERYONE THINKS I'M SOME KIND OF MONSTER.
THE QUEEN OF SNOW AND ICE AND COLD.
I TRIED SO HARD.
I TRIED TO KEEP IT IN.

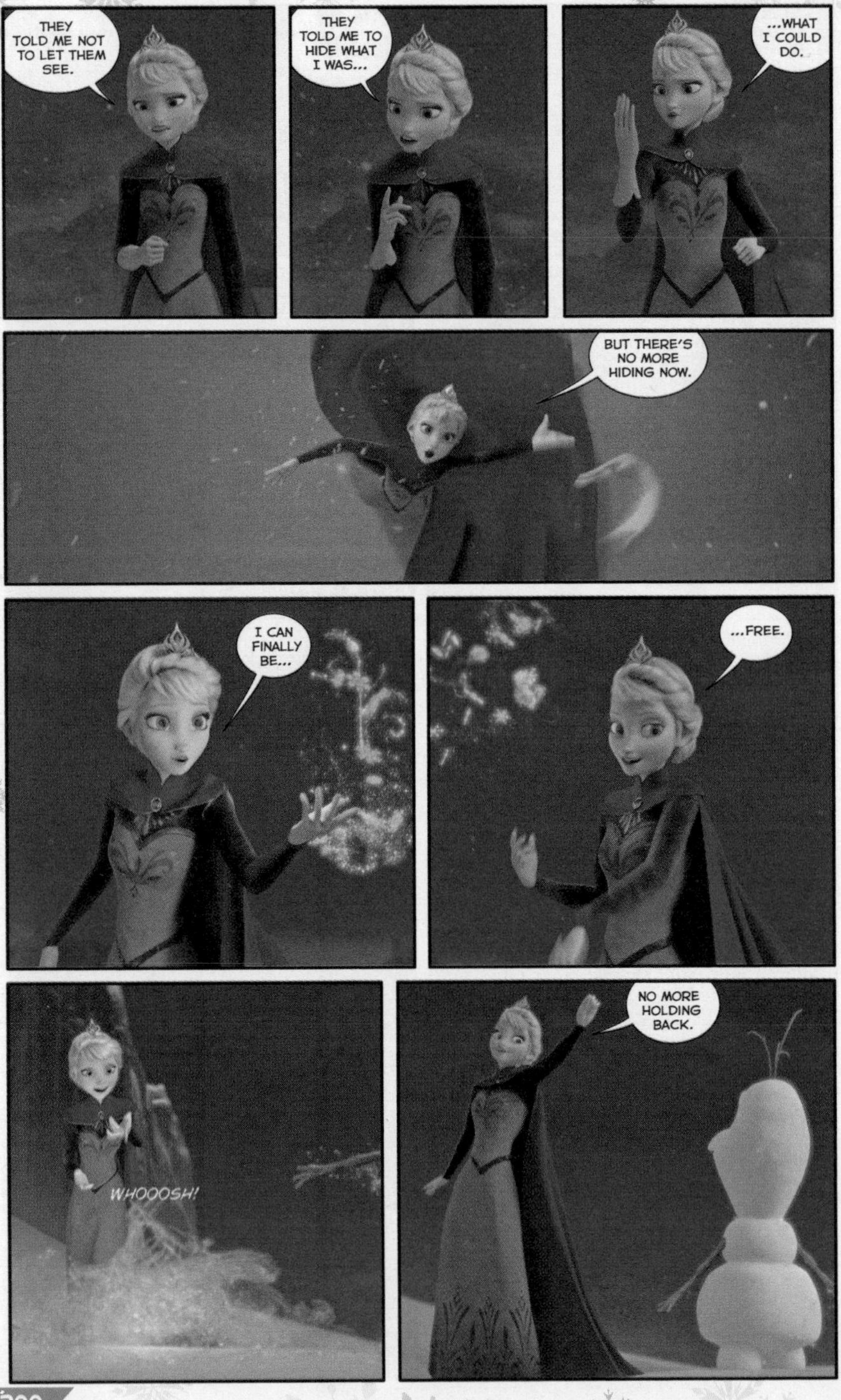
THEY TOLD ME NOT TO LET THEM SEE.
THEY TOLD ME TO HIDE WHAT I WAS...
...WHAT I COULD DO.
BUT THERE'S NO MORE HIDING NOW.
I CAN FINALLY BE...
...FREE.
WHOOOSH!
NO MORE HOLDING BACK.

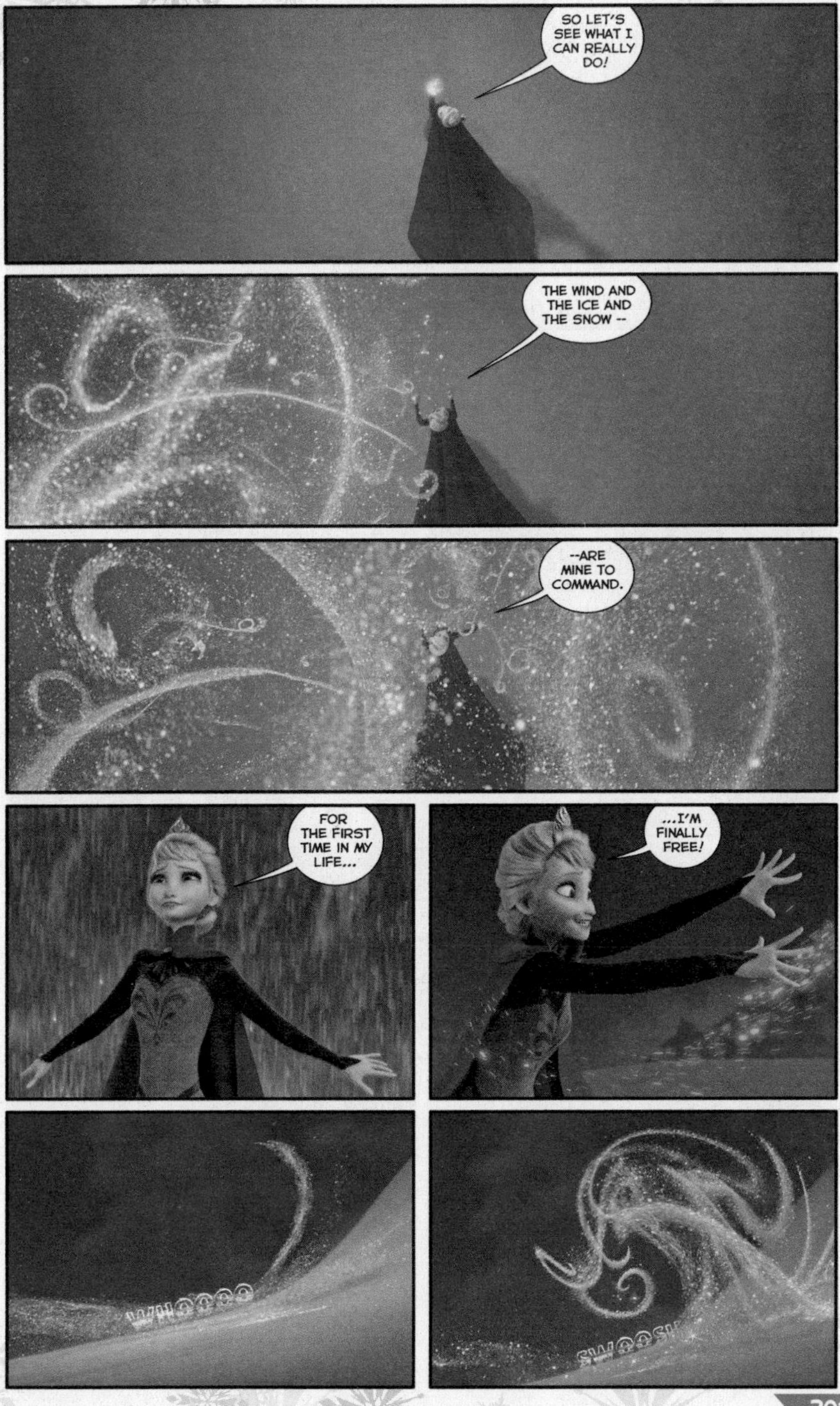
SO LET'S SEE WHAT I CAN REALLY DO!
THE WIND AND THE ICE AND THE SNOW --
--ARE MINE TO COMMAND.
FOR THE FIRST TIME IN MY LIFE...
...I'M FINALLY FREE!
WHOOOO
SWOOSH

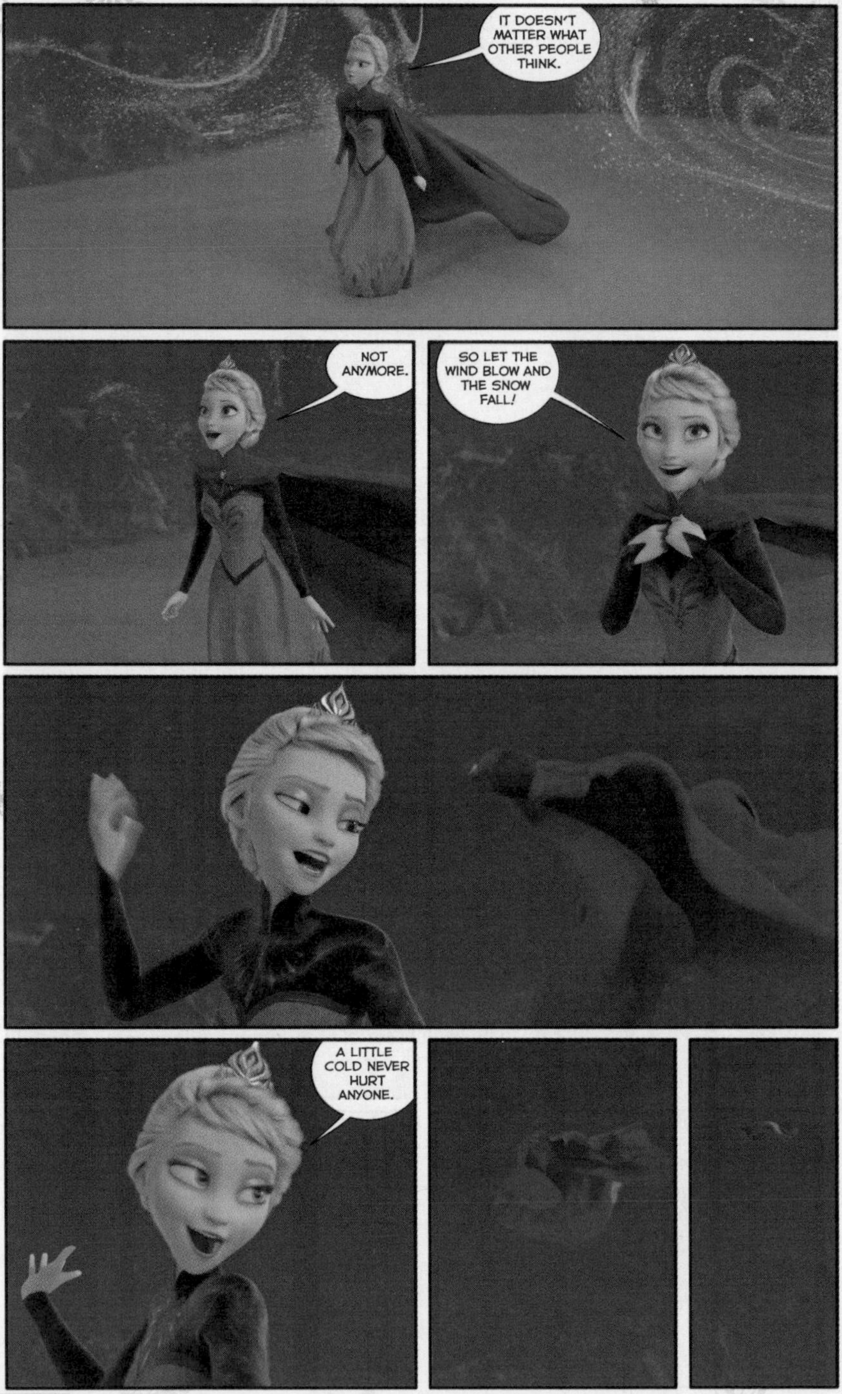
IT DOESN'T MATTER WHAT OTHER PEOPLE THINK.
NOT ANYMORE.
SO LET THE WIND BLOW AND THE SNOW FALL!
A LITTLE COLD NEVER HURT ANYONE.

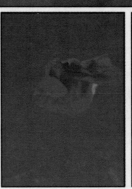

FROM WAY UP HERE...

...EVERYTHING LOOKS SO... DIFFERENT.

IT'S LIKE I'M SEEING CLEARLY FOR THE FIRST TIME.

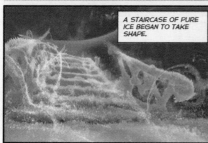

A STAIRCASE OF PURE ICE BEGAN TO TAKE SHAPE.

ONE THAT WOULD TAKE HERE EVER HIGHER INTO THE MOUNTAINS.

THIS IS INCREDIBLE!

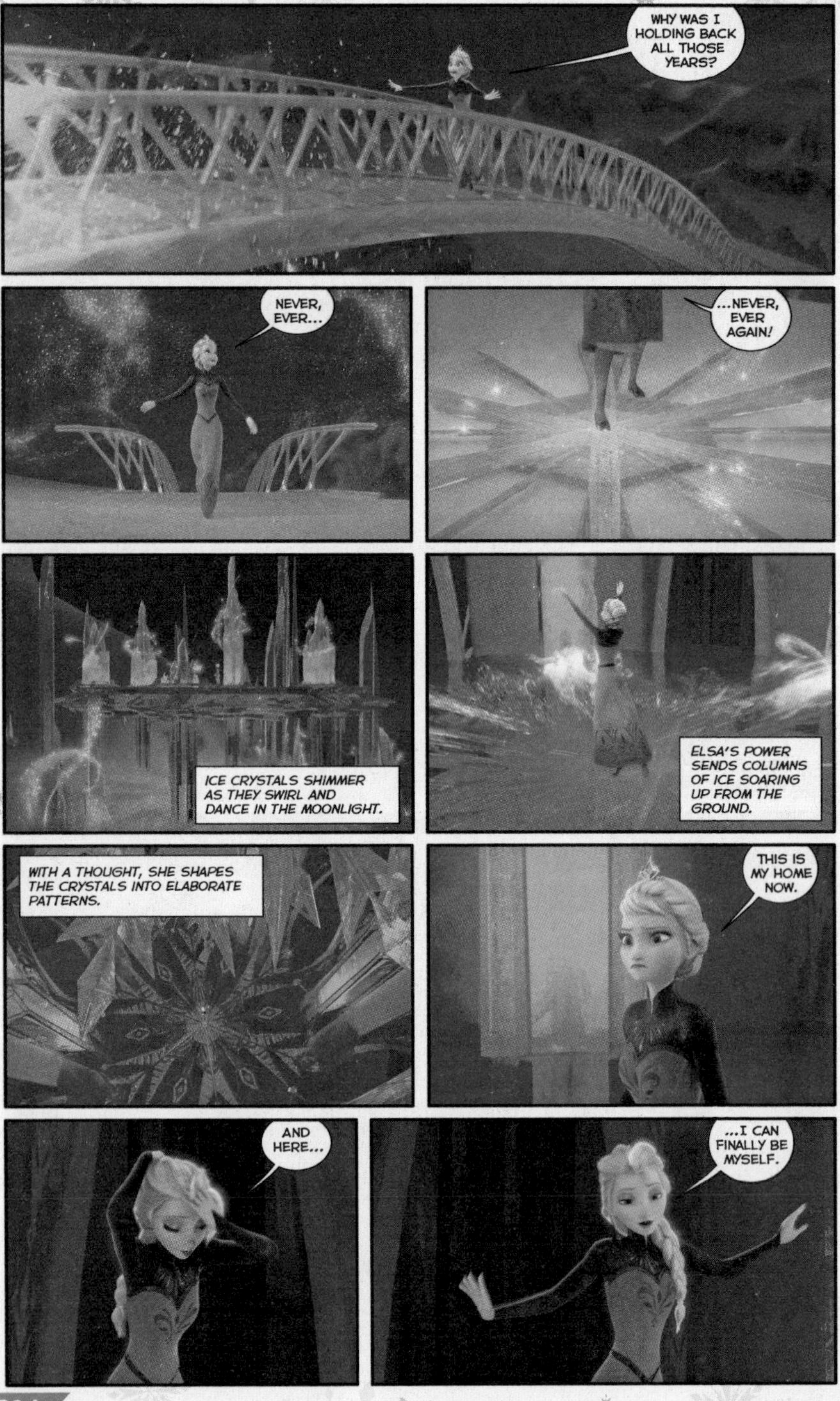
WHY WAS I HOLDING BACK ALL THOSE YEARS?
NEVER, EVER...
...NEVER, EVER AGAIN!
ICE CRYSTALS SHIMMER AS THEY SWIRL AND DANCE IN THE MOONLIGHT.
ELSA'S POWER SENDS COLUMNS OF ICE SOARING UP FROM THE GROUND.
WITH A THOUGHT, SHE SHAPES THE CRYSTALS INTO ELABORATE PATTERNS.
THIS IS MY HOME NOW.
AND HERE...
...I CAN FINALLY BE MYSELF.

THE OLD ME...

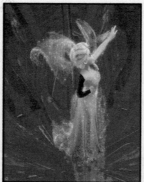

...IS GONE.

NO MORE HIDING IN THE SHADOWS.

I'M GOING TO STAND IN THE LIGHT!

I TRIED TO BE WHAT THEY WANTED ME TO BE.

BUT NO MORE!

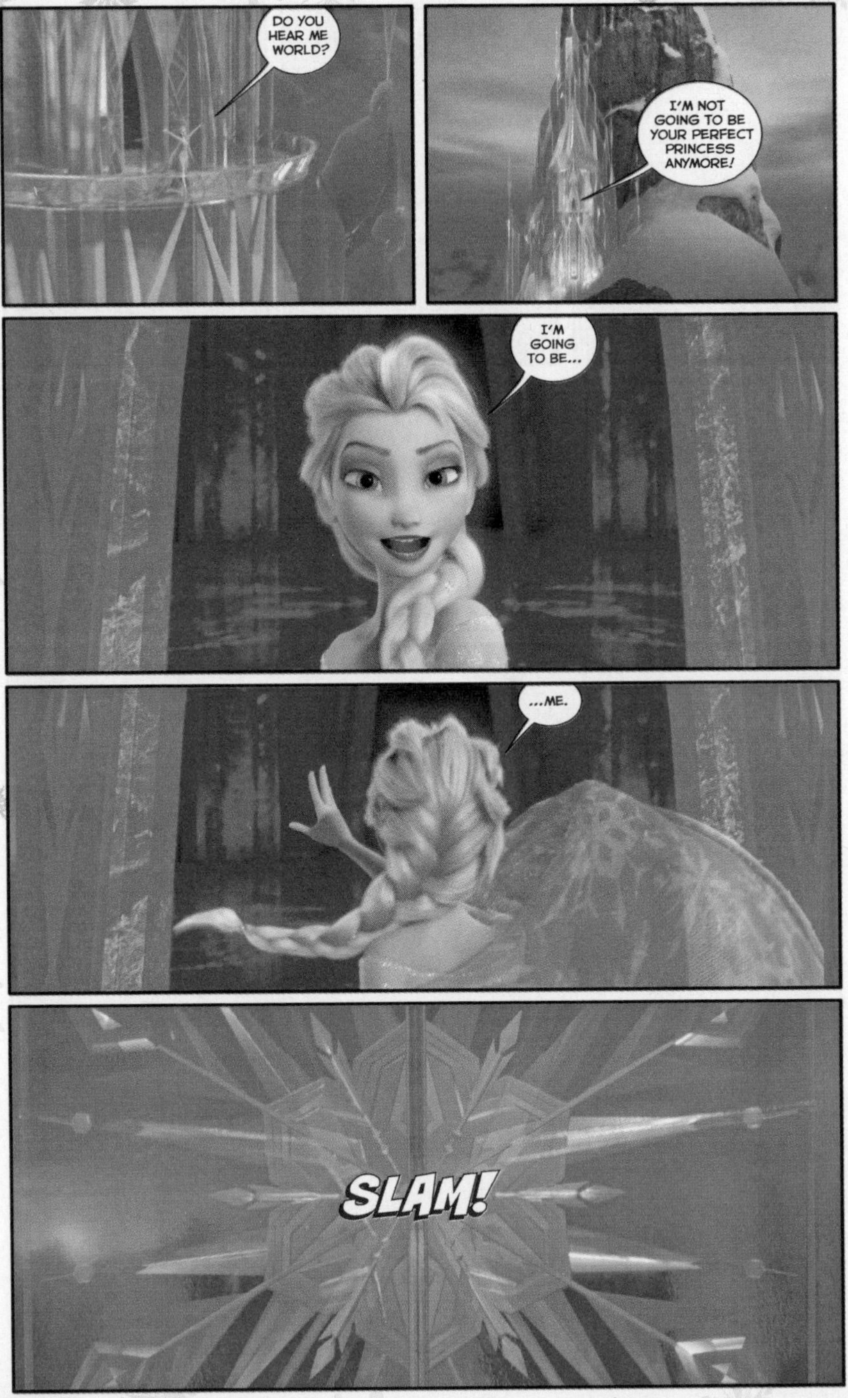
DO YOU HEAR ME WORLD?
I'M NOT GOING TO BE YOUR PERFECT PRINCESS ANYMORE!
I'M GOING TO BE...
...ME.
SLAM!

Disney

FROZEN FEVER

Cinestory Comic

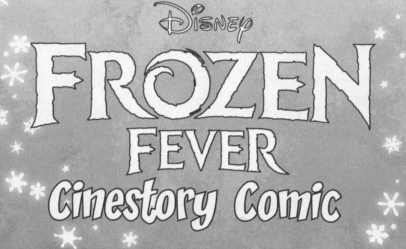

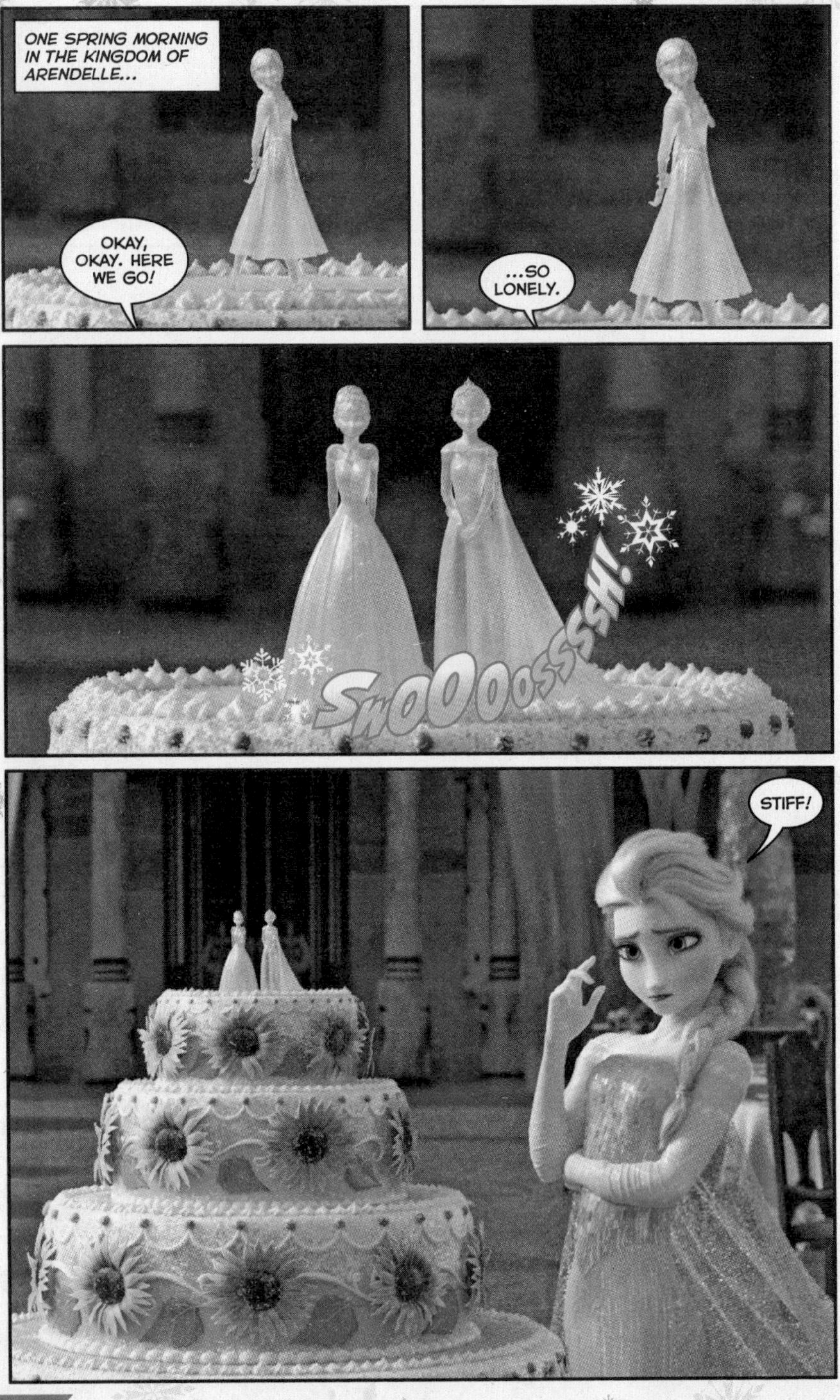
ONE SPRING MORNING IN THE KINGDOM OF ARENDELLE...
OKAY, OKAY. HERE WE GO!
...SO LONELY.
SWOOOOSSSSH!
STIFF!

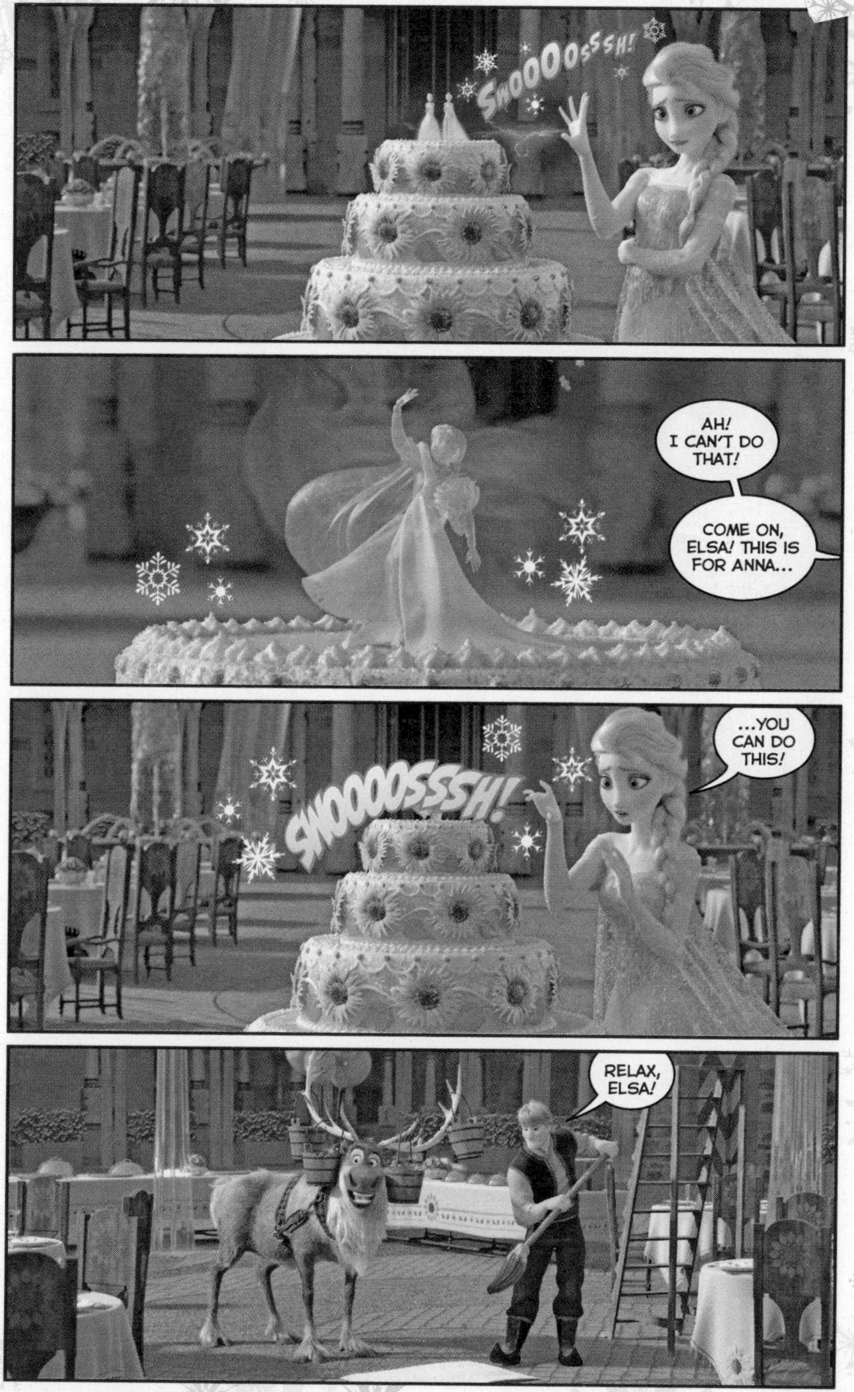
SHOOOOSSSH!
AH! I CAN'T DO THAT!
COME ON, ELSA! THIS IS FOR ANNA...
SHOOOOSSSH!
...YOU CAN DO THIS!
RELAX, ELSA!

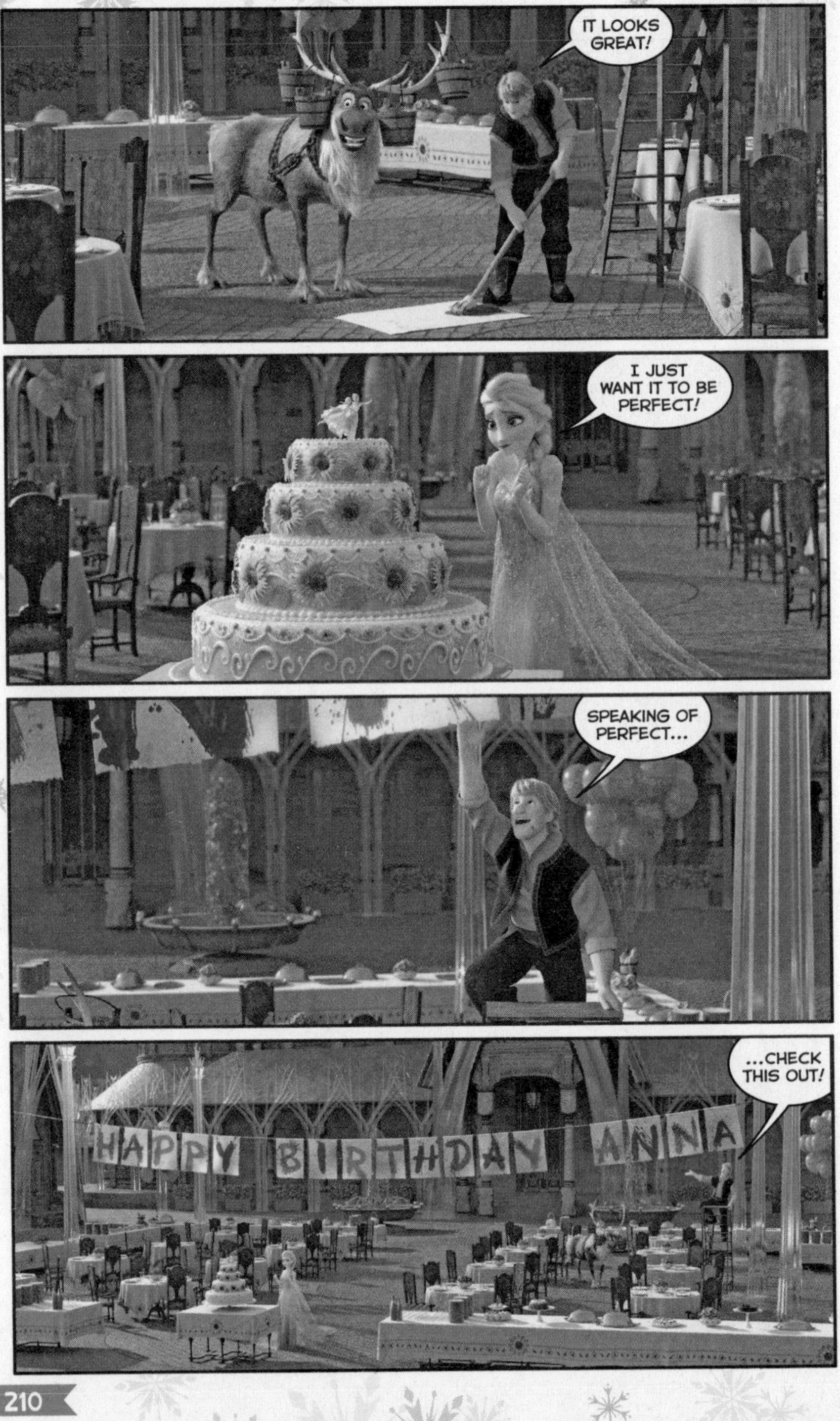
IT LOOKS GREAT!
I JUST WANT IT TO BE PERFECT!
SPEAKING OF PERFECT...
...CHECK THIS OUT!
HAPPY BIRTHDAY ANNA

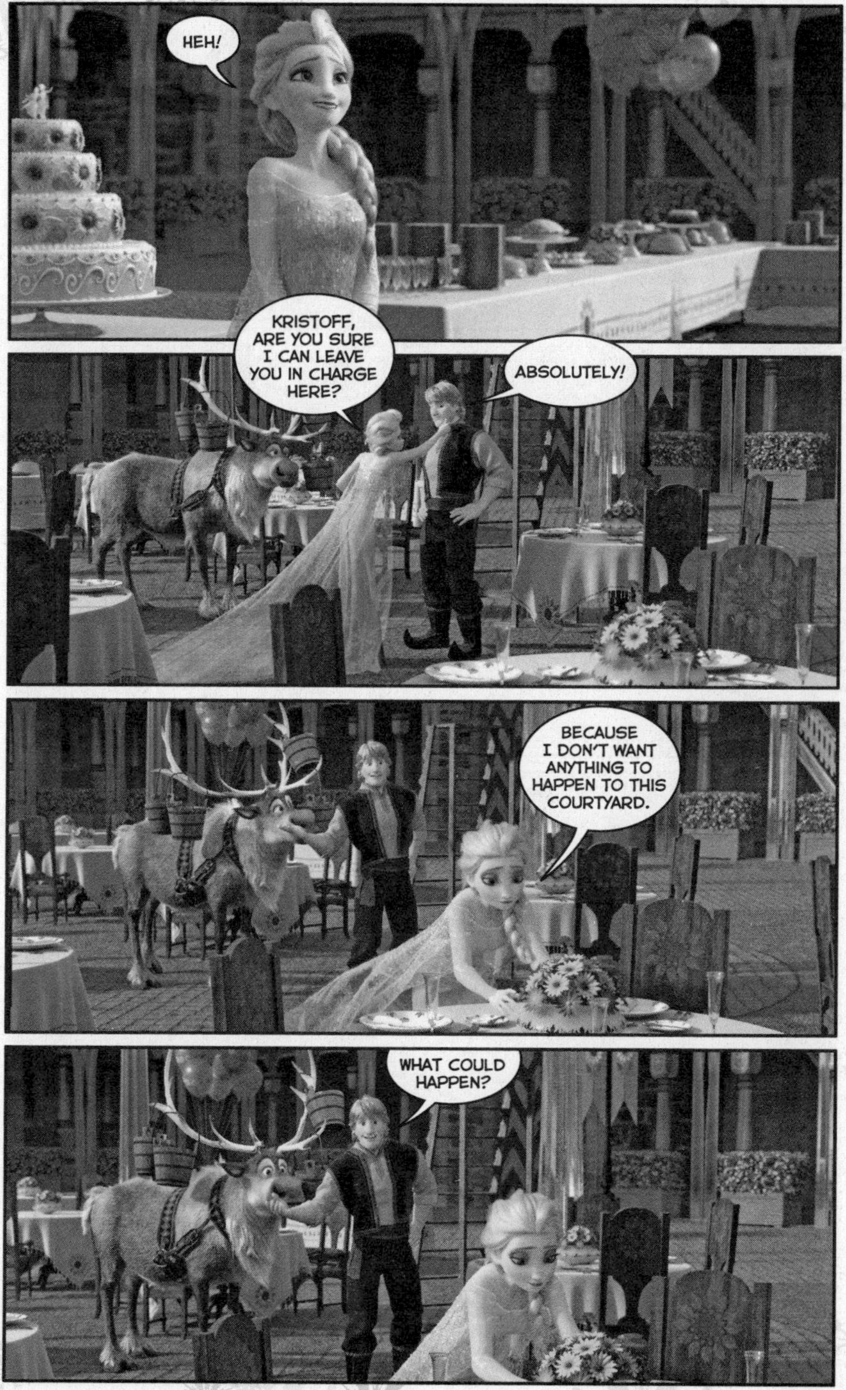
HEH!
KRISTOFF, ARE YOU SURE I CAN LEAVE YOU IN CHARGE HERE?
ABSOLUTELY!
BECAUSE I DON'T WANT ANYTHING TO HAPPEN TO THIS COURTYARD.
WHAT COULD HAPPEN?

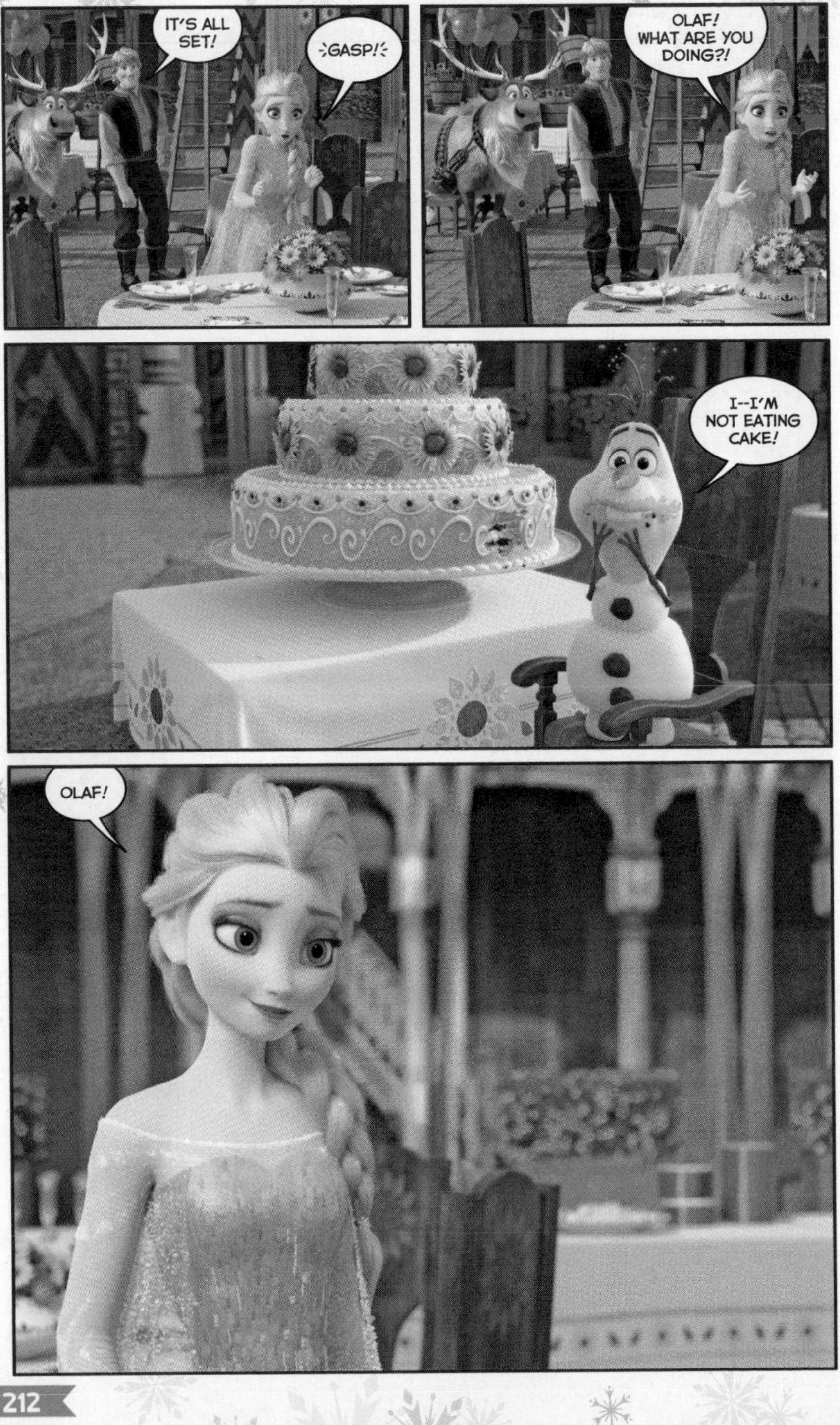
IT'S ALL SET!
GASP!
OLAF! WHAT ARE YOU DOING?!
I--I'M NOT EATING CAKE!
OLAF!

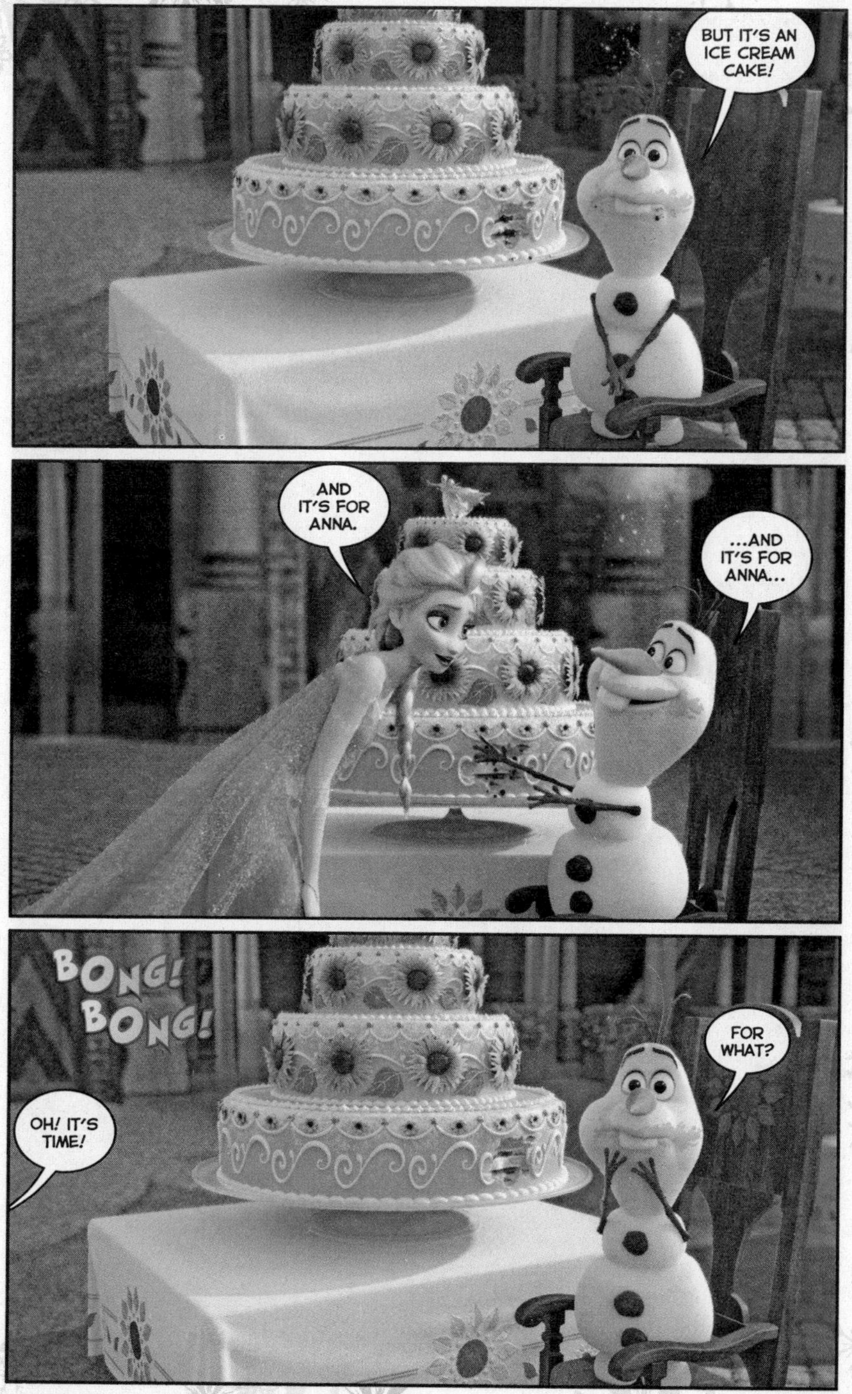
BUT IT'S AN ICE CREAM CAKE!
AND IT'S FOR ANNA.
...AND IT'S FOR ANNA...
BONG! BONG!
OH! IT'S TIME!
FOR WHAT?

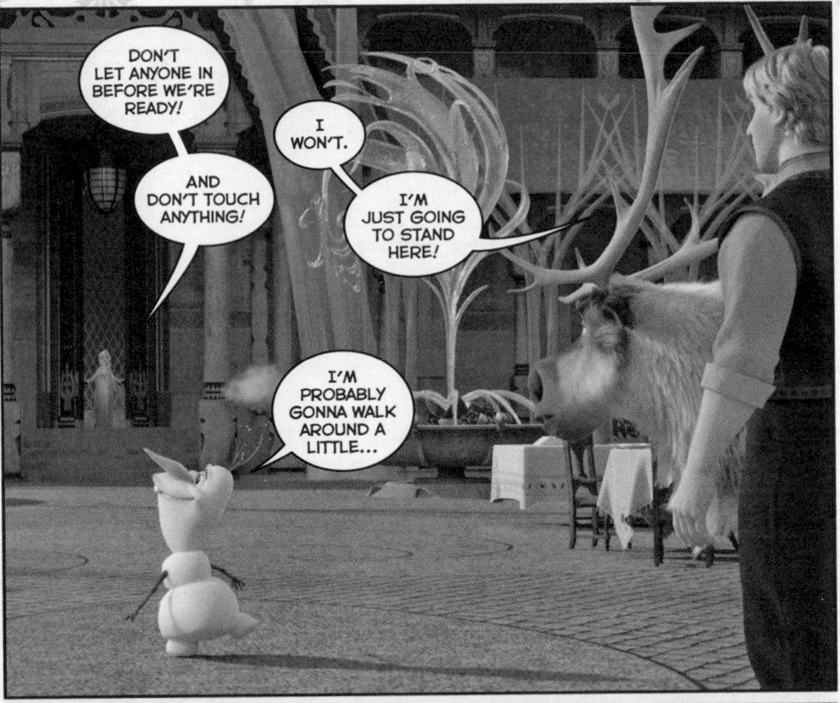
DON'T LET ANYONE IN BEFORE WE'RE READY!
AND DON'T TOUCH ANYTHING!
I WON'T.
I'M JUST GOING TO STAND HERE!
I'M PROBABLY GONNA WALK AROUND A LITTLE...

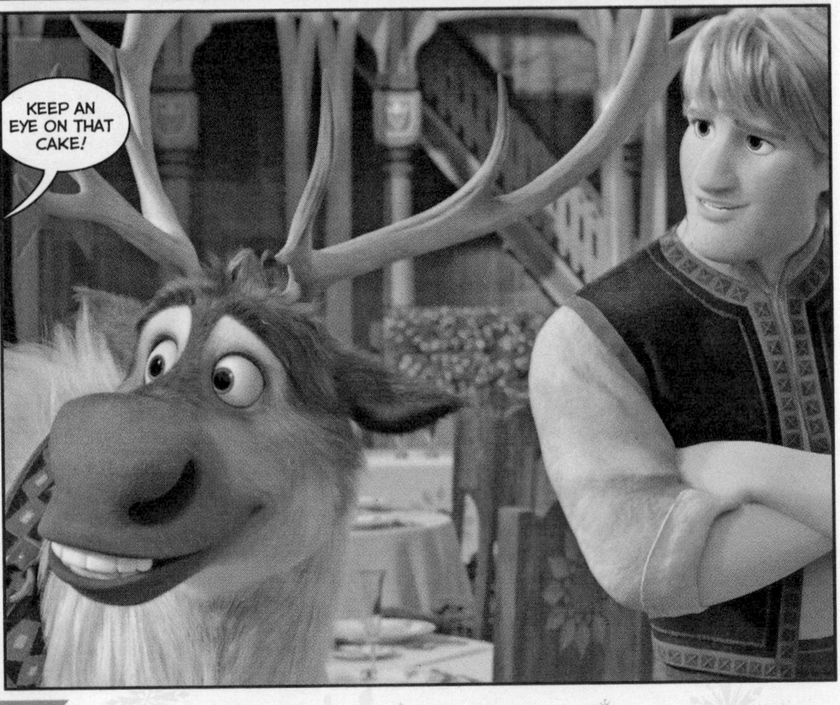
KEEP AN EYE ON THAT CAKE!

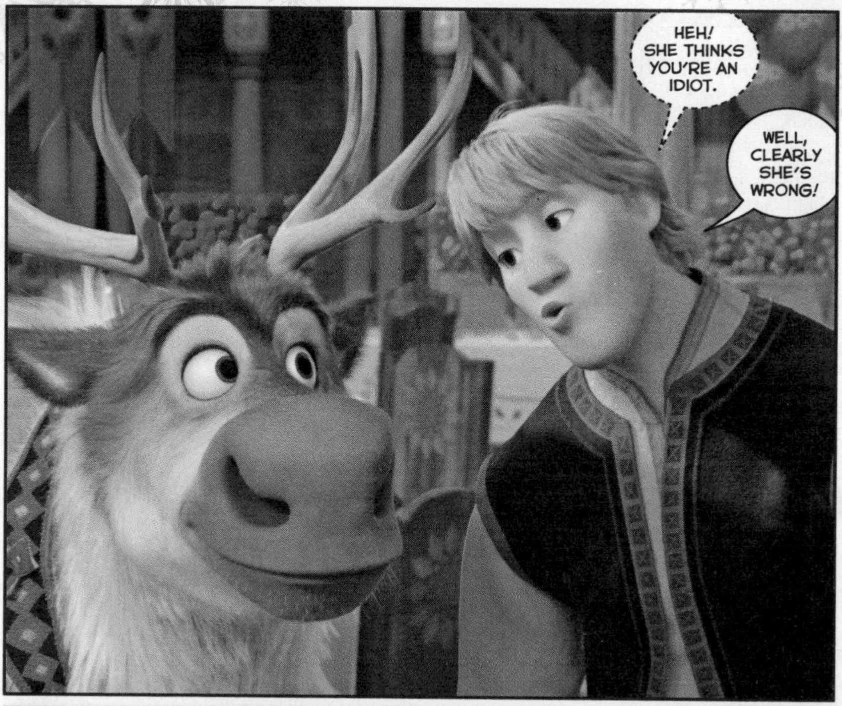
HEH! SHE THINKS YOU'RE AN IDIOT.
WELL, CLEARLY SHE'S WRONG!

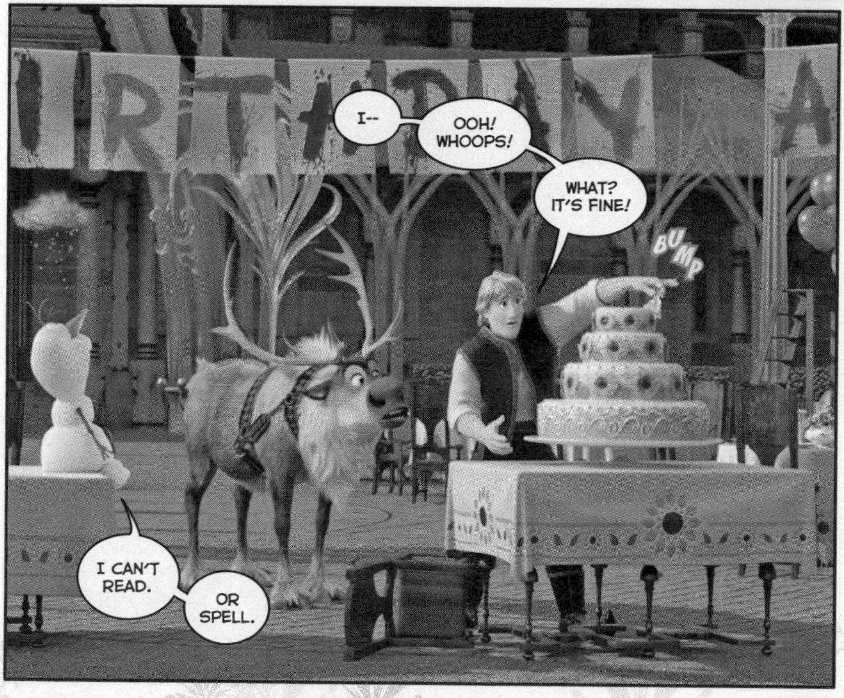
I--
OOH! WHOOPS!
WHAT? IT'S FINE!
BUMP
I CAN'T READ.
OR SPELL.

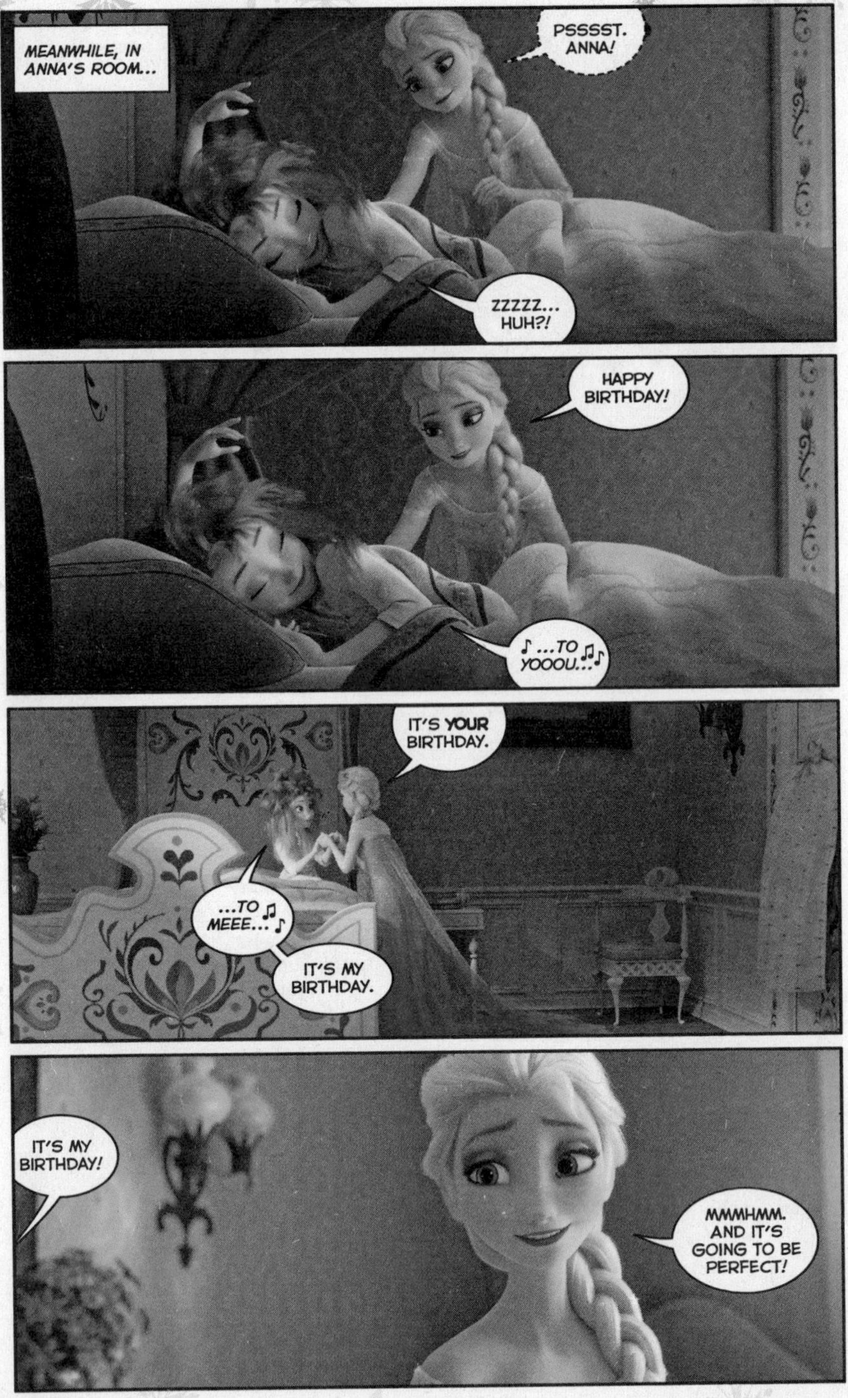
MEANWHILE, IN ANNA'S ROOM...
PSSSST. ANNA!
ZZZZZ... HUH?!
HAPPY BIRTHDAY!
♪ ...TO ♫♪ YOOOU...♫♪
IT'S YOUR BIRTHDAY.
...TO ♫ MEEE...♪
IT'S MY BIRTHDAY.
IT'S MY BIRTHDAY!
MMMHMM. AND IT'S GOING TO BE PERFECT!

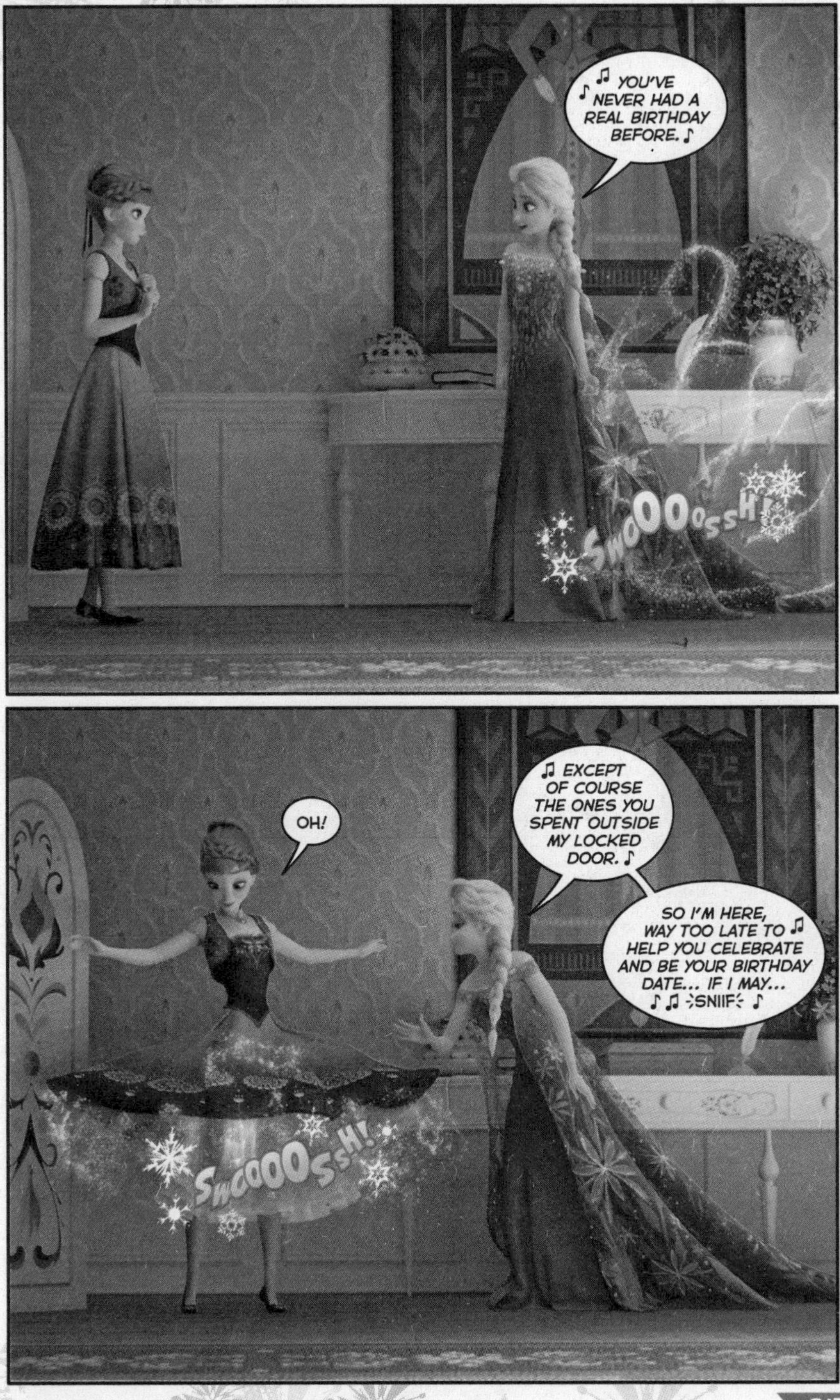
♫ YOU'VE NEVER HAD A REAL BIRTHDAY BEFORE. ♪
SWOOOOSSH!
OH!
♫ EXCEPT OF COURSE THE ONES YOU SPENT OUTSIDE MY LOCKED DOOR. ♪
SO I'M HERE, WAY TOO LATE TO ♫ HELP YOU CELEBRATE AND BE YOUR BIRTHDAY DATE... IF I MAY... ♪ ♫ SNIIF ♪
SWOOOOSSH!

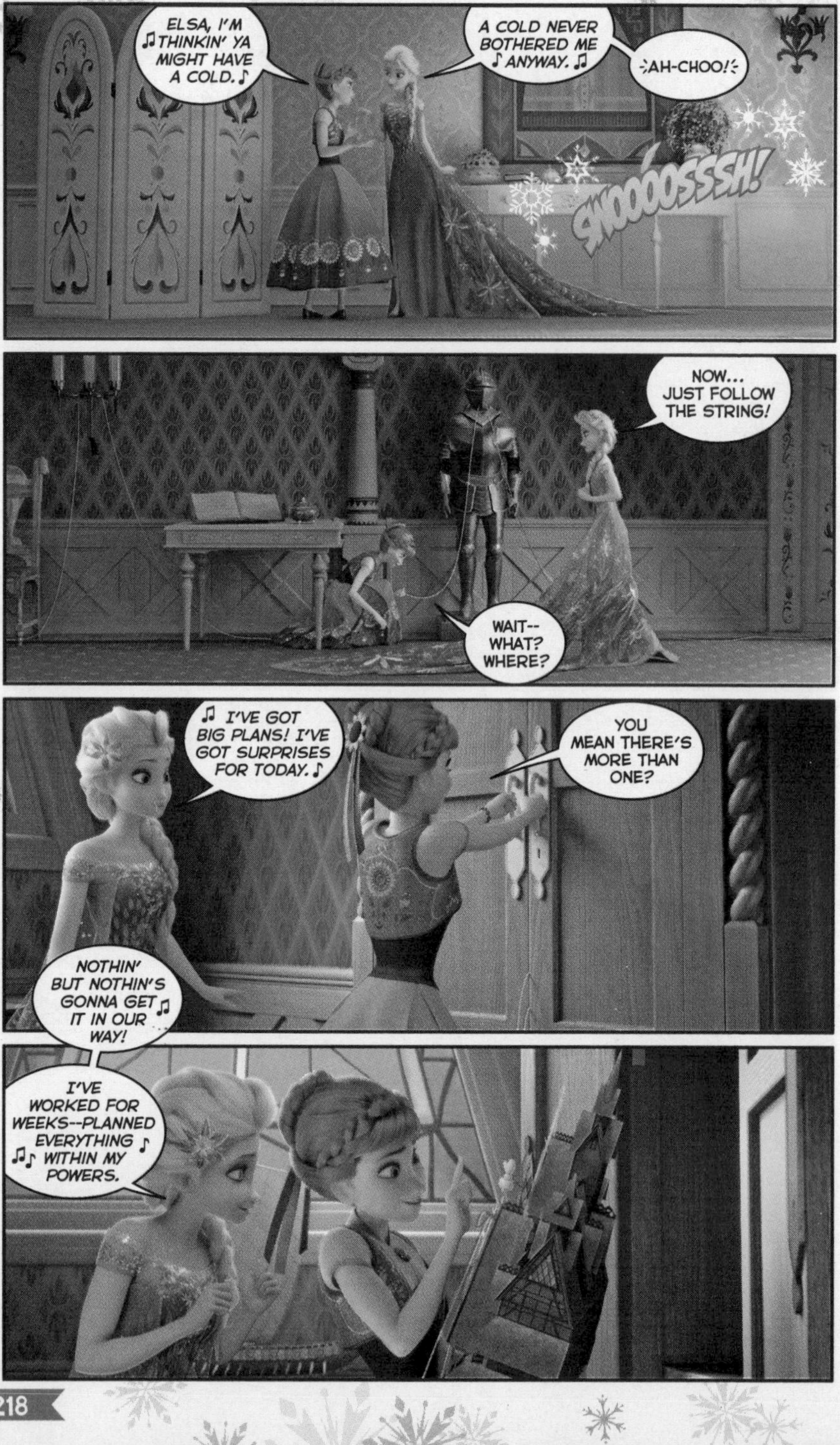
ELSA, I'M ♫ THINKIN' YA MIGHT HAVE A COLD. ♪
A COLD NEVER BOTHERED ME ♪ ANYWAY. ♫
AH-CHOO!
SNOOOOSSSH!
NOW... JUST FOLLOW THE STRING!
WAIT-- WHAT? WHERE?
♫ I'VE GOT BIG PLANS! I'VE GOT SURPRISES FOR TODAY. ♪
YOU MEAN THERE'S MORE THAN ONE?
NOTHIN' BUT NOTHIN'S GONNA GET ♫ IT IN OUR WAY!
I'VE WORKED FOR WEEKS--PLANNED EVERYTHING ♪ ♫♪ WITHIN MY POWERS.

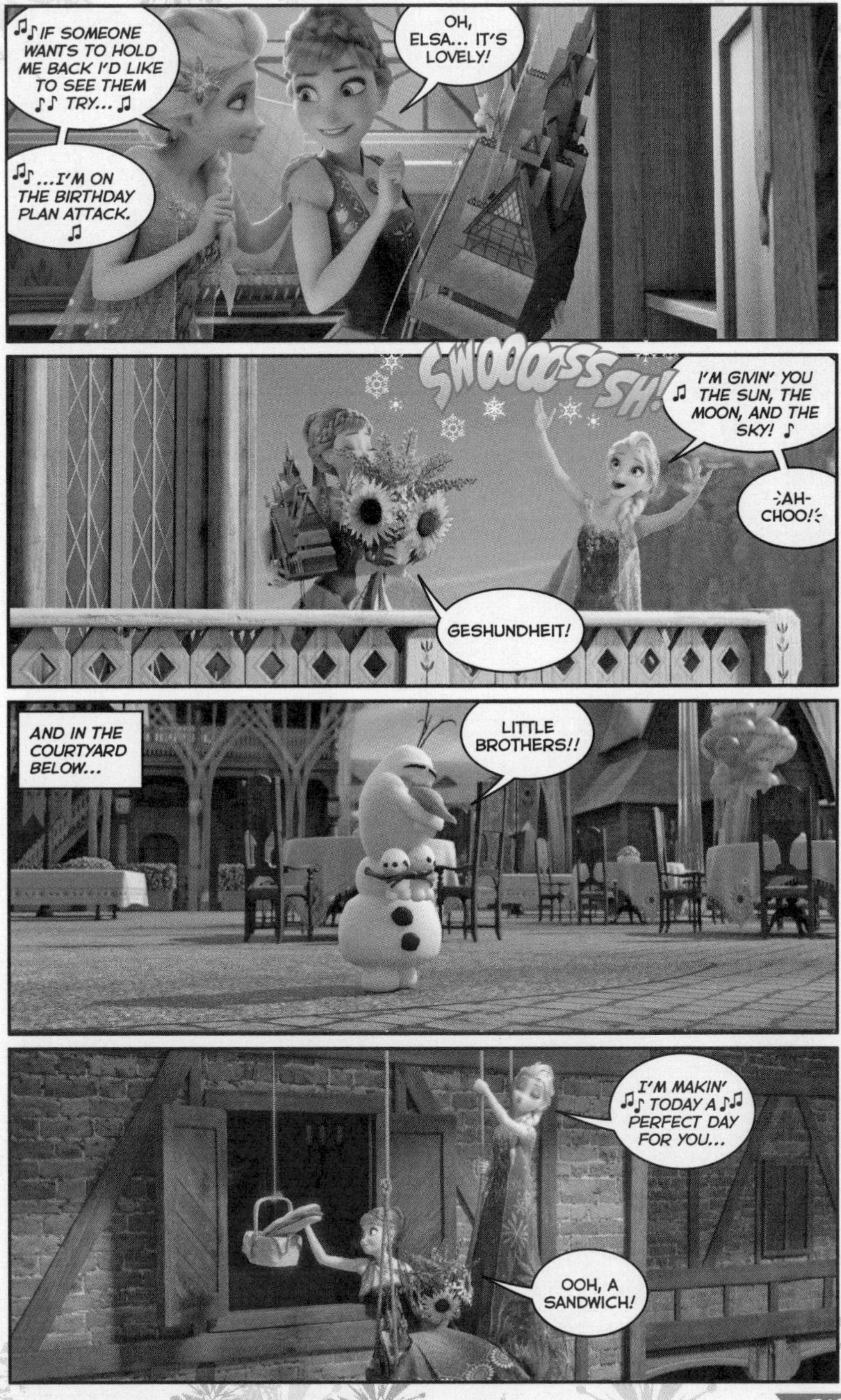
♫♪ IF SOMEONE WANTS TO HOLD ME BACK I'D LIKE TO SEE THEM ♪♪ TRY... ♫
OH, ELSA... IT'S LOVELY!
♫♪ ...I'M ON THE BIRTHDAY PLAN ATTACK. ♫
SWOOOOSSSH!
♫ I'M GIVIN' YOU THE SUN, THE MOON, AND THE SKY! ♪
AH-CHOO!
GESHUNDHEIT!
AND IN THE COURTYARD BELOW...
LITTLE BROTHERS!!
I'M MAKIN' ♫♪ TODAY A ♪♫ PERFECT DAY FOR YOU...
OOH, A SANDWICH!

♫ I'M MAKIN' TODAY A BLAST IF IT'S THE LAST THING I DO. ♪
OOOH!
WHERE ARE WE GOING NOW?
♫ FOR ♪ EVERYTHING YOU ARE TO ME... ♫♪
♫ ♫ ...AND ALL YOU'VE BEEN THROUGH... ♪

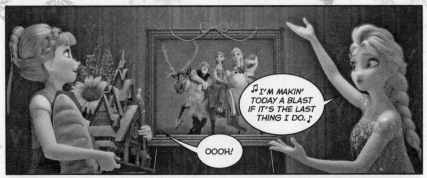

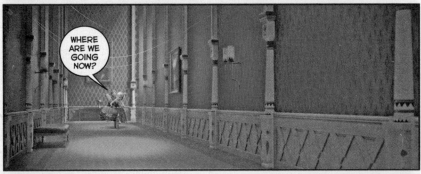

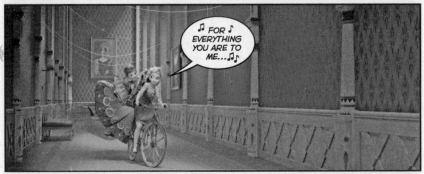

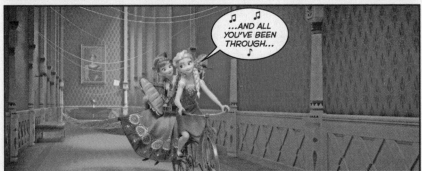

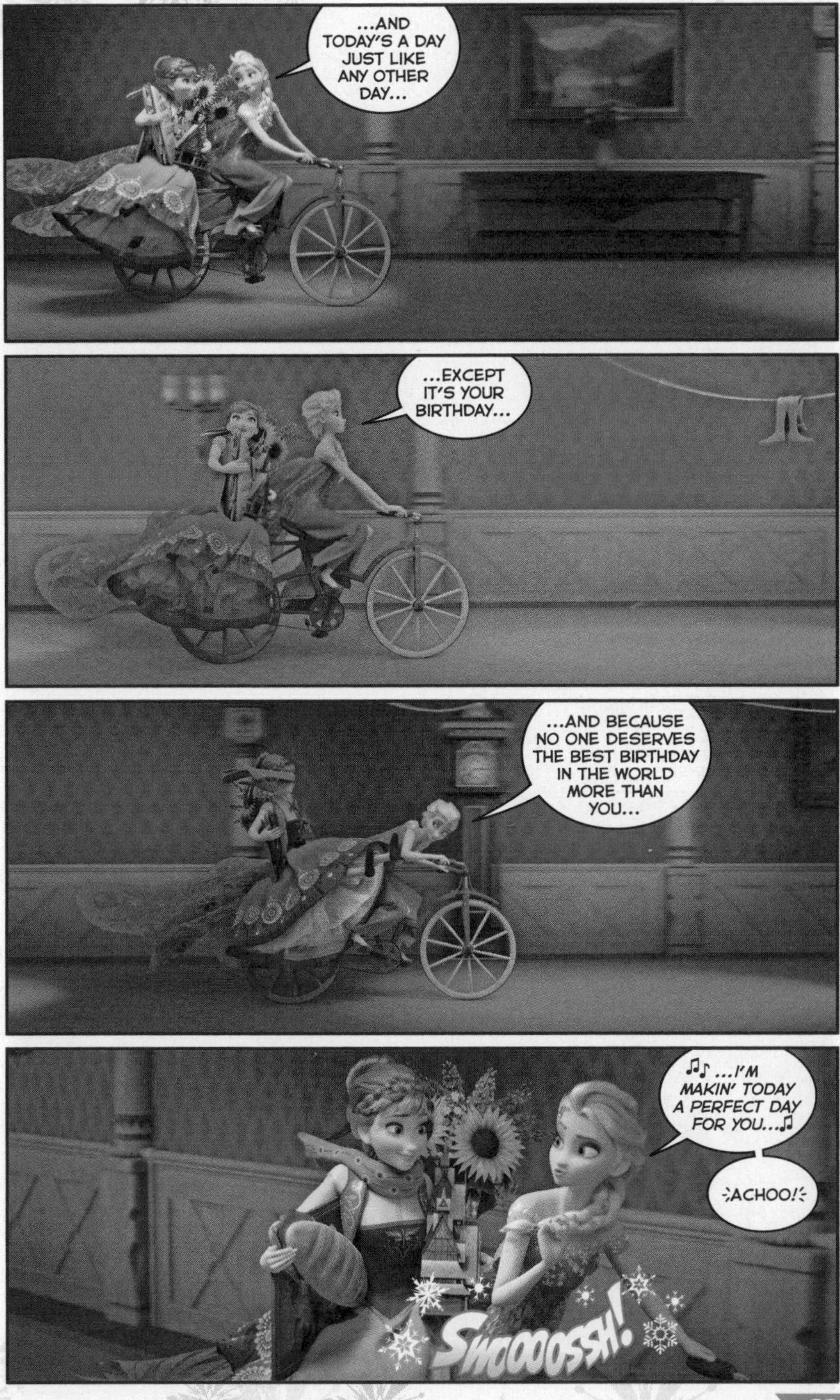
...AND TODAY'S A DAY JUST LIKE ANY OTHER DAY...
...EXCEPT IT'S YOUR BIRTHDAY...
...AND BECAUSE NO ONE DESERVES THE BEST BIRTHDAY IN THE WORLD MORE THAN YOU...
♫♪ ...I'M MAKIN' TODAY A PERFECT DAY FOR YOU...♫
ACHOO!
SWOOOOSSH!

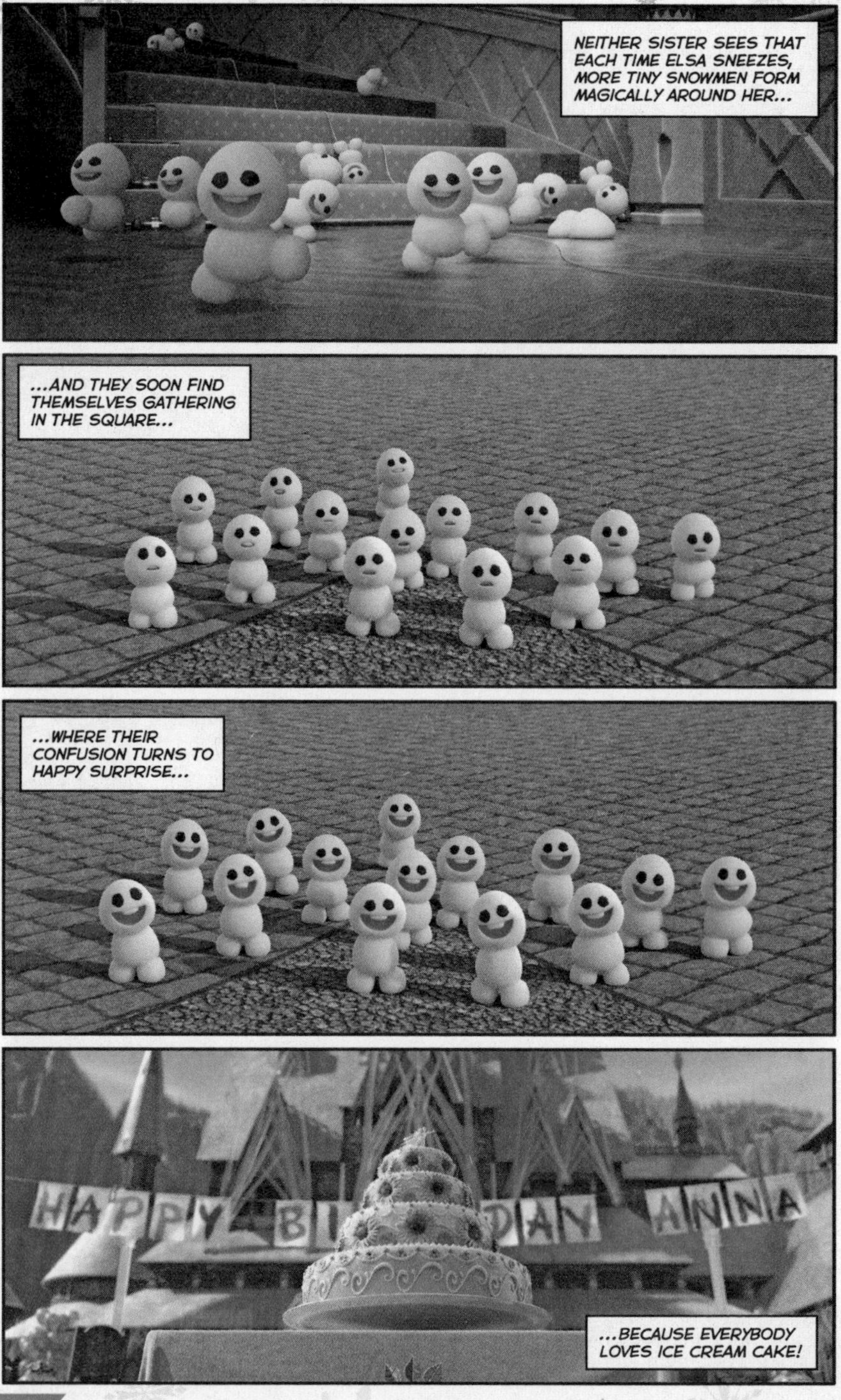
NEITHER SISTER SEES THAT EACH TIME ELSA SNEEZES, MORE TINY SNOWMEN FORM MAGICALLY AROUND HER...
...AND THEY SOON FIND THEMSELVES GATHERING IN THE SQUARE...
...WHERE THEIR CONFUSION TURNS TO HAPPY SURPRISE...
...BECAUSE EVERYBODY LOVES ICE CREAM CAKE!

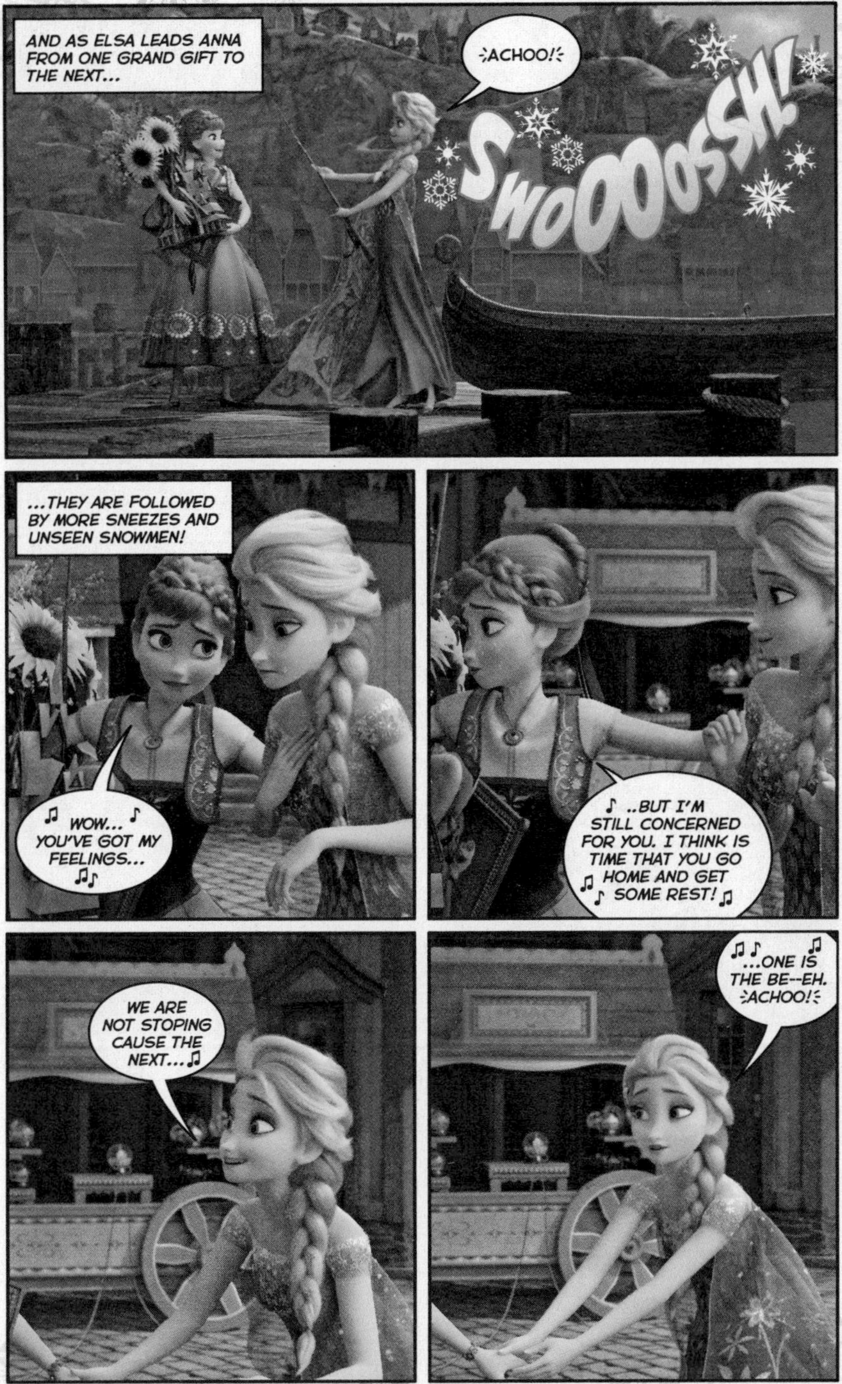

AND AS ELSA LEADS ANNA FROM ONE GRAND GIFT TO THE NEXT...
ACHOO!
SWOOOOSSH!
...THEY ARE FOLLOWED BY MORE SNEEZES AND UNSEEN SNOWMEN!
♫ WOW... ♪ YOU'VE GOT MY FEELINGS... ♫♪
♪ ..BUT I'M STILL CONCERNED FOR YOU. I THINK IS TIME THAT YOU GO HOME AND GET SOME REST! ♫
WE ARE NOT STOPING CAUSE THE NEXT... ♫
♫♪ ♫ ...ONE IS THE BE--EH. ACHOO!

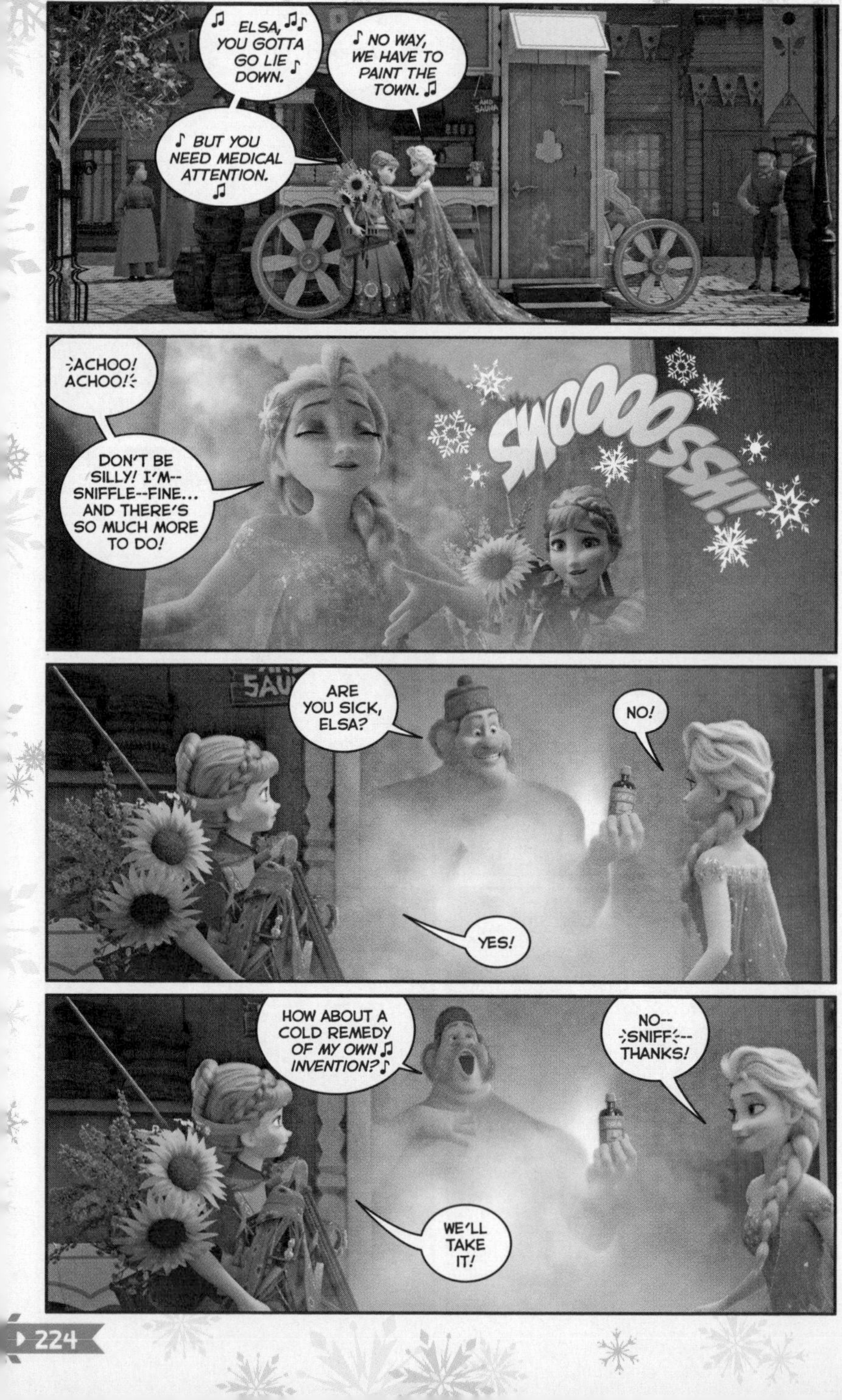
♫ ELSA, ♫♪ YOU GOTTA GO LIE ♪ DOWN.
♪ NO WAY, WE HAVE TO PAINT THE TOWN. ♫
♪ BUT YOU NEED MEDICAL ATTENTION. ♫
ACHOO! ACHOO!
DON'T BE SILLY! I'M--SNIFFLE--FINE... AND THERE'S SO MUCH MORE TO DO!
SWOOOOSH!
ARE YOU SICK, ELSA?
NO!
YES!
HOW ABOUT A COLD REMEDY OF MY OWN ♫ INVENTION? ♪
NO--SNIFF--THANKS!
WE'LL TAKE IT!

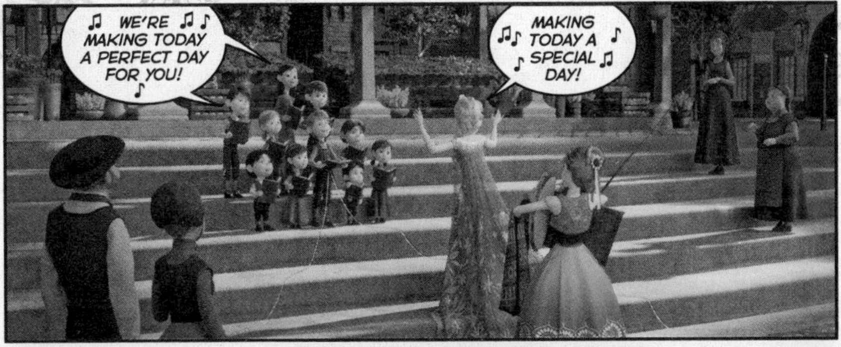
♫ WE'RE ♫♪ MAKING TODAY A PERFECT DAY FOR YOU! ♪
MAKING ♫♪ TODAY A ♪ ♪ SPECIAL ♫ DAY!

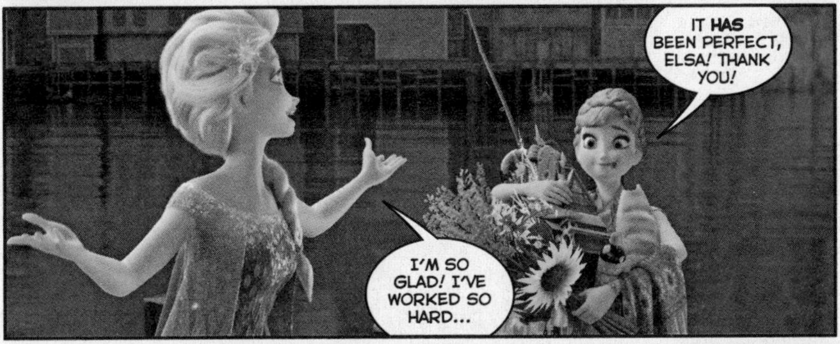
IT HAS BEEN PERFECT, ELSA! THANK YOU!
I'M SO GLAD! I'VE WORKED SO HARD...

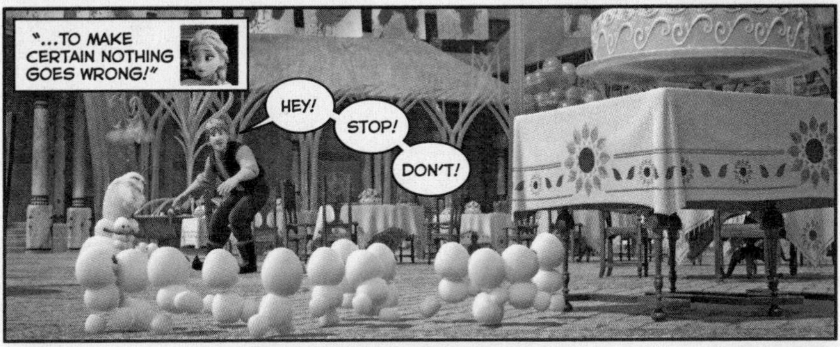
"...TO MAKE CERTAIN NOTHING GOES WRONG!"
HEY!
STOP!
DON'T!

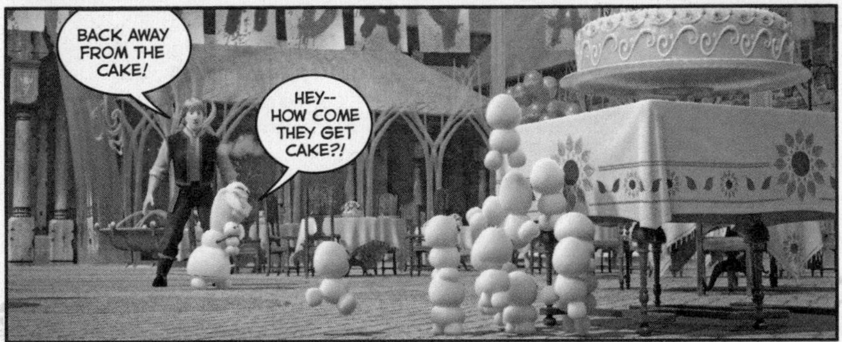
BACK AWAY FROM THE CAKE!
HEY-- HOW COME THEY GET CAKE?!

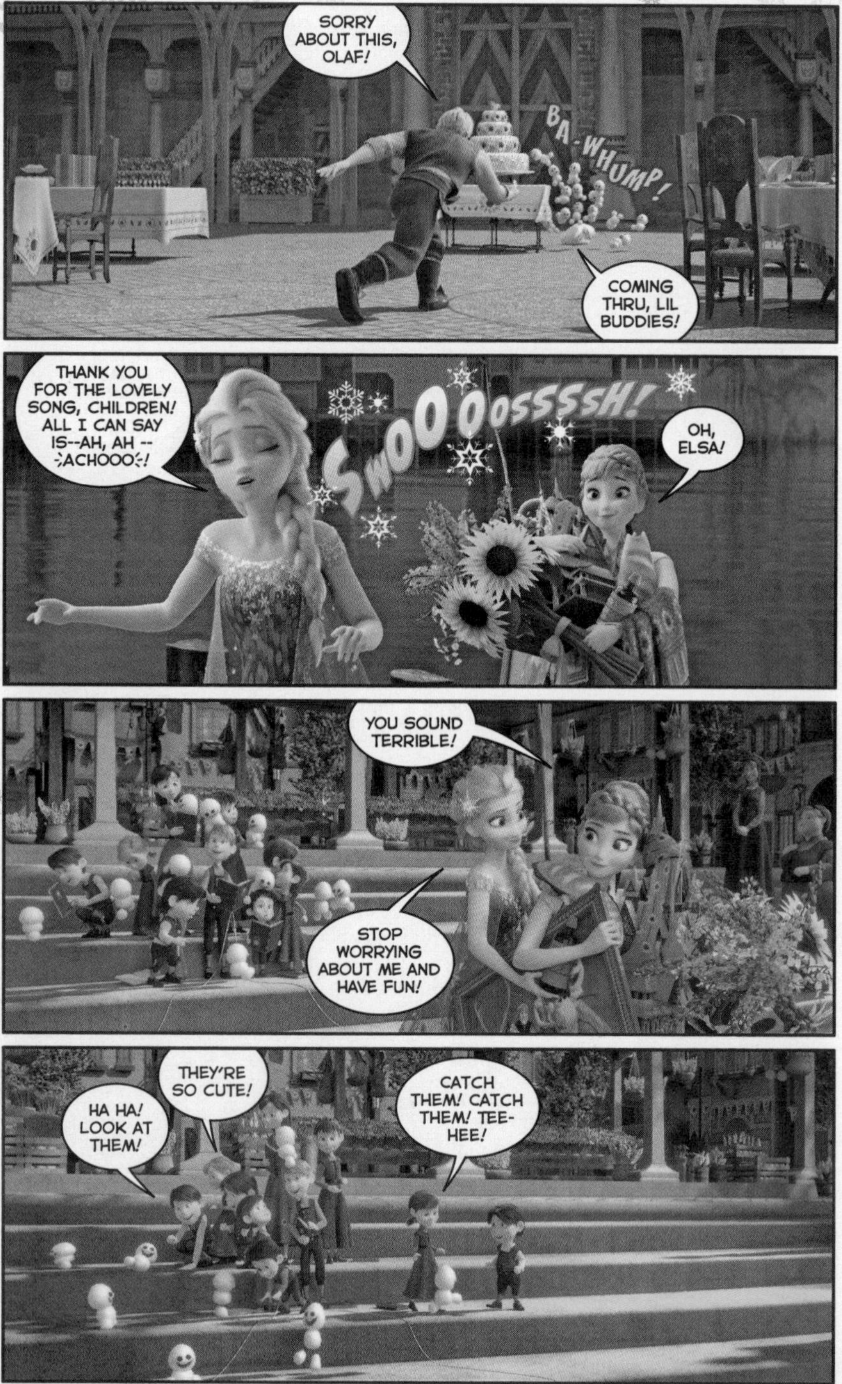
SORRY ABOUT THIS, OLAF!
BA-WHUMP!
COMING THRU, LIL BUDDIES!
THANK YOU FOR THE LOVELY SONG, CHILDREN! ALL I CAN SAY IS--AH, AH --ACHOOO!
SWOOOOSSSSH!
OH, ELSA!
YOU SOUND TERRIBLE!
STOP WORRYING ABOUT ME AND HAVE FUN!
HA HA! LOOK AT THEM!
THEY'RE SO CUTE!
CATCH THEM! CATCH THEM! TEE-HEE!

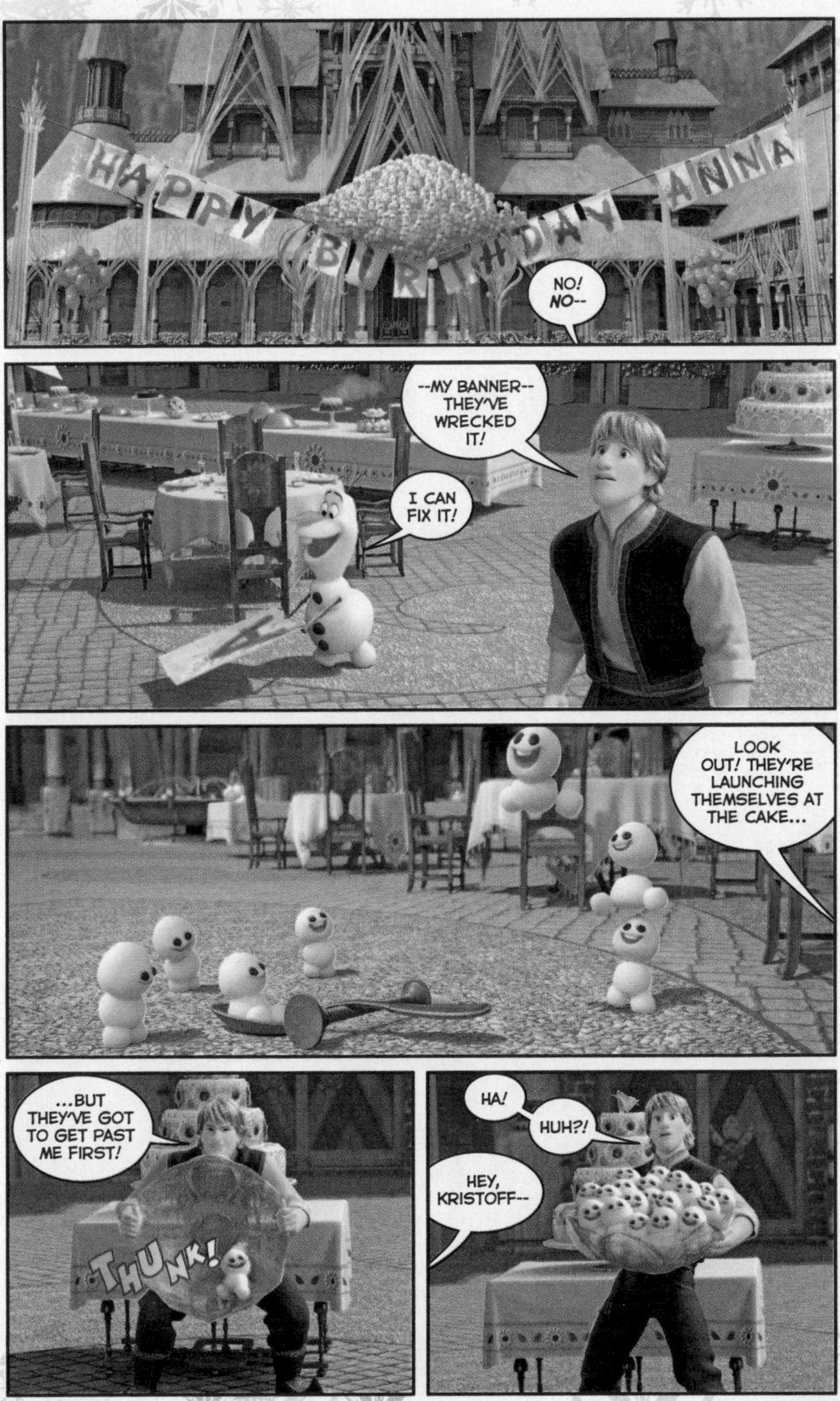
HAPPY BIRTHDAY ANNA
NO! NO--
--MY BANNER-- THEY'VE WRECKED IT!
I CAN FIX IT!
LOOK OUT! THEY'RE LAUNCHING THEMSELVES AT THE CAKE...
...BUT THEY'VE GOT TO GET PAST ME FIRST!
THUNK!
HA!
HUH?!
HEY, KRISTOFF--

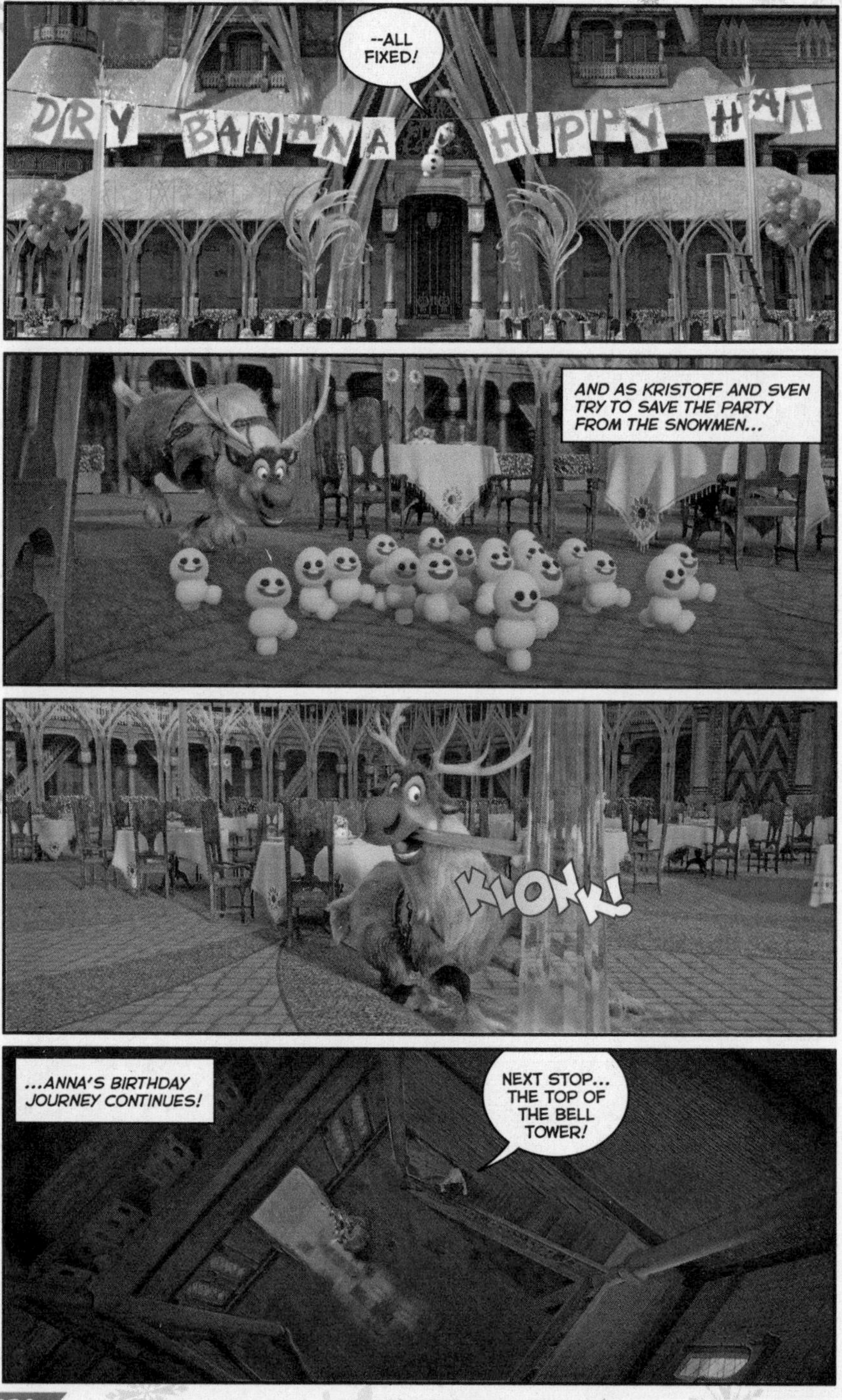
--ALL FIXED!
DRY BANANA HIPPY HAT
AND AS KRISTOFF AND SVEN TRY TO SAVE THE PARTY FROM THE SNOWMEN...
KLONK!
...ANNA'S BIRTHDAY JOURNEY CONTINUES!
NEXT STOP... THE TOP OF THE BELL TOWER!

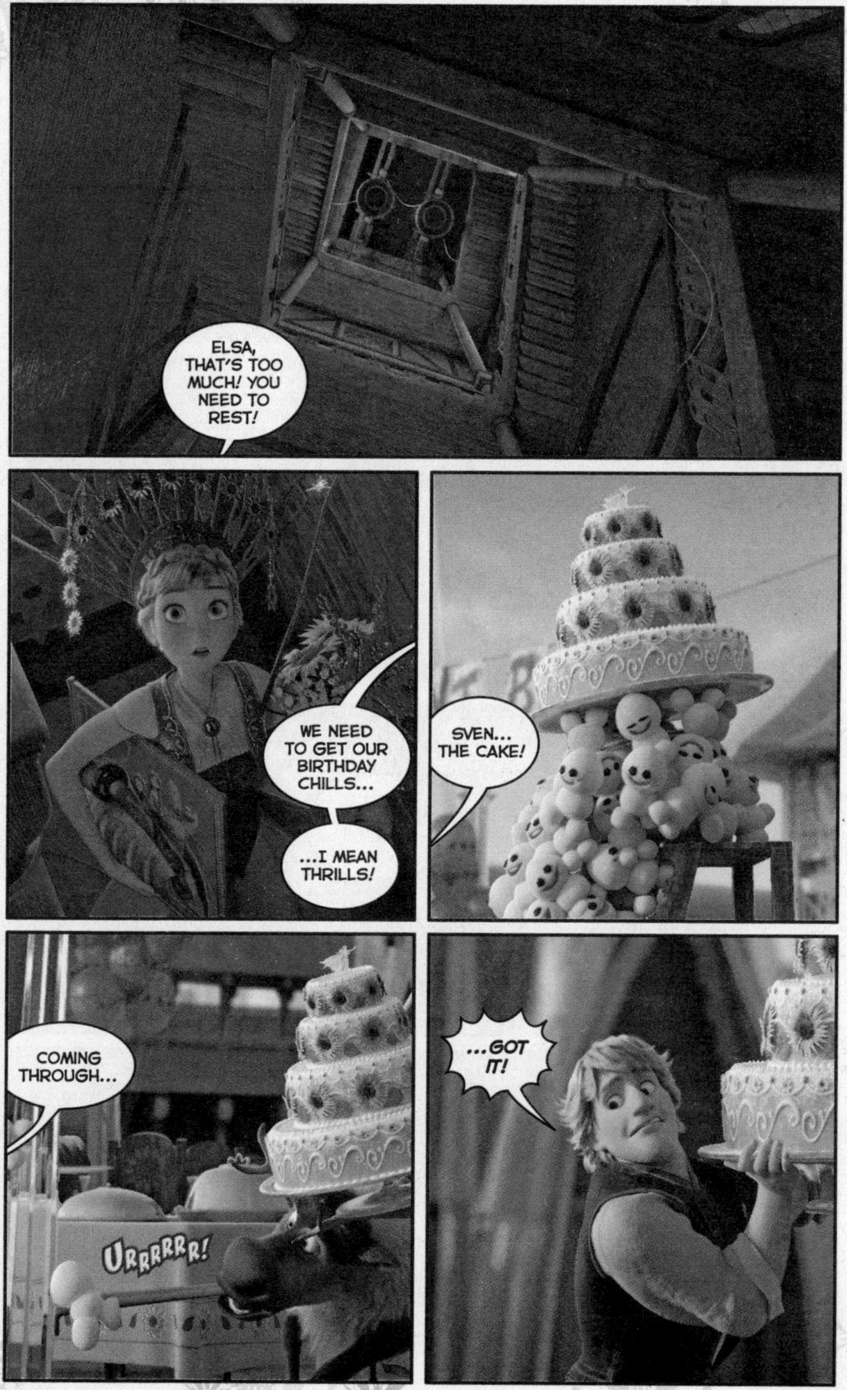
ELSA, THAT'S TOO MUCH! YOU NEED TO REST!
WE NEED TO GET OUR BIRTHDAY CHILLS...
...I MEAN THRILLS!
SVEN... THE CAKE!
COMING THROUGH...
URRRRRR!
...GOT IT!

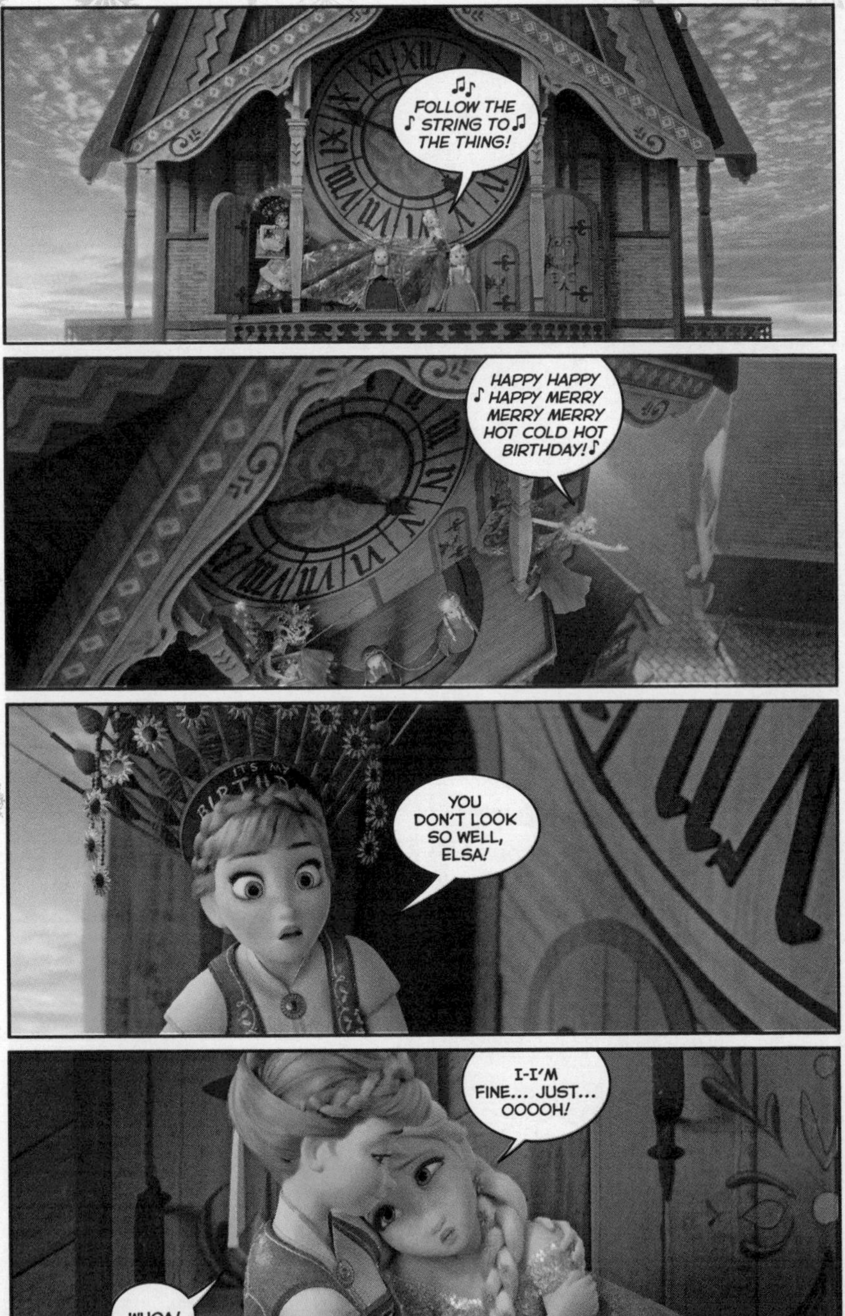
♫♪ FOLLOW THE ♪ STRING TO ♫ THE THING!
HAPPY HAPPY ♪ HAPPY MERRY MERRY MERRY HOT COLD HOT BIRTHDAY! ♪
IT'S MY BIRTHDAY
YOU DON'T LOOK SO WELL, ELSA!
I-I'M FINE... JUST... OOOOH!
WHOA!

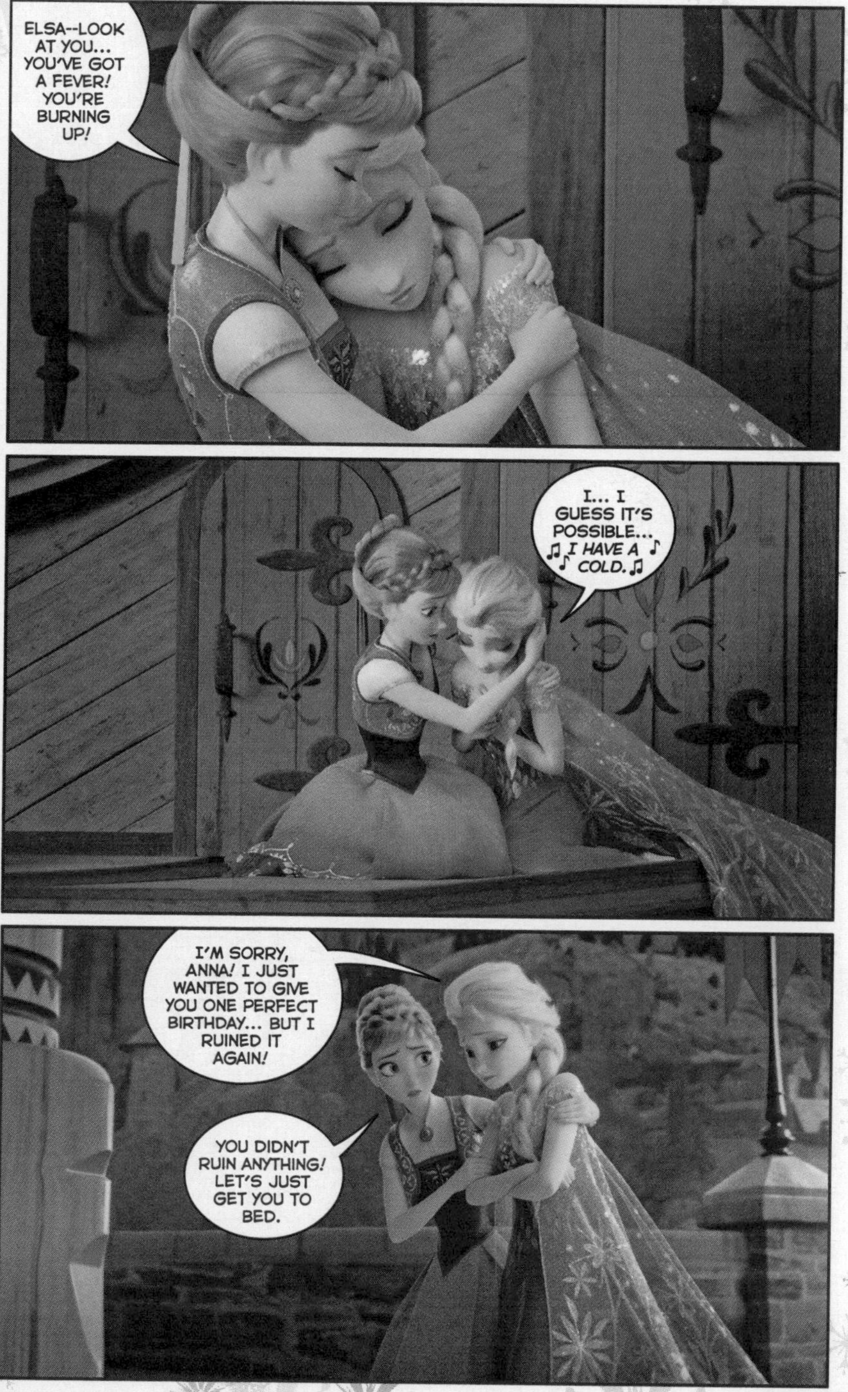
ELSA--LOOK AT YOU... YOU'VE GOT A FEVER! YOU'RE BURNING UP!
I... I GUESS IT'S POSSIBLE... ♫ I HAVE A ♪ ♪ COLD. ♫
I'M SORRY, ANNA! I JUST WANTED TO GIVE YOU ONE PERFECT BIRTHDAY... BUT I RUINED IT AGAIN!
YOU DIDN'T RUIN ANYTHING! LET'S JUST GET YOU TO BED.

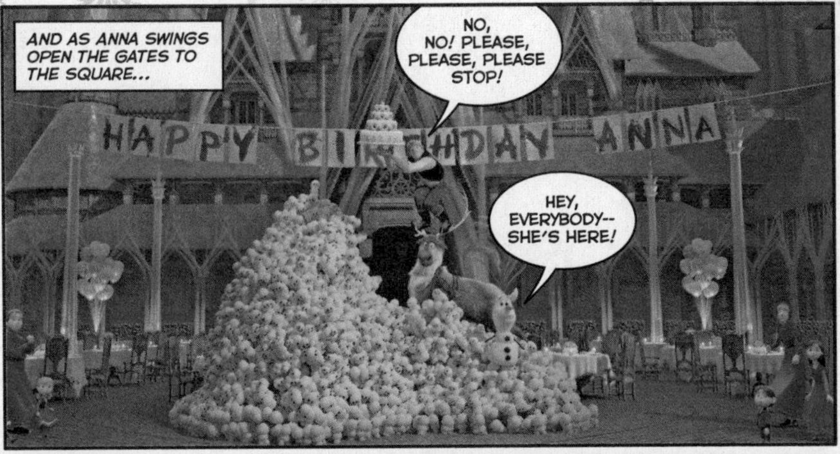
AND AS ANNA SWINGS OPEN THE GATES TO THE SQUARE...
NO, NO! PLEASE, PLEASE, PLEASE STOP!
HEY, EVERYBODY-- SHE'S HERE!
HAPPY BIRTHDAY ANNA

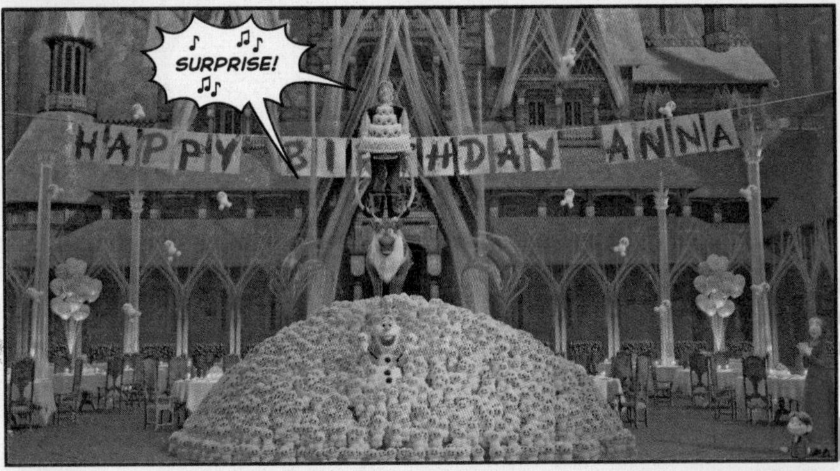
SURPRISE!
HAPPY BIRTHDAY ANNA

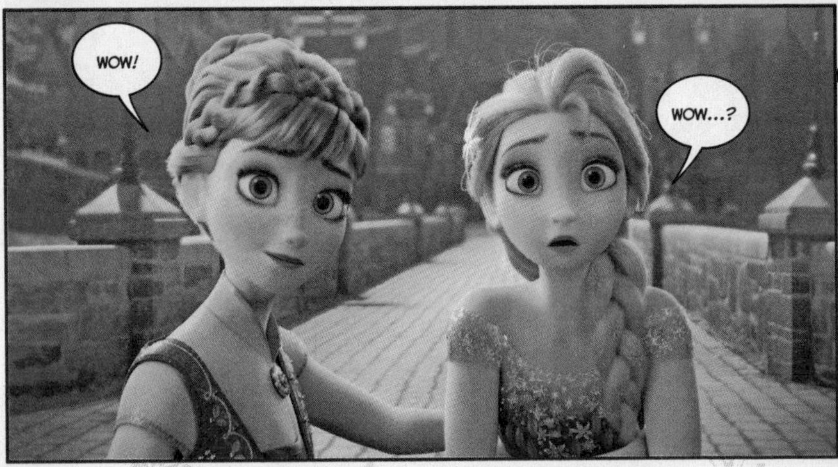
WOW!
WOW...?

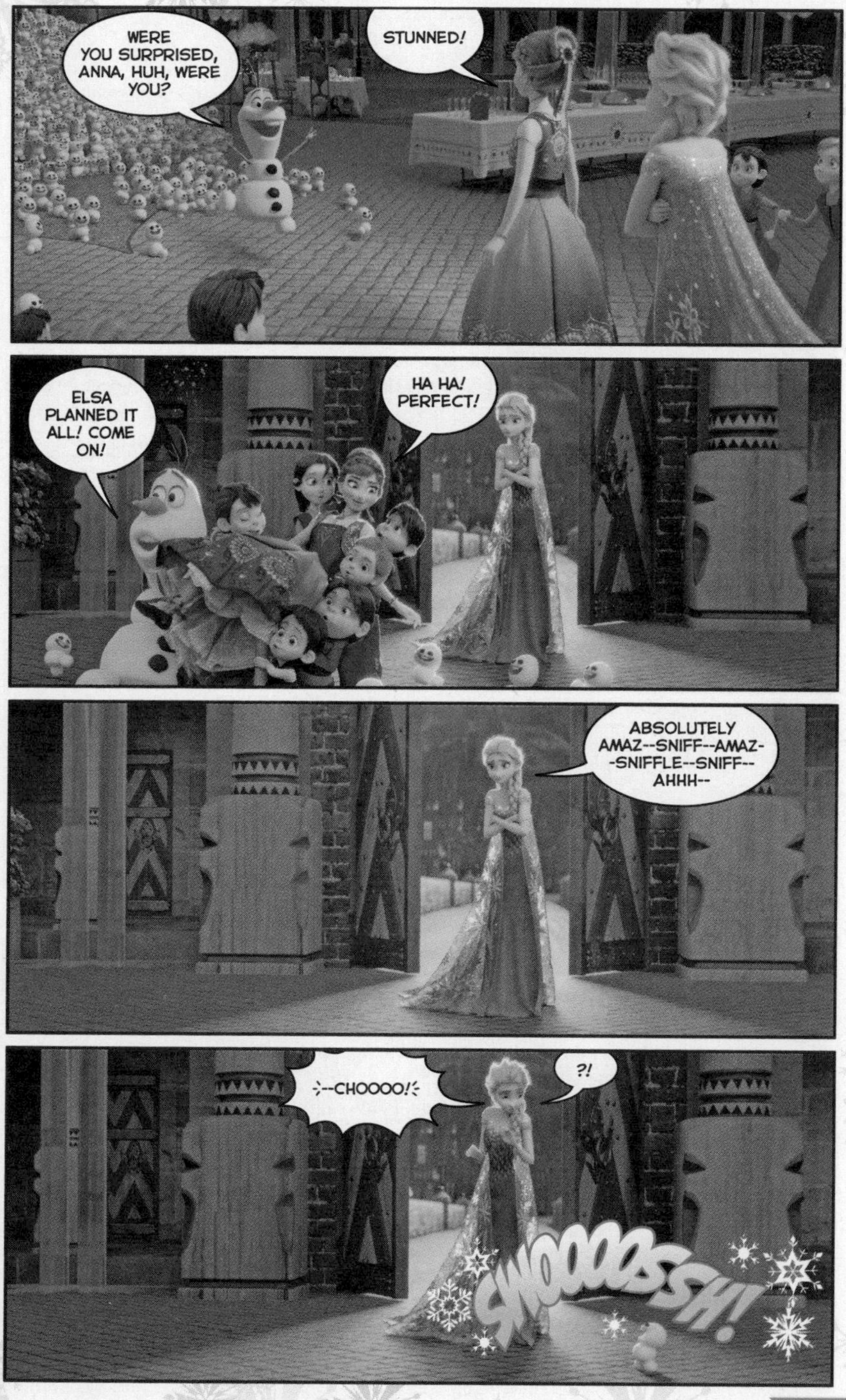
WERE YOU SURPRISED, ANNA, HUH, WERE YOU?
STUNNED!
ELSA PLANNED IT ALL! COME ON!
HA HA! PERFECT!
ABSOLUTELY AMAZ--SNIFF--AMAZ--SNIFFLE--SNIFF--AHHH--
--CHOOOO!
?!
SHOOOOSSH!

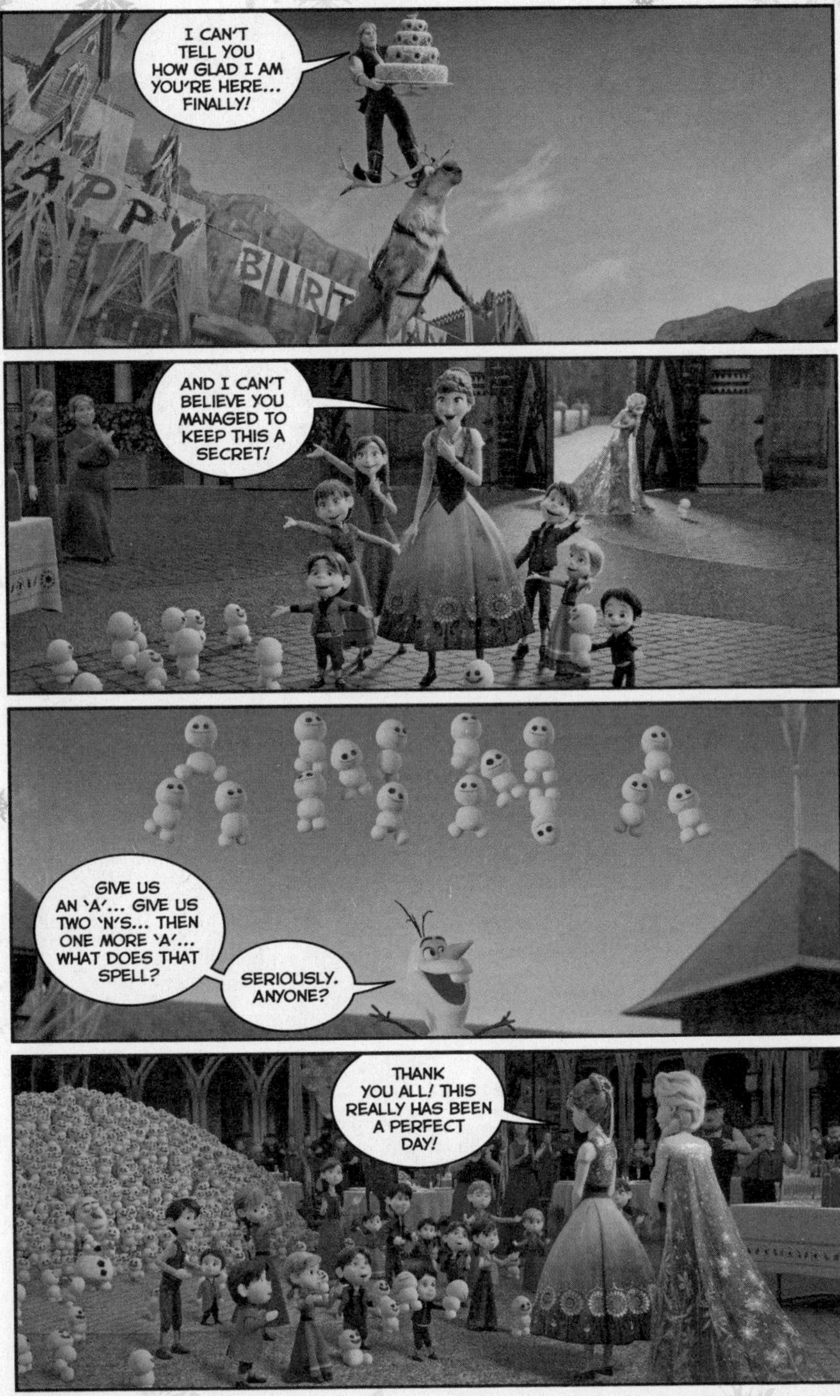
I CAN'T TELL YOU HOW GLAD I AM YOU'RE HERE... FINALLY!
AND I CAN'T BELIEVE YOU MANAGED TO KEEP THIS A SECRET!
GIVE US AN 'A'... GIVE US TWO 'N'S... THEN ONE MORE 'A'... WHAT DOES THAT SPELL?
SERIOUSLY. ANYONE?
THANK YOU ALL! THIS REALLY HAS BEEN A PERFECT DAY!

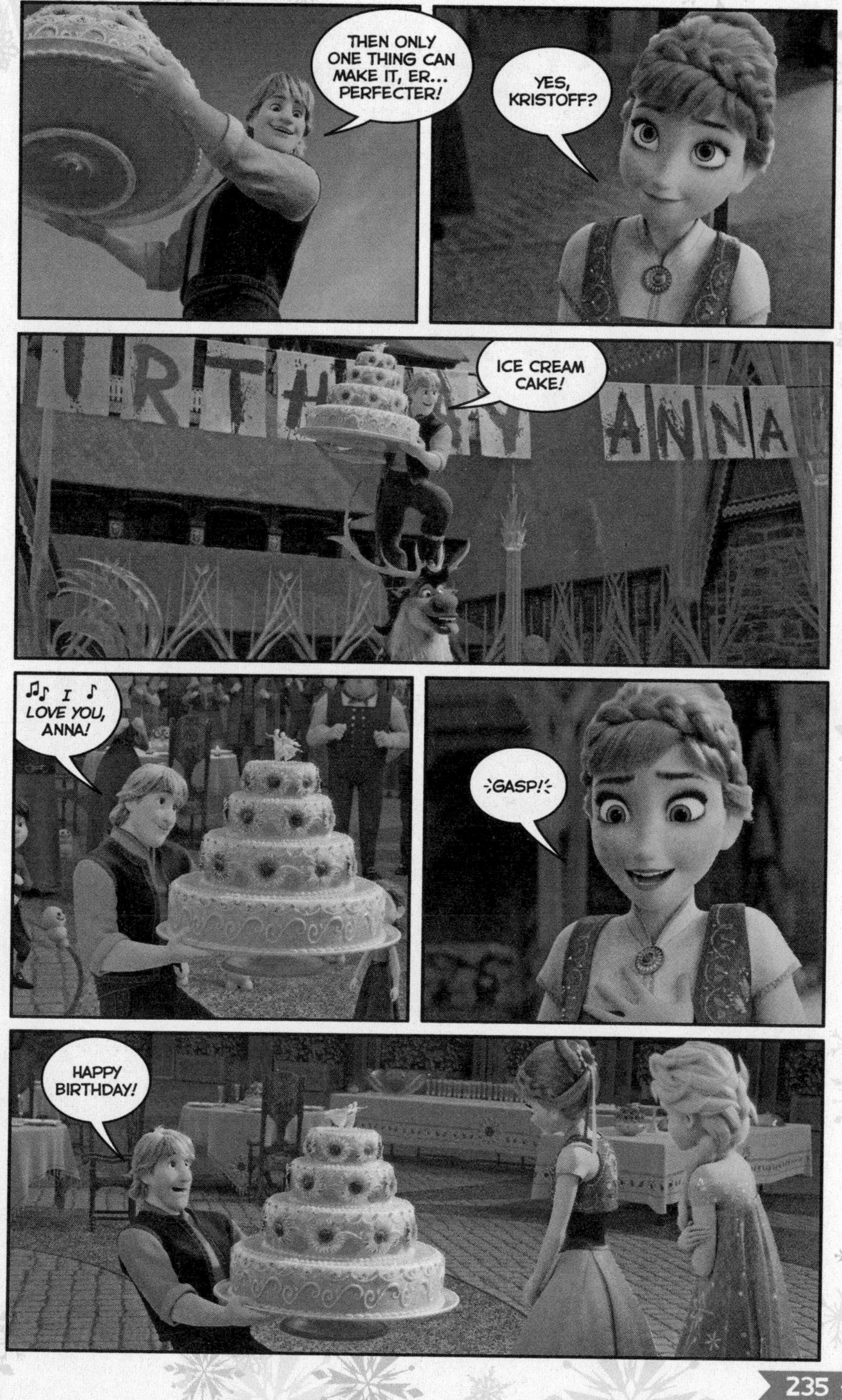
THEN ONLY ONE THING CAN MAKE IT, ER... PERFECTER!
YES, KRISTOFF?
ICE CREAM CAKE!
♫♪ I ♪ LOVE YOU, ANNA!
GASP!
HAPPY BIRTHDAY!

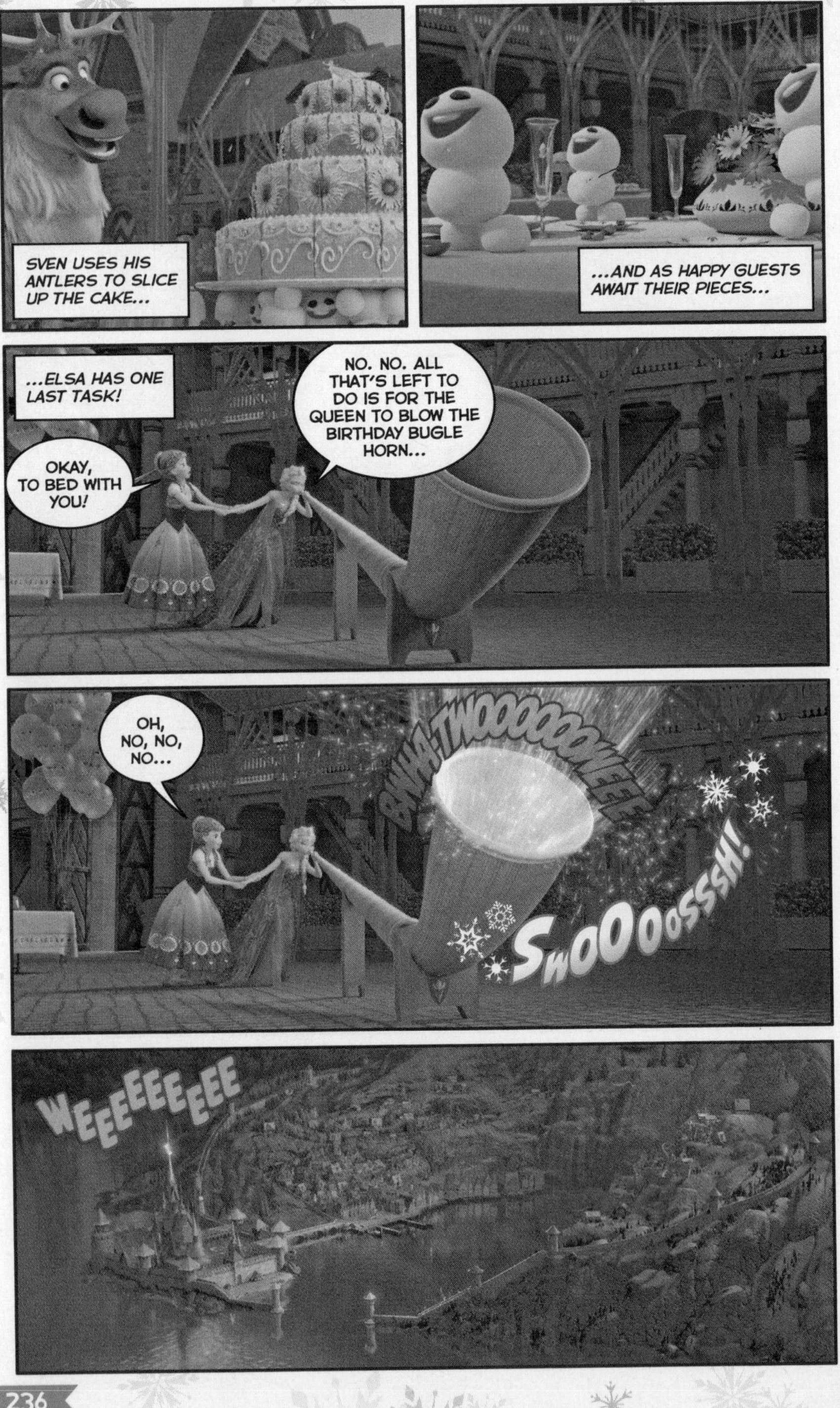

SVEN USES HIS ANTLERS TO SLICE UP THE CAKE...
...AND AS HAPPY GUESTS AWAIT THEIR PIECES...
...ELSA HAS ONE LAST TASK!
NO. NO. ALL THAT'S LEFT TO DO IS FOR THE QUEEN TO BLOW THE BIRTHDAY BUGLE HORN...
OKAY, TO BED WITH YOU!
OH, NO, NO, NO...
BWAA-TWOOOOOOOWEEEE
SwOOOOSSSH!
WEEEEEEEEE

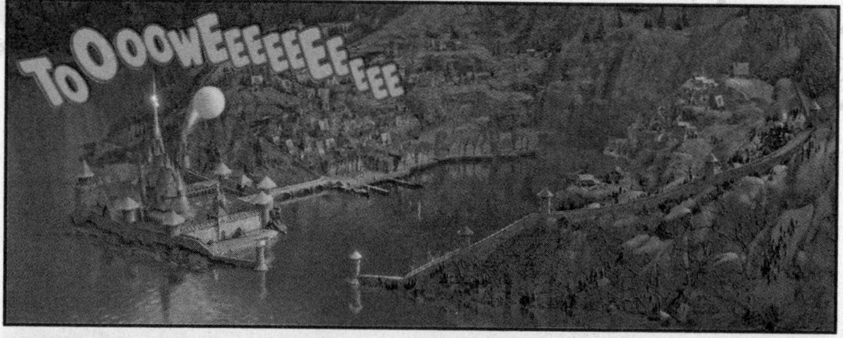
TOOOOWEEEEEEEEEEEE

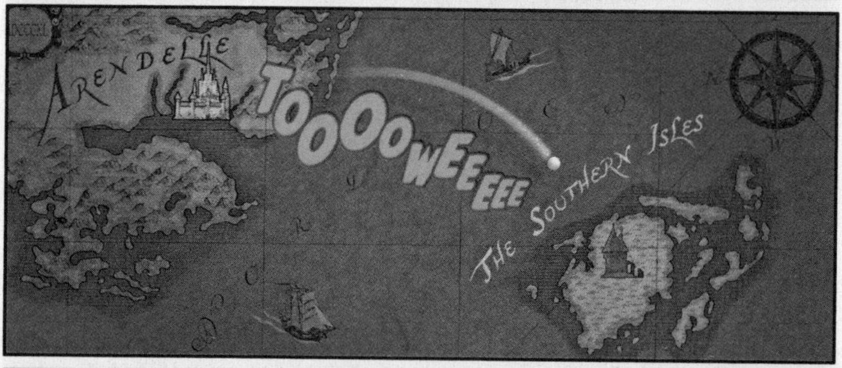
ARENDELLE
TOOOOWEEEEEE
THE SOUTHERN ISLES

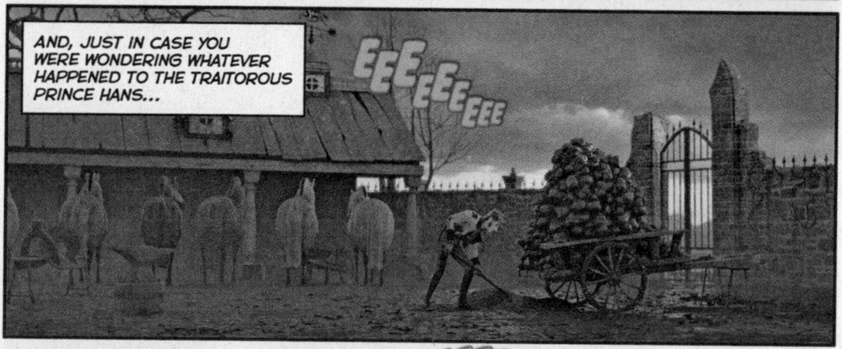
AND, JUST IN CASE YOU WERE WONDERING WHATEVER HAPPENED TO THE TRAITOROUS PRINCE HANS...
EEEEEEEEEE

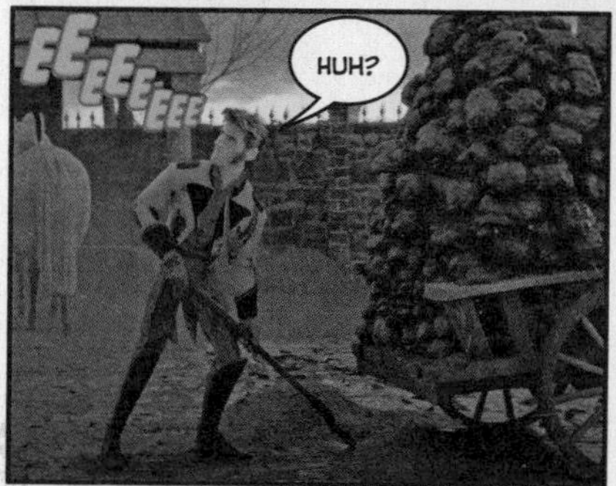
EEEEEEEE
HUH?

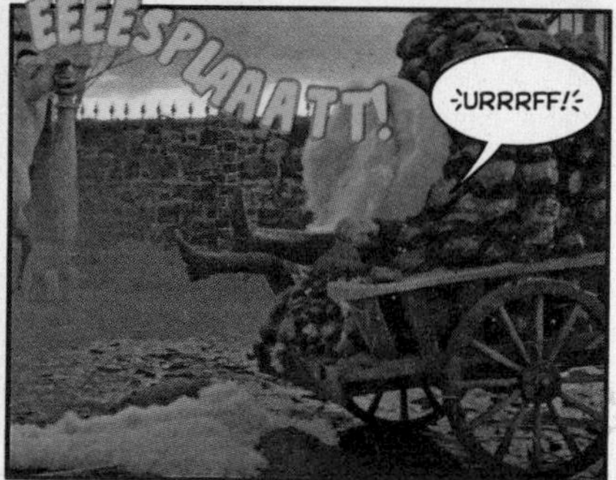
EEEESPLAAAATT!
URRRFF!

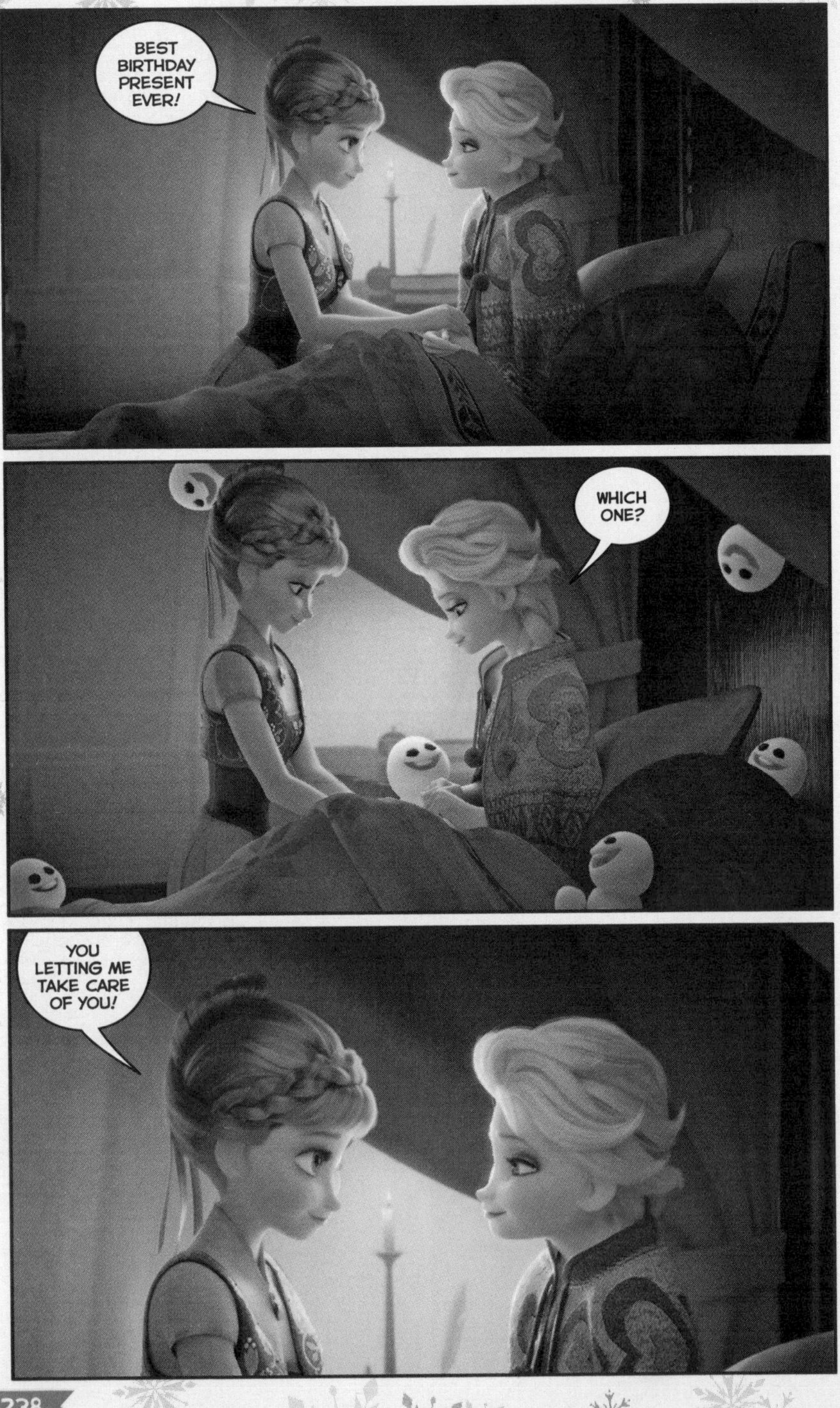
BEST BIRTHDAY PRESENT EVER!
WHICH ONE?
YOU LETTING ME TAKE CARE OF YOU!

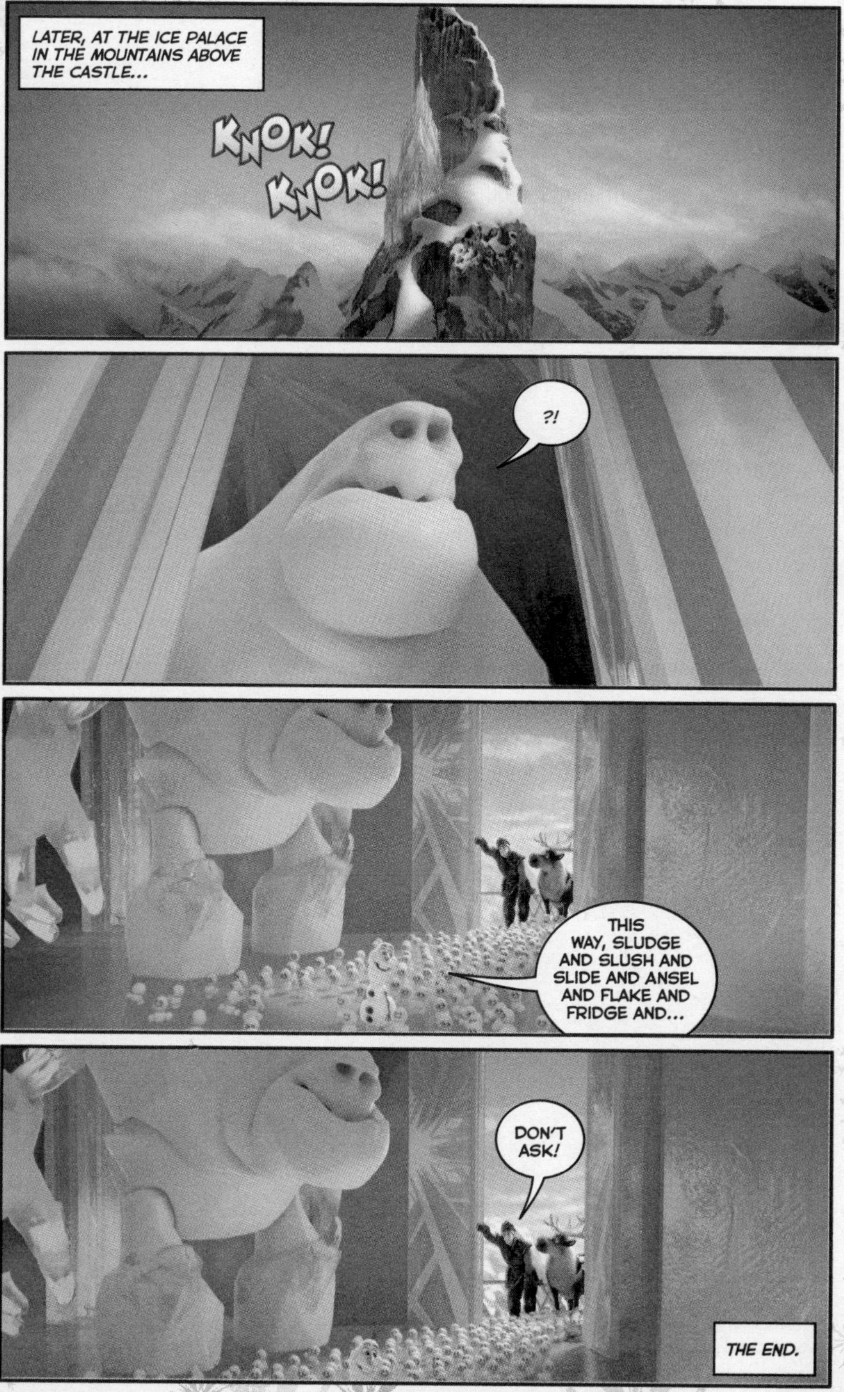
LATER, AT THE ICE PALACE IN THE MOUNTAINS ABOVE THE CASTLE...
KNOK! KNOK!
?!
THIS WAY, SLUDGE AND SLUSH AND SLIDE AND ANSEL AND FLAKE AND FRIDGE AND...
DON'T ASK!
THE END.

Solutions

PAGE 108-109

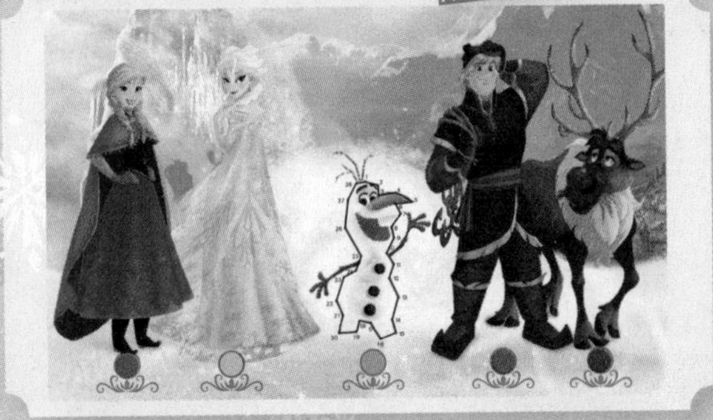

PAGE 110

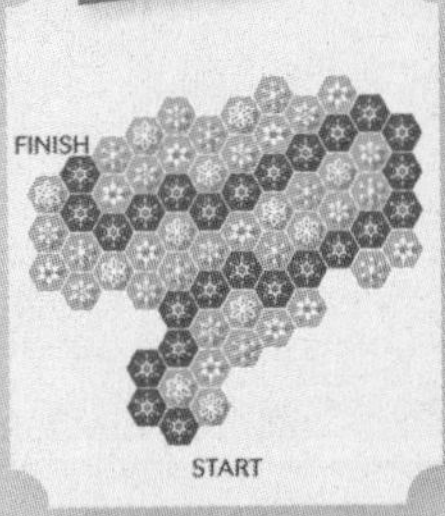
FINISH
START

PAGE 111

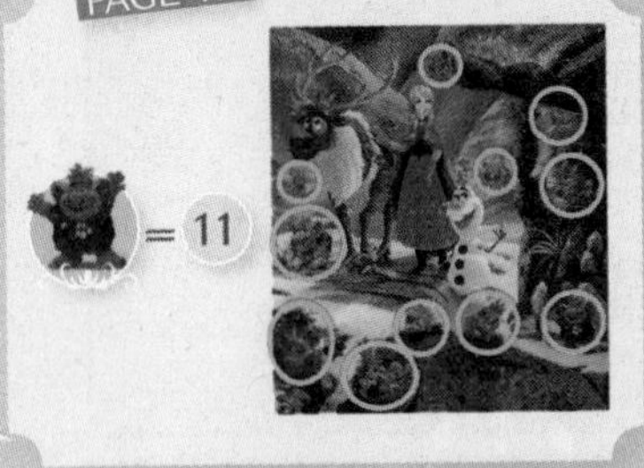
= 11

PAGE 112

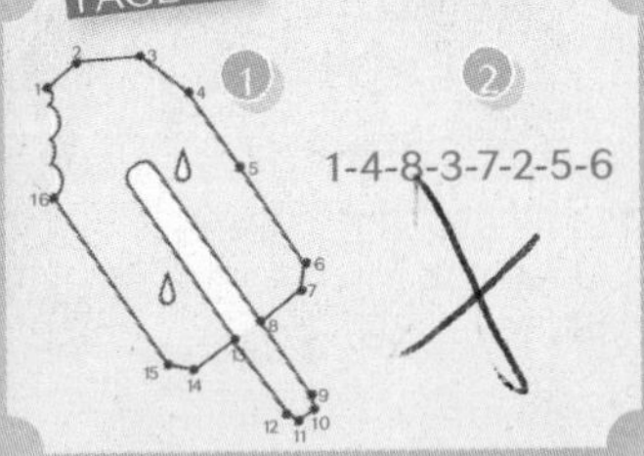
1
2
1-4-8-3-7-2-5-6

PAGE 113

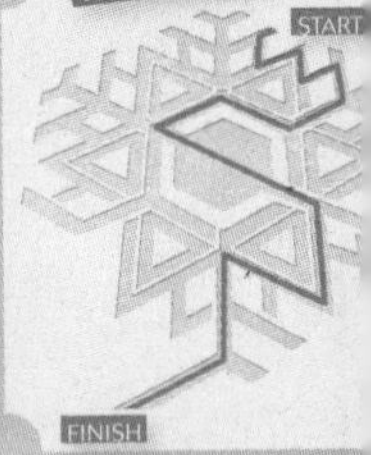
START
FINISH

PAGE 114

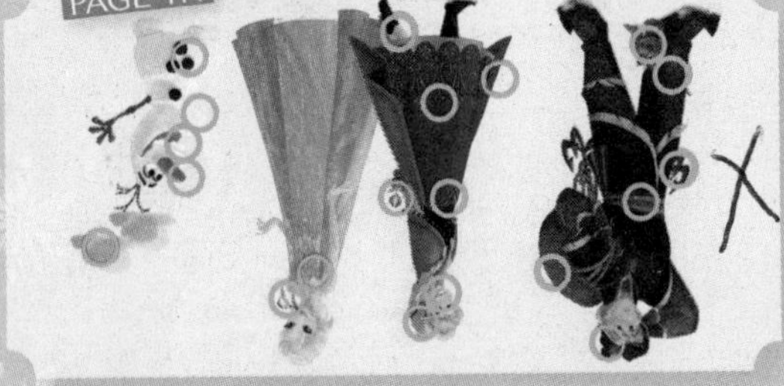

PAGES 130-131

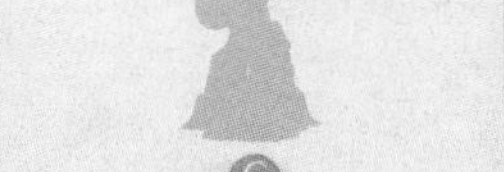
CHOCOLATE CAKE
C

PAGE 132

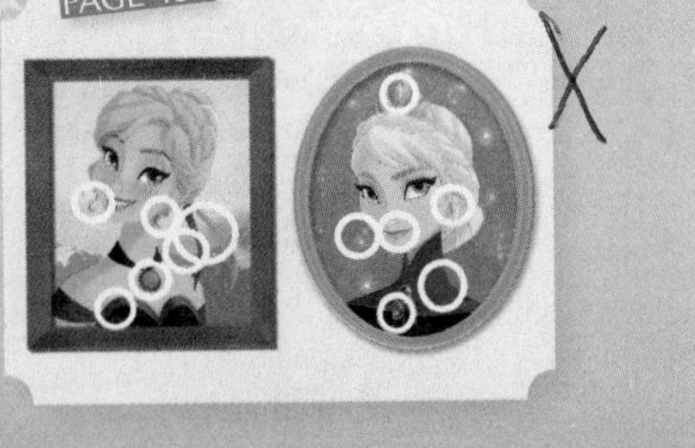

PAGE 133

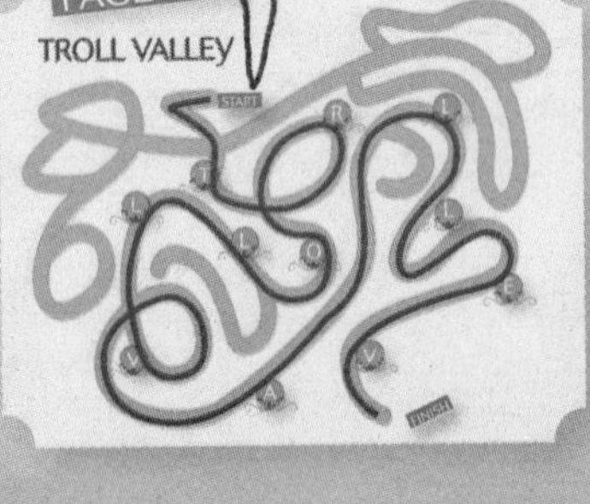
TROLL VALLEY
START
FINISH

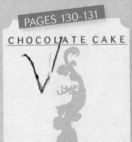

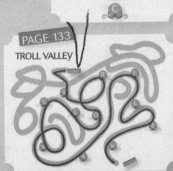